COERCION

A MAFIA ROMANCE

COERCION

A MAFIA ROMANCE

ELLIE SANDERS

CONTENT WARNING

This is my take on the Andromeda and Perseus Myth with a little artistic license thrown in.

Instead of keeping Andromeda as a one dimensional figure who should be saved purely because of her beauty alone, I made her a more worthy, fierce creature, who in the end, is fully capable of saving herself.

This is a modern, mafia romance. If you haven't read the first book 'Vendetta' then you can still read this without any major plot issues or confusion.

This book contains numerous triggers and as such, is only suitable for adult readers.

These triggers include: on page, descriptive rape, dub con, physical assault, emotional trauma, forced marriage, murder of immediate family members, grief, loss, anxiety, fear, kidnapping, manipulation, coercion, suicidal thoughts, mentions of pregnancy / breeding, and torture.

There are a number of detailed and descriptive sexual scenes, including praise, degradation, choking, voyeurism, a jacob's ladder (IYKYK), - if this is not your thing, then this book really isn't for you.

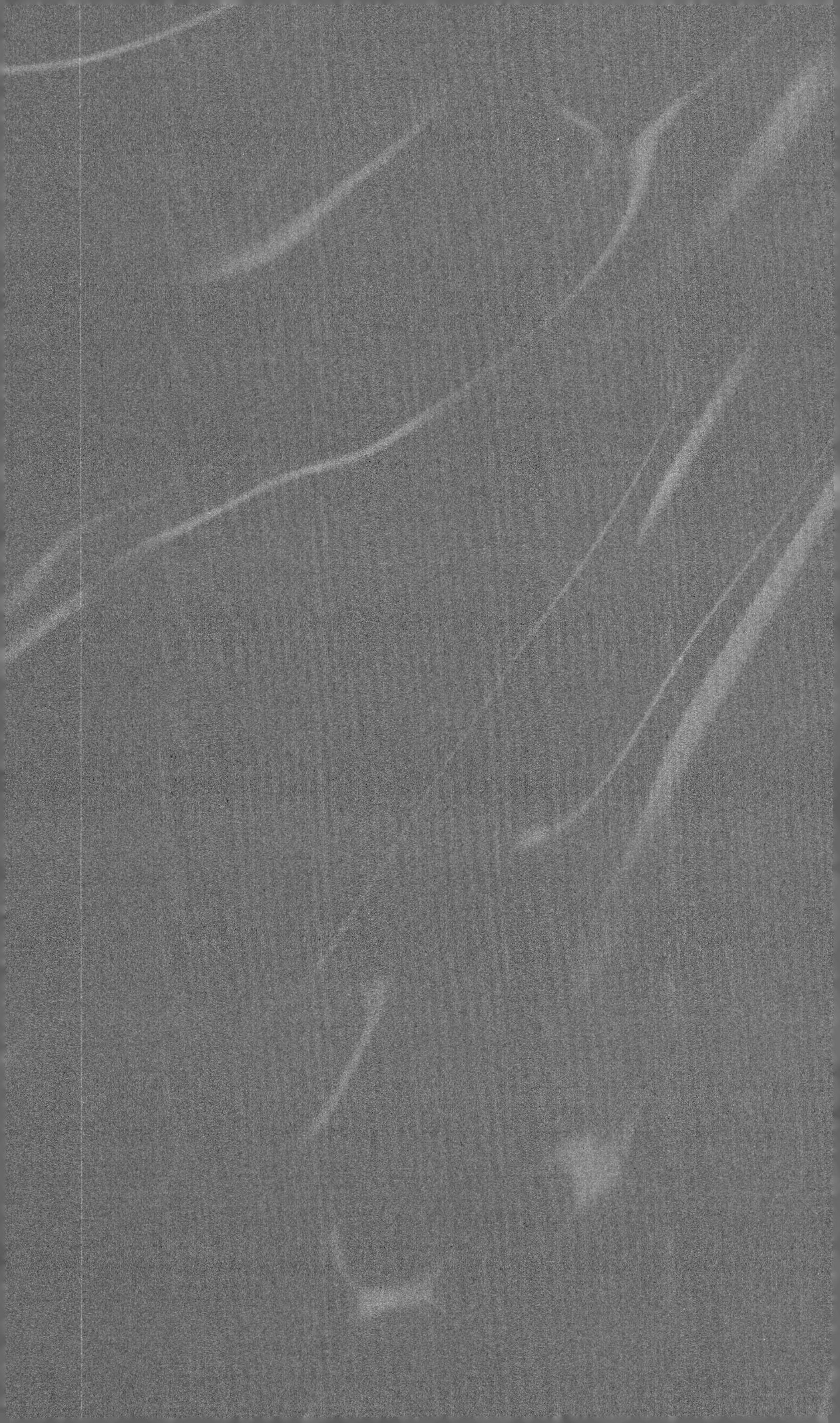

Andromeda; she was meant to die because of her beauty
but she refused to be a sacrifice for the sins of her parents.

Ruby

CHAPTER

Run.

That's the only word screaming in my head as I scramble through the darkness. I don't know what time it is. I don't know where any of my family are. I only know one thing…

Someone is in the house.

Gunshots echo from the floor below. For a second, sheer panic makes me freeze and then I come back to my senses. I have to get out. I have to get as far away from whatever this is as possible.

I know I could climb out of the window and hide in the garden but if there are men in the house chances are they've already taken out our guards so there's no guarantee they're not waiting for one of us to make that move.

In the crystal glass that spans the entire front of the house, I can see my petrified reflection staring back at me. My parents always had a thing for luxury. I guess when your entire business revolves around smuggling diamonds you get used to a certain way of life.

My hand fingers the chain around my neck. A solitary diamond more costly than most people's annual income hangs between the dip of my collar bones. It's a family heirloom, it belonged to my great grandmother and was gifted to me for my last birthday, to mark the apparent enormity of turning sixteen.

Another shot rings out followed by a scream - both of which make me jump like I've been shocked.

I know it's not my mother, but the sound still petrifies me. It must be one of the maids, but that doesn't give me much comfort; if they're taking them out then I don't stand a chance.

And then a shadow moves near me. I barely have time to register it before I hear the sound of my brother's voice calling my name and within seconds I've thrown myself into his arms.

"It's okay." He says, holding me tightly. "But we have to get out."

"What about mum and dad?" I gasp back.

He shakes his head.

"No…" I wail and he's quick to clamp a hand tightly over my mouth to stifle the noise.

"We have to go, now." He growls as loudly as he dares.

I let him carry me away like a child, down the hall, towards what he thinks must be a safe route out. He puts me on my feet before sliding the window open and he stares down as surreptitiously as he can.

"We need to keep to the foliage. Keep your body pressed tight and we should make it." He says.

I nod back, wiping the tears, trying to must what little bravery I have left and focus on the task ahead. I don't mention the potential of armed men waiting for us. I keep that thought to myself.

I can do this. I have to do this.

He climbs out first, offering his hand for me and despite my resolution, I can feel myself trembling as I take it. If we fall, we'll be lucky to simply break a few bones, and yet if we stay, whoever is here will certainly put a bullet in our heads.

But I can't think like that. I have to stay focused on the now.

Slowly, we climb down the trellis. The damned leaves stick to my face, they dampen my pyjamas and I can feel the material sticking to my chest. If I'd been smarter I would have put something on over the tiny shorts and top I was sleeping in, but it's too late now. I just hope wherever we're headed, we get there fast because it's absolutely freezing outside.

"Keep going." He murmurs.

We were on the second floor when we started but I used to spend my most of my childhood climbing trees across the estate, this is child's play compared to that and yet it feels like I'm scaling a mountain.

When my feet hit the grass, I let out a sigh of barely muffled relief.

"We have to run now." Jett says. "Head for the trees. Run as fast as you can."

Again, I nod, giving him a look that hopefully fills him with the belief that I can do this.

He turns and starts sprinting.

I draw a ragged breath and then race after him.

The freezing grass makes every step I take treacherous. My feet slip and slide as I pummel my hands to force my body to go faster.

I can hear yells. Shouts behind us.

I already know in my heart that we've been spotted but if we can make it to the treeline, I'm certain we can get away.

Jett is way ahead of me. His legs are so much longer than mine. I guess it helps that he's got seven years on me and he spends most of his days in the gym, working out, building muscles like he's planning on competing in the Olympics.

I keep my eyes focused on his back. I keep my legs pounding one after another. As long as I can see him, I know I'll be safe, I know I'll make it.

But just as that thought manifests in my head, something heavy collides with me, and I land hard on the ground with a scream.

Jett turns, his eyes widening, as he realises I've been caught. He's at the treeline. He's made it while I've barely gotten halfway.

"Run," I scream at him.

He pauses, like he's going to come back, like he's going to risk his life for me and I can't have that. If they've come for my parents then we're just as much of a target as they are. I have to save my brother, I have to be the hero here.

"Run," I scream louder as I'm dragged up to my feet. A hand wraps around me, pulling my body against the awful strength of someone twice my size.

Jett turns, running further into the woods and all the men around me pick up their guns and start shooting.

I scream, I jerk, I try to get free, and the man holding me laughs as he tosses me over his shoulder before carrying me back to the house, while I pummel his back with my fists.

I'M DUMPED ONTO THE FLOOR OF MY FATHER'S OFFICE. MY KNEES slam hard into the marble and I let out a cry that no one bats an eye to.

I'm not allowed in this part of the house. Daddy always made that abundantly clear. That this part was for him and his men, that this was so off limits even my mother's access was restricted.

The room looks ransacked. It's complete and utter carnage. His great leather chair is upturned on its side. Paper is strewn about the floor like confetti.

"And the boy?" An only too-familiar voice asks.

"He's in the woods but we'll get him." Someone behind me says.

I blink, forcing myself to look, forcing myself to meet my uncle's glare. He tilts his head, stepping closer to me.

"Where is your mother?" He asks in a voice so cold I shiver.

I shake my head but as I do, I register what else is in the room, or rather *who* else. My father is there, on the floor, lying face down like he simply tripped up and forgot to get back to his feet.

Only his head is wrong.

His face is wrong.

I blink rapidly as my mind refuses to register exactly what I'm seeing.

And then it hits me. Why there's a dark stain spreading around him. Why he isn't moving. Isn't even breathing.

Why half his face is gone.

"Daddy," I scream, crawling on my hands and knees but my uncle grabs me by my hair, yanking me back.

"Where is your mother?" He asks again, hauling me to my feet to face him.

"I don't know," I whimper.

He lets out a snarl, dropping me onto the floor and I land in the pool of my father's blood, beside his horrifically still body.

Maybe it's my shock, maybe it's something else entirely but I can't believe he's dead. I just can't. I shake him harder, willing him to get up, to start barking orders, to protect me the way he always has. Afterall, I was his princess, his favourite.

"Daddy," I whisper, as if that alone might just wake him up.

He doesn't respond. But of course he doesn't.

"He's dead." Uncle Levi states, like I don't already know it. Like he clearly isn't the reason why.

Someone else storms into the room. Levi turns as he mutters something I can't work out and then they drag Abraham, my father's right hand man, in.

His eyes find my father first, then they settle on me and I see that same look of horror reflected back at me.

"Levi." He says looking across at the man responsible.

Levi smirks. "Come on, like I wasn't going to do this eventually. Like I wasn't going to take what's mine."

"It was never yours. Issac built this empire from…" Abraham begins.

"And now I've taken it." Levi says cutting across him with a smirk.

"Diana will fight you…"

Levi throws his head back and laughs. "Let the bitch try. My men have seized all the warehouses, all the mines, she has nothing to fight with."

"And Ruby?" Abraham says, glancing at me then back again. "What about her?"

Levi tilts his head, stepping over the body of his brother to haul me back up. I shut my eyes, hating the fact that I'm defenceless, that I can't even fight him.

He strokes my hair back from my face, studying it. "You've grown since last I saw you. You look so much like your mother now…" He says in a way that makes my skin crawl.

I spit at him. It's the most I can do and, instead of reacting with anger, or even surprise he just laughs.

"I see you have her temperament too." He states before twisting my arm around, forcing my wrist into a position I know it can't make. I scream as the bone snaps, as it gives way under the horrific pressure. "Don't worry, Ruby, I'll beat that side out of you." He mutters. "I'll make sure you learn your place."

"Levi," Abraham snarls.

Levi drops me, letting me fall into a heap as I cradle my now useless limb while the tears stream down my face. I'm so scared to make a noise now, too scared to even cry out. All I can do is make weird whimpering sounds like I'm some sort of broken animal.

"Let the girl go." Abraham says. "You've said it yourself, you have everything, all your brother's mines, the girl is nothing to you..."

"The girl is of my blood." Levi snaps. "My family's blood. That makes her valuable enough in our world."

"Please..." I whisper, not even understanding what it is I'm begging for. Jett is dead, my father is dead too. What do I have to live for now?

Levi ignores me, pulling out a gun, and points it at Abraham who instantly stiffens more.

"Tell me Abs, with all your professed loyalty to Issac, why should I trust you to be loyal to me?"

"I'll never be loyal to you." Abraham spits back.

"As I thought." Levi muses before pulling the trigger and Abraham slumps back onto the marble, his eyes staring right at me, with an awful hole right between them.

He used to look out for me, used to take me to dance class when I was little, used to shield me when my mother was having one of her moments. In a way he was as much a parent to me as they were.

And now he's dead. Just like they are.

I cry then. I scream out and someone slaps me to shut me up.

No one is going to stop this. No one is coming to save me.

The realisation hits me like a ton of bricks and I sink down further onto the blood stained floor. I don't understand how this is happening. I don't understand why my uncle is suddenly betraying us like this. It's not like he and my father were ever close but still, we're family. He's his brother.

"Get the girl." Levi barks as he struts out.

I shut my eyes, wishing I knew how to fight, how to stop this.

Hands reach around me, picking me up from my waist and I'm carried out over someone's shoulder like a sack of potatoes.

My room is cramped. Dark. There's bars at the window as if they really have locked me in a dungeon. I don't know how long it took for us to arrive here, wherever we are. A doctor saw to my wrist, putting it in a cast and then I was locked away, out of sight, while Levi cemented his victory.

I huddle under the meagre blanket. The room is cold. Dank. I can smell the moisture in the air. I don't know what time it is. I'm so hungry my stomach has twisted around with the pain.

All I had to wash with was a freezing cold bowl of water and I know my skin is still smeared with blood. My father's blood.

I want to get it off, to get fully clean, but once I do that, the last remnants of him will be gone. I'll have nothing left to remember him by because I don't doubt my uncle will destroy every photo, every trinket, everything that belonged to my parents. He's stolen their business, stolen the mines, if my mother is even alive, she'll have nothing but the clothes on her back.

For a moment I think of Jett. No one has said whether he's alive. No one dragged his body back. I can only hope that he did as I asked, that he ran and never came back. That he's out there, somewhere, that he's alive and he at least as escaped whatever horror I have to face now at my uncle's hands.

I stiffen at the sound of footsteps. It's been days since they locked me here and for some reason I'd convinced myself that they'd leave me alone. That perhaps I'd been forgotten. I was even happy about that. I could hide away, disappear, forget myself in my grief and die in this darkness.

Only, that's clearly not what they intend for me.

The door creaks open.

I wince at the noise. My head feels fuzzy and I don't know if it's from lack of food or lack of sleep, or something else entirely.

A huge form is illuminated against the light of the hall beyond. I hold my breath, staring back at whoever it is, hoping that maybe they can't see me. That maybe with all the darkness I'm invisible.

Only, I'm not that lucky, am I?

He steps inside, shuts the door, and hits a switch. I cover my eyes to shut out the sudden blazing brightness while he clearly takes the moment to assess me.

"Get up."

His voice is gruff, harsh, as cold as my uncle's. I don't move, I just blink, trying to force my sight into clearing.

He's almost twice my height, a great brute of a man. His hair is completely shaven off, his eyes are so black it's as if he has no irises at all. It makes him look almost demonic. But it's the scars that reach up either side of his mouth that are the worst. Sometime, years ago by the looks of it, someone cut his face, gave him a Chelsea smile, and though the wounds have clearly healed, they dominate his already harsh features, morphing his face into something truly horrific.

He crosses the room, grabs my arm, and hauls me out of the bed, leaving me swaying in front of him.

"Little whore." He murmurs.

"I'm not." I whisper back. It's as much as I dare and, somehow, I know he's going to punish me for it.

He grabs my face, striking me hard before pushing me back and I stumble, falling over myself, and end up colliding backwards with the hard bed.

"Do you know who I am?" He asks as he moves closer.

I shake my head. I don't know who any of these men are, none of them beyond my uncle. He had to hire mercenaries, outsiders, because none of my father's men would have betrayed us. They were too loyal to even consider such a thing.

"Your uncle's asked me to teach you some manners." He says, as he starts undoing his buckle, and my fear multiplies.

Is he going to beat me with it?

When he undoes the button on his jeans, I realise that's not it. It's going to be much, much worse than that.

My eyes dart to the door, to the exit so impossibly far from where I am.

"We're going to have some fun, you and I." He murmurs. "Though I suspect I'll be enjoying it more than you."

I shake my head, pushing my body back, pushing myself into the wall like I might be able to melt into the brickwork.

My tears are streaming.

My fear takes over everything.

I know what's coming.

I know what he's going to do and my helplessness is making this even worse because I know I can't stop it.

I'm locked in this room, trapped with this monster and there's no way out.

He lets out a laugh that tells me everything. He's not going to stop. He knows exactly what he's doing and if anything, my fear is making this even better for him.

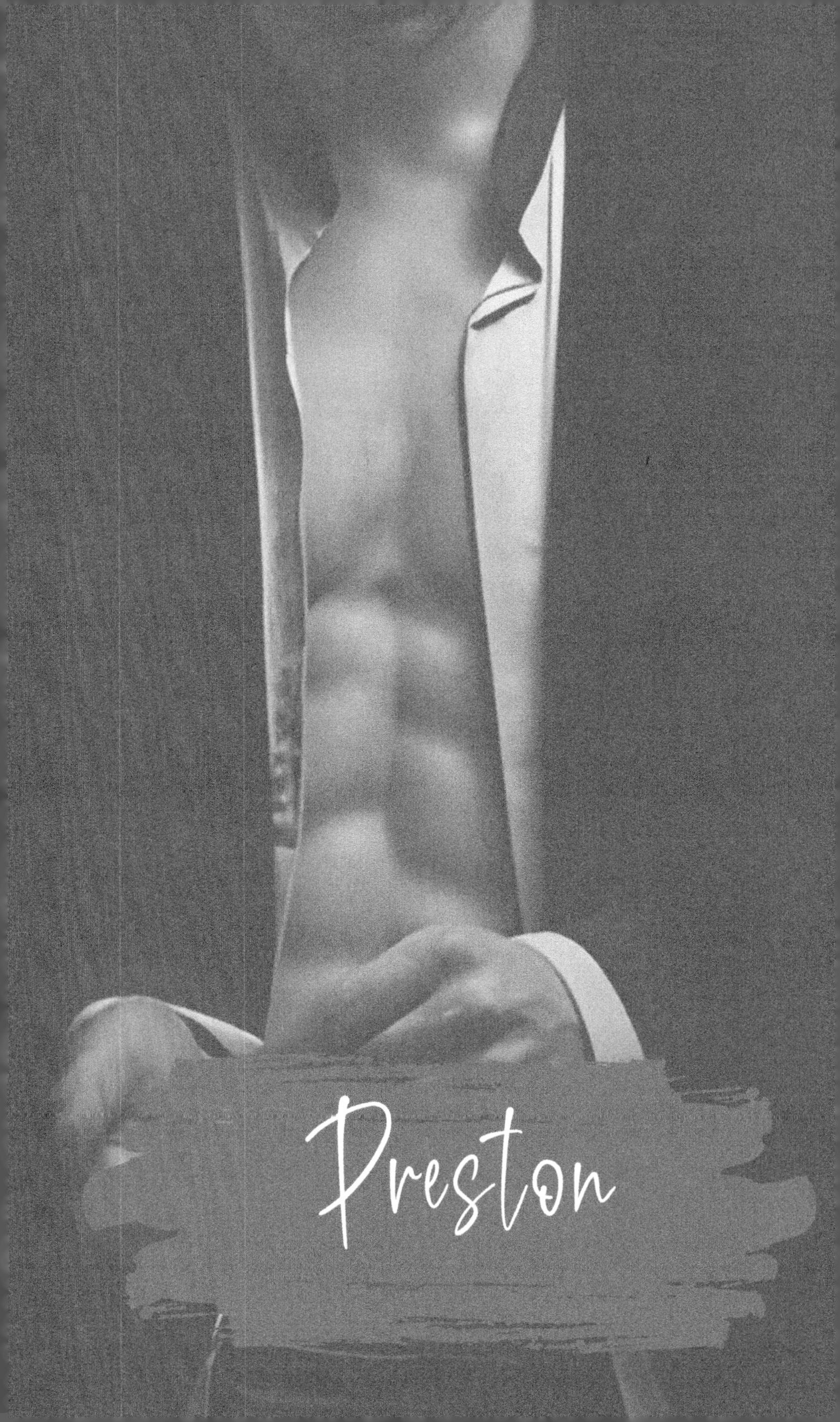

Preston

CHAPTER
Two

Five Years Later

The air is tense. Fraught. There are enough egos in this room that it will only take one flippant remark and it will all erupt into carnage.

The long table is laid with whiskey and enough glasses for everyone to drink. I've deliberately steered clear of it because in my experience, alcohol and politics don't mix. At least, not with this sort of company.

Blaine is stood behind us, flicking a lighter on, burning the tips of his fingers like he finds nothing more pleasurable, while the men opposite are watching like they desperately want to look away but can't.

"You certain about this?" Nico says quietly, checking in with me one last time.

I nod. It's not like I'd say no, we need this alliance, we need to expand operations and besides, why would we turn down a chance to use the Holtz trade routes when they're offered so readily?

"This is your life..." He murmurs.

I shrug. "If you weren't married to Eleri you'd do it yourself, wouldn't you?"

He tilts his head, clearly considering my question before he answers, "Yes."

And that says it all; that this needs to be done. It's a business deal. Nothing more. No need to overthink it. No need to be dramatic.

"Nico Morelli." Levi Holtz says as he finally saunters in. My eyes dart behind him expecting to see another figure, only he's alone and that makes me pause.

We've all been sat here, waiting for his arrival like he's some sort of king. He's greyer, fatter around the gills than last time I saw him but he still looks like he could gut you.

"Levi." Nico says, extending his hand and the two shake like they're trying to break the others' bones.

Levi casts his eyes about the room and smirks. "I see the whole gang is here." He murmurs.

"You were the one who asked for this." Nico states, not giving an inch.

Levi sinks into the chair and Gunnar, his righthand man, sits down beside him. Up until today we've been dealing with him, with Gunnar, and to say we've had more than enough of him is an understatement. I can see why someone cut him up the way they did, why they mutilated his face. The smug piece of shit no doubt deserved it and I'm only sorry I wasn't there to witness the act.

"Call me old fashioned but I like to do the final sign off in person." Levi says as if he's the one making all the decisions.

I can see Nico bristle at that, I can see the way he's itching to put him in his place after the way he's treated him, but we need this alliance. We need it just as much as Levi apparently does.

Good thing all the paperwork is drawn up. All the negotiations are done. The alliance between us is as good as sealed.

Levi looks across at me, folding his arms smugly. "I hope you'll treat my niece well." He says.

I give him a cold hard stare in reply. In less than a week she will no longer be his niece and though I've never met the girl, I don't doubt she'll be happier in my house than she ever has been in his considering how he managed to acquire her.

"She's very pretty." Levi continues. "That's the only good thing she inherited from her mother." He pulls out his phone, swiping through it and places it down for us to see the picture.

Gunnar snickers like there's some hidden meaning to his words and once more my eyes flicker to him while my hand itches to pull my gun and put a bullet between those black eyes.

But that wouldn't do much for our alliance, would it now?

I grit my teeth, biting back the irritation and stare down at the screen in front of me, at the image of the woman who will soon be my wife. Only, she doesn't look like a woman at all.

She looks young.

Too young.

Her dark hair hangs down in loose, natural waves. She's not wearing any makeup. She looks the exact opposite of what I'd expect a Mafia Princess to be.

But it's her eyes that get me; within those deep brown irises is a sadness that seems to swallow me whole. It's like she's never learnt how to smile, never felt an emotion akin to joy.

I'm not sure why it bothers me so much. I'm not sure why I care. Women are expendable, our women even more so. But then, all of us are in a way. This deal is proof of that fact. We all have our parts to play and it's far better we remember that than let idiotic notions like sentimentality confuse things.

"How old is she?" I ask before I can stop myself. Up until now I'd never considered what age she was. But she barely looks like an adult. The t-shirt she's wearing engulfs her body, but there's no hint of a chest, no hint that she's even fully past puberty.

"She's legal." Gunnar says.

"She's twenty one. Just turned twenty one." Levi smiles. "Like a fresh peach ready to be eaten."

The way he says that makes my skin crawl. The way they both speak about her makes me feel something akin to fury.

My eyes drop back to the girl.

Twenty One? I'm over twice her age then.

Nico lets out a grunt before getting up. "A word." He says into my ear and we exit the room, walking far enough that all the men lurking outside can't hear.

"What do you think this is?" I ask because we can both sense something is up. No normal marriage pact would go like this. We wouldn't simply be shown a picture, normally both families would meet, the bride and groom would meet too. That's what I was expecting from today. That she would be here, that we'd exchange some pleasantries, some pretence at getting to know one another under everyone's watchful gaze.

Nico shrugs. "He's playing us but we know that. He wants to make us look bad so if this deal goes south he's got mud to sling at us before the other families."

I narrow my eyes, "You think he wants us to say no to the girl?"

Nico pauses. "He knows I won't." He says. "And what they're offering is worth too much to say no."

"She's a child." I state.

Nico shrugs. "You heard what they said, she's twenty one. Besides you're only marrying her. No one said anything about anything else."

"Meaning?" I raise an eyebrow.

"She'll be your wife in name only. Put on a show for the other families but in private keep your life separate."

"Is that an order?"

He nods. "Yes. We don't even know if the girl can be trusted. She's a Holtz after all."

I grunt back. Like that isn't obvious. The girl is probably a snake, all primed to pass on any and all information about the Morelli Family and our doings.

I'll have to watch what I say, watch how I act.

From the moment I put a ring on her finger I won't be able to let my guard down for a second. I'm literally opening my home up to a potential enemy and inviting her inside. It's reckless in the extreme, but then, Nico wants this, he wants this alliance. Who am I to deny him?

Nico walks away and I follow after him. It's Gunnar who meets my eyes as we walk back in and I'm itching to wipe that look right of his face.

"We agree." Nico says. "To all the terms. Preston and Ruby will marry."

Ruby

CHAPTER
Three

I knew this day would come. I wasn't stupid. I knew my uncle only kept me alive as cannon fodder. Something to use. A spoil of war to be traded when the right opportunity presented itself. And I've played the game as best I could; kept my head down, kept away from him and all his men. I've become so compliant I've forgotten who I am now. Who I was too. My father must be turning in his grave at the perfect obedient daughter I've pretended to be for the man who murdered him.

But not anymore.

I can't do it anymore.

If I stay, if I let them get away with this, I'll become just like her, like my mother. My life will be a repeat of hers. Sacrificed for the greater good of my family. Shackled to a man, forced into a marriage I don't want, forced to endure the brutality and violence and everything else that comes with this life, with being Mafia.

I gulp, trying to steady my nerves. My hands are shaking. My heart is hammering as I stand here waiting in the shadows. I just need a little bit of luck and perhaps the entire trajectory of my life will change.

Dear Uncle Levi had me packed and onto a private jet this morning, surrounded by his men, naturally. I've been guarded better than the crown jewels. Whoever it is I'm marrying, Levi is definitely getting a hefty payday from it.

As soon as we landed, I was shoved into an SUV and driven to this nondescript house. The only saving grace is Finn is here. Over the years he's gone from lackey to trusted guard. And between us a friendship has grown. He's protected me when he can, when it won't put himself at risk, and for that alone I'm grateful.

But tonight he was the one who approached me. I don't know what made him do it. I haven't really stopped to question it, but when he said he could get me out, I didn't hesitate to follow him.

His head pokes up between the stacked up barrels. "Let's go." He whispers.

I get to my feet, shadowing his footsteps. I don't know this compound, I don't know where the cameras are and where the blind-spots are. I won't risk putting a foot in the wrong place and ending up caught.

I haven't got anything with me. I didn't have a bag to pack or anything to put in it. All I have is the battered old jeans and top I'm wearing.

"Climb in." Finn says lifting the tarp off the back of one of the trucks. I hesitate for a millisecond.

He thinks we can simply drive out of here?

"They'll let me pass." He says, answering my unspoken question. "Just keep silent. Once we get to the city we'll get you on a train and away from here."

I nod. Get on a train. That sounds as likely as flying to the moon right now.

But I don't voice that. I just clamber in, huddle up, praying that some greater power is looking out for me right now.

He straps it back in place and I sit in the strange hue of light created by the plastic covering me. I don't know how long this journey is going to take. I don't even think we're near the city. The compound we're in is isolated. I didn't see a single building nearby.

As the engine roars to life, I can feel the base beneath me vibrate. I doubt there's much suspension in the back. This is going to be a seriously uncomfortable ride but it doesn't matter.

Nothing matters.

If I had to be strapped to the damned wings of a plane to get away, then I would do it. I would risk everything.

And in truth, I am.

I'd rather die than let myself be sold on like this. Be used like this.

No, they've taken enough from me, stolen enough.

I'm done playing along like the little victim.

I'm done letting these arseholes dictate my life.

Preston

CHAPTER *Four*

It's late in the evening. I've spent most of the day clearing the house, making it secure. If I'm going to be sharing it with a potential spy then I want to make sure I'm not leaving us wide open to attack. Not for the first time I consider renting somewhere else and sticking my new wife there, but I get the feeling Nico will not be happy about that - he's already said he wants to keep an eye on her. And besides, it hardly fits with the whole happy marriage thing, does it? I need to at least put on a show.

As I'm locking the last of some papers away into the safe, the knocker goes. I know Sidney will answer it so I don't bother moving but I look up when I see Nico standing there in the doorway with a bottle of whiskey in one hand.

Normally we meet at the bar to discuss business and anything urgent he would have called ahead, so though I know this isn't a good sign, whatever he wants, it can't be a complete catastrophe.

I gesture to a chair and he struts in the same way he enters everywhere; as if he owns the place and if he chose, he'd have it wiped off the face of the earth with barely a second thought.

He sits down in one of the oxblood leather chesterfield wingbacks like it's a throne.

For a moment he doesn't do anything but watch the fire crackling away, it's not giving out much heat but I like the aesthetics of it and it's helped deal with a few items I deemed not worthy of keeping.

He grabs the bottle, opens it, and I get up to put two crystal cut glasses down.

"This business with Levi…" He begins before sighing like he suddenly has the weight of the world on his shoulders. The whiskey gurgles as he pours out two extremely generous portions.

Neither of us are old men by any stretch of the imagination but if you look closely you can see the whisps of grey in his dark hair, you can see the peppering of it in his stubble.

"What is it?" I ask, because clearly something is rattling him.

"She's my goddaughter." Nico says quietly.

"Who?" I frown.

"Ruby Holtz." Nico mutters sounding almost weary. "Her father was a mentor of sorts. A long time ago. In a previous lifetime."

"Why does no one know this?" I ask. I didn't even know they were friends. In truth I know little about the family beyond the fact their marriage was something of a shock. Diana, Ruby's mother, was not what you'd class a traditional 'Mafia Bride', not from one of our families– she was Nigerian, or Ethiopian, heiress to half the diamond mines of Africa by all accounts and, no doubt, why Isaac chose her in the first place. It was tactical, strategic, it benefited his business interests.

He shrugs. "Things were different back then. It didn't always please people to have rival families like ours working in tandem."

"If she's your goddaughter why didn't you claim her when her father died?"

He takes a long sip of his drink, scowling at the flames like they've personally insulted him. "I should have. I should have done more for her, more for the Family, but by the time Levi made his move it was too late. Issac was dead. The son was dead. The mother was presumed to be dead. Only Ruby survived."

"And Levi doesn't know?"

"He knows nothing." Nico states, fixing those deadly eyes on me. "And that's how I want it to remain. Ruby can't find out. Levi certainly can't. I want them to think this connection is purely what they're setting up."

"You *were* playing him." I smirk.

"Of course I fucking was." Nico growls. "A man like Levi, he would never have handed her over if he knew. Besides, we need these routes, we need this alliance."

I narrow my eyes at that. He's right, we do need it but, while I'm as ruthless as the next bastard, I don't like the idea of ignoring Levi's more nefarious activities. Afterall, it's not just diamonds and rubies he's smuggling, it's a far less palatable treasure. Girls. Young ones. I guess that's where the notion of selling his own niece came from. He's trading children already, what's another to add to the list?

I take a sip of my drink, savouring the taste and allow it to distract myself from that thought. Nico always has the best bottles, the best vintage. "Is that why you're ordering me not to touch her?"

He gives me a look that would make an ordinary man shit himself but I've learnt to hold my own.

"She's off limits. That's how she remains."

I nod. I can do that. From what I've seen of her so far she looks barely old enough to vote, so it's not like that's going to be an issue. I'll house her, clothe her, feed her, but beyond that, she won't exist.

"She was intended for me." Nico murmurs.

"What?"

"That's what Issac wanted, to tie our families in marriage. His first daughter was closer to my age but she died. She had Leukaemia and passed before they even had Ruby."

"If she was meant to be your bride why did Issac make you her godfather?"

He shrugs. "He knew I'd take care of her if anything happened, and he never trusted Levi or Diana for that matter. When she was old enough then we'd get married. At least, that was the plan."

"So you've met her?"

"Once, she was young then, probably too young to remember. Besides, I married Eleri."

"Did you not consider…"

"Levi had her." He says, fixing me with a hard look. "As far as I knew she was either dead or as good as. And I had my own shit to focus on, I had Roman to deal with."

I stare back at him, knowing that's true. Roman was kicking up a shit storm when everything went down with Ruby's parents. Nico could hardly avenge them while he was fighting tooth and nail for his own empire.

"So how do you want to deal with Levi moving forward?"

"We'll do what he does to everyone else. We'll use his resources, learn where his weaknesses are, and when the moment is right I'll bring that bastard down."

"I'm not convinced that the information we have on him is accurate." I say. Oh, I know Jace did a lot of digging, that he spent months working on getting eyes and ears inside the Holtz network but when you look at the detail, when you look at the numbers, it just doesn't add up.

"I agree." Nico says. "It's another reason to watch our backs. Once we have Ruby you can question her, find out what she knows."

"You think we can trust her?" I ask, curious to see if he thinks the same as me.

He shrugs. "Time will tell. Let's see how she is at the wedding. See how she interacts with her uncle." He downs the rest of his drink eyeing the fire once more, no doubt seeing the pile of papers waiting to go on it. "Are you cleaning house?"

"Can't be too careful considering." I mutter and we both know what I'm hinting at.

He grunts in reply before downing his drink and leaving me to it.

Ruby

CHAPTER *Five*

The truck careens to the right. My body slams into the side, my face smacks into the solid metal frame and the impact makes my nose stream with blood.

This isn't good. This isn't good at all.

When the truck comes to a stop and that awful silence fills the air, I know it's over. That I'm done for. And yet I can't accept it. I can't just wait here for my fate to come and kick me in the arse again.

I crawl out from under the tarp and drop to the ground.

I can hear them. I can hear how close they are.

One of the tyres has blown. They must have put a stinger out to bring us down.

My breath sounds ragged, my body already feels too beaten up, but I refuse to surrender now. I crawl down into the muddy ditch, feeling the stinking water seep into my shoes and between my toes, knowing that's the least of my worries right now.

But as I make it to the other side, as I manage to scramble behind the spikiest bush imaginable, his voice calls out.

"Come out, Ruby..."

I shut my eyes, that wave of fear hitting me once more, as my uncle's taunt rings out across the desolate landscape ahead of me.

"Come out now or your little friend gets a bullet in his head."

I shouldn't look. I know I shouldn't. But I do it anyway.

A whimper escapes my lips as I see Finn stood, with a gun rammed under his chin. He looks like he's already taken a beating. There's blood all over his shirt. One of his eyes is so swollen he can't even open it.

I bet they started laying punches the minute they opened the driver's door.

"You've got until the count of three." Levi snarls, like I have a choice.

He's going to kill him, even if I surrender. Finn betrayed him, he's going to make an example of him. Levi isn't merciful, he's not simply going to let Finn go if I hand myself over.

I huddle further into the spikes, welcoming the pain. Maybe if I wait long enough he'll think I'm gone. That I got away.

Only, I know I'm naïve to even believe that.

"One." Levi shouts out.

I don't move. I'm too paralysed by my fear to do anything now. My hands are wrapped around my head like a shield but I know it won't do any good.

"Two."

Maybe he'll kill me too.

Maybe he'll decide I'm not worth all this drama or whatever the hell this deal is.

I close my eyes, praying that's the case. That a simple bullet to the head might finally end this all for me.

A boot kicks into my side. I grunt as it makes contact and the pain radiates down my ribcage. It's not enough to break them, just enough to really hurt.

"Get up, Ruby."

The guard hauls me to my feet before I can move. But I'm quick to react, kneeing him in the groin and he falls back, groaning in the dirt.

"She's a feisty little bitch when she wants to be." Another one laughs, dragging me out by my hair and tossing me into the dirt in front of everyone.

I look up, staring at Finn. Levi has him in a headlock now.

Levi tilts his head, sneering, with the gun rammed into Finn's temple.

"Don't kill him." I whisper but I know he hears.

His response is to pull the trigger. To blast half of Finn's head off.

I scream, shutting my eyes but that horrific image is still plastered there along with the ones from before. My father. Abraham. All of them dead at Levi's hands.

He tosses Finn's body into the ditch, then grabs hold of me by my throat. "You're lucky you're worth so much." He mutters. "Otherwise I'd put a knife in your belly and leave you here to bleed out and die."

"Maybe I wish you would." I spit back because right now I'd prefer death. I'd prefer even a lonely agonising death than the awful future this man is forcing on me.

His lips curl. Ordinarily he'd hit me for my insolence but I know he won't this time. Not when the wedding is so close. He wouldn't want to have a battered bride showing him up now, would he?

He tosses me into the waiting car.

The partition is already up. I frantically try the door and it's locked from the outside.

There's no escaping this.

No last minute reprieve.

I'm so totally fucked now.

I sink into the leather of the seat, silently sobbing as I'm driven back to purgatory.

THEY LOCK ME BACK INTO MY CELL LIKE ROOM. I DON'T EVEN HAVE the strength to wash the dirt off me. I just collapse onto the bed, too exhausted and defeated to even attempt to take care of myself.

No doubt tomorrow Levi will ensure I'm all done up and presentable, ready for my new husband to use and abuse.

I scowl, biting my lip. I never wanted to get married. I never wanted to live this life. Her life. My mother's. I dreamt for so long of escape. And I told myself it was possible, that one day when I was old enough, Levi would either no longer see me as a threat or that I'd fool him enough that he'd let me go.

I guess that was wishful thinking but a girl has to hope, doesn't she? You can't spend your life in the dark and not dream of seeing the stars.

As the key turns in the lock, I freeze.

Something in my gut tells me already who it is.

Who's there.

As his scared face appears, my stomach turns and a wave of bile flares up. Of course he would be here, of course he would want one last hit before his fucktoy is gifted away for another to use.

I drop my gaze, shame and revulsion already sweeping through me because, just like always, I can't do a thing to stop this.

"You were stupid to run." He says quietly.

Maybe my fear is making me reckless now because I scoff at him, folding my arms, showing him for once the real me, the girl that still exists deep down and not the petrified creature he always turns me into.

He crosses the room, sinking onto the end of the bed and I jerk away, far enough that his disgusting hands can't touch me.

"Listen to me very carefully, Ruby," He says. "This is what you're going to do…"

I blink, listening to the words he speaks as if they're not real. As if this is all some delirious nightmare of my imagination. God, if only.

"…Marry Preston Civello. Play the good wife, the good whore I know you are. Seduce him, make him believe you love him." He instructs. "And all the while you'll pass on every bit of information, everything you can to bring him and Nico Morelli down."

I grit my teeth so hard I'm surprised they don't shatter.

Preston Civello? That's who they're essentially selling me off to? Oh, I know who he is, I know all about him. They say the man is so cold he's made of actual stone. That he doesn't show emotion, that he sees it as weakness - and yet Gunnar somehow thinks I can make him fall in love with me? As if that's possible. Hell would sooner freeze over than a man like Preston Civello would fall for me.

And worse, I'm meant to spy on them, him and Nico Morelli, I'm meant to pass on secrets; Christ, if they find out they'll skin me alive, irrespective of if I'm this Preston guy's wife or not. They'll torture me, beat me, make sure my death is a warning to the entire world.

I can feel myself shaking, I can feel my fear growing. Seduce him? How can I possibly do such a thing? I don't even know the first thing about sex, consensual sex anyway.

"Do what I ask and you can have your freedom." He states, like he can promise me that. He might be Levi's righthand man but ultimately he doesn't have the power to offer such a thing. He's not a Holtz. He doesn't run this Family.

He shifts closer, placing his hand on my thigh and I shudder a wave of revulsion threatens to erupt from the pit of my stomach.

"Be a good girl, Ruby, be smart and make the right choices."

Do I even have a choice in any of this? Besides, I don't doubt the man I'm marrying tomorrow will be just as bad as Levi. Just as controlling and, no doubt, just as abusive.

My shoulders slump as I realise I'm going from one prison to another.

And as his hand begins to move over me, grabbing at me, I shut my eyes, I shut down.

I retreat back into myself and try to ignore the horror of what's about to unfold.

Preston

CHAPTER
Six

Most men don't dream of their wedding day. Most men don't even consider what it will be like, if they even have one. But then again, most men aren't in the line of business I am.

I stand stiffly with Nico beside me. My parents had an arranged marriage, as did my grandparents. It's nothing unusual with our way of life and yet I'd never considered it for myself. Truth be told, I'd never imagined getting married at all. With death stalking your every move it seems a selfish thing to want to build a family, to want to put others at risk.

Besides, I'd never met any woman that seemed worth it.

Maybe that's why I'm so stoic about this. I'm not leaving some loved one behind, I'm not making some grand sacrifice, in reality, this decision was pretty easy to make. It was logical. This is for the good of the Morelli Family and it's the least I can do considering what Nico's family have done for me.

As the music begins to play out, I don't react. Nico and I have already agreed how we're going to handle this. It's a marriage of convenience, a way to seal the deal and while I'll smile for the cameras, that's all this is; a show. I'll pretend until this alliance falls apart, if it falls apart, and at the least it'll appease Nico's conscience to have his goddaughter safely out of the way.

Nico shifts beside me. The church is full. Levi has his side packed as though he really does consider Ruby to his actual offspring. All his men have that trademark diamond pinned to their suit pocket. God knows how much those things cost. Each diamond shows the rank of the man wearing it. The bigger the diamond, the higher up the food chain they are, with Gunnar having a full five carat monstrosity that looks almost ridiculous as it glints under the stained glass window.

On relatively short notice it's our men that fill out the pews to the right, making this look even more of a shotgun wedding than it already is.

Behind me I can sense them approaching. I can hear the tell-tale ruffles of a wedding dress, but I can hear something else too, above the music, above the merry little tune that's ringing out around us.

She's *crying.*

Something in my chest seems to thaw. I haven't even laid eyes on her and already I feel something akin to sympathy - as if that's an emotion I'm even remotely familiar with. Like I'm the kind of man that allows themselves to feel such weakness as that.

But some pathetic part of me suddenly wants to stop this, to pull her aside and tell her what's really going on, but that's crazy thinking. Besides, it could all be an act, a way to get me on side, while underneath, she's Levi's creature through and through - and I'm not going to be stupid enough to fall for it.

Only, she starts actually fighting, giving up all pretence and, as we all watch on, I realise she's either the best actress I've ever seen in my life or this is real.

She really doesn't want this.

She really is fighting as if her life depends upon it.

She digs her heels into the thick carpet and Levi curls his fist, clearly wanting to beat her, but he refrains under all our watchful gaze. So instead, he deepens his fingers in her arm and jerks hard enough that she stumbles forward and he can haul her down the last bit to where I'm stood.

As they come up beside me, it takes all I have not to punch the bastard in the face, but then I look at her, at my bride, and my heart seems to stop entirely.

She has a long veil covering her features but underneath a satin dress clings to a naturally curvaceous body that makes my mouth water and my dick come to life.

I know Levi said she was twenty one but she looks older.

She looks nothing like the blurry photo he showed me on his phone.

Perhaps it's the makeup, perhaps it's the dress, but this girl here, she doesn't look like a child. She looks every bit the Mafia Princess I'd first imagined her to be.

And it's the tears streaming down her beautiful face that seem to captivate me in a way I didn't expect.

I've never had much time for women's tears, much time for emotions in general. I'm a firm believer in being in full control of yourself, of keeping a hard mask in place, especially in public. Ordinarily, such a reaction would irritate the fuck out of me, but on Ruby it makes me even more curious.

I'm a sick bastard because all I can think is how she'd look as I slammed my cock down her throat, how she'd plead and beg and how pretty she'd be on her knees as I gave her a real reason to be crying.

She keeps her eyes down, refusing to look at any of us. Levi is gripping her arm in a way that I'm certain will bruise badly and I'm quick to pull her free. In less than an hour she'll belong to me anyway, so I'm staking my claim, making him see that from now on she's untouchable to him and all his cronies.

Something feral consumes me.

Some innate need to make the point that she's mine now. Mine to touch, mine to control.

All fucking mine.

Levi's lip curls as he looks at me and then he slinks away to sit on the front pew beside Gunnar, who is scowling like someone has shat on his bed and made him sleep in it.

The ceremony is quick. The priest has clearly been bribed because he doesn't seem to care that the bride wants no part of this. When it comes to her vows she stumbles, sobbing harder, too distraught to say any articulate words and Levi gets up, slapping his hand over her mouth from behind, and speaks them for her as if none of us would care.

Nico and I exchange a look while the priest acts like this is all perfectly normal, like every blushing bride behaves like this, as if they have a gun pressed right to their temple.

Putting the rings on is even worse.

I have to wrench her hand open and practically jam the thing down her finger. The diamonds seem to sparkle in jest, their light catches on the tears still streaming down her cheeks. She doesn't make any attempt to pick up the gold band meant for me and in the end, I pick it up and put it on myself.

When he says the words 'man and wife' she seems to deflate more, practically collapsing so I have to hold her up. It's like she's just been handed a death sentence. Like life as she knows it is over and I guess, in a way, it is.

She'll smile now if I allow it, she'll feel joy too when I decide.

She might have lived under her uncle's strict rules up to today but from now I get to decide every aspect of her life and deep down, I'm already revelling in that power.

I take her hand again, trying to ignore how small it feels in my grasp, all of her looks so fragile, so utterly breakable.

And I haul my new wife back down the aisle, while glaring at every man we pass, daring them to try something.

We only have to get through the reception now and then finally I'll have her all to myself.

Levi and Gunnar are drinking like this really is a celebration.

Eleri is sat stiff, with her eyes continuously darting to Ruby, who hasn't looked up once. Her veil is off her face, every few seconds she sniffs. Her makeup, that no doubt was immaculate hours ago, is smeared down her cheeks and a weak part of me wants to scoop her up and take her away from all the jackals surrounding her.

To her left is Levi and then Gunnar. I'm on her right, our chairs placed close enough that my leg should be touching hers and it takes a lot of effort to keep it twisted at an angle so I'm not. Nico is beside me with Eleri placed on the nearest table to ours.

I wonder if they did that on purpose, to try to goad Nico. To insult him further.

Eleri doesn't make a fuss. She takes her place beside Blaine and they seem to make conversation. If anything, I wish I could join them. I bet they're having a far better time than all of us sat on the top table.

It's a five course meal. Each one seems to drag out. I don't speak, I just eat, wanting this damned day over with. I don't think Ruby has more than a bite the entire time. The cutlery shakes in her hand so much I can hear it chinking against the plate like a fractured little tune. By the time desert comes, Levi is making blatant innuendos about his niece; comments no decent uncle would say.

"She comes from good breeding stock." He says, slapping Ruby's thigh as she jolts like she's been hit by lightning. "I expect you to use her well, after all, this is about binding our families together."

Ruby physically recoils, except there's nowhere for her to go; she's caught between the monster to her left and me, her new husband, a man over twice her age and one she clearly doesn't trust.

My eyes fix on her face, I study the way she reacts, the way she falls apart further as insult after insult lands.

"Her mother was easy enough to train." Gunnar says, leaning right over his plate to look at me. "In time, I'm sure you'll get her to behave exactly the way you want. Turn her into a proper whore for you."

My fists clench at the way they just spoke about my now wife, even though she clearly does not want me as a husband. I've never been this emotional, this reactive before. I don't know why now, why here, I seem to be taking complete leave of my senses.

"Keep it together." Nico mutters beside me, low enough that only I hear.

"Alright for you." I say back through gritted teeth. "Would you do the same if they spoke of Eleri like that?"

Nico tilts his head, his eyes flashing. "The situation is not the same."

"Eleri is your wife just as Ruby is now mine."

He shakes his head. "No…" He begins but Gunnar cuts across him.

"As a wedding gift, from our family to yours, we booked you the honeymoon suite at the Astoria."

My eyes connect with his as I take in the words. "What?" I half snap.

"Come now, Preston." Levi says. "Surely you want this wedding to get off to a good start? Afterall, my niece is used to the finer things in life, I expect you to treat her with respect."

Like they have up until now? They've already stated how much they want me to fuck her brains out. Hardly the words of a respectful family.

It feels like the room tenses.

I can't read the expression on Nico's face as he side eyes me. "The honeymoon suite?" I say, acting like I'm suddenly so honoured.

Beside me, Ruby looks like she's crying again. Like the prospect of spending the night with me has sent her right over the edge. God, this is fucking awful.

My anger spikes and, before I can stop myself, I'm on my feet. Levi looks at me like he wants this fight, like this was the entire point of today's proceedings.

My eyes drop to Ruby. She's huddled up like she just wants to disappear entirely and I can't say I blame her.

"Fine." I growl back. If they want to play this game, then I'll meet them head on. I grab Ruby's arm, hauling her to her feet more roughly than I mean, and she lets out a yelp. "Enjoy the rest of the party." I say before leading her out to what feels like a frat house round of applause.

Ruby

CHAPTER

Seven

I tried to keep it together. I really did. I even drank down the champagne at breakfast, knocked it back like it might make this all better, like it might numb everything, but as soon as we pulled up to the church everything went to shit.

The closer I got to the altar, the harder every step took. It felt like I was trying to swim through liquid concrete and the fact that Levi had to drag me the last few metres – yeah I doubt anyone will forget that in a hurry.

I couldn't look at them. At any of them. And especially not at my new husband.

Now, I'm sat beside him in the car, barely daring to breathe. I know he's angry and I'm more than aware what happens when men like him get angry. I bet Gunnar did that on purpose, made those remarks to get him as irate as possible. What a nice final fuck you now that he can't hurt me any longer.

I'm trembling so much he must see it, but he hasn't said a word.

He hasn't tried to touch me either.

It feels like he's trying to give me space, pressing his huge body as close to his door as he can possibly fit. But why would that be? What possible benefit would he gain from that? Especially when we both know what the rest of this night entails. Afterall, my body is his to do as he pleases, right?

I don't know whether to beg, to plead, to try to appeal to his sense of mercy – as if a man such as him even knows what that is. It feels like I'm getting neckache from the way I'm hanging my head so low.

"We're here." He says quietly. His voice is deep. He doesn't sound annoyed at me. He doesn't sound like he's angry that I'm making a scene, not behaving the way one would expect a bride in my position to be. A bride from *our* kind of family.

He gets out, walks around and opens my door, holding his arm for me and, reluctantly, I let him help me out of the car. My dress is so tight it's hard to move without assistance, and besides, I want to shore up whatever goodwill I can at this stage.

I can't afford to offend him now.

I can't afford to make him more angry because I know exactly what the consequences will be.

I belong to him now. He can treat me however he likes and no one will say a word otherwise. If he decides to beat me black and blue, to turn me into a human punchbag, no one will challenge him.

No, this man is now my destiny.

My fate.

And I've already fucked myself by losing control the way I did back at the church. I don't doubt my husband will make me pay for that offence as soon as the doors are shut on us, after all, he's

Nico's second in command, he's used to be treated a certain way, used to being respected. He will hardly let it pass that his own wife has behaved in such a manner. No, he's going to hurt me. I already know that, it's just a case now of what I can do to limit the pain.

The entire foyer falls silent as we walk into the hotel. A few people start to applaud as if this day is one of joy. I don't want to think about how I look. My makeup must be smeared down my face. My mascara must be everywhere. I half want to pull my veil back over my face to hide myself but I don't; something tells me my new husband will not like that.

I cling to his arm as if I need him to help steady me, and I see his eyes dart down to take note. Does he assume I'm behaving like a dutifully submissive bride? Or is even this displeasing to him?

When we get to the suite, I just stand there. Frozen. Mute. Perhaps, if I act obedient now, he might not beat me so badly?

It feels like a fool's hope – but that's what I am, what I've always been; a fool.

The suite is so luxurious, a complete contrast to the bare room I woke up in. There's crystal and gold covering almost every surface. The place gleams brighter than a jewellery shop. Part of me wants to feel some sort of elation that at least now I won't fall asleep shivering from the cold, at least now I will have proper meals, and clothes, and some sort of life, but that's all dependent on my husband's generosity and I've done nothing to earn it. Nothing at all.

Preston walks about, tossing his jacket over a chair, searching the entire space like he's looking for bombs. He pulls something out from under a side table and my eyes bulge as I register what it is.

"That won't be the only one." He murmurs, meeting my gaze, only I'm quick to drop it.

It's a bug. This room is bugged.

I cringe, realising what the implications are. My uncle didn't just gift us this room out of the benevolence of his own heart.

This is part of his plan. He wants to hear everything that happens tonight. He probably has cameras set up as well to record it.

My face flushes with more shame. Will he and Gunnar watch it together? Will they let their men watch it too? God, what must Preston think of my family, of me?

Maybe he won't care.

Maybe he will just fuck me regardless, even put on a show to make it clear who I belong to now. My stomach churns again and it's all I can do not to hurl up the meagre contents.

Preston comes to a stop in front of me and without thinking I look up.

He's handsome.

That thought alarms me more than it should. Should I be grateful for that? That my family didn't sell me to a grotesque pig? That I won't have to fuck a repulsive old man but an attractive one? He eyes me with what could be misconstrued as concern and I bite my lip to stop the sarcastic response I so dearly would love to say but would never have the guts.

I can see the hint of wrinkles at the corner of his fierce blue eyes. I can see the tanned colour of his skin, the way his strong jawline tenses like he's gritting his teeth just a tiny bit. His light brown, sun-kissed hair is swept back from his face but it's long enough that you could run your fingers through it, you could yank on it too - if you had a death-wish. He must be twice my age and some. I don't know how to feel about that, I guess there's nothing *to* feel. The deed is done. He's my husband now. I'm as good as his property.

"Would you like a drink?" He asks quietly, with that same emotionless, controlled tone of his.

I nod quickly. I'll take anything right now, anything to ease the horror of this. Hell, if he offered to drug me, I think I'd say yes. I think I'd willingly slip into oblivion for a few hours and let him do what he wants to my body so I don't have to face what's about to come next.

He comes back with a glass of whiskey for both of us. I sip mine before choking on the sharpness.

"Would you prefer champagne?" He asks, like he actually cares.

"No." It's the first word I've said all day. The first word I've ever spoken directly to him. It feels like an omen. Like we're already doomed from the start but then we are, aren't we? Nothing about this marriage is set for success.

He frowns, clearly confused by my response, and I take the opportunity to knock the entire glass back before spluttering once more. I'd rather have something strong. I'd rather numb my senses with something I know will not only kick in fast, but will last.

He swears under his breath, taking the weighty crystal glass from my hand and then shots back his own, though I suppose he can handle it better than me because he doesn't choke. He just swallows it like it's water.

He walks back over to the bar, setting the glasses down with his back to me.

I can feel the tension between us. I can feel every single one of those glances he's been giving me when he thought I wouldn't notice.

So I don't fight it.

It's easier not to.

Far easier.

It's a lesson I learnt long ago and one far too painful to repeat. My body seems to give up as I silently make my way past the couches, past the balcony with the enviable view, and into the room beyond.

The bed is massive. It's strewn with rose petals. My breath catches as I take it in because this would be any other girl's dream. A wedding night spent here, in the very heights of luxury.

His footsteps give him away as he walks up behind me. When he places his hands on my shoulders I physically jump, though mercifully I bite back the strangled cry before it can truly form.

"Ssssh." He soothes me quietly. "I'm not going to hurt you or do anything you don't want."

I don't reply. It's already been made perfectly clear by Gunnar what he expects of me. What my duties are. This marriage has to be consummated. Add the fact they bugged the place and I know my actions will be scrutinised, that everything we do will be checked and if I don't act the way I'm supposed to, Gunnar will certainly make me pay.

Besides, I'm under no illusions what my new husband is capable of if push came to shove. He's literally the same mould as all of them, as Levi, Gunnar, Nico Morelli too. Different name, same predatory behaviour.

Slowly, he begins to slide the clips out of my hair. It tumbles down my back but, I'll admit, it feels good to no longer have the metal pressing against my scalp.

The only sound beyond my rapidly increasing breath is the little tapping noise the clips make as he tosses each one onto the carpet.

When it's all free, he sweeps it to one side, lowering his mouth to my exposed neck. I gulp, waiting for the inevitable feel of his lips on my skin.

"We need to put on a show." He says quietly, right into my ear, like he thinks someone *is* listening in.

"What?" I frown.

"The other room was bugged. It's almost certain there are cameras in here."

He doesn't need to tell me that because it's obvious, isn't it?

"...I can try to find them but I doubt I'll get them all." He continues.

I nod. He's right. Levi and Gunnar would have had days to prep this. There's no way we'd be able to find them, even if we spent all night searching.

But why do we need to put a show on? Why does he care what they do and don't see? I blink as I realise what he means, what he must be thinking.

"I'm not," My face flushes with more shame, "I'm not a virgin." I whisper. He's going to be mad about that. He was probably sold the notion that I was some sort of untouched prize when I'm anything but.

I tense up, waiting for the inevitable fallout of that confession, for the hand in my hair to tighten, for my body to be slammed to the ground before the blows start landing – only, it doesn't come.

He lets out a low breath that warms the back of my neck in way that's almost soothing. "It doesn't matter." He says. "You're my wife now. I'm not going to let them see anything. To expose you any more than I have to."

I turn, forcing myself to face him properly. He sounds so protective right now. He sounds like he might actually help me. His eyes scan my face and, for the first time, I allow myself to *truly* look at him too, to bury the fear and truly take in his appearance, without shame, or whatever other twisted emotions have been clouding my vision.

He's tall. I know I'm above average height for a girl but he still towers over me.

His jaw is angular, his skin is tanned. His eyes seem to hint at what I want to believe is a kindness under all that brooding mass of muscle. I want to indulge in that notion, that this man might be less of a brute, that perhaps even, he might show me softness, gentleness, if I'm careful enough about my own behaviour. If I act the way my mother did with my father.

His hand moves to catch my face, his fingertips brush my cheek and my breath stops for a second.

'Seduce him.' Gunnar's words ring out in my head. He was more than clear what he expected me to do, what the consequences would be if I disobeyed.

As I hold his gaze, I move my hands, fumbling with the zip at the back of my dress. The fabric slips, the satin slides down my body and pools at my feet, and his eyes widen just a little.

He swears under his breath, staring at me now I'm fully exposed. This morning I hated the lingerie that was laid out for me because I knew it was all part of this sham but now, now I'll admit that the look in his eyes, the way he seems to be devouring every inch of me, makes me feel something, makes some part of me want to be desired in a way I've never dared to seek before.

I have to put on a show now. I have to act like I want this.

Only, under my fear, under those words that keep repeating in my head I think I do want this. Inexplicably, incomprehensibly, I think I'm less fearful of what's about to happen, as if I'm the kind of girl that understands pleasure, that knows what it feels like when sex isn't forced. When it's wanted.

And if I can control this, if I can make him believe that I'm a person worthy to be his wife then perhaps I might just survive after all.

"You can touch me." I say, giving permission like he isn't used to simply taking what he deems as his.

He tilts his head, tangling his hands into the mass of my hair further and as he angles my head back he captures my lips in a devastating kiss. I lean into him, letting his lips ease mine apart and then his tongue slides in, caressing mine as he groans.

I've never kissed a man before. Never kissed anyone. I let him take control, let him dominate every moment but I'll admit some part of me enjoys the way he's devouring me right now.

He tastes of whiskey. He tastes of danger. He tastes of everything I fear and everything I want to hope might just save me.

His arms wrap around my body and he carries me backwards onto the bed. It feels like he's stopped caring about who could be watching this scene play out, that he's so lost in his lust that he no longer gives a damn, and then he seems to come to his senses. He gets up, pulls his clothes off and tosses them, before he yanks the duvet up and over to conceal us both.

I blink, staring at him and his lips curl into an almost cruel smirk before he reaches over and turns off all the lights, pitching us into near total darkness.

Our breathing sounds so much more exaggerated under the covers. I can't see him but I know he's touching distance from me and I can feel the heat radiating off him.

I reach out and my fingertips meet the hard, smooth skin of his chest. He's so warm, like under that skin he's on fire. It makes me want to snuggle up into him, to seek the safety of his body, as irrational as that thought is. Only, his hand curls around mine, keeping it still, preventing me from doing so.

"Ruby." He murmurs and it sounds like a warning.

But I lean in closer anyway. Maybe it's the alcohol making me behave like this, maybe it's the relief that this man, this stranger who is now my husband clearly isn't going to hurt me like I first thought. Perhaps he isn't as much of a monster as the ones I've grown up with. At least, not in this moment, he's not.

He pulls me closer and I can feel it, his dick, it's hard, pressing into me through his boxers which he's curiously still kept on.

"Can you pretend?" He murmurs quietly.

"Pretend what?" I reply.

"They can't see anything now but they can still hear."

My face flushes. He wants them to think we're having sex rather than actually doing it. But why?

"I need you to make the right noises. Can you do that? Can you fake it?"

"Why?" I ask.

"Because they're listening." He states again, like I'm stupid.

"No." I say. "Why only pretend?"

That makes him pause. "I'm not fucking you here. Not like this. If I fuck you there won't be witnesses."

"If?" I repeat in confusion. What man doesn't want to fuck their new bride? I'm not exactly ugly, I know that, despite how disgusting I feel inside there's no visible taint, nothing that shows what I really am, and it's clear from the way Preston reacted when I stripped that he's attracted to me, that he wants me.

He cups my cheek with his hand. "You've spent almost the entire day crying. It's clear you don't want this. Do you really think I'm going to force you?"

I don't know how to respond. What to say. What man in his line of business doesn't just take what he wants?

"Ruby…"

"You can fuck me." I say, cutting across whatever he's about to. It's better to get it over with. Better to just be done because refusing him is only going to cause more pain for me. Besides, I'm his wife now, he can do what he wants with me.

He growls, pulling me around so that his body is more on top of mine and instinctively I shut my eyes ready for the feel of his hands grabbing at me, for my legs to be forced open.

"I'm not doing that." He says. "But I need you to moan, to pretend that I am and that you're enjoying it."

I blink back. Enjoy it? Since when did someone care if I enjoyed it? "Okay." I whisper, hoping I can do that.

"I'm going to kiss you. It will make this feel less awkward."

I nod, not that he can see and then his lips are on me, his tongue is back in my mouth and all thought, all reason seems to dissipate. He wraps his arms back around me and I lose myself in whatever magic he seems to be creating.

"Moan," He murmurs against my lips.

Right. Pretending. I'm meant to be acting like we're having sex.

I let out a noise. It feels constrained. It feels wrong. I don't even know how to moan, not the way he clearly wants or expects.

He kisses me deeper, as if he's trying to make this all feel less contrived. I moan again, at least I think I do. It sounds even worse than before. I must be the worst actress in the entire history of the world.

He stops, cupping my cheek. "Not like that." He says. "Pretend that you're enjoying this. Pretend that I'm touching you, giving you pleasure, making you come."

My face flushes with shame. I make another noise. I try so hard to do what he asks but I can tell it's wrong. All of it is wrong. He's going to be angry. He's going to hurt me now because I'm failing at this.

"I don't know how…" I mumble. I don't even know this man and all of this suddenly feels too much. Way too much.

"You've never come before?" He says after a moment.

"No." I manage to say, though god only knows how I get the word out.

"I thought you said you've had sex?"

I look away for a moment, not that he can see me but it feels like even through this darkness, all of this is far too intimate.

"I have." I say jutting my chin. "I've fucked loads of men." I don't want him to know the truth. Right now I'd rather he think me a whore of my own choosing than what I really am.

He lets out a snort. "And none of them have made you come?" He murmurs. "Do you not touch yourself?"

"Why would I?"

The air seems to tense. Like he's learning all my awful little secrets.

He lets out a sigh. "Alright." He says but it sounds like he's talking more to himself than to me. Like I'm so disgusting he needs to give himself a pep talk before he can even consider sinking his cock into me.

He holds me tighter, turning my body so that I'm now tucked against him with my back to his stomach. It's so hard to ignore his erection from this position. He feels huge, he feels colossal.

"Let's just sleep." He murmurs.

My eyes widen. "You don't want to pretend more?"

"No."

I've disappointed him. I've failed. I hang my head, not sure what to do. In so many ways it feels like my prayers have been answered. He's not touched me. He's not done anything other than kiss me and I'm not ashamed to admit that I like his kisses. I like the way it feels when his tongue is in my mouth, when he's wrapping his hands around my hair like I'm something to actually want.

But this won't be the end of it.

This man may act nice right now but he's going to flip, he's going to use this against me. Just as Levi and Gunnar would. I've failed a task and my new husband is going to make me pay.

"I can be better." I say quickly.

"Better with what?" He asks, sounding confused.

"I can pretend better. I can. I…" His hand over my mouth silences my pleas. I'm pulled onto my back, with him leaning right over me once more. His head lowers to my ear and I know I'm so fucked. Clearly this isn't a man you can beg, you can plead with. I've completely miscalculated who my new husband is and now I'm going to suffer the consequences.

"Listen to me carefully, Ruby." He says so quietly. "I'm not like Levi. I'm nothing like him. I don't want you to pretend. I don't want you to be afraid of me. I'm not going to hurt you or do anything you don't want, do you understand that?"

I don't. I don't understand at all. Why the fuck is he saying that? Why the fuck is he pretending to be a decent person when we all know men in our world are not like that?

I stare up at him through the darkness, trying to figure out if this is some sort of test. If it is, then I'm definitely failing and I can't have that, I can't face the inevitable pain that comes with failure. So I take his hand, moving it to where the lace of my thong is. I can feel him jerk, I can feel the surprise as he realises what I'm doing.

"If you want me to moan then make me." I say, summoning the last of my confidence, the last of my bravery. Whatever it is he's talking about, whatever it sounds like when you come, if that's what he wants and that's what will save me a beating later, then fine, he can do it.

I'll be a performing monkey, I'll jump through whatever hoops he creates, if that's what it comes down to.

It feels like the air tenses more. Perhaps I've pushed him too far.

But as that thought forms, I feel his fingers move, feel him sliding further down under the fabric. I let out a gasp, shutting my eyes as he starts to explore me like this is what he wanted all along.

I spread my legs wider, instinct telling me that that's what my husband wants, how I should be behaving.

His touch feels light and yet so possessive all the same. I bite my lip, unsure what to expect. Gunnar never touched me like this. No one has touched me like this. Ever. I'm a thing to fuck, a hole to be used.

As his fingers circle my entrance, I brace myself for the same pain there always is, the same awful intrusion – only, it doesn't come. Instead, he traces back up, spreading what I realise with horror is my own wetness.

I'm wet.

I'm aroused.

My body clearly wants this and though a part of me is ashamed, another is so relieved. This will make my husband happy, won't it? It will make him think that I really do want his touch.

He murmurs something but under my heavy breathing I can't make out the words and then he's slowly circling some part of me, some secret part I didn't know existed, but fuck me does it feel like I might just lose my mind at that.

I let out a noise. A deep, loud sound that vibrates through me as if I'm actually enjoying this.

"Does that feel good, Ruby?" He asks gently.

I nod, grasping at the sheets as my body leaks out more liquid. Fuck, it feels so good. How is that possible?

"If I could, I'd teach you what it feels like…" He says in more of growl, as if he too is holding some part back.

"Teach me what?" I gasp. It's hard to think, hard to register any of his words as he manipulates me to perfection.

His lips find mine, he kisses me like this moment here is everything he wanted and, as his tongue delves into my mouth, I fall apart. I writhe, I arch my back, I clench my eyes so tight as an explosion detonates inside me.

"Scream, Ruby." Preston all but orders. "Let it out."

I want to. I want to scream so loudly. But as my mouth opens no noise comes out. I know I'm coming. I know that's what my body is doing right now, that as my legs kick and more pleasure than I can fathom explodes in my mind, I'm coming like the whore my family believes I am and yet I can't scream, I can't make a sound.

Preston keeps me there, right on edge as if he really is trying to make a point about his total possession over me. And for one fearful moment I think he might pull the covers off and reveal what we're doing to the cameras. That he's going to parade me, shame me even.

Only he doesn't. His sole focus seems to be on me.

When I slump back, I can feel the sweat on my brow, I can feel the beads of it on my skin. My heart is thumping so violently in my chest I think it might smash through my ribcage but that euphoria is still there, still on the peripheries, like I've tasted heaven and stolen a little piece of it.

He brushes my hair back, but he's giving me a look like a mask has come down, like that emotionless cold monster is once more taking over. "That wasn't meant to happen." He says quietly.

"You didn't want me to..." I trail off embarrassed by the word as much as what I've just done. Was I stupid to have let that happen, to have just given in like that and submitted?

"No," He says. "I'm not meant to be touching you."

I frown, staring back at him. "Why not?"

He shakes his head like he doesn't want to say but he's pulling me around, wrapping his arms around me like he wants to protect me. Only, I know it's madness to even think it.

"You can trust me." He says.

I know that's another lie.

Another thing he's probably saying to lull me into a false sense of security. I can't trust him anymore than I can trust Levi or Nico Morelli for that fact.

My heart is racing. Some stupid part of me wants to believe it but my survival instincts are rapidly overriding it.

So I don't reply.

I just shut my eyes and let him think I'm agreeing. It's far safer that way. Act the way they want, behave the way they want.

Don't show weakness, don't disobey. Ever.

If I want to survive, if I want to escape all of this, I need to be smart, focused. I need to play the game just as well as all the bastard men around me.

Preston

CHAPTER *Eight*

She drifts off in my arms. In a way I'm relieved that she has because it gives me thinking time. It gives me a reprieve.

I don't know what the fuck is happening to me, why suddenly I seem to have lost all control, all sense of reason but it's like my heart has melted, like I'm suddenly feeling for the first time, as if every moment up until now was spent existing in simple black and white.

Oh, I know she doesn't believe me. I can tell that my words of kindness, that my behaviour is confusing her. Scaring her even. Hell, it's confusing me too. I don't even know why I'm reacting like this, why I give a damn, because let's face it, I never have before - but the moment we were alone, the moment our eyes connected, my entire plan crashed and burnt.

I can't simply lock this woman away.

I can't simply pretend that she doesn't exist, because she's already wrapped herself right around my stone cold heart before she even spoke a word. If I didn't know better I'd think she'd done it on purpose, that this is all some sort of trick.

God, it would be so much easier if it was.

If she really was just playing a part, I could handle it, I could handle her; but she's not a snake. She's not a spy. This girl is clearly petrified of her own shadow and that kind of fear, it doesn't come from nowhere.

She lets out a little whimper. It's so quiet it's like she's fearful of making noise even when she's asleep. She's so used to Levi and Gunnar controlling her. She's grown up in their toxic, fucked up world, no wonder she doesn't know how to react when someone shows her a tiny bit of kindness.

It's going to take time to bring her out of her shell, to show her that she is safe and I'm not sure I'm the man to do it.

I've already crossed boundaries, already stepped over so many lines I said I wouldn't do.

I promised myself I wouldn't touch her. I wouldn't even kiss her. I wouldn't do anything that made this relationship even close to being real. She's too young, far too young to understand all of this and but she took her dress off, the minute I saw her body, I wanted her more than I could put into words.

Except, she wasn't consenting. It doesn't matter that she spoke the words, that she tried to act like she was willing. She wasn't actually okay with this. I've already seen enough of her behaviour to realise what she's doing; that she simply plays along, that she doesn't fight. Whatever the fuck Levi did to her family, it's clearly taught her that asserting herself, raising her head above the parapet for any reason, only results in punishment.

And yet the minute she put my hand into her thong, I couldn't resist. I couldn't fight the overwhelming urge to claim her. To possess every inch of her.

On the side, my phone buzzes, and I pick it up reading the message. Apparently the party turned into a fight after we left.

Nico, Eleri, and Blaine made their excuses and got out but we kept enough men there to watch Levi just in case.

Ruby shifts just a tiny bit, and I brush her frazzled hair back off her face.

She feels too fragile. She feels too young. The kind of women I usually go for, the kind of women I fuck are so different than the girl laying in my arms right now. I'm used to confident, assertive, sassy women that can take charge, that know what they want and aren't afraid to go get it. Women I can use and toss aside without guilt, without concern.

Ruby feels like an animal that's been caged so long she's forgotten she even has claws or how to use them.

But I'll admit there's a small part of me that wants to be the one to teach her. To turn her into something ferocious, someone to be reckoned with.

To show her that all the cruelty she's experienced up till now is done. That I'm going to protect her. That I'm going to look after her.

I'm up with the sun. We didn't draw the curtains and I'm quick to pull them across and block out any light. My new wife is still out for the count and, though I let her sleep for a few more hours, in the end my need to get out of this damned suite is what makes me wake her up.

She stirs, letting out a soft moan and then, as she opens her eyes, she recoils back as that fear takes over her completely.

"It's okay." I say in what I hope is a reassuring way.

She doesn't meet my gaze but her eyes dart around like she's trying to assess how much danger she's in. I can practically see the way she's folding herself inward, taking all those tiny pieces of herself and hiding them away behind the docile mask she wears so well.

"What time is it?" She whispers.

"It's early," I reply. "But we need to leave."

"Has, has something happened?"

"No." I say. But I want us both as far from Levi's reach as I can get now. I hold up her dress, giving it a shake as she gets out of the bed. Thank god it's got a zip and not some fancy corset back because I wouldn't have the patience to do it back up, nor would I be able to stop myself from touching her given the opportunity. "We can eat back at my house. I'll have a breakfast prepared for us."

"Okay." She says like she doesn't have any opinions, like she doesn't have any thoughts of her own, like she's some simple minded creature that lets the entire world control her.

I'm going to change that.

I'm going to bring out the real Ruby, the girl that she's buried so deep inside she's forgotten who she is.

She takes the dress from my hands, slipping it up over that beautiful body that I'm trying so hard not to leer at. I do the zip back up, half wishing I could rip it off and devour her and the cameras be damned.

"Let's go." I say, taking her hand and she lets me lead her out.

There's still champagne on the side. If I were more of a romantic I'd let us enjoy the view from the balcony, I'd indulge in everything this suite has to offer; we'd sit out in the hot tub, watching the city come to life, we'd have a lazy breakfast, wearing the fluffy white robes and matching slippers.

Only, I'm not that sort of a man.

Romance is as obscure a concept to me as mercy is, as forgiveness is.

And truth be told, I want the security of my own house. The safety of my four walls.

If Ruby wants to soak in a hot tub then I'll buy her one. I'll have an entire spa complex built if that's what will make her happy, though I suspect she'll never voice that want for fear of displeasing me in some way.

At the door Noah and Jace greet us. Ruby's eyes widen as she stares from one overbearing tattooed man to the other. We might have technically arrived here with just the driver but we weren't going to remain that way. A part from anything else, I wouldn't put it past Levi to gut me in my sleep.

The car journey takes long enough that she falls back asleep. Her head lulls against the leather and I've got the best view of her cleavage if I choose to look. Which, naturally I do. I can't seem to stop looking. To stop staring at her. My hands are itching to touch her, to just reach out and take what's technically already mine.

In my head I told myself she was a barely more than a child. From the pictures, that's what she looked like. I never expected to be attracted to her. I never expected to want her.

But now, now I can't take my damned eyes off her.

She's my wife; and that thought alone makes my dick harden.

But Nico and I had an agreement. I'm not going to fuck her. I'm not going to touch her any more than I already have. I'm the one in control here. I'm not going to let a little desire change who I am. Maybe we shouldn't even be sleeping in the same bed because she feels like a temptress come to bring me to my doom. Some siren sat out on the rocks, calling to me with a secret song only I can hear.

As we pull up to the security gates, she wakes up. Her eyes meet mine and she gives me a shy half-smile.

"We're here." I say. It's same line I said when we got to the hotel. It sounds stiff. I sound almost pompous.

She lets out a sigh that could be a shudder. Her eyes drift past the walls and to the huge house beyond and her jaw drops.

"Do you like it?" It shouldn't matter. Not really. If everything goes to plan she won't be here long enough for this place to truly become home. But I want her to like it. I want her to be happy here.

"It's not what I expected." She admits.

My lips curl at what feels like a rare show of honesty. "What did you expect?"

"More concrete." She says. "Like Levi's compound."

"Ah." That makes sense. She's used to walls and prisons. She's used to the great monstrosity Levi built that resembles more of a bunker than a home.

"Are you not afraid?" She asks. "With all those glass windows?"

"Afraid of what?"

"Attack."

I shake my head. "It's all reinforced. Bullet proof. And no one can get past the perimeter."

"You're sure?"

The car door opens as she speaks and she bites her lip, like she thinks questioning me is speaking out of turn. I get out, holding my hand for her and she once again takes it like she's taking the very hand of death.

"You're safe here, Ruby." I say, leading her up the stone steps. "I want you to feel safe, to feel at home."

She side eyes me like she doesn't believe a word I'm saying but I let it go. It's going to take time but I am going to get her trust me.

I don't bother giving her a tour, that can wait, instead I take her straight to the master suite. "Grab a shower, freshen up. Breakfast will be ready when you are." I say before leaving her to it, giving her what I suspect is her first moment of privacy in the last twenty four hours.

I head down to the dining room, taking the time to pour an extra strong coffee while I go through my emails.

When I hear the patter of her bare feet on the stairs, I look up in surprise. She was quick. Like she was afraid of keeping me waiting.

She's wearing a silk robe that more than hints at her pebbled nipples beneath. And the turquoise colour accentuates how pale she is. With her mother's heritage her skin should be so much darker. Maybe Levi kept her locked inside and that's why she looks like she's never felt the sun on her skin.

She stands awkwardly, just inside the room, waiting for something.

Her hair is damp. Her face is finally free of all the smeared makeup and, though she looks beautiful, I can see the faint hint of bruising against her right cheekbone. Someone hit her. And recently. A flash of rage surges in me and I clench my fists, forcing it back down, reminding myself that she's mine now, no one is going to hurt her ever again.

"Sit, Ruby." I say, realising that's what she's waiting for. God damn permission just to breathe.

She does it quickly, sliding into a seat that's far enough out of reach from me but not so far I'd take it as an insult.

"Do you like coffee?"

She nods.

I get up, taking the cafetiere from the side and pour out a fresh mug for her. When I place it in front of her, she wraps her hands around it like she wants to warmth to reach her very soul.

"Are you hungry?" I ask as I sit back down.

"A little."

"What do you like to eat?"

She shrugs, all noncommittal, and my jaw tightens with frustration. She's so afraid of saying anything, of voicing any opinion. It's fucking infuriating.

"Fine." I murmur before clicking my fingers and quietly make the staff bring up everything there is.

She keeps her eyes down. Every so often she sips her drink and I'll admit I catch myself fantasising about what those pouty lips would feel like wrapped around something other than just that cup.

When the food is laid out, her eyes widen. She looks up at me in alarm. "I, I can't eat all this." She stammers.

I let my lips curl. "You wouldn't say what you liked so I decided to give you options."

She blanches. "I didn't mean…"

I get up, moving to sit in the chair next to hers and she immediately stiffens. "Eat as much as you want." I say before reaching over and piling up some bacon onto my plate. I'd put some on hers too but if she doesn't want it then I know she'd eat it to be polite and that's the exact opposite of what I'm trying to achieve.

She waits until I'm done and then starts doing the same, taking some bacon, some waffles, and some other bits. I note it all. Clearly this girl has been conditioned into just accepting whatever scraps are thrown her way but I'm not going to let her live like that from now on.

I'll give her a cage far bigger than the one she was locked in. I'll let her spread her wings but only so far. Afterall, she's still my wife, and that puts a target on her back.

I tuck in quickly. As much as I'd like to spend the day here, things are already piling up my to do list.

My phone buzzes loudly and I pick it up to hear Noah issuing commands in the background.

"What is it?" I ask.

"Sorry, boss. This Tang shipment has gone to shit." He says.

"How?"

"Half the stock has been quarantined."

"What?" I snarl. Beside me, Ruby flinches and I get up, stepping away, cursing myself for my reaction.

"Apparently it's contaminated." Noah states.

"Contaminated with what?"

"That's just it, boss. Can't seem to get the answer to that."

"For fucksake." I growl. This is the last thing I need right now. More government bureaucracy. I glance at Ruby and she's sat, no longer eating, instead she's staring at her plate like she's ready to be held responsible for whatever the fuck is going on. "Give me ten and I'll be there."

I hang up before I get a reply.

"I have to go." I say, like my wife hasn't heard it.

She gives me a small nod but she doesn't look at me. The anger I feel is unfounded, but I want those eyes on me, I want her to *want* to look at me, to want her to devour me the way I almost did her last night.

Without thinking I grab her jaw, jerking her head up and those frightened eyes go so wide.

I can practically hear the hammering of her heart. I can see the pulse at her neck thumping so quickly with a burst of adrenaline.

"Explore the house. Take a bath if you want." I state, easing my grip. She's not meaning to be disrespectful and I need to remember that. "There's a library if you'd like to read."

"Okay."

"The staff can get you whatever you want, just ask them and they will oblige."

She nods again with the tiniest of movements but already I know she won't ask for shit. She'll probably hide away, pretend she doesn't exist rather than be noticed for even a second.

"Will you be back later?" She says quietly, like she's petrified of whatever answer I give.

"I'll try." I say, planting a kiss on her forehead before I can think not to.

She shuts her eyes, her body jolting like she wants to pull away but is too afraid of pissing me off more.

Maybe it's better if I'm not back.

Maybe a few days of just adjusting here might reassure her. I know Sidney will happily cater to her every need and it's clear my presence is making her more fearful. Besides, I need some time to think, to clear my own head, to stop looking at me new wife and obsessing over all the things I'm not allowed to do to her.

As I go to leave, I tell Sidney to look after her. That whatever she wants she gets, no questions asked.

And then I message to have the townhouse readied for me. I'll sleep there tonight. I'll give her a little space and see if that helps her adjust.

Preston

CHAPTER *Nine*

"Well?" Eleri says as I walk into the room.

Nico is sat beside her, his eyes fixed on me like he already knows I've fucked up and taken a bite of the forbidden fruit.

"She's fine." I say.

Even Blaine snorts at that.

"Alright." I sigh, pouring myself a stiff drink despite the fact it's still very much early morning. "She's all over the place."

"In what way?" Nico asks.

I shrug. "She's so she's scared of her own shadow she barely breathes. She says whatever she thinks will placate me. She does whatever she thinks will make me happy."

"Sounds like the perfect wife." Blaine mutters and Eleri shoots him a look.

"She's fucking traumatised." I snap, feeling my anger flare. She's not fucking perfect, she's so far from it though none of it is her fault exactly.

"Traumatised by the sight of your cock?" Blaine teases and Eleri gets up and slaps him before I can.

He grins, rubbing the red mark like it's something of pleasure not pain. The fucking psycho that he is.

"Have you spoken to her?" She asks as she sits down, because apparently assaulting Blaine is now a thing she doesn't think twice about.

I fix her with a look. I'll admit I used to avoid staring at her face, when I first laid eyes on her the scars used to make me cringe but since she's been with Nico she owns them, like they're battle wounds. She styles her hair not to hide herself but to show off. She's beautiful in a devastating way and the contrast between her and my ghost of a wife couldn't be more apparent.

"About what?" I ask back.

"Any of it. Has she talked about her mother? About Levi? Anything?" Nico says.

I shake my head. "No. She doesn't talk. And when she does it's mainly one word answers."

"Sounds perfect to me." Blaine says and I pick up the nearest glass and lob it at his damned head.

He responds by laughing as it bounces off and smashes.

"There were cameras in the room." I say. Like they didn't know. Like I didn't tell them already.

Nico leans back in his chair. "What benefit could they have to watch you?"

"Maybe Levi gets off watching others fuck." Blaine shrugs.

"That's not it." I say. Levi isn't a voyeur. This wasn't some sort of kinky sex thing. It was a power trip, I just don't get why. It's like they're intentionally trying to piss me off, despite our alliance.

"I don't understand what he's doing." Nico murmurs, glancing at the paperwork he sent over to us.

"Me neither." I say. Even this marriage seems odd. Why would Levi have sought an alliance with us? There are enough big players about, the Puccini's, the Gambino's. All of them are powerful enough to have been a good ally and, considering our history… I sigh shaking my head slightly. I feel like I had the worst night sleep of my life because I spent the majority of it watching over my wife, unable to take my eyes from her, afraid that if I dropped my guard either Levi would be there, in the shadows, or worse, I'd lose what little control I mustered and I'd be touching what I'm not permitted to.

I rub my temples, trying to ease the headache that's already forming. I'm not even one day into this marriage and already my wife is fucking with every carefully constructed piece of my world.

"Has she said anything about her mother?" Eleri asks again.

"Not a thing but then I haven't asked." I replied.

She chews her lip. "It sounds like she needs a friend." She mutters.

"She needs therapy." I state bluntly. "And a lot of it."

"Can you blame her with what she's been through?" Nico growls.

No, no I can't. Watching your family be murdered right in front of you is enough to fuck anyone up - I of all people know that.

"I want to see her." Eleri says. "Maybe a woman might put her more at ease."

Nico takes her hand and nods his approval.

"Call in whenever you want." I say. "I'll be staying at the townhouse for the moment so she's on her own, apart from the staff."

"Why are you staying at the townhouse?" Nico asks, narrowing his eyes like he's caught me in some sort of lie.

"She needs space." I state. "She needs time to adjust to all of this."

He tilts his head, assessing me. "You better not have touched her."

"I haven't." I snap. "But she's weird about that too."

"In what way?"

"She knew the cameras where there, I even stated it, and yet she told me I could fuck her anyway."

Blaine chokes. Eleri goes pale like she knows something I don't.

"What?" Nico growls back at me.

"I didn't obviously. I could tell it was bullshit. But the way she was…"

"What?" Nico repeats.

I shake my head, not able to properly form the words that are in my head. I don't even know what I mean. But there's something. My gut tells me that. There's obviously some trauma there, some trigger, after all, she couldn't even imitate the right sounds, she couldn't even fake the feeling of pleasure despite her bravado about being some sort of nympho.

"I'll go see her." Eleri says. "Maybe she'll open up to me."

"Be careful with her." I say, feeling a flash of protectiveness. I trust Eleri but even so, this is my wife. She's fragile. I won't have her harmed any more than she is already.

She gives me a reassuring smile. "I will be."

"Are we done talking about Preston's wife?" Blaine asks.

Eleri throws him a look but Nico picks up the paperwork, looking through the routes Levi is now offering to us.

Diamonds and drugs. It even has a ring to it, doesn't it? I guess it makes sense to be smuggling them together. They're both worth enough that you would kill for them. I just find it curious that Levi is being so open, so forthcoming. He's willing to throw his hand so easily in with us when his business should be one that sets him apart. That keeps him apart.

I don't know any other smugglers that would share their secrets, so what does he gain beyond our protection? And why does a man such as Levi even need *our* protection in the first place? What sort of shit has he created that means he has to come crawling to another Family for help?

I guess sooner or later we're going to find out the answer to that.

And when we do, I know Nico is going to use it, he's going to turn this to our advantage. Levi Holtz thinks he's leading this dance, when the truth is, we've got him by the balls – he just doesn't know it yet.

Ruby

CHAPTER

Ten

This house is so big. Not that I expected my new husband to live in a one bed apartment considering who he is. But there are little things, odd things that give me flashbacks to my old home, to the one where my mother and father lived.

Once he's left, I eat quicker, all but scoffing the food down. I'm so hungry I could cry because I didn't eat a thing yesterday. Only, I didn't want him to see that. I didn't want him to think I behave like that. Like I don't have any manners.

Once I'm done, I get up, my mind already fixing on a plan.

I don't know how long Preston will be gone but if I'm going to get away, then this is my chance. I can't believe what Gunnar said, I can't trust that he'll let me go once this is all over.

I have to take the chance now, when everyone thinks I've given in and accepted all of this.

I sneak into Preston's rooms, yanking out a t-shirt and shorts from amongst his clothes. It's not ideal. I have to roll the shorts up over my hips and the t-shirt hangs down like a dress. I look ridiculous but I don't care. This isn't about fashion, this is about my life, about claiming it back, proving that I'm not that broken thing they made of me.

His shoes are far too big and, with a sad realisation, I decide to go barefoot. It could be worse I tell myself as I make my way back downstairs.

Technically, Preston said I could explore the house, so none of the staff seem to be watching me and yet I know, if I even try to walk out the front door, I'll be yanked back. Instead, I make my way to the garden, pretending that what I need most is fresh air, as if mere oxygen could fix all my woes.

I make a show of smelling the roses, of running my hands through the freezing water of the fountain. I want them to think I'm as pliant as possible but all the while my eyes are scouting out the walls, seeing where would be the best place to make my escape and when I spot it, it's hard not let out a squeal.

It takes a full ten minutes to meander over to it, to make it look like I'm just enjoying being in the sunshine but, once I know I'm hidden from view by the massive camellia bush, I don't waste a second, scaling the walls, scraping my hands as I clamber up. I drag my body over, earning another scrap across my belly and then I flop onto the other side.

As I land in a heap, I take a moment to collect myself, before I'm sprinting away, down the street, darting as quickly as I can into another street and to where I hope there might be a crowd, or a subway, or anything that means I can get out of view.

As I make my way, I can feel people staring. I must look a sight, barefoot, clearly dressed in men's clothes. I need to cover myself, I need to hide myself. I duck into a side street, find a massive rubbish bin and start hauling out whatever I can. There are a pair of sneakers, old, a size too small but I ram my feet into them all the same. And there's an anorak too. It's stained, it stinks but I wrap it around, realising that I look like a tramp, but I don't care.

For the first time I feel inconspicuous. I feel invisible.

As soon as I'm done, I head back out, walking fast, ignoring the blisters as they rapidly spring up along my heels. It'll take more than a few cuts to stop me now because this is the first real taste of freedom I've had in forever.

I freeze as I realise that.

A man collides with me and then curses like I'm the one at fault.

I ignore him because right now nothing can dampen my mood.

I've done it. I'm free.

A giggle escapes me and it's hard to contain. I haven't laughed in so long. I haven't felt real joy in so long.

I slump back into the brick wall of a building. Despite the food I ate, I feel exhausted, and I'm half tempted to take a nap, after all, no one bats an eye at a sleeping homeless person, do they? But, just as I contemplate it, the hair on the back of my neck pricks up. I can feel goosebumps all along my skin like my body knows something I don't.

I look around trying to figure out why I sense danger and my eyes connect with a man I know is Mafia.

I gulp, taking a step backwards, then another. With every step I take he does the same. Within seconds I'm spinning on my heels rushing through the crowds, frantically trying to get away.

Only, there's two of them now. Two men hot on my heels.

I let out a cry. The blisters are tearing into my feet, the coat I found is no longer hiding me but is flapping in the wind, slowing me down. I turn a corner, then another. They're right behind me, hunting me down like a dog.

I don't know if it's Levi's men, if it's Preston's or even Nico's, but whoever they are, I know they're going to drag me back.

As I make a last minute duck to the right, I realise I'm at a dead end. A wall of dirty bricks blocks the path ahead. My stomach drops as I turn to face them.

I'm trapped. Cornered.

I grab a random piece of broken pallet wood, raising it up like a bat.

The man on the right tilts his head like he's trying to assess if I'll actually do anything and then the pair of them separate, they part, and Levi walks between them.

My eyes widen. My fear multiples. My legs seem to collapse under me and I whimper as it feels like the entire world implodes.

I'm sick of always being a failure.

Of always being the loser in these games.

"Where the fuck do you think you're going?" Levi growls.

I can't speak. I can't make any noise except a pathetic whimper. The wood that barely minutes ago felt like a viable weapon is now lying useless by my feet, though I don't know when I dropped it.

He grabs me by my hair, hauling me along.

"I thought I made this perfectly clear…" He snarls, before throwing me face first into the waiting van. "You've already shamed this family once with your performance yesterday."

I glare back at him. That's how he viewed the entire sham that was my wedding day?

"You fuck this alliance up, Ruby, and I will make you wish you were never born."

Like he hasn't already.

Like I haven't spent every day of the last five years dreaming of death, begging for it.

Preston

CHAPTER Eleven

"How is she, Sidney?"

The pause tells me everything.

I can hear him walking about, searching, going from room to room. No doubt she's tucked herself away, maybe even hidden herself in a cupboard.

"You were meant to be taking care of her." I say irritated. "Has she even eaten since I left?

"Yes, sir." Sidney replies. "She ate breakfast."

"Breakfast?" I snap. That was hours ago. Did no one think to offer her lunch because it's not like the girl would ask for it.

I can hear his breath picking up. I can hear him murmuring with someone and the words 'outside' mentioned. Is she in the garden? Is she hiding under a damn bush like some sort of faerie?

"What is going on?" I snap into the phone, finally losing what little patience I have.

"Your wife isn't here." Sidney says. "She went outside and now she's vanished."

"Where the fuck is she?" I growl, pushing my chair back, jumping to my feet.

"I, I don't know sir…"

Jesus fucking Christ, how long has she been MIA? I only called for a check-up, what if I hadn't bothered? What if I'd been too busy? I left two guards to watch over her but apparently that wasn't enough.

I hang up before I really lose my temper and I'm quick to pull up the surveillance footage, scanning from screen to screen until I find what I'm looking for.

"Something amiss?" Blaine says with a smirk.

I shake my head, biting back the retort.

She's good, I'll give her that. I watch as she wanders around aimlessly amongst the roses, as she sniffs the flowers like she's in some sort of drug induced haze. And then she disappears, vanishing behind a bush like we wouldn't be able to put it together.

I dial Noah's number and he picks up after two rings.

"Yes, boss?"

"My wife is MIA." I state, meeting Nico's eyes across the room. "I want her tracked down and located immediately."

"Yes, boss." Noah says hanging up.

"Not a good start." Nico comments, folding his arms, fixing me with one of those looks that would quell an ordinary man.

"Little ole wifey has run away…." Blaine taunts and Nico smacks him over the back of the head.

"That's my god daughter." He growls.

Eleri shifts and from the look on her face I can see this isn't new information to her. What Blaine thinks about it, I don't know.

Nico gets to his feet but, before he can say anything else, my phone rings in my hand once more.

I narrow my eyes at the withheld number. Surely not?

"Are you missing something?" Levi's less than dulcet tone echoes in my ear.

"You have her?" I reply.

I can practically hear the smirk in his voice. "It's been less than twenty four hours, I'd say I'm disappointed but I know my niece likes to play hard to get…"

"Is that right?" I snap.

"I'll send you the address. We'll have her gift-wrapped for you." He says.

"No need to do me any favours."

"I'm not. Besides, we're family now, aren't we?" Levi says before hanging up.

"Well?" Nico snaps as soon as I lower my arm, like he doesn't know what's going on, like everyone in the damned room isn't aware that my new bride has already made a bid for freedom.

I stalk out as my anger flares and I slam my fist into the wall just to lose some of the pent up fury.

Why the fuck would she run? I was nice to her, kind even. I didn't touch her, at least not in any way she didn't want. I didn't hurt her. I treated her better than her family have up until now and this is how she behaves?

And how the fuck did Levi even know where to find her? Neither of them have been in this city before, neither of them know their way around. Have they been watching the house? Waiting in case she pulled a stunt like this?

For fucksake, I thought the girl was broken, I thought the girl was so afraid of her own shadow she wouldn't even leave her room.

I guess I was wrong there.

Little Ruby Holtz does have a backbone after all.

THE ADDRESS HE SENDS TURNS OUT TO BE IN THE DOCKS.

As I approach the security gates a man waves our SUV through. Evidently, they've been primed to anticipate our arrival and they're all smiling like this is the biggest joke they've seen all year.

I get out, slamming the door shut. Ahead, I can see a circle of about twenty men. I can see Levi. And in the midst of them all, is Ruby.

On her knees.

With a darkening mark across her cheek that I know is from being hit.

Her eyes cast up, she meets my gaze for a millisecond before she succumbs to her fear.

"Ruby," I murmur, like me saying her name might save her from the situation she's in. Except, she brought this on herself, didn't she? She was the one who ran when I'd given her the peace and safety of my home. When I'd shown her I could be trusted.

"You should keep a better watch on your wife, Preston," Levi lectures as he grins at me.

I walk past him without a word, though I suspect that will only piss him off more.

When I'm in front of her I take in the dirty clothing she's wearing, clothing I don't recognise. "You look like shit." I murmur before sniffing hard. "You smell like shit."

She narrows her eyes at me. "What do you expect?" She half snaps before her face returns back to one of abject fear.

It's hard not to feel delight at that spark of personality. It's just a shame she's chosen this moment here to show it.

"You should teach her to hold her tongue." Levi says, walking up beside me.

She looks between us, huddling up more, waiting for the blows to continue.

I offer my hand for her to take but she shakes her head, obviously refusing and, technically, disrespecting me even further.

"I expected better of you." Levi spits at her. "I brought you up to be obedient." He raises his fist and I quickly move my body to block him.

"Do not touch my wife." I growl.

He smirks more and I seize the moment to grab Ruby, wrenching her up to her feet by her arm as she yelps. I've had enough of this shit, enough of this grandstanding or whatever the fuck this all is.

"Let's go." I say, dragging her past them all. Her legs kick out beneath her but I don't give her time to get any footing.

"I'd tie her to your bed if I were you, Preston." Levi shouts after us. "Make sure your wife understands exactly what is and isn't expected of her."

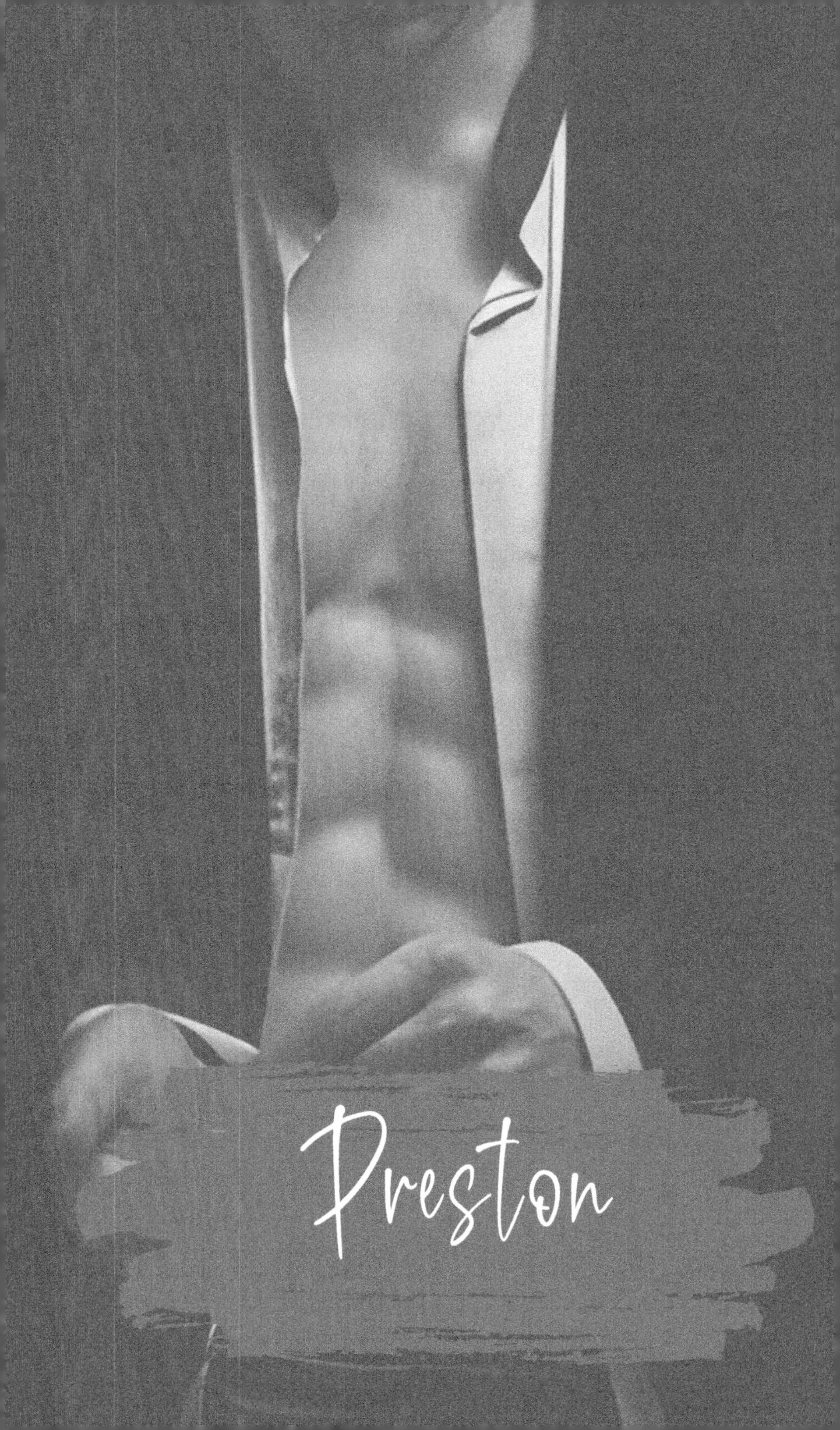

Preston

CHAPTER *Twelve*

I don't speak to her as we drive back. She's in the back while I'm up front and though I don't want to treat her like a prisoner, if she's going to act like one, then I will have her heavily guarded, I will have her locked up, monitored, the full-fucking-shebang. I'll lock a cage around her so tight she'll realise that the one Levi made was a thing of fancy in comparison.

When we pull up outside, I jerk my head for the doors to open and she's hauled out, landing on her knees in the gravel.

She's sniffing, hanging by her arms, still wearing the stinking anorak that has come from god knows where.

I walk up to her, tucking my hand under her chin to lift her head so she's forced to look at me.

She glares for the briefest of seconds before that same empty expression comes down.

"You shouldn't have run, wife." I say quietly.

She curls her lip down, showing her distaste and my dick instantly comes to life. I like her feisty, I like her when she's not pretending to be someone else. For a second I contemplate what it would feel like to do it, to rip those damned clothes off and to fuck her here, in front of everyone, to show her under no uncertain terms exactly who she belongs to. Exactly what kind of man she's goading.

Fuck Nico for making this so damned difficult.

And fuck Ruby for being such a fucking temptation that I'm close to stripping her naked and doing it anyway.

Behind me I hear as the two guards who were meant to watch her are brought out. She looks from me to them in confusion.

I tilt my head, hoping she understands exactly what the situation is and I slip my hand into my jacket, pulling out my hand gun that is holstered there, out of view. I usually only use it for emergencies but I'll make an exception this time.

"No." She cries, as it dawns on her what this is.

"They let me down." I state. "Their job was to watch you and they failed."

"Please Preston…"

It's the first time she's spoken my name, first time she's uttered it. It's a shame she chose such circumstances really. It's a shame she's ruined that moment for me. I tut, brushing my thumb over her beautiful pouty lips. "When I want you to beg, wife, you'll know it."

In my head those words are for show, for my men, that this is just another performance in our pretend marriage, only, I know that's not true. The thought of Ruby on her knees begging for my cock makes me so hard I can't even think straight.

She shuffles forward, her hands snatching at the one of mine that holds the weapon. Her fingers curl around my wrist.

"Please don't kill them."

I jerk my chin up at the tone of her voice. She cares so much for these men? My men? And yet she willingly risked her life without any care for her own.

"Please…"

All eyes are on me. Every one of my men are watching to see what I'll do. If I'll give into the pretty face and sad tears.

And while so much of me wants to, I can't be seen to be weak. If I let this go, where will it end?

But another thought registers that if I kill them in front of her, she'll never forgive me. She's witnessed enough death in her short life, I don't need to add more horror to it.

My eyes connect with Noah. He gives me a quick nod of understanding and I pocket the gun, taking hold of Ruby and pull her inside. The rest of this lesson will be in private, out of view.

Her eyes seem to come to life, a tiny spark registers with something akin to hope, as I shut the front door behind us.

"You're sparing them?" She says.

"No."

Her face crumples at that one word, she steps back and I'm quick to tighten my hold on her.

"But…" She begins and the sound of a gunshot echoes, followed quickly by a second.

"No." She cries, jerking violently to try to get herself free, and in response, I wrap my arms more tightly around her.

"Stop, Ruby." I growl. "You knew this would happen."

"I didn't." She gasps.

"You chose to run. Your actions have consequences."

"Then punish me." She pleads, flailing against me. "Punish me, just don't hurt someone else for my crimes."

The way her body presses into mine, the way the heat of her melds into me should be illegal. Under the surface my anger is still raging. She might be traumatised, she might be messed up but that doesn't mean I can simply give her free rein to misbehave. And especially not when I have Nico and now Levi breathing down my fucking neck.

I carry her up the stairs. She hangs her head as if she already knows where this is headed.

In what should be our bedroom, I throw her onto the bed. She lands in a heap of dirty clothes and tangled hair.

For a moment I just stand there, waiting to see what she'll do, if she'll finally fight me but she doesn't move, she just lays there, waiting, like she's defeated.

I yank the anorak off her roughly, seeing that underneath she's wearing one of my t-shirts and a pair of my rolled up shorts.

"Where the fuck did you get this?" I growl, holding the stinking black coat up. I know it's not mine. Did one of my men procure this for her? If they did I'll have their fucking head.

"I found it." She sniffs. "In a rubbish bin, along with the shoes."

I stare at her feet, seeing the way the back of her heels are bright red and cut up from how badly fitting the trainers are. I hadn't noticed the torn footwear before but now I want them off too.

I rip them off, ignoring the yelp from my wife and I toss them into the pile that I'll have burnt.

"You're my wife." I state. "Do you think people won't take note of what you're wearing, how you present yourself?"

"I had nothing else." She sobs.

Before I can think not to, I rip the t-shirt off. It has to stink from the contact with that disgusting coat and I sure as hell won't wear it again. Once it's gone, I rip the shorts off too.

She's not wearing a bra. Under the top she's completely naked except for the same thong she wore on our wedding day. She curls herself up into a ball, twisting her neck to bury her face into the duvet.

I clamber onto the bed, my anger driving me more than reason now. As I yank her body around I can see the tears streaming down her face, I can see the fear in her eyes, but I see something worse, the way she seems to accept whatever I'm about to do, the way she's already withdrawing further into herself.

"I'm not going to hurt you." I murmur, but I can tell she doesn't believe me. She clearly thinks I'm as much of a monster as the ones she's grown up with.

I let out a growl of frustration. God, it would be so much easier if I was a monster, it would be so much easier to simply fuck her into submission the way I would any other woman that fought me. But with Ruby, that's not an option. She's too damaged, too far gone to take such action. She needs someone kind, someone gentle. Not a brute like me.

I get up, walking to the bathroom and come back with the first aid kit. Carefully, I clean up the cuts on her ankles, then stick a plaster on both. She winces, letting out a gasp when I apply the antiseptic wipe but beyond that, she makes no movement.

"Has he done that before?" I ask, looking at the obvious mark on her face.

"Done what?" She whispers.

"Hit you."

She meets my gaze then drops it, shrugging like it doesn't matter.

"You're my wife now." I state. "No one will lay one hand on you from now on without facing the consequences."

She lets out a little huff like she doesn't believe me and, before I can think not to, I wrap my body around hers. She freezes, her body going stiff as a board. It's as if she's expecting me to pin her down and do whatever I want.

Like I've not been dreaming of doing exactly that.

Carefully, I stroke her hair back. I can still smell that stink but underneath it I can smell something else, something softer, more feminine. Something I think I'd give my soul just to have a taste of.

My dick is so hard it hurts. A voice in my head is screaming at me to throw all logic out the window and just claim my wife the way any other man would in this situation. I should at least beat her ass, punish her in some way for what she's done, but even that I can't bring myself to do.

I trace my fingers down the bare skin of her arm, watching as she erupts into goosebumps.

"Why did you run?" I ask as calmly as I can.

She sniffs but doesn't answer.

"Ruby?"

Again, nothing but silence.

"I can't help you if you don't talk to me." I growl.

"You don't want to help me." She barely speaks above a whisper and yet I hear every syllable.

"What makes you say that?"

She buries her face more as if she's too afraid to reply and my anger spikes again.

I yank her around, forcing her onto her back and though I know her tits are right there, bared for me, I keep my eyes on her face, though it practically kills me to do it.

"Tell me, Ruby. Just fucking tell me."

"You think I wanted this?" She suddenly screams. "You think I wanted *her* life?"

"Whose?"

"My mother's."

I frown at those words. What the fuck is she talking about?

"She didn't want to marry my father either." She gasps. "But she did it. She pretended. She acted as she was expected to and what did she get for it? Nothing but pain, nothing but misery, and then my uncle murdered her."

"Your life will not be like hers."

"No?" She scoffs. "It's already starting out the same. Forced marriage..."

I cup her cheek and she falls silent. "I know you didn't want this, but I promise you, I'm on your side."

She shakes her head, shutting her eyes, but the tears begin to stream down her cheeks anyway.

"You have to learn to trust me." I state.

"Trust." She repeats, like the word makes no sense to her, like it's not even in her vocabulary.

"There are people out there, people who will happily hurt you just to get to me." I state. "And you running off like that will only make their job easier."

She gulps as that knowledge sets in. As she realises how damned stupid she really was.

My eyes drop. I don't mean to. Hell, I wish I didn't look but I stare at her body, at her breasts, at the fucking incredible way her dark nipples are so hard right now I can actually imagine how they'd feel sliding past my lips, into my mouth, how they'd react as I bit them.

She's skinny. Her ribs are showing enough to tell me she doesn't eat properly.

She needs someone to nurture her. To take care of her. She needs a parent not a husband.

For a second I think about doing it, about touching her, about cupping her breast just to know what she'd feel like. Would she moan? Would she arch her back into my hold and urge me on? Or would she recoil as if I repulse her? She already let me touch her back at the hotel, she spread her legs for me like she was willing to let me do whatever I wanted, but now I'm wondering if the reason behind that was simply the alcohol she'd drunk.

I glance back at her face and thank god her eyes are shut.

Does she know I'm leering at her? Acting like a teenager that's never seen a naked woman before? My dick weeps with need and it's all I can do not to unzip my pants and give myself what I so desperately want.

My thumb drags across her mouth. Her lips are so full, so fuckable. She licks them just a little and though I doubt she realises what she's done, that turns this entire situation into an inferno.

I lean down, catching her mouth, my tongue claiming what legally is mine anyway. She opens enough for me to slide in, she lets me take what I want, just like the last time we kissed, but there's no real give on her side. Once more she's like a robot, she'll submit but she's not mentally consenting in any actual way.

I pull back, staring at her now open and obviously hollow eyes.

"Fuck." I growl, getting to my feet, forcing myself to move. How does this woman have this effect on me? How is this possible?

I know if I stay I won't be able to stop myself, I'll have my cock buried so deep down her throat I won't care for the consequences. I'll break her while I'm busy finding nirvana.

Christ, this girl is temptation.

This girl is the very epitome of desire.

And yet I will destroy her if I touch her, I can see that, I can feel that. She doesn't want me. She doesn't desire me. She will act any way she thinks will save her a beating but, deep down, I think she despises me as much as she despises her uncle and that arsehole Gunnar too.

I prowl the room while she sits up, bringing her arms up to cover herself.

"Did, did I do something wrong?" She whispers and if anything that confirms everything. That her actions can't be trusted. That she won't actually respond in a way that shows me what she really wants. She's buried her needs so deep I doubt they'll ever resurface.

And yet I want them to.

I want her to want me.

I want her to come out of whatever this broken state is and be the woman I keep getting glimpses of. That fiery, feisty, creature I know still exists. That true Mafia Princess.

"I have to go." I state. It's not a lie - I have shit to do. I can't stay here. I can't be close to her until I learn how to control myself.

And I sure as hell can't look at her while she's wearing nothing but a tiny lace thong.

"Where…?"

I cut across her before she can finish whatever she's about to ask. "Stay here. In the house. If you try to run again then I will punish you for it and, believe me when I say, you won't enjoy one moment of it."

She grits her teeth, nodding.

"Say it, Ruby, say you won't run." I bark.

"I won't."

"Look your husband in the eyes when you're talking to him." I growl, becoming more possessive as my frustration builds. She might be broken but she will damn well show me some respect all the same.

She gulps, her throat bobbing, and then she jerks her chin in a tiny show of defiance before she meets my gaze. "I won't run." She says more clearly.

I turn to go but as I reach the stairs I realise what other actions I have to take. What I have to do to ensure Ruby is compliant, that she understands that I have total control over her because, apparently, my wife will say anything, will agree to anything but the moment she thinks she has an opportunity she will take it. She will seize it and I know we'll just be back here again.

When I walk back in the room her eyes widen. She's off the bed but she hasn't covered herself. She's just stood, taking stock, no doubt contemplating her days' adventure. It's so damn hard not to stare at her, not to pin her against the wall and just lose myself for a few hours in that fuckable body.

"Give me your arm." I say.

She narrows her eyes before dropping them to the instrument in my hand.

"What, what is that?" She half-whispers.

"Give me your arm, Ruby." I order.

She takes a step back, a tiny one, but I've already closed the distance because in this, she won't have a choice.

I grab her left wrist. She quickly moves her right to cover both her breasts like I'm some sort of caveman, though I can't blame her considering how much I've perved on her so far.

"This will sting." I state as I push the metal end into her flesh and quickly pull the trigger.

Her whimper tells me the thing has done its job and as I pull away, I can see the bead of blood.

"It will heal in a few days." I murmur, swiping it gently with my thumb.

"You, you tagged me?" She gasps.

I meet the furious look in her eyes before she drops them, staring at her feet in a show of submission I know is put on simply to lull me into believing she's obedient.

"Now I will know where you are, wherever you are." I say. "So it's pointless to run."

She bites her lip and the tears start to stream again.

"Be a good girl, Ruby." I say, cupping her cheek. "And I will only use this as a form of protection."

"As opposed to what?" She snaps.

I take another step, boxing her in as my hand wraps around her neck, because I need her to understand how deadly serious I am right now. "If I have to, I will hunt you down, wife. If I have to do what your uncle said and tie you to a bed then I will. Your actions dictate how kindly I will treat you."

She mumbles something so quietly I can't make it out.

But it doesn't matter.

I've played my trump card. She knows escaping me is a pipe dream. She knows any attempts are futile.

I've forced her obedience in this and once she accepts it, hopefully she'll stop fighting me and start to come out of her shell.

And perhaps then I'll meet the real Ruby Holtz.

Ruby

CHAPTER *Thirteen*

He tagged me. Like a dog. Like a damned pet.

Does he have an app where he can log in and see when I go to the toilet, when I eat, when I sit in the library?

My fury is matched only by my helplessness in this. I can't escape now. I cannot get away because he will know before I even take a foot out the god damn door.

I let out a snarl, slamming my fist into the wall, and get another whiff of that awful stinking coat I had on.

I need to wash.

I'm surprised Preston didn't fling me straight into the bathroom and make me take a cold shower while he watched. I guess I should be grateful he's not that kind of a pervert.

I run my thumb over the tiny wound in my arm and I'm half tempted to grab a knife and try to gouge the tracker out, though I suspect that won't work.

I'm fucked.

Completely and utterly fucked.

I slump against the wall, sink down to the floor and let my despair take me, heaving as each sob racks through my body. Once more, I'm on the losing side. Once more, I'm at the mercy of all these arseholes surrounding me.

Only when I can cry no more do I force myself to take a shower.

The bathroom is so big it has an actual antique couch in it, complete with a gilded frame. I drape a towel over the back before turning the handles for the multiple jets that make up the shower unit.

It sprays out at so many angles that, when I step in, my body instantly relaxes despite how frazzled I am. The only toiletries are the ones Preston uses, so I wash my hair with an all-in-one shampoo and conditioner and then I use a shower gel that smells so much like him, I can't decide if I love or hate it.

Still, it beats the old cracked bar of soap I had back at my uncle's house.

When I get out, it takes a full ten minutes to ease the knots out of my hair. I don't have any brush so I have to use my hands, working each strand free. I used to be so prideful of my looks. I used to spend hours learning how to apply makeup from online tutorials and then removing it all before my parents would find out and tell me off.

With my ancestry, my hair is seriously prone to frizz but there's nothing I can do to help that. I don't have any products, I don't even have a band to tie it back. When I was younger my mother used to braid my hair, create intricate styles and weave it all on my head like it was some sort of crown. I wouldn't even know where to begin trying to replicate it.

I let out a sigh, making my way back to the master suite, where a huge dressing room is stacked with my husband's things.

My husband.

He had me sprawled on that bed, he could have done what he wanted and yet, once again, he didn't hurt me. Didn't even beat me for publicly insulting him the way I did by running. Am I fooling myself that Preston isn't quite the monster I believed him to be? Sure, he's dangerous, possessive, damned right deadly when pushed, but then the fact he hasn't fucked me doesn't exactly make him a saint, does it?

My fingers brush against the fine suits that hang, one after another on the racks. He has shirts too. And ties. It's all so organised like he's a neat freak and that thought makes me smile. My father had actual OCD. He had a place for everything and nothing was ever put away wrong or there was hell to pay.

I let out a sigh, pulling a shirt from a hanger. I can hardly stay in this robe all day. As the silk touches my skin, I shut my eyes. It feels so soft. And the fact that it smells of him? Yeah, I'll admit that I like that, that in a way it's calming, grounding even.

In the mirror, I check I look decent enough. My legs are so long that the shirt comes to a stop well above my knees. I look sexier than I mean to but I guess that can't be helped.

When I make my way downstairs, there's a man waiting for me. He's in a suit that tells me he's staff but he's smiling kindly enough as if I hadn't made a bid for freedom and gotten two men killed as a result.

"Mrs Civello," He says. "I'm Sidney, the butler, your husband has asked me to give you a proper tour of your home."

"Please, call me Ruby." I say trying not to flinch at the word 'home'. Besides, Mrs Civello sounds so formal. It sounds so not me.

"As you wish." Sidney smiles, before putting his hand out, directing me ahead.

I don't know what I had planned, I only came down because I could hardly hide up in my room all day and yet a tour doesn't sound so bad. At least then it might feel like this house is less of a gilded cage.

We walk from one ornate room to the next. Sidney tells me what each one is and for some it's hard not to giggle because it's so obvious I don't really need someone to announce that it's the 'kitchen' or the 'library'. But I let him continue. Clearly, he has a set route for this.

When he opens the door to Preston's office, I pause, staring back at him in disbelief. I'm allowed to see this? I'm allowed to even be in this part of the house?

"Nowhere is off limits." Sidney says, as though reading my mind.

I can't understand that. How can I be allowed in there? Surely my husband has secrets he doesn't want me to know about? Would Preston know if I rifled through his papers, through his drawers? Is this another test for me?

My mind flickers back to Gunnar's words, that I'm to be a spy, it's like Preston already suspects it, like he's laid a trap and is just waiting for me to fall right into it.

I let out a nervous sigh, deciding that right now, I need to do exactly what my mother did when she first married my father. I need to play it safe. Learn the lay of the land.

I can't escape - Preston has already seen to that, but I am safer here than I was with my uncle. Maybe I can win my new husband to my side. Maybe I can do what Gunnar instructed me to do, seduce my husband, make him fall for me, only, I won't betray him the way Gunnar wants, I won't screw him or Nico Morelli over the way they have planned. Preston has had so many opportunities to hurt me, to treat me the way Levi and Gunnar expect and yet he hasn't, not once. He keeps asking me to trust him and while that feels so far from possible right now, maybe staying here *is* my best option.

Afterall, if I did run, where would I go? I have no money, no belongings, I don't even have any clothes.

And if I run, Preston will know. He'll track me. I doubt I'd even get halfway down the road this time before he had me hauled back and then what would he do? Would he tie me to the bed? A shudder runs through me at the thought, at being so helpless and incapacitated as that.

No, running is not an option. Not that it ever really was.

But betraying Preston? Helping my uncle after everything he's done to me, after murdering my parents? No, that's not an option I'm willing to entertain either.

"Ruby?" Sidney says, peering at my face, and I realise I've been staring into the office, lost in my thoughts for far too long.

"Sorry." I mumble.

"I asked if you'd like something to eat? You haven't had anything since breakfast and you must be hungry."

I smile, nodding. I *am* hungry. I'm starving. I'm not used to actual regular meals. It feels like a novelty but I'm not sure I want to get used to it, what if I start to expect it and then someone takes it away? I'll only set myself up for more pain. More heartbreak.

And yet, I should eat to keep my energy up. I should eat because I don't know for definite when the next meal *is* coming.

And I want to be ready for when Preston returns. I want to charm him, to show him that I've learnt my lesson. I just wish I knew how to be the kind of woman I know this man would normally go for.

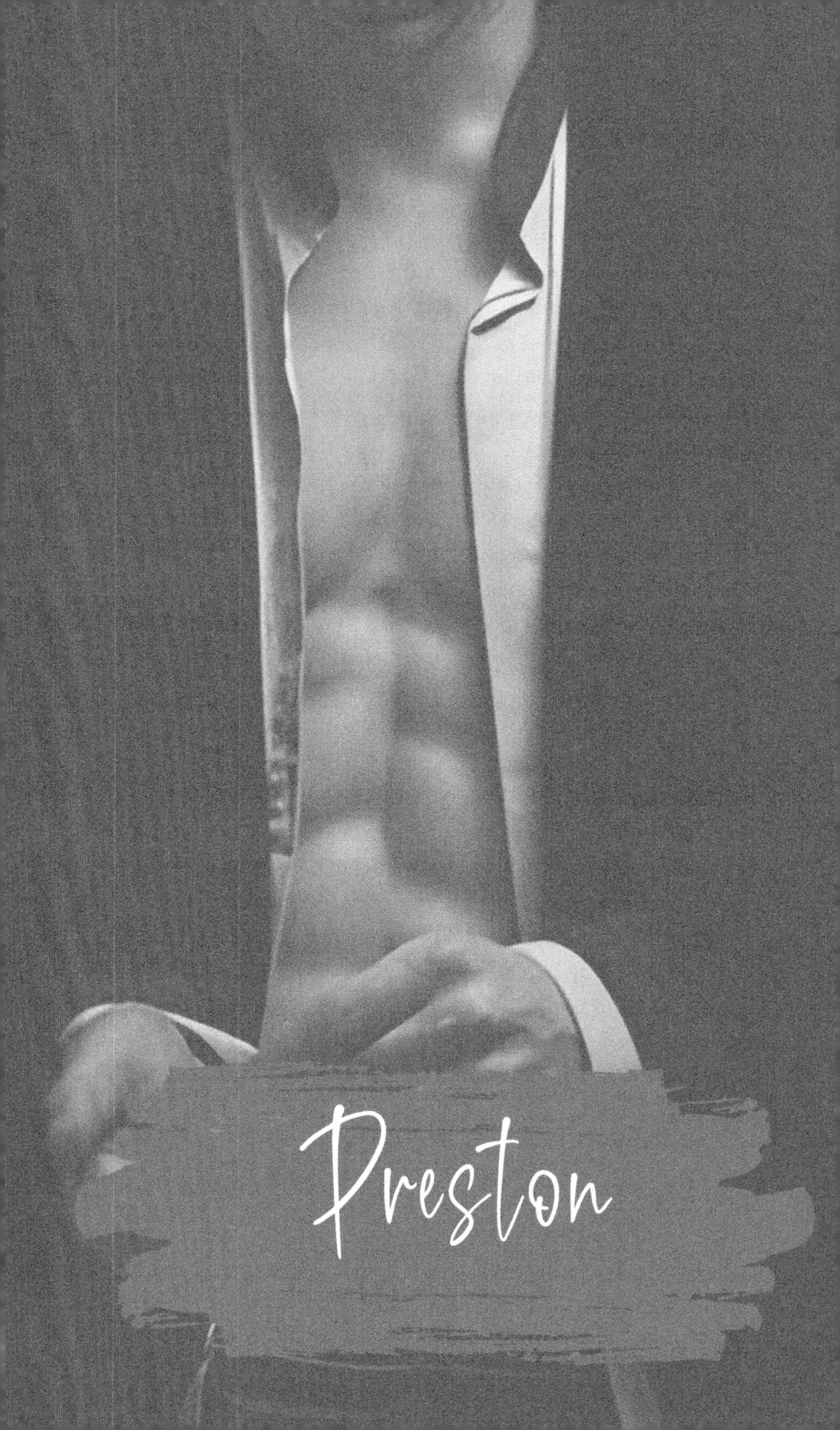

Preston

CHAPTER *Fourteen*

I'm sat in the town house, watching the sun slowly set out the window, while around me my men are all relaxing, drinking, gambling, enjoying the downtime while we can get it.

In the middle of the room a man is tied to a chair and Noah and Blaine are busy tormenting him. I don't really give a shit what the consequences are, if the man lives or not – it's his name on the paperwork that quarantined our stock so as far as I'm concerned, he deserves whatever he gets. And so far, he's not given any adequate justification for it. He's just sat there, blubbering and begging like we'll just change our minds and let him go. No harm, no foul and all that.

Cold beer hits my throat as I knock back another mouthful. It's not my drink of choice but the good stuff, my whiskey, is back at the main house and, right now, I don't want to go anywhere near that place. Only problem is my mind keeps drifting to it, to her, to wondering what she's doing, if she's hiding somewhere, if she's thinking about me, if she's lying in my bed, smelling my scent on the pillows, if she's touching herself… no, she won't be doing that. No normal woman who's been put in her situation would do that and Ruby sure as hell is not normal.

"Boss," Jace sits down on the couch beside me.

I grunt back but I keep my eyes fixed on the bound man. I feel in control, I feel me again but I'm certain the second I lay eyes on my wife, all of that will dissipate. I just need to understand why. Why her? Why now? I've fucked enough women, I've been in enough relationships, why is this girl so different? Sure, she's pretty, but she's also a fucking headcase.

"How's the wife?"

I turn my head, glaring at Jace. He really wants to poke the dragon?

"Fine," I murmur, hoping he takes the blatant hint that I don't want to talk about it.

"Fine," He repeats smirking. "It's been what, twenty four hours and you're sat here, drinking with all of us instead of at home with her?"

I shake my head, feeling another spike of emotion I have no good reason for. It shouldn't matter what anyone thinks, after all, my marriage is a business deal, nothing more, who gives a shit if everyone around me talks? And yet some furious part of me does, if not for me, then for my wife, for her, for the fact that they're even speaking her name, speaking about her like they have a right.

"She's taking some space." I mutter, like I even need to justify myself to him.

"You fucked her that good?" He jokes before slapping the arm chair and laughing.

The bottle in my hand shatters. I feel the cut of the glass slicing into my skin and I welcome that pain, I welcome that spike in adrenaline.

As I turn to face him, Jace is pale as a ghost and he clearly realises he's overstepped the mark. He starts spluttering about drinking too much, about not thinking before he speaks, about how he's so used to be being around Levi's crew that he forgets how to behave now he's back.

"Tell me," I state, seizing upon the fact that he's been there, mixed up in the Holtz business for near on three years. "Tell me what you know of her, of my wife."

He gulps, dropping his gaze like he knows some dirty little secret.

"She claims to have fucked loads of men." I say, studying his reaction for any tells, "Who are they? Is it true?"

He draws in a breath, shrugging a little with an obviously nervous laugh. "I didn't really interact with her. No one did. Levi and Gunnar kept her locked up and out the way…"

I guess that fits with her behaviour. But why then is she pretending to be some sort of whore? Is that what she thinks I'm into? Is that what she thinks will please me?

"There was talk, I mean…" He trails off, running his hand over his face like he's trying to figure out the right way of explaining something to me.

"Talk of what?" I growl.

"When they arrived in the city, there was some sort of incident. A boy, he was dealt with."

My eyebrow raises at that. "How is that relevant to my wife?"

"The rumour is they were trying to escape. I think the pair of them were together, in a relationship, and they were trying to run away. They got caught. The boy ended up with a bullet in his head and well, Ruby…"

Ended up married to me.

I narrow my eyes, remembering the tears, remembering the way she was as she fought so desperately the entire length of the church. Was that her plan then? Was she and this boy in love? Were they planning to run off into the sunset together and that's why she was so upset at our wedding? Had she imagined him waiting there at the altar for her and not the brute of a man she ended up shackled to?

I feel a flash of jealousy, of fury too. Whoever this boy was, he had no right to intervene, no right to try to steal my bride; good thing he got a bullet to the head because, if I'd caught him, I would have done far worse.

Ruby is mine. No one is taking her from me.

But Nico is going to do just that.

I know once Levi has been dealt with, then this marriage will be annulled and my young bride will no longer be mine.

I can't let that happen. I won't let that happen. She's my responsibility and I refuse to give her up.

But that thought is just as illogical as my sudden lack of control. What do I really care for a girl I don't even know? What does it matter if our marriage is annulled? I grit my teeth, hating the voice in my head, hating the swirling emotions. I owe Nico my loyalty, I won't let something as benign as a pretty face fuck over everything I've worked so hard to build.

"Boss?"

I don't reply, I just get up, stalking past where the man in the centre of the room is currently screaming out as they hack away at bits of him.

I step out, onto the balcony, staring past the bright lights to where the dark hillside is, where my main home is, where right now, my wife is technically safely locked away. Is she wondering where I am? Is she missing me? I pull my phone, checking the tracker for what must be the umpteenth time. I know she's there and yet seeing it on the screen seems to ease some of the tension inside me.

It's a pitiful way of dealing with this – and I already know a far better one and it's so tempting despite the stakes involved.

"What's a handsome man like you doing out here all alone?"

I don't turn, I don't even react as Justine waltzes up to me. Her and a few of her buddies are clearly having a night off from the bar. I know they hang out here, I know they fuck my men, help channel their anger into a more productive outlet

Her hand brushes up my spine, touching me in a far too familiar manner.

"Go away, Justine," I mutter. It's not that she's unattractive, far from it. And it's not like I haven't fucked her more times than I can count.

"You seem tense." She says, positioning herself between me and the balustrade.

I narrow my eyes, taking in the heavy makeup, the heavily done up hair, and the knowing smirk. All so very different from the woman I married.

"It's been a while…" She adds, like I don't know it.

"I'm married." I state, as if that explains my absence.

She tilts her head, dropping to her knees, and her hands reach to grasp my belt. "I won't tell if you don't." She giggles.

"Justine." I say in warning.

"Preston," She replies, sliding the buckle loose. "You need to relax. Clearly your new bride isn't giving you what you need, so use me, I'm more than happy to do whatever it takes to satisfy your needs." Her hands grab my cock as she speaks the last of it, freeing it from my boxers, and it hardens more as the cold air hits it.

In my hand, I can still see the screen, the dot, the marker that my wife is right now in my home. It would be easy to do it, easy to fuck Justine and work out some of this tension. Hell, it would probably help whatever bullshit it is messing with my head.

As I shut my eyes, I see her face, Ruby's, and for a moment I imagine it's her, her mouth, her hands, *her* so eager for my cock.

Only, it's not her.

The movement is too confident, the licking is too familiar. Ruby wouldn't touch me like this, I doubt she'd even know how, and while the sensation isn't exactly unpleasant, it's not Justine I want. It's not her I need to hear moaning, gasping, gagging on my cock.

"Get the fuck off," I mutter, but she clearly doesn't hear me so I grab a fistful of her hair, wrench her head back and all but toss her onto her arse at my feet. "I said get the fuck off."

She blinks, staring up at me, her tits heaving like she's still so ready for me.

"Preston…" She begins but I don't stay to hear it. I just storm back into the house, doing my pants up, half cursing myself.

I should just fuck her, I should just use Justine like the whore that she is, but she's not what I want, not who I want. My eyes fix on the man in the chair and before anyone can stop me I start laying in punches as if he's responsible, as he's the cause of all my troubles.

Blaine whoops beside me. Noah and a few others step back, silently watching, no doubt surprised by my sudden show of barbarism. Oh, they all know what I'm capable of, the level of violence I can happily stoop to, but I don't do this, I don't lose control, my punishments are measured, exact. I don't act without reason but right now, reason is the farthest from my mind.

The only thing I can think about is Ruby. About how she writhed and moaned and clung to me back in that honeymoon suite, back when I wasn't meant to be touching her, when I wasn't meant to be doing anything with her. The pain helps, the punches seem to bring it all into focus, but that frustration still lingers under the surface all the same.

By the time I'm done, the man's face is unrecognisable. His eyes are so swollen and black he barely looks human. Half his teeth are smashed from his jaw and there's blood splattered all over me. Gone is the party atmosphere, gone is the bravado and laughter, that is except for Blaine, who claps me on my back and cackles.

I don't have to check his pulse to see that he's dead. Sure, that's what we had planned but we wanted information first but I guess that ship sailed. I stand back, glancing at all the figures around me and silently leave the room. I don't care what they think, I don't give a shit what anyone has to say.

I need to think.

I need to breathe.

I need to get Ruby Fucking Holtz out of my system.

Ruby

CHAPTER
Fifteen

He doesn't come home. I sat up waiting for him the first night. I didn't want to eat without him in case he got angry and, when it got past ten, Sidney brought up a tray.

Is this how it will be then, him asking me to trust him one minute and then abandoning me the next? Will he come back tomorrow once he's decided a suitable punishment for me?

I don't eat the food. I can't bring myself to. I've been married barely more than twenty four hours and already my husband despises me. So much for winning him over then.

I spend the night in a fit of restlessness and because no one locks the door, I end up sleepwalking, coming around in a room I don't know, and then panicking that it's off limits and I'm in even more trouble.

By the time I find my way back to my bed I'm in a full blown panic attack and I can't calm myself.

When the first streaks of sunlight come in through the window I'm both exhausted and relieved. Night time is always the worst for me. Night is when the monsters come out. When everything feels horrific and there's never a glimpse of hope.

I get up, shower, put on another of Preston's shirts because, once again I have nothing else to wear, and then I wander from room to room, trying to learn my way around without looking like I'm snooping.

Whenever I bump into the staff they all smile at me and ask if I need anything but I don't know what to say. I don't technically need anything. I know if I want, they'll bring me food. I know there's a clean comfortable bed upstairs and as yet, Preston hasn't done anything awful to me. Hasn't tried to touch me. Hasn't hurt me in anyway.

And yet I feel lost. So lost.

All the emotions I've kept buried since my family's demise seem to keep coming to the surface. I keep finding myself crying, sobbing, like I'm suddenly reliving my past all over again.

Everything now seems to remind me of her, of them. Both my parents. When I managed to eat some dinner one of the staff asked if I wanted salt and all I could think of was how my mother was so superstitious and used to throw salt over her shoulder whenever she spilt it.

When I decided to check out the library, the first book I saw was Huckleberry Finn – my father's favourite, and the desk, it's antique with a green leather top just like the one he had, like the one I found him lying beside with his face blasted off.

In the end, I retreat, no longer leaving the bedroom at all.

Preston doesn't come back the night after, or the night after that. I guess he really is angry with me, isn't he?

But if he doesn't return, if he stays away, how can I apologise? How can I show him I'm sorry? How can I even start to make this supposed marriage work?

A TAP AT THE DOOR ROUSES ME FROM WHERE I'VE BEEN EFFECTIVELY languishing for what feels like forever.

"Ruby?"

I look up at the stranger's voice. It's one of the staff. A girl I don't recognise. Not that I know any of them really.

"You have a guest downstairs."

My heart leaps. A guest? Is it Preston, is he back?

No, stupid, he wouldn't be a guest would he?

And he certainly wouldn't send someone to get me. Unless he really was punishing me. Maybe that's his plan, have me hauled down to some sort of basement where he can take his time exacting out his own form of justice.

I bite my lip, wincing. Maybe I'd take the pain now if it meant he'd stop ignoring me.

"Who is it?" I ask. My voice sounds so husky, like it's forgotten how to work.

What if it's Levi, what if he came here? Or worse, it's Gunnar? Would they have the balls? Would Preston's men even let them in? They're in an alliance with my new husband, I doubt he'd turn them away.

"It's Eleri Morelli." She says.

My stomach drops. What the fuck? Nico's wife?

I scramble to my feet, feeling my legs shake. I'm wearing another of Preston's shirts. When I glance down I can see how wrinkled it is. Christ, I must look an absolute state.

"Tell her I'll be a few minutes." I say quickly, before racing to the bathroom. I haven't brushed my teeth all day. I haven't washed my face. My hair is all skewwhiff from how I was lying and it's more frizzy than ever.

But as I sort myself out, I realise it's Nico's wife I'm keeping waiting. Will he see that as an insult? Will she? Maybe that will anger Preston even more.

I sprint down the stairs, almost skidding across the beautiful parquet floor in my haste. All I can think is how pissed my mother would be when someone kept her waiting. She had zero tolerance for tardiness. You'd think it was a crime worse than murder the way she acted.

When I get to the room she's sat in, my heart is thumping so loudly and then it hits me that I don't even know what to say to her. What I'd even talk about.

She stands up, running her eyes over me and I flush with shame.

She's pristine, in a dress that clings to her body and highlights every gorgeous curve. Her hair is coiffed perfectly to one side, and though one half of her face is covered by a massive scar, she's devastatingly beautiful all the same.

"Come sit down." She says gently. Like this is her domain and not Preston's house at all.

I gulp, taking small measured steps, and sink into the couch opposite. I've not actually been in this room beyond peering in. It's too fancy. Too polished. Sitting here makes me realise how much of a state I really am. How close to a rabid animal I've become.

"I've ordered some tea. Is that okay or would you prefer something else to drink?" She says.

I shrug. I'll drink whatever she does. It makes it easier.

She smiles again before nodding to the girl, who drops a curtsey like Eleri is actual royalty. But then again, I guess she is. She's Nico's wife. You piss her off and you have to face the full wrath of him.

I twist my hands, hoping that whatever this is, I don't fuck it up, but I feel so wholly unprepared.

"Did Preston send you?" I whisper. I don't know if I want her to say yes or not. If she does, at least it will put an end to this torture, but if she doesn't, then what?

She frowns before shaking her head. "No. I meant to pop in earlier to see how you were after the wedding but some things came up."

"What things?" I say before biting my lip, practically drawing blood, because I shouldn't ask. It's none of my business. I don't want them to think I'm trying to rifle for information. I want them to like me for me, not see me as just another piece on the chessboard.

She shakes her head smiling. "Just business." She says like it doesn't matter. "Tell me, Ruby, how are you settling in?"

"Okay."

"Preston has a beautiful house." She says, looking around.

"He does." I agree. It's hard to deny that. It makes me wonder if he bought it like this or paid someone to decorate it. Or did he have someone before, a woman who made this home and now I've come in and usurped her space? Is that where he is now? In her arms, wishing he never married me?

She fixes me with a look just as the tea arrives. It's placed on the table in front of us and, as soon as the girl leaves, she kicks off her ridiculously high heels and tucks her feet under herself leaning back into the cushions as she sips from the mug.

"How are you finding all of this?" She asks.

"It's fine."

"Fine?" She smiles, like she knows that's not exactly true.

God, is this some sort of test? Did Preston send her here to see if I'm properly apologetic now? Is that what all this is about? He tagged me and left, so he knows exactly where I've been all this time. Will this be how it is from now on? Him showing me how much power he has, how he can treat me however he wants and the minute I do something he doesn't like, he'll have me locked away out of sight until he decides I've learnt my lesson.

"Please," I half-whisper. "Please tell him I'm sorry."

She narrows her eye. "Sorry about what?"

I gulp, hanging my head my head. "I…"

She gets up, putting the mug down and comes and sits right next to me. My body instantly tenses at our sudden proximity. I've heard so many things about this woman. About how she charmed *the* Nico Morelli, how she helped him to kill his brother and every other person that was betraying him.

She sounds fearless. She certainly looks it with that scar marring her face like a battle trophy. Compared to her, I must seem pathetic.

"Ruby," She says gently. "I don't know what you think you have to apologise for but…"

"He's angry at me." I blurt out, almost frantic now.

She frowns with confusion. "Who?"

"Preston."

"Why would he be angry at you?"

I shrug as a tear escapes, sliding down my cheek. "I had to try."

"Try what?"

"To escape." I whisper it, wincing as I remember who exactly I'm talking to. Eleri chose this life. She chose to marry Nico Morelli and become everything a Mafia wife is, while, so far I've done everything I can to try to escape it. "…And now he won't come home. He won't see me."

She lets out a low breath, gently taking my hand in hers. "Ruby, he's not staying away because you've done something."

"Then why..?"

"You've been through a lot. Not just with the wedding but before that. Preston wanted to give you some space. He didn't want to overwhelm you."

I shut my eyes, burying them into my palms, not sure how to respond. Why would he care if he overwhelms me? I'm his wife. His property. My feelings don't come into this. And besides, we all know Preston isn't the kind of man who considers feelings. He's logical. Calculated. I doubt the man even has warm blood in his veins.

But I need him to thaw, I need him to want me, if I'm to survive any of this, if I'm to stand a chance I have to win Preston over.

"None of us want to overwhelm you." Eleri says gently.

"But I'm okay." I say but it barely comes out because, suddenly, I'm sobbing. All my fear, all my self-loathing over the last few days hits me like a tidal wave and I can't contain it any longer.

If I were back in my old room in the basement, I could deal with this, I could compartmentalise this, shut my headspace down but everything is so different here.

Everything is so confusing.

Eleri wraps her arm around me and it's all I can do not to flinch from the contact. "No, you're not." She murmurs, "But that's to be expected."

When I've finally cried myself out, she calls for more tea.

I don't talk much after that. Eleri talks away, talks about non-consequential things, about her husband too. I want to pay attention but a big part of me wants to shut out her words. I don't want her to tell me anything secret, I don't want to learn anything that Gunnar might force out of me later.

It's safer if I remain ignorant.

By the time she leaves, I'm exhausted. I feel like I've spent so long doing mental gymnastics, watching what I say, what I ask, how I behave. I want her to like me, I want her to see me, maybe not as an equal, but someone good enough to be her friend.

As if someone as glamourous and powerful as Eleri Morelli would ever consider me as that.

"We should have dinner." She says, as I walk her to the front door. "You and Preston should come round. I'll ask Nico to sort it."

The way she says it, the way she acts is like Nico is the sort of man who arranges dinner parties and is not in fact a ruthless killer, the head of a Mafia Family so powerful my own seems to pale in significance.

I smile, nodding, but would Preston allow that? Will he ever even let me step foot outside this house again? Maybe he will because he'll want to show Nico how well he can control his new bride. I'd have to be careful, really careful, I'd have to put on such a good show.

I let out a silent sigh, realising how utterly exhausting such an evening would be.

And if I fucked it up, my new husband would never forgive me.

And he sure as hell would punish me badly for such an insult.

Preston

CHAPTER Sixteen

I didn't intend to stay away all week but in the end that's what happened. One thing after another came up and I found myself busy. Really busy. Though in truth, I think that's an excuse.

I still can't control myself, I still feel like a damned freight train that is hurtling towards almost certain destruction.

Besides, she's too fragile and I'm too much of a brute. I shouldn't be looking at her, contemplating all the ways I want to fuck her after everything she's been through, everything she's suffered, - she deserves better than that.

And anyway, Nico will skin me alive if I lay one finger on her. Like I haven't already.

The door slams as Eleri storms into the office and slaps me hard around the face.

"What the fuck?" I stammer as Blaine grins.

Nico mercifully is out because whatever the fuck I've done to upset Eleri, he will undoubtedly be pissed at me for too.

"You complete and utter arsehole." Eleri cries, throwing her arms up to emphasise her point.

Blaine sits back, lighting that damned zippo, his eyes showing how much he truly loves a fight.

"What have I done?" I ask.

"Done?" She hisses. "Done? Do you know where I've been today?"

I frown. Like I'm supposed to know her damn diary now?

"Ruby." She says.

My stomach drops. "What..?"

"She thinks you're punishing her."

"Punishing her for what?" I growl. "She hasn't done anything."

"Exactly." Eleri snaps like that explains it. "She's traumatised. She's frantic. She's spent so long having to second guess everyone else's behaviour because no doubt Levi has treated her like a punchbag this entire time…" She runs out of steam before shaking her head. "Have you not even thought to check on her?"

"I stayed away to protect her." I say.

She snorts. "So, that means no. Did you not even check all those camera's I know you've rigged the place with?"

I haven't. I haven't dared. I didn't want to look and catch her in a compromising position. To get a glimpse of her when she was getting in the shower, to see her at moments when she thinks she has some privacy, because I know what will happen if I do. I'll open the box, I'll lose what tiny control I still have and I'll be driving like a mad man up that hill to get to her.

Christ, how can one woman have such an effect on me? Me?

"Eleri…"

"Don't you fucking dare." She hisses. "You're going to go home right now and explain yourself."

"I can't do that." I state.

"Why not?"

I glance at Blaine, who any minute now, is going to pop out a load of snacks over the front row show he's getting. "Get out."

Blaine tilts his head, eyeballing both of us, no doubt trying to gauge how far he can push this.

Eleri shoves her hands on her hips and tells him to clear off and thankfully he has enough sense to listen to her.

Once he's gone she fixes her gaze back on me. "Speak, Preston."

I'll admit my lips curl at the way she's gotten so haughty. Five years ago she'd never have dared speak to me like this. Five years ago she'd never have looked any of us in the face. I guess Nico really did mould her into a queen.

"I want to keep her safe. To protect her."

"How does locking her in your house and ignoring her do that?" She snarls.

"It protects her from me." I say coldly.

"Excuse me?"

"Christ, Eleri," I growl. "She's already offered herself up to me. She's already acting like she won't even put a fight up if I decide to fuck her."

"But you won't." She says pointedly.

I glare back because this is weird enough as it is. Like I want to be having any such discussion with her of all people. Like I want to be talking about this to anyone. I'm a grown man for Christ sake, I don't need to justify myself to anyone.

"Preston, have you touched her?" She asks.

"No." I lie and for a second she looks relieved before I admit a tiny part of what I have done. "I kissed her."

"Excuse me?"

"The cameras where on us. It was in the honeymoon suite. I wanted Levi to think that we were having sex. I wasn't thinking straight." Christ, now I'm rambling, like a teenager.

"But you didn't have sex?"

"No." I growl more forcefully, like that's not what I want, like my mind is constantly imagining how it would feel to sink my cock into her, like I'm not continuously imagining what she'd feel like, how she'd moan, if she'd enjoy it, but then I'd make sure she enjoyed it, I'd dedicate hours to just that.

I'd break my young wife in all the best ways, mould her to me, train her…

"If Nico finds out you've kissed her…" She says make those thoughts jar in my head and she runs her eyes over me with disgust.

"I know." I say. "But that's not what I'm concerned about."

"What are you concerned about?"

I turn my back on her. A vision of Ruby as she was, in that suite, as her dress fell away, flashes before my eyes and it's all I can do not to groan as I fight the way my body wants to respond.

"Oh fuck off," Eleri hisses. "You want her, that's it, isn't it?"

I stiffen more, fighting the urge to tell her where she can shove it.

"You can't fucking have her." Eleri continues, jabbing me in the back. "She's not in any fit state to actually consent."

My anger spikes, something inside me rages and before I can register that I'm doing it, I've flipped the table over, sending all the contents across the room as I yell, "I know that. Why do you think I've been staying at the townhouse?"

She pulls a face, looking at me like I'm utter trash. "Oh I get it. You've been so busy trying to get a hold of yourself you forgot what all this is about. That at the very centre of this is an twenty one year old girl."

"I haven't forgotten her. I haven't stopped thinking about her."

"Because you want to fuck her, right?" She glares at me.

"Eleri…"

"No." She says, shaking her head. "You're a grown man. A decent man. At least I thought you were. So you're going to go back to your home, back to your child-bride and put her needs above yours."

"She's not a child." I snarl, as a vision of her more than perfect body flashes in my mind. No child looks like that. Christ, it would be so much easier if she was a child, then I wouldn't want her.

"As far as you're concerned she's off limits."

I wince because those words should have the complete opposite effect of what they do. Eleri is turning my wife even more into forbidden fruit. Making her a great, untouchable prize.

"I'm going." I say, picking up my things.

"And keep your damn cock in your pants." Eleri shouts as I walk out the door.

Ruby

CHAPTER Seventeen

It's been another long day. After Eleri left, the house felt so quiet, as if the whole place is waiting dormant for its master's return.

I've been languishing in the sun room, staring out the window, watching two tiny birds flitter about and yet, I don't dare go out there. Preston told me to stay in the house and I know he'll know if I take even one step over the threshold.

But it's not the fear of punishment that makes me obedient. I want him to check, to see, to realise that I am being good now, that I'm doing what he asks, and perhaps then he will come home and reward me with his time, with his presence.

I let out a snort.

It feels like a pipe dream now. Preston will return when it suits him. It's what my father did. How he managed my mother, though truth be told I think some days she managed him. The pair of them were tempestuous at best and you learnt very quickly how to read the signs.

The minute the air changed, the minute one of them pulled a certain face you got up, you got out, you fled the house if you could and left them to their carnage. And that's what it was. Both of them would fight it out. Would act like every argument was a battle to win the war. It wasn't a healthy environment. It certainly wasn't the sort you'd chose to grow up in and yet in so many ways we were happy, as strange as that sounds. My parents doted on me and my brother. They made sure we had the best of everything and with the diamond business, that was never much of an issue.

And then Levi came and stole it all.

Stole all my joy. All my family. And pitched my life into darkness.

I sigh, rubbing my eyes with my palms, I'm sick of my mind keep going over the same shit again and again. What is in the past is just that; the past. I don't know why I keep spiralling, I don't know why I keep focusing on it. I want to move on, to forget. If this is my new life then I want to make it work and forget the shit that came before it.

When I drop my hands I realise with a jolt that I'm not alone, that someone is stood in the doorway, watching me.

My eyes widen as I take him in. He's wearing a crisp white shirt, a dark tailored suit that clearly costs more than most people's annual wage, and his hair is slicked back in a way that makes him look roguish.

"Preston." I more whisper than say his name.

He tilts his head, smiling at me in a way that is so disarming. "You're wearing my shirt."

I glance down as my cheeks heat. "I, I didn't have anything else to put on."

He frowns shaking his head slightly. *Is he mad that I've taken his things again? That I've just helped myself?*

"I should have thought of that." He murmurs. "Levi was meant to send over your belongings but they're still yet to arrive."

"My belongings?" I repeat. I didn't have anything bar a few measly things that I'm not sure I'd miss. Would he be so brazen as to send that here, to show Preston how shit my life was?

He steps up to me, placing his hands on my shoulders. "I need to apologise to you, Ruby."

"What about?" My voice comes out as a squeak, high pitched, desperate. I hate how weak I sound, how pathetic I must look to this man who wears his strength and control like a pieces of armour.

"Being away this week. About not letting you know. Eleri told me you thought I was angry with you."

I nod quickly, dropping my gaze. She could still be wrong. He could be mad. I did run away after all and it's not like he left on the best terms.

"I wasn't angry with you." He says, lifting my chin. "And I'm sorry I upset you."

"It's okay." I say.

"No, it's not." He replies. "You deserve better."

I wince. He thinks that now but soon he may well realise that's not the case. That I'm not the kind of person anyone would actually choose to marry. That I'm sullied. Unclean. Disgusting.

"I want to take you out."

My eyes widen. Out?

"Have you seen much of this city?" He asks.

I shake my head. Beyond being flown in, escorted like a criminal, and then my brief escape attempts, I've seen nothing.

"I'll have my driver ready the car."

"I, I don't have anything to wear." I say quickly.

He glances at my shirt. It's a dark blue one, it covers me enough that it doesn't matter that I'm not wearing any underwear. But still, I don't have any shoes except the ones I got married in and, with the blisters still healing, the thought of wearing them is not appealing at all but I guess that's another thing I don't have a choice in.

"We'll get that sorted today. We'll go to a boutique. You can buy whatever you want."

"I," I bite my lip, not wanting him to think I'm ungrateful.

"What is it?" He asks.

"You want me to walk around the shops like this?"

Didn't he say before that everyone will judge him based on what I wear? That as his wife I need to look a certain way. I doubt hobbling around in my heels and an oversized shirt will present the image this man is wanting.

He lets out a chuckle. "No, Ruby, I'll have the shop closed for us. No one else will be there."

I don't know what to say to that. He clearly has a plan so it seems pointless to argue but I'll admit I am excited at the prospect, at the fact that I'm leaving these four walls, and that Preston is going to be there, spending time with me.

This is a start. This is my chance.

I just have to be amenable. I have to be convincing. I have to act the way Preston expects, be charming, seductive – I have to win him over because god knows he may spend the entire next seven days away again.

He's as good as his word. An hour later and he's watching me as I walk around the most luxurious clothes shop I've ever seen. If my mother were here I think she'd already have half the items off the racks.

I freeze as that thought hits me.

She's never going to do that again, will never take me shopping again.

Our last trip was so long ago. I was in a mood, in a huff about something so inconsequential I don't even remember now, and I stomped from store to store, making sure she knew I was pissed.

I wish I'd known. I wish I'd realised how truly numbered our days of happiness were. I would have treasured each and every one. I would never have snapped at her, never picked fights. Never played my parents off the way I did when I wasn't getting what I wanted.

In truth, I was a spoilt brat. A daddy's girl through and through, and at times I think my mother actually hated me.

"You okay?"

Preston's voice makes me jump. I turn to face him and he's there staring down at me with the same familiar look of concern I'm starting to believe might actually be real.

"I'm okay." I say back.

He takes my hand. "Where did you go just now? What were you thinking about?"

I look away, shutting my eyes. Sharing something so personal feels like a risk. But not sharing comes with risks too. I don't want him to think I'm hiding things, that I can't be trusted.

"I was thinking about my mother." I say quietly.

His eyebrows raise. "What made you think of her?"

"She would have loved this place. Would have loved to be here."

He squeezes my hand but he doesn't pry any further and for that I'm so grateful. I want to keep my memories secret, I want to keep them as mine, like tiny treasures that I can lock up and protect, and in a way it feels like I'm protecting them too.

"Have you seen anything you like?" He asks.

I nod, surreptitiously wiping away the tear that I hope he hasn't noticed.

"Why don't you try some on? See how they fit."

"Do you want to see?" I ask.

He shrugs. "Only if you're comfortable with that."

In the end, I show him everything I put on. Maybe I'm seeking his approval, maybe I just want him to feel like I'm giving him a choice in what I wear. Either way, he neither criticises nor puts down any of the items I pick. The few that I dislike, he hands back to the assistant without comment.

When we're done, one of his guards ends up carrying the humongous bags and I feel like I'm in some Hollywood film. Like I'm Pretty Woman or something.

I'm wearing new shoes. Comfortable heels that don't pinch the way my awful wedding shoes did. I feel attractive, I feel worthy of him.

As we walk down the street I lean into Preston and he glances down at me, smiling in a way that makes my heart flip. Is he happy right now? Is he enjoying spending this time with me as much as I am with him?

People are looking our way. I realise this is the first time since our wedding that we've been seen as a couple. Do we look like we fit? Do I look good enough now to be on his arm, as his wife?

"Where would you like to go next?" He asks, cutting through those thoughts.

"Aren't you done buying me things?" I say.

He takes my hand in his, intwining our fingers. "No. I'm happy to buy you whatever you want. As my wife you should have the very best of everything. If there's something you want you only have to say."

I bite my lip, hesitating because there is something I need, but it feels risky, really risky to ask. And yet on some level, I know it will also help in my plan to seduce him.

"What is it?" He asks, like he can read my facial expressions now.

"I need underwear." I say bluntly.

His eyebrows raise. "Underwear?" He repeats.

"I don't have any."

He drops his gaze, staring at the shirt I'm still wearing, despite all my new purchases. I know what he's thinking, where his head is at, that under this fabric I'm completely starkers.

"My wife wants to go underwear shopping." He murmurs.

"I can go by myself." I state quickly. "If you'd rather…"

"Absolutely not." He says. "Whenever you're out in public my men will be with you for your own safety. I'm not going to let you try on lingerie, surrounded by them, if I'm not there."

He sounds so possessive right now. Jealous too. Like I've already done something to warrant it.

"I," I begin but I'm not sure how to respond. I like the fact he's jealous, I like the fact he cares enough to be jealous. That's a good sign, surely? I need to build on that, I need to make this man of ice thaw entirely, need to make him rage with it.

He cups my face. "My wife wants underwear." He murmurs. "Then she shall have her pick."

Preston

CHAPTER *Eighteen*

Is god testing me right now? Is that what this is? The one person I'm not allowed to think about is currently stood behind the flimsiest of curtains trying on various pieces of lingerie while I'm supposed to act like it doesn't bother me?

My men are stationed by the door. I made it more than clear where they could keep their god damn gaze. I don't want them even seeing what she picks up, what grabs her attention.

None of it.

If they even glance in her direction, I will carve out their eyes and make them eat them.

The assistant flitters about, picking up pieces she thinks my wife will like. Apparently, Ruby didn't know her size so she had to be remeasured, whatever that means.

Turns out my wife is a 34E. I know I shouldn't have memorised that fact but I have. Maybe I'll buy her something sexy as a treat. Yeah, if I want Nico to cut my dick off and shove it down my throat.

"Preston?"

I narrow my eyes, staring at the fabric from where she's called.

"Everything okay?" I ask. God, I sound like a teenager with his first ever boner.

"Can you come here?"

I shake my head. Not a fucking chance. I step in that cubicle, I'll end up either losing my mind or worse, I'll shove her to her knees and start fucking her mouth till she chokes.

"The assistant can help." I reply as monotone as possible.

"Please?" She says in that sweet, innocent pleading she seems to have suddenly learnt. A tone that seems to linger in my head, as if I'm imagining she's begging for an entirely different outcome.

I get up, my head already telling me how utterly stupid this action is, and I walk into the cubicle.

She's stood, with her arms covering her chest wearing some sort of contraption. It crosses over her back, it highlights every delicious inch of her body. I stare at her perfect, plump arse in that thong bottom and I so badly want to sink my teeth into it. To mark her right here for everyone to know.

"It's stuck." She states.

"What?"

She's so bright red you could fry an egg on her face. "I can't get it off."

"I'll get the assistant."

"No." She hisses, grabbing my hand and pulling me back. "Please, help. Please."

I tilt my head and let out a laugh at the ridiculousness of this situation.

"Please?"

"You don't have to beg me to take your clothes off, Ruby." I say before I can stop myself and if anything, she flushes even more.

She drops her eyes like she's just realised how compromising this situation is and I mentally chastise myself for being such a brute. She might not be a virgin but she's as good as from what I can tell, despite all her protestations about 'fucking loads of men'.

Sex clearly makes her uncomfortable. It's a no go area for more reasons than simply because she's Nico's goddaughter.

"Turnaround." I murmur.

She does as she's told, staring back at me from the reflection in the mirror.

The lingerie is all twisted around itself. No wonder she can't get it off.

"I thought you were just buying bras." I say as I begin to untwist it. The outfit she has on is not something you'd simply wear under a dress.

She bites her lip. "The assistant said this would suit my skin tone. That my husband would like it…"

As my eyes run back over her, I can't disagree, even with the straps all wrong she looks fucking gorgeous. Is that where her head is at, that she wants to wear these sexy little things for me? That she wants to dress up in expensive lingerie and let me rip if from her body before I devour her?

My hands brush against her skin and I love the contrast, my pale fingers against her dark, perfect flesh. She feels so soft. So fucking malleable. Before I can stop myself I'm tracing a pattern down her back, hearing how her breath hitches, seeing the way her body responds so delightfully.

"Preston." She whispers.

I look back at her through the mirror. She's dropped her hands, I can see every delicious curve of her body. My hands wrap around her, I pull her hips back into me, wanting her to feel how hard I am and she lets out a gasp. One of both shock and underneath, that obvious excitement too.

"I can't touch you, Ruby." I say hoping she hears the regret. Hoping she hears how much I want to pin her against this wall and slide aside that tiny bit of fabric keeping me from the very gates of paradise.

She turns, staring at me before taking my hands and cupping her breasts with them.

"You're touching me now." She states, suddenly so confident.

I let out a groan, palming her breasts, feeling the way her nipples harden under the silky material. She arches her back, wrapping her arms up around my neck and goes on tip toes to kiss me.

Her tongue snakes into my mouth, she isn't just a spectator this time, she's here, wanting this, urging me on, and suddenly I'm incensed, I'm rabid, I push her back, needing more, demanding more. She writhes into me, rocking her hips against my cock and I groan at the feel of her.

I nip at her lips, then delve my tongue deeper into her mouth in my desperation to taste all of her.

I can't stop now.

I don't give a fuck what anyone says, I need this too much. I damn well deserve this too.

"...here it is." The assistant says, walking in before letting out a shriek of shock.

We break instantly.

Ruby's face is flushed, though I'd put money on it being more than just embarrassment at how we've been found. In one quick movement she flicks her hair over to cover herself.

"I'm so sorry, Mr Civello." The assistant says, stepping back quickly. "I, I didn't realise."

"It's okay." I reply. Perhaps it's for the best. The universe is stepping in, preventing me from crossing a line I'm forbidden from going near.

Ruby bites her lip and reluctantly, I let her go, leaving her stood there, though how I can walk away with the size of my erection right now, I don't know.

My men glance at me then quickly look away. Apparently everyone is aware of what I was up to just now. How I was indulging in my wife. I guess it's a good thing none of them directly report into Nico or he'd have my dick served on a platter by sundown.

Ruby

CHAPTER *Nineteen*

I can't look at him. I'm too embarrassed. I don't even know where it came from, why I did it, but one minute he was helping me and the next, well, the next I just couldn't stop.

I wanted him to touch me, to realise that I'm not some child, because that's what I think is the issue.

He must be over twice my age. Does he think I'm too young? Does he find my body too juvenile for him? Why else would he not be fucking his wife like any normal man would?

He keeps going on about how he can't touch me, like it's forbidden, like he's made some rule in his head about what we can and can't do and yet I felt him, I felt how much his body wanted me.

If I want to win him over, if I want to show him that I've accepted this, then I need him to fuck me. I need him to want me, as much as that thought in so many ways scares the shit out of me.

We sit in silence on the journey back. Preston flicks through his phone, replying to messages and takes a few calls. I don't speak. I stare out the window taking in the unfamiliar sights of this new city as it whizzes by.

It's so bright. Every street seems to have flashing advertisements and the entire place is buzzing like it's built from gold.

For a second, my hand wraps around my neck, remembering that diamond necklace my parents gifted me. Levi stole that too. I don't even know if he still has it or if he had it taken from the setting and sold along with the others he got from our mines.

Maybe if I ask nicely Preston will buy me one. I glance at him, seeing the concentration on his face as he responds to something.

He's so serious.

I like that about him. In fact, I think now that I'm understanding him a little better, I think I'm starting to actually like him as a person. Sure, under that beautiful exterior I know he's just as deadly as Levi but he's more controlled too, he doesn't fly off the handle for no reason, he doesn't hurt me just for the sheer amusement of it. With Preston, I don't feel like I'm constantly waiting for him to go on the attack.

When we pull up to the house, he gets out before walking around, opening my door, and holding his hand for me to take. He's acting like a perfect gentleman. The perfect husband. Yeah, I think my father would have liked him too, though perhaps he'd not be too amused at the whole tracker in the arm situation.

Inside, Sidney is stood waiting for us. He gives a small courteous incline of his head as we approach.

"Your things have arrived." He says.

Preston looks at me and I frown.

"What…?" I begin.

"Mr Holtz had one of his men deliver them an hour ago." Sidney states.

My things? What the fuck? I follow Preston though to where it's all been placed and there's a lot of it. Bags that is. I take a step forward, opening one up and a sleeve of some fine fabric slides out. It's not mine - but I knew that before I even opened the bag.

"Do you want to unpack and go through it?" Preston asks.

I think I'm too dumbfounded to reply and he takes my silence as a yes, leaving me to it.

Slowly I start pulling things out, shaking my head. It's all fine clothing, all way too old a style for me, and some isn't even in my size. Did Levi do this? Did he order this all to be bought? For what cause, to pretend that he took care of me, to pretend that I wasn't as a good as a slave in that house?

I shudder, wondering if my new husband will believe this, if he'll think Levi was in fact a good guardian all these years.

In one of the bags something vibrates. I rifle through, pulling out a phone and see the message that flashes up.

'Little whore'

My stomach twists. There's no sender's name but I know who it is. Who sent it.

Another message appears. I scan the contents realising that this is part of Gunnar's plan isn't it? It's how he gets to me, how he ensures I do exactly what he wants.

Except, he can't make me do this. He can't physically force me to do anything anymore.

I let out a little laugh as I realise how powerless that bastard now is. He thought planting me here would set them up, that they'd make their moves and I'd be the snake in the Morelli camp.

But I'm not a snake.

I'm not their creature. Their little puppet.

All this time he thought he'd beaten me into submission, that he made me the perfect spy and yet he didn't even stop to consider that the moment I got free of his clutches, he would lose all his power over me.

I turn the phone off, creep out of the room, I don't want Preston to find this and think I'm helping them. I don't want to run the risk of him thinking I'm a traitor.

In the library, I grab the first book I can, the copy of Huckleberry Finn. In a way it feels poetic to hide this phone behind it, like my father is somehow protecting me from all the shit I'm now turning my back on.

I place the phone flat against the wall then put the book back. No one would ever know it's there. Hopefully it can stay there until I figure out a better way to dispose of it. I don't want to risk putting it in the trash. I don't want to risk anyone finding it.

I leave my supposed belongings where I found them. For all I know Levi has bugged them and I'd rather see them burnt than still in this house. Upstairs, Preston has already ordered the walk in wardrobe to be reorganised so half the space is now mine.

It's odd to think that I now have this. I have this tiny tangible thing. The maid offers to hang my new clothes up, the ones Preston has bought me, but I want to do it, I want to go through everything, to take a moment to relish that I have belongings now, that I own things of my own.

I hang it all carefully. Perhaps there's some special way you're meant to sort everything but for me just seeing the clothes, the splashes of colours, just knowing they're all mine, makes my heart leap. While I didn't mind wearing Preston's shirts, now I can at least look decent if Eleri calls again.

I can walk around and not look like some sort of forgotten part in all of this.

In the drawers, I lay out all my new underwear. I like that I have options with this too. I like that if the time calls for it, I can actually look sexy for my husband. I can be the wife he expects me to be.

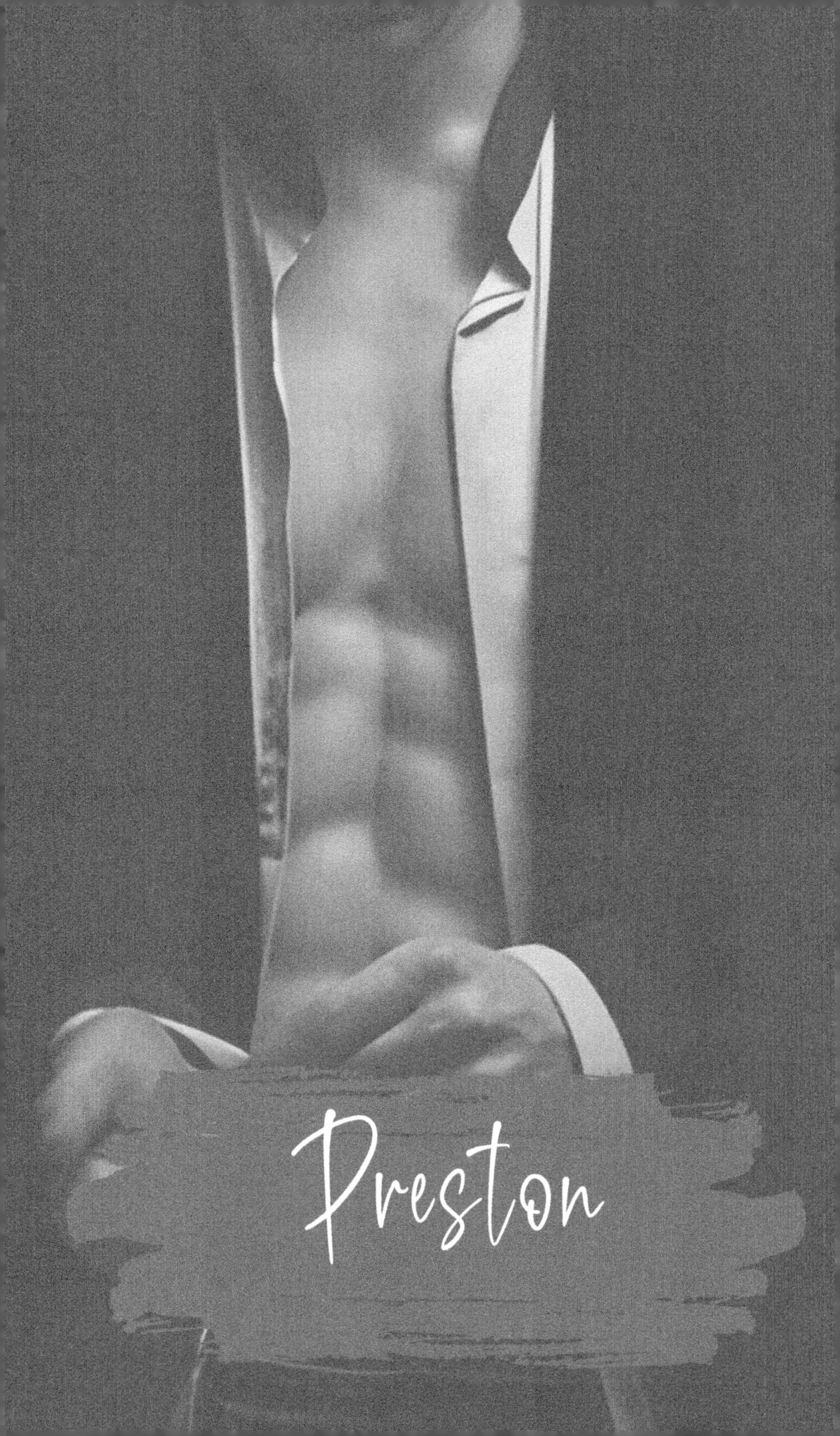

Preston

CHAPTER *Twenty*

I'm leaning against the doorframe, watching her, though she's completely oblivious. She's just been sat there staring at all those new clothes, looking up at them sat on her knees on the plush carpet like she can't quite believe her luck.

I glance at the items all hung up. Something tells me that she did it, that she hung each and every one. But I note something else too, all of it is what I bought her today. All of it still has tags on. All of it is brand new.

She's not hung up one item from the things Levi delivered.

"They weren't your things, were they?"

She jumps, turning around, and slowly shakes her head.

"All of it?"

"All of it." She confirms, getting to her feet.

"Where is your stuff?"

She chews her lip, hesitating for a second. "I didn't really have anything."

"No clothes?" I growl. How the fuck does that even make sense?

She wraps her arms around herself, shrugging. "I had a pair of jeans, a couple of old tops. Nothing much."

"What about other stuff, jewellery, photos, sentimental shit?"

"Sentimental shit?" She repeats with a little laugh but I can see the tears in her eyes all the same. "I don't have any of that."

"Not even photos?"

She shakes her head. "No. He destroyed everything. He burnt the house, got rid of every last possession we had."

I can hear the pain in her voice. Her hand is wrapped around her throat, as if it's clinging to some imaginary thing that's also lost with all those memories.

"I see." I reply before pulling out my credit card. "It's not the same," I begin, "But anything you want, anything you need, you can have it."

She stares at the shiny plastic, hesitating for a moment before she slowly takes it.

"I don't really need anything now," She whispers, glancing at the new clothes hanging so neatly, as if a few dresses can heal the gaping hole in her heart.

She's like driftwood in the ocean, smashing from wave to wave with nothing to anchor her down.

I clench my fists to fight the sudden emotion that seems to swirl inside me and again, I wonder who the fuck I'm becoming. How does one woman have such an effect on me? How is she able to make me *feel* when I've never wanted to feel, never needed to before?

In my head, I make a note to hunt down some pictures, to somehow find some images of her parents, of her brother too. I can't bring them back, I can't undo all the shit that happened to them but I want to fix her, I want to take all those broken parts and make her whole again.

I'll buy her jewellery too, I'll fill the house with flowers, and ornaments, and whatever Eleri says will cheer her up. I'll fill her future with happy memories and...

It hits me then that her future doesn't belong to me.

I have no business planning any of it.

This marriage is temporary. Our time together is temporary.

"Your parents died..." She says quietly, hesitantly.

My eyes snap to hers and for a second, something violent seizes me. "Yes," I reply almost coldly because, unlike her, I've never mourned their death, never felt the need to.

"Do you, did you..." She sniffs, looking like she's afraid to finish whatever sentence she's trying to get out. "You moved on?"

I draw in a deep breath, taking her hand and pulling her to me. She gulps as she lets me guide her out of this space.

"They died a long time ago." I state. "And in entirely different circumstances to yours."

"But it wasn't..." She pauses, glancing at me then away.

I don't know what she's heard, I don't know if it's merely rumours because let's face it, there are enough of them, but she's clearly trying to reach out, to understand me, and some selfish part of me likes it.

I want her to know me, to see me, to understand the man and not just the image I project.

But that's dangerous too. I like having distance between me and everyone else, and yet the idea of Ruby knowing my secrets, of knowing my very soul and not flinching when she looks at me – yeah I'm a fucking fool to want that, to crave it.

"Do you really want to know, Ruby?" I ask.

She chews her lip, nodding. "Tell me."

"Fine," I grip her hand, ensuring that for the moment, she won't turn and flee, that she's forced to hear my secret, to understand exactly what happened that day, exactly who I am. "I killed my father." I state. "He was a Capo for Nico's father and he was a rat, he was betraying Nico's parents, passing information to the Feds."

She shudders but she keeps her eyes fixed on me, and for that alone, I admire her. She could easily shy away, let her fear override her thoughts but she doesn't, under that exterior, Ruby has got some guts.

"He used to beat my mother up, come home drunk, take out his rage on her." I explain. "He'd beat me to when I was stupid enough to stand in his way and yet she stood by him, despite his treachery."

"But you killed him?" She says, still obviously shocked.

I shrug back, my lips curling into a smirk because I won't apologise for it, I don't feel guilt, remorse, I've never second guessed my actions – I knew what I was doing, even as a twelve year old pulling the trigger. "The bastard deserved it." I state. "Anyone who snitches deserves what they get."

She swallows, trembling just a little, and I wonder if I've gone too far. I didn't mean to scare her, I didn't mean to turn this into a conversation about me when she was clearly taking a moment to grieve her own loss.

"Are you hungry?" I ask.

She nods.

"Let's eat then," I say, leading her down the stairs. She needs to be fattened up and food right now is as good a distraction as anything else.

Ruby

CHAPTER
Twenty-One

He left with the sunrise. I guess I can't expect him to spend all his time with me and, considering he spent the entirety of yesterday afternoon and all evening here, I can hardly complain. Compared to the last week, he's spoilt me with his attention.

While he's gone, I take the opportunity to have all my supposed belongings that are currently downstairs taken away. I have Sidney send them to a charity shop. I don't want them in the house. I don't want them anywhere near me.

I still haven't dared to retrieve the phone. Maybe in a few weeks, once Preston trusts me more, I can sneak it out and drop it into the river, or better, leave it on a park bench and let some stranger find it. Maybe Gunner will message them, maybe they'll fuck with him for a bit.

I smirk at the notion. Yeah that would be some good comeuppance, him thinking it's me and some complete weirdo stringing him along.

But Preston's words from yesterday repeat in my head, that he killed his own father, murdered him because he was a snitch – if he can do that to his own flesh and blood, what would he do to me? I don't want to think about it but the thought scares me shitless all the same and it cements the belief that I can't do it, I absolutely cannot betray him.

For a second I consider confessing the truth, telling him exactly what Gunnar wants me to do and begging for mercy but I know that's madness.

Preston won't show me mercy, he killed his own father for godsake, even if I haven't done anything wrong, he won't believe me.

He'll see me exactly as everyone else sees me; cannon fodder. Expendable.

No, I have to keep my mouth shut, I know that much. I have to pretend that this marriage is what he thinks it is, that I'm here simply to sweeten whatever the deal is between our two families.

But if I can make him fall in love with me then surely that will protect me from Gunnar and Levi too? That, as his wife, he will make sure nothing bad happens to me. I just wish I knew what I was doing, how to actually seduce him, what does a man like Preston even like?

In my desperation, I ask to borrow one of the maids phones, promising that I only want to look up something, but I haven't used a modern phone in so long that the one Annabell lends me is like something out of star wars. I stare at the large screen. There are no buttons, nothing but shiny glass. The phone Gunnar slipped into my fake things was a billy-basic compared to this.

After minutes of sheer desperation, I give in and ask for help.

Annabell smiles as she shows me what to do, how to pull up what she calls "a browser" and says I can type in anything I want into the search bar. I swear you can fry an egg on my face as I start searching how to seduce my husband.

Annabell stares over my shoulder and what she must think I don't know, but she's clearly satisfied that I'm not trying to break out again, and then she starts giving me tips too. Bits of advice like we're friends and not technically employer and employee.

By the time I'm done, I feel like I've got a whole libraries worth of information, most of which seems to be about being confident, that confidence is sexy, confidence is what men want in a woman, but how the fuck can I be confident around a man like Preston Civello?

I can barely hold his gaze most days. He's too handsome, too fearsome too. I feel like a pathetic excuse of a person and not nearly worthy enough of his attention.

Annabell tells me it's all about the foundations, looking confident means feeling confident. So we spend a good few hours of her preening my hair, doing my nails, turning me from some street rat into what feels like a supermodel.

She does my hair, styles the frizz into a smooth mirror like finish that I want to continuously run my fingers through. And she helps pull out a ridiculously sexy dress from my wardrobe, one that is made from some clinging material that hugs every curve of me.

As I hear his car pull up in the drive, my stomach is a bag of butterflies, but I tell myself that I can do this, I can be confident, I can be sexy – I have to be. I have to make him fall in love with me, to want me - my very life depends upon him seeing me as his wife in every single way.

The door opens, he stalks in, tosses his impeccable suit jacket to the waiting man and then his eyes fall on me as I stand at the top of the stairs.

I want to smile, to laugh at the shocked look on his face, and it takes everything I have to remain composed as I slowly make my way down to him.

"How was your day?" I ask quietly, trying to master my fear.

He scans my face, tilting his head, before running his eyes down the entire length of me. It feels like the air heats, it feels like the entire room is holding its breath, waiting for what this man will do.

"Where did you get that dress?" He says, ignoring my question entirely.

I glance down, seeing the way my breasts are heaving, I'm not exactly small chested but this dress cuts low enough to emphasise that point to the max.

"You bought it for me." I reply. "Don't you like it?"

He blinks, staring again and I wonder if I've somehow rendered him speechless.

Preston

CHAPTER Twenty-Two

It's been a long day. A shit day. Apparently, Levi's trade routes aren't nearly as secret as he'd led us to believe and we've had to deal with the repercussions of that fact, losing men, stock, tens of thousands of revenue too.

But as I walk through the door, as I toss my jacket, all thoughts of Levi, of Gunnar, of Nico too disappear from my head.

My wife is stood, clearly waiting for me, and my jaw practically hits the floor as I take in what she's wearing.

"Ruby," I murmur her name under my breath, feeling like it's the only part of her I can lay claim to.

She slowly makes her way towards me, taking each step almost gingerly in those ridiculous heels. I swear I'm about to go full caveman just watching the way her hips sway, the way she holds my gaze like she's about to strip right here and beg me to fuck her.

"Where did you get that dress?" I manage to get out, trying to focus on the present, trying to force my blood-flow to retreat, to turn around, to go back to my brain and not to the almost ever present hard-on I have around her.

She glances down, a momentary flicker of uncertainty covers her features, and I'll admit, that in itself makes her even more beautiful.

I see her lips move but whatever words she says make no sense above the pounding in my chest. I take a step forward, then another, closing the distance like I'm an assassin going in for the kill.

"Don't you like it?" She asks, clearly seeing the look in my eyes.

Like it? Fucking hell, I can't even formulate words in response to that.

She pauses, letting me look my fill, and then she turns as if she knows the exact game she's playing, heading to the dining room, and leaving me to follow in her wake.

I don't know who the fuck my wife has just transformed into, I don't know where the shy, timid creature has gone and who this temptress is before me, but I know one thing; I am completely and utterly fucked.

I consider running, I consider retreating back to the townhouse, but I've never backed down before and I sure as hell am not starting now. No, whatever happens, wherever this ends, I'm here, I'm seeing it through.

Sidney has dinner already laid out. It's like this entire evening has been planned. We sit and while I'm trying to wrangle what little self-control I have left, she's there, eating away, acting like this sudden change in her is completely normal.

I manage to force down a few mouthfuls but it's hard to eat, hard to focus on anything when she's sat there, looking like that.

After the meal is done, we head to the lounge and she saunters over to the bar in the corner and pours out two glasses like all of this is perfectly normal.

"Drink?" She says handing one to me.

"I thought you didn't drink whiskey." I say, surprised that out of everything in my cabinet, this is what she chose for herself.

She gives me a smile. "I like the idea of it."

"Maybe you'll get used to the taste." I say before taking a sip.

She nods, taking a sip of her own and trying not to wince as the sharpness hits her throat.

"Come on," I murmur, taking the glass. "Why not drink something you actually like?"

"I don't know what I like."

I raise an eyebrow at that. "You don't drink?"

"I wasn't allowed." She says, pulling a face that suggests there's more to it than just that.

"What about before, when your parents were still alive?" She was sixteen when all that shit went down, even with strict parents, most sixteen year olds would have learnt to sneak a drink here and there.

She lets out a laugh. "Jett used to. He used to steal bottles from my father's study and we'd sit out, drinking it on the hill top while they were fighting."

"Your parents fought?"

"Like cats and dogs." She says, her face going so serious.

Internally, I wince, not meaning to turn this conversation into one of sadness, of bitterness. "Alright, let's find out what you like then."

Her eyes widen at my words. "What?"

I get up, going to the art deco bar in the corner, and start pulling out various bottles and glasses.

"What are you doing?" She says, coming up behind me.

I give her a smirk, making them up, mixing them, pouring them out like it's her own taster board. "Give them a sip, see which ones you prefer."

She eyes them with suspicion then turns that beautiful gaze onto me. "Is my husband trying to get me drunk?"

I let out a laugh, wrapping my arm around her waist, while raising the first glass to her lips. "Drink Ruby, tell me what you think."

She takes a sip. Her lips pucker over the creamy liquid and her tongue darts out to lick it up. My eyes drop to stare at the movement. Christ, what I wouldn't give to have that tongue wrapped around me.

"Do you like it?" I ask.

She nods. "I like it." She breathes, her chest rising and falling in that tight little dress she has on.

"Try another."

"This is good."

"Try another, Ruby." I order.

She pouts, picking a glass up and shots the entire thing back.

"You couldn't possibly have tasted that." I state.

She shrugs. "It's not about the drink."

"No?"

"No." She says, jutting her chin, raising her lips so they're so close to mine. "If my husband wants to get me drunk, he just has to say."

I tilt my head, lowering my mouth to her ear. "I won't get you drunk, Ruby. I'm not the kind of man who needs alcohol to get what I want."

"And what do you want?" She replies, battering her eyelashes like she doesn't know the game she's playing, like she really is as innocent as she's pretending to be, despite the slutty way she's dressed.

I'm so close to just ripping that dress right down the middle.

I'm so close to picking her up and showing her exactly what I want.

But that voice of reason echoes in my head. I can even see Nico, in all his rage, losing his shit because I've devoured his precious goddaughter, even though she's my wife now, my property.

"Preston?" She says softly.

I cup her face, stare back into those bewitching eyes. "I can't, Ruby." I murmur and her shoulders slump like I've just denied her every dream she's ever wanted.

I pour out another drink, passing it to her, then avoid her gaze as I sit back down. She stands still, watching me then tiptoes to where I am before planting herself right beside me.

She can't see it, but I clench my fist, digging my nails into my palm, reminding myself of why she is untouchable, why she is off limits, why I'm married to this incredible creature but I'm not allowed to fuck her.

"Why won't you touch me?"

I shut my eyes, letting out a low breath. "Because…"

"Am I that repulsive?"

"What?" I snap. How can she think that? She's the complete fucking opposite, that's half the problem. "Ruby," I begin. "You didn't choose to marry me…"

"But I'm okay with it."

I shake my head. "Are you really? Because from what I've learnt about you, you've been conditioned to give into everyone else. You never say what you actually want. You never say what you're actually feeling."

She winces and that makes me feel even more of an arsehole.

"I didn't mean to hurt you." I say, cupping her cheek as gently as a brute like I can.

"I know."

I tuck my fingers under her chin, making her meet my eyes. "I don't want to hurt you, Ruby. Ever. That's why I won't touch you."

She bites her lip, staring back at me. "What about what I want?"

"Ruby…"

"You said the last night that whatever I want I just have to ask."

I feel my lips curl and before I can stop her, she's leaning in and kissing me.

I groan into her mouth. I know I should stop this. I know I should stop all of this, but I've spent the last I don't know how long, smelling her perfume, staring at her in that tight little dress, all the while imagining how it would feel to get just one taste. Just one moment.

"Preston." She murmurs.

Her hands start undoing my belt. My dick is already so hard it hurts.

I can't fuck her. I cannot fuck her.

But I'm not stopping this either. Right now, I'm just sat here, letting her reach down and take hold of me. I guess, technically, this isn't breaking the rules right, she's touching me, not the other way around. We never made any agreements about that, did we?

And then she freezes when she realises exactly what I've been hiding.

"You're…"

"It's called a Jacobs ladder." I say.

She blinks, staring at my cock with a look that seems half-awe, half-fascination. "Did it, did it hurt?"

Yeah, it fucking killed. And add the fact you can't have sex for months after. But the way women react, the way they come on my cock, it makes it all worth it.

I stare back at her, imagining what she'd feel like to be wrapped around me. How good her cunt would fill as she came just for me.

She's off limits. She's un-fucking-touchable.

She wraps her hand around me, carefully placing her fingers so she doesn't grip right on the piercings and slowly she brings it up.

"Fuck." I hiss.

Maybe I'm a masochist.

Maybe I'm a complete fucking idiot but right now I'd happily let Nico gut me for just a second of her. Just a taste.

She lowers her mouth, kissing me again, only this time I'm not letting her tease me the way she did before. I wrap my hand around the back of her head, taking control, possessing her mouth the way she's possessing my cock.

She moans against me. A real moan. A sexy little noise that I know from our wedding night she hasn't just faked.

That noise seems to drive me over the edge.

I can't stop now. I won't stop.

I don't give a fuck about the consequences.

I grind my hips, accentuating every movement she's making. She's teasing my cock like she knows exactly what I want. And then she takes my hand, sliding it under her dress and into her underwear.

"Make me come." She says. "Make me come the way you have all the women before me."

I growl, opening my eyes, grabbing her jaw tightly with my spare hand. "You are nothing like them." I say. "You are so much more. You are my wife. I married you." But I can feel how wet she is. Christ, she actually wants this, she actually wants me to touch her.

I push her back, taking control as she relinquishes her grip on me. "You really want this?" I ask.

She nods, hiking her dress up so the only thing separating me from the best view of my life is the tiny strip of red lace I bought her.

"Please, Preston." She whispers.

My lips curl at the way she says it. At the sweet way my wife is begging me.

"My wife wants to come." I say, pulling her underwear aside, staring at her glistening pussy that's bared just for me. She's so pink, so plump, god I can just imagine how she'd welcome my dick home. "Fuck."

She nods, encouraging me on. "Please."

I look back at her face. "I told you before, Ruby. You can have whatever you want, you only have to ask."

"I want you." She says reaching out, grabbing my cock that's weeping with its need for her. "I want you, Preston."

I run my fingers down between her lips. She arches her back as she gasps and she spreads her legs a little wider for me.

"My sweet, innocent wife." I say. "By the time I'm done with you, you won't be so innocent."

She whimpers, rocking her hips, showing me every way she can that she wants this.

I slip one finger inside her, then another. She feels so fucking perfect. So fucking wet. As I curl them up, she loses herself in the feel of it, and she shuts her eyes.

Only, I can't have that. I won't have that. I want her to know who's touching her, who's giving her this, I want her to remember exactly who owns her now. Who grants her pleasure. Who gives her everything she ever needs.

"Open your eyes." I order. "Look your husband in the face when he's fucking you."

She does it immediately. Staring back at me like she thinks she's pissed me off.

But her cunt is dripping.

She lets out a moan, reaching out like she wants my cock back in her hands.

"Not yet." I say. I want to taste her. I want to have her juices all over my mouth before I get my finale.

I slide off the couch, spread her legs wide, holding her thighs in place and lower my lips to her. She lets out a whimper, not one of pleasure, but fear.

"Let your husband show you what his tongue can do." I say, staring up at her.

She looks like a goddess, she looks so regal, bared wide just for me, and I'm ready to worship at her altar for as long as she allows me access.

She gulps, staying still, obviously trusting that whatever this is, I won't hurt her.

As I sashay my tongue up between her lower lips she gasps in shock.

"That feel good, Ruby?"

She nods.

"You like my mouth on you?"

She nods again, like I've made her speechless.

"How about you show me how much you like it, wife." I say. "Come on my mouth. Come for me and make your husband proud."

She gulps but I don't give her time for any more of a reaction. I'm too lost in this, driven half mad by the delicious taste of her.

I suck her clit in between my lips. She moans louder, rocking her hips. With two fingers, I spear her once more. I want this time to be memorable. I want it to be earth shattering. I want her to fall apart beneath me.

She starts riding my mouth, shoving her cunt as hard into me as she can. I wrap a hand under her perfect, peachy arse and hold her in place. I want to control this, I want her to come on my terms.

She starts writhing, kicking out, but I don't relent. I swirl my tongue, I tease her, never taking my eyes from her face.

"Oh god." She gasps. "God."

I can hear she's close. I can see the way she's getting so flushed.

"Come for me, Ruby. Come for your husband like the good girl you are."

She whimpers, shutting her eyes and this time I let her. I suck her clit harder, forcing her over the edge and suddenly she's screaming, locking her legs around my head, thrashing like some creature possessed.

Her arousal pours out of her. Hot, salty, utter fucking perfection. I lap it all up. Lap every last drop as she slumps back onto the couch.

I sit back on my heels, watching her for a moment like she's the finest piece of artwork I've ever seen.

Her chest is heaving.

Her body's got tremors like it doesn't know what to do with all the pleasure she's just experienced.

"So fucking perfect." I say, sweeping her hair back from where it's stuck to the sweat on her forehead.

She blinks, staring back at me and then what seems like shame, or embarrassment, or something, washes over her.

"No." I growl, scooping her up. "Don't you dare."

I carry her out of the room, up the stairs, and to where our bed is.

"Preston." She whispers, as I lay her down.

"Did you enjoy it?" I ask.

She bites her lip but she nods and then she stares down at where my cock is still so damn hard.

"You didn't come." She says.

"It doesn't matter."

"Yes, it does." She replies, reaching down, taking hold of me.

I shut my eyes, allowing myself to indulge in the moment, to really savour every delicious movement of her hand on my cock.

As she starts to pick up pace, I ease her legs open and slide my left hand back where it belongs.

She frowns as I do it. "You already made me come." She says.

I let out a chuckle. "Did you think I'd be satisfied with just the one orgasm?" I reply. "Now that I've taught your body what to do, I'm going to demand more. A lot more."

Before she can respond, I claim her mouth. I claim every one of her moans as we both start humping the other's hand.

She comes first. I make sure of that.

I hold myself back long enough to watch as she topples over the edge and her grip around me is gone. And then I'm leaning over her, pumping away, covering what little exposed skin she has with my come.

She blinks, staring down at the mess I've created.

And then her lips curl. She smiles for the first time. A real smile. A genuine smile.

It's the best most fucking incredible moment of my life. My wife smiles and I swear in that moment something deadly locks around my heart.

I get what Nico and Eleri are now. I get what all of their passion is about.

I will kill for this woman. I will start wars for her.

If all this shit with Levi ends and Nico tries to split us, I will go to war against him too.

I'm never letting her go.

I get up, walking to the bathroom, and turn on the taps to fill the bath. We've not really done anything close to what would require aftercare and yet that urge in me is there anyway. I want to show her, now more than ever, that I'm not like the bastards she's grown up with.

When I scoop her up, she gives me a look like she has no idea what I'm doing.

"Let me take care of you." I say, carrying her through.

Her eyes widen when she sees the tub. "A bath?"

I don't reply beyond a smirk but when I set her on her feet, I realise she's still wearing that dress and I've never actually seen her fully naked in any decent light.

The realisation seems to hit her at the same time. I expect her to shrink away. If she does then I won't force her. If this is a step to far then I'll hold my hands up and acknowledge it.

Only, her hands move to slide the straps down. I follow every tiny movement as she waggles her generous hips and the fabric slides off her. The lace bra she has on matches the thong I've already become intimately acquainted with. Her breasts are heaving. But I can see the outline of her nipples. I can see how hard they are and it's making my mouth water.

She reaches around, unhooks the thing and lets it fall.

My eyes instantly drop to stare at her breasts.

She doesn't try to cover herself. She just stands there letting me look, letting me take every delicious inch of her in.

"Do you like what you see?" She says quietly.

I step up, grabbing her ass in my hand, pulling her hips into my crotch. She's so fucking soft, so fucking perfect. "You're beautiful." I say. "Stunning."

She smiles again, a softer smile than before but one that melts my heart all the same.

"You need to get undressed too." She says, putting her hands gently on my chest.

"We're sharing the bath?" I reply.

"Isn't that what you wanted?"

It's not what I planned but I don't say it. Why the hell would I give up the opportunity to have her naked body against mine? I let her go and she steps so gracefully into the water, leaning back as the ripples lap against her breasts.

I pull my top off, pull the rest of my clothes off. She hasn't seen me naked either so I stand still, letting her look where she wants, the way she did for me.

I'm not ashamed of my body. I never have been. I work out, I work hard, I'm in the best damn shape of my life but I am aware that I'm over twice her age.

Has she even seen a man as old as me? Has she ever been with someone not her own age?

She holds her hand out, reaching for me, and I take it as I climb in. The water is perfect. Her body resting against me is sublime. This moment here really is a slice of the kind of heaven men like me do not get. Nor do we deserve.

She puts her hand on my thigh, gripping it in a way that makes my cock thicken despite its release. "Thank you." She says quietly.

"For what?" I ask.

She shrugs like there's some sort of secret. "Just, thank you."

I plant a kiss on the side of her head.

For the first time she feels at peace. She feels content.

If I have to lie here all night not to disturb her joy then I will.

Ruby

CHAPTER Twenty-Three

He washes me. He brushes my hair with a comb he's produced from what feels like thin air, teasing out all the nasty little knots that my fingers neglected to find. And when the bath water grows cold, he helps me out and towels me down.

I stand there, letting him do it, letting him take care of me the way he clearly wants to, but some part of my mind seems to be panicking.

Seems to be screaming that all of this is wrong.

That any minute now he's going to flip, he's going to turn to anger and I'm going to feel the full force of his fists.

I gulp, staring at his hands as if I can imagine them curling up already, and then I remind myself that Preston isn't like that. That he's kind, at least, kind to me. That I can trust him.

But can I? Can I truly trust any of them?

"You're trembling." He murmurs.

I glance up, meeting those concerned eyes. "I'm just tired." I lie. I don't want him to know what I'm thinking, I don't want him to realise how conflicted I feel.

"Then let's get you to bed." He replies as if the only thing in the world that matters to him is me.

I take his offered hand, I walk silently beside him and when we slip under the covers, I let him hold me, I let him seek whatever it is he needs in my body.

Perhaps this is what a normal marriage is meant to feel like. But Preston right now, he seems so different from the Mafia monster I've come to expect.

Preston right now feels so safe.

And I don't know how to deal with it.

How to process it.

I lie awake, telling myself that this is part of the plan, that it's all coming together. I'm seducing him, turning him to my side, but I'm not sure that's all of what's happening. I can feel my walls starting to ease. I can feel something inside me, something changing, altering, and truth be told, it's scaring the shit out of me.

I don't want to like Preston.

I don't mean that in a horrible way, but if I fall for him, if I let myself truly trust him, then all I'm doing is opening myself up to danger, to heartbreak, to more pain.

It's better if I can remain as I am, with a heart so broken from trauma that I'm not capable of true emotions. At least, not positive ones.

When I eventually fall asleep, I feel like I drift from one nightmare to another. Nothing too awful mind, just enough to torment me.

I dream that I'm running, racing, desperate to catch up with Jett but he's moving too fast and there's no way I can. Behind us are those same gunmen. But as I glance back, I see him, I see my father, I see him alive.

I see him trying to escape and then, I see Gunnar.

I see him raising a gun, taking aim, and that bullet flies through the air, it obliterates my father's face and I'm screaming, collapsing onto the grass, falling back into that awful pool of his blood.

I wake with a jolt.

I'm not in the bed, I know that much.

The rug beneath my knees is so plush, so soft. I squint, and with horror I realise exactly where I am, what room I've unwittingly entered; Preston's office.

I gulp, trying to get to my feet as a voice in my head screams at me to move, to get out.

If Preston finds me here in the middle of the night he'll think I've been snooping, he'll think I've...

My panic turns to something incomprehensible as a shadow moves, as a figure steps through the doorway, and with horror, I realise it's too late.

He *has* found me.

And I'm in so much trouble now.

Preston

CHAPTER Twenty-Four

She's trembling, whimpering, shaking her head like I've just caught her red-handed.

Only, it's more than obvious what happened, even if I hadn't woken up as she slipped from the bed, even if I hadn't followed her the entire way, in her sleep-addled state.

"I didn't, I didn't." She whispers over and over like I'm about to beat her senseless.

I try to soothe her, I try to reason with her but she's too lost in her panic to hear it.

In the end, I carry her back up to our bed and wrap the covers around her. It's clear she's having a panic attack, I just don't understand what brought it on.

"You're okay." I murmur, trying to sound comforting, trying to *be* comforting, as if I even know what that looks like. "Nothing's going to happen."

"I didn't mean…" She gasps, burying her face into my chest. "I wasn't snooping. I wasn't…" Her voice trails off as her words turn to sobs.

So that *is* it. She thinks she's in trouble for being in my office? She thinks I'm going to punish her for doing absolutely nothing wrong.

I shake my head, tightening my arms around her in a way I hope feels protective rather than aggressive. "I know you weren't." I state. "You were sleep walking. I followed you from our room. I was behind you the entire time…"

She looks up at me as if trying to hear the lie and her eyes widen as those words sink in.

"You, you followed me?" She repeats.

"When you got up, I asked where you were going and you didn't reply. You seemed off. I just wanted to make sure you were alright."

She shudders, relaxing a little, but I can hear her breath is still shaky; she's still not back to normal.

I place a kiss on her head, I stroke her hair, trying to flatten some of the frizz.

"I trust you." I state.

She gulps, blinking at me. "You, you trust me?" She says in obvious disbelief.

"I trust you." I repeat. "You can go anywhere in this house, you can look through any drawer, anything you like." I don't add that the reason is there's nothing here of merit, that I've already taken all the sensitive papers and locked them away because that won't ease her fears right now, that won't calm her.

"Why?" She asks.

"Why what?"

"Why do you trust me? You don't even know me, I could be a spy, I could be…" My fingers over her lips silence her rushed words.

"You're not." I say simply. "You're not a spy, you're not up to anything nefarious. You're my wife, and you have every right to do as you wish in this house."

She gives me a look like she doesn't quite believe me. As though this is a trick I'm playing. Luring her in only to punish her later.

"Do you often sleepwalk?" I ask.

She shrugs, dropping her gaze. "I guess so. My room was always locked so I couldn't even if I'd tried."

"They locked you in?"

She draws in a breath like she wanted to keep that fact a secret. "It was for my safety." She murmurs but we both know that's bullshit. Clearly, Levi really did keep her like a prisoner.

"What were you dreaming about?" I ask.

She bites her lip, shuts her eyes and then those tears are streaming down her cheeks.

"Ruby?" I coax.

"I saw him," She sobs. "I always see him."

"Your father?" I guess.

She nods, palming her face with her hands. "I can't help him. It doesn't matter what I do, I can't save him."

"Ssssh," I rock her in my arms, soothing her as best I can. The rumours were they shot him right in front of her, though I don't know how anyone but those present would know, and it's not like Levi wants to shout out about it.

For a moment I think of my own parents. Of that day. Of standing over my father's body, gun in my hand, staring down at him. My mother had rushed from the house, had fled while I'd stayed motionless, as if waiting for the bastard to spring back up.

And then Nico's father had appeared. He'd taken the gun from my hand, ordered his men to clear up the mess and welcomed me in as another son.

I'd been lucky that he believed me, lucky that the Morelli's had my back.

But Ruby, she'd had everything stolen from her and no one was there to help pick up the pieces. No one was there to save her.

"I'm here." I say, "I've got you."

And I'm never letting you go.

Preston

CHAPTER Twenty-Five

I shouldn't do it. I should walk out the door, go to work like normal, but after last night, I don't want to just leave Ruby on her own.

So I send Jace in my place, I bark out my orders then clear the house out entirely. I want it to be just us, me and her, no Sidney, no staff, no eyes watching any of this.

She's still tucked up in bed as I bring the tray of food in and she shifts, her eyes widening in that familiar flash of fear before they settle on what's in my hands.

"Breakfast in bed?" She says, half in confusion, half in tease. "What did I do to deserve this?"

"I wanted to do something for you." I murmur, feeling awkward, stupid, vulnerable too.

I'm not this person, I'm not soft, I don't give a shit about anyone and yet, for Ruby, apparently I'm becoming a lap dog.

She sits up, pulling the covers back and I get a glimpse at her perfect body as she waits for me to clamber in.

God, if my men could see me now, if Nico could see me now.

I know most of them would feel derision at such behaviour but I let her snuggle up beside me as I fork some eggs and for a moment, I wonder if this is it, this is what all those books and movies and poems and bullshit– all of it talking of love and romance, this is what it feels like. This is what living is.

"Preston?"

Even the way she says my name, it's pathetic and yet my heart reacts to that as if she's gasping it out in the throes of ecstasy.

I give her a smile, then tell her to open her mouth and begin feeding her. She takes each bite without comment but her eyes are questioning me all the same.

"I'm just taking care of my wife." I state like it's that simple. Like that's all this is. Duty. Obligation.

"Are you not going to have some too?"

The hint of concern in her voice makes my stupid heart flip. I take a few mouthfuls before focusing back on her. She's the one that needs fattening up, she's the one who needs taking care of. But as my eyes study her, I can see she is looking healthier, that tinge to her skin has gone, that bruise on her cheek has faded.

Give her a few more weeks of care and attention and I don't doubt she'll be completely transformed.

I finish feeding her then take the tray away. When I come back, she's there, still in bed, waiting for me and it feels so perfectly normal to slide back in, to wrap my arm around her, to feel her body pressed against mine.

She takes my hands, studying them for a moment with a serious look on her face. "How many men have you killed?" She asks.

The question catches me off guard. It's not like I'm ashamed of answering, I'm just not sure why she wants to hear it.

"More than I can count." I state honestly.

She chews her lip, "Was it easy?"

"To kill?"

She nods.

My lips curl. "Every person has deserved it in one way or another."

Her hand tightens, she looks up at me with those innocent brown eyes. "Would you kill for me?"

I don't hesitate. I don't question why she's even asking. "Yes."

I can't tell if that's what she wants to hear or not. On some level she seems surprised, but she's also frowning, like she doesn't quite believe it, like she thinks I'm teasing her.

And then she leans in, kissing me, and I realise I don't give a shit either way.

My hands tangle in her hair, I pull her down, push her further into the plump pillows as my body engulfs her. I'm not a small man, but Ruby isn't tiny either, she may be skinny but she's got long legs, she's lithe, lean, a perfect fit against me.

And then that voice repeats in my head; that I can't fuck her, that I can't have her the way I truly want.

I let out a frustrated growl and she instantly tenses.

"What's wrong?" She whispers.

"Nothing," I lie.

She sighs, leaning back, staring up at me, "Don't you want me?"

Of course I fucking want her. I've never wanted anything more than her right now, but in the cold light of day I can't just ignore my loyalty to Nico, my duty to him.

"Please, Preston. Please." She says, staring at me like right now I hold the key to her salvation.

I groan, pulling myself off her and stalk out of the room.

When I come back in she looks almost surprised to see me, as If she'd expected me to fuck off out the house and then her eyes drop to the thing in my hand.

This is a mistake, I know it, and yet, it also feels like an answer, a reprieve. She gets what she wants and me, well, I'm not a saint because, if this plays out the way it does in my head, I'll be more than satisfied with the outcome.

"You want to play, wife," I say, sounding nothing like the man I am, nothing like someone in control, as I toss the toy at her. "Spread your legs then, put on a show for me."

Her eyes go so wide, she sits up, holding the vibrator like she doesn't even know what to do with it and I can see she's uncomfortable.

I should stop. I should tell her I went too far, and yet I don't.

Maybe I'm a sick bastard because I like watching her squirm, I like watching her suffer the consequences too, after all, I've suffered enough so far, forcing myself to retreat, to hold back, to do everything possible to protect her, while she's been goading me the entire time.

"Spread your legs." I repeat more aggressively.

She lets out a gasp, pushing the covers off, and she lays her legs wide enough that I've got a perfect view of her pretty little cunt.

"I don't, I don't…" She trails off, her face bright red with what could be shame.

Good, the little minx needs to learn what happens when she pushes me, she needs to understand that, while I've been treating her more than fairly, I am at my core, a beast, and if she pushes too hard then I will turn around and bite her.

"Don't what, Ruby?" I ask, already knowing the words she's going to speak.

She glances down, staring at the bulge in my boxers. "I've never used one before, I've never done anything like that before."

And yet she claims she fucked "loads of men"... I knew that was bullshit the day she said it but I'm not letting her off so easily. She wants to pretend, she wants to lie to me, then this is the consequence.

"Then I'll teach you." I reply, climbing onto the bed, positioning myself on my knees, between her ankles, close enough to get a fucking fantastic view.

Her cunt is glistening, she's so pink and flushed that on some level I can see she's turned on by this, by the prospecting of pleasuring herself under my unwavering gaze.

"Turn it on." I state.

She hesitates for a second and then she complies, those years of conditioning obviously kicking in, telling her to behave, to do as she's told.

I toss the lube at her and it bounces off her thigh. "Get yourself nice and wet, it'll feel better."

She gulps, picking up the bottle and again, does exactly as instructed, squeezing a good amount onto her fingers before she runs them between her lips. Beside her, the toy is quietly vibrating, I know there are enough fancy options, but if this is a lesson, then my wife is going to learn my way, through repetition.

Practice makes perfect after all.

"Run it over yourself, you need to explore to start with," I instruct.

She looks dubious, she looks more than a little unsettled but she does it, she runs the tip up and she jolts as the vibrator hits her clit. "Oh god."

My lips curl at the tone of her voice. "That feels good, doesn't it, Ruby?"

"Yes," She sounds almost afraid, as if she's regretting putting herself in this situation but it's too late for remorse now. I'm not backing and down, and she's not going anywhere until she performs.

"I'm going to watch as you fuck yourself." I state.

She balks, shaking her head a little.

"You want to play games, Ruby, then we'll play on my terms."

"But," She whimpers, staring once more at my groin with that hungry look in her eyes. "I wanted you…"

"You can't have me, not right now." I growl, feeling all the frustration of those words. "But you are going to do this, you're going to give your husband what he wants, because you're a good girl, aren't you, Ruby?"

She nods again, so reluctantly, but I watch as she lifts the toy, as she adjusts it and as she slowly slides it into herself.

Her cunt sucks it in greedily, she moans, though I'm not sure if it's in pleasure or something else.

Once it's fully inside, she leaves it there, staring back at me like she's unsure how to deal with the sensation of it.

"Slide it out," I say, not giving her the reprieve she's so desperately begging for with those beautiful, innocent looking eyes.

"Preston…"

I shake my head, not caring that I'm crossing a line, not caring that I'm meant to be a spectator in this, and I reach forward, taking the toy and yank it out.

She shudders, heaves, no doubt thinking that it's done with, but I'm not even close to being done.

I push it back in, one hand holding her right thigh wide, forcing her to take it again.

She moans, arching her back, trying to find a comfortable angle but I'm too lost to care, this is my moment now, mine. I gave her a chance, I gave her the opportunity to take the easier route and yet all she did was keep begging for me like she expected any other outcome.

I start pumping it in and out, upping the speed, practically punishing her pussy. And all the while I'm staring down at her, seeing how wet she's getting, seeing how red she's turning, seeing the way her cunt keeps expanding around to meet the silicone.

My free hand reaches up, without thinking I slap her breast, making her yelp. If it were me inside her right now, I'd be devouring those breasts, letting her realise exactly who I am.

But I'm not meant to touch, am I? Not meant to taste.

Ruby is off limits to me, so fine, I'll get her off the only way I can.

I pick up speed, fucking her pussy more mercilessly and she's moaning, crying, responding in a way that tells me she's enjoying it, even though on some level it hurts.

"That's my good little wife," I taunt, "Look at you, taking what I give you, enjoying it like you were made for me,"

She shudders, rocking her hips, and I can tell she's getting close. Her cunt is so red, it's practically pulsating.

"Preston," She cries, digging her hands into the sheets like she needs some sort of anchor, "Preston, I..." Her words turn into a scream as she topples over and it's the most incredible thing I've ever heard.

My wife, my woman, screaming for me.

I know I could ease off, could let her ride out this orgasm but that's not who I am, I'm not kind, I'm not gentle, I'm not the kind of man who buys flowers and chocolates and has romantic candlelight dinners.

I'm a monster, a beast, and I need my wife to understand that.

I want her to crave it, to crave all the dark fucked up parts of me. To love those parts, to relish them as much as I do.

So I show her no mercy, I keep fucking her, keeping shoving that vibrator so deep into her cunt as she's writhing and trying to get away.

"You'll take what I give." I snap, holding her down, delighting in the way I can manipulate her body.

She's full on sobbing but I can't tell if that's simply the after effects of coming so hard and still being so close to the edge.

I guess there's only one way to find out, isn't there…

I leave the toy where it is, buried right to the hilt and, with my spare hand, I spread her labia wide. As my thumb brushes her exposed clit, she whimpers.

"I can't…" She pleads, trying to close her legs like that would stop me. "I can't…"

"Oh, but you will," I reply, smacking her thigh to force them back open. "This is a lesson, remember," I circle her clit, starting gently enough. She's so over-sensitised that it takes barely a second before I can see her rocking her hips, desperately seeking more, as she bites down on her lip.

Turns out my wife *is* a whore for me. "That's my good girl," I murmur, rewarding her the best way I know.

She whimpers, she grinds, she's so covered in sweat that beads of it are trickling down her skin, pooling between her breasts. I lean down, snaking my tongue up to lap it up, it's not as sweet as her pussy but she still tastes divine.

When she comes again, her muscles contract so hard she pushes the vibrator out and it pops onto the sheets. God, what would it feel like to have that around my cock? To truly experience her coming like that?

I'm so tempted to do it, to pull my dick free and to just fuck her.

But that was the point of this, wasn't it? To be able to play while not technically breaking the rules.

I palm my cock, wondering if a bullet to the head would be worth the pleasure of it, but I know Nico, if I cross this line it won't be a quick death, it won't be pain free.

He'll make me pay for disobeying an order, and rightly so.

"Fuck," I groan, feeling my dick weeping. I want to shove it down her throat so badly, I want to have her choking on me while I'm punishing her pussy but that's an impossible dream.

A reality I'll never be granted.

Anger flashes through me, I pinch her clit, not to be nasty, not to be mean, but it feels like I'm the one taking all the shit right now, I'm the one suffering while Ruby lays here, enjoying every second, blissfully unaware of the consequences.

She gasps, but that hit of pain seems to do something, I see it in her eyes, I see the way she likes it, my wife doesn't want soft either, she enjoys being used, she enjoys me dominating her.

I pinch her clit again, holding my fingers together to keep the pressure. She shudders, arching her back, squirming like it's getting her off.

"You're so fucking beautiful." I say, before I can think.

And she is, lying like this, fully splayed out for me to look my fill, with her cunt dripping and her skin flushed, she's a literal goddess.

Her hands reach for me, she grabs hold of my dick, and she pulls it free from my boxers. Once more she's careful of the piercings and I wonder if they intimidate her, maybe that's something to work on, showing her how she can pleasure me, after all, that's not *me* touching *her* is it?

Technically that's within the rules too.

She's not being shy right now, she's not being cautious, she's jerking me off, almost desperately panting as if she needs me to come right this very second.

I pick up the vibrator, start fucking her once more with it, matching my speed to hers like we're now in a race, both us hurtling towards our end.

Only, she's already come twice. She's had her reprieve. I deserve a little attention, I deserve a little thanks for my efforts.

I shut my eyes, enjoying the feel of her, the way she's so devoted to me right now and, as I realise I'm about to explode, I grab her hair, pulling her around, and come into her hastily opened mouth.

If I thought she looked beautiful before, she looks majestic with my come splattered upon her lips. Her tongue pokes out and she licks them enough to tell me she's enjoying the taste.

For a second, I stay there, waiting till my breath comes back, and then I'm pounding that toy into her, forcing her to give me one more orgasm of her own.

"Oh fuck," She practically shrieks and I grab her leg to keep her still.

I know she's close, I know she's right there and she will give this to me, she will behave exactly as I expect.

"Preston," She gasps, "God, Preston, I…" She blinks, shuddering, her tits heaving like she's about to collapse from all the writhing she's been doing.

"Thank your husband." I order, as I stare her down. "Thank him for being so kind."

She kicks out, she jerks, but she's screaming it anyway. Screaming her thanks, as if I'm a man of mercy, as if I've granted her the best damn moment of her life.

As I toss the toy, she lies there in a post-haze stupor and I can't resist tweaking her hardened nipples.

"Was I good?" She asks, like her sole existence is to please me.

"Perfect," I say. "More than perfect."

She blushes, sitting up, and licks her lips once more. "You tasted good," She says, "I want to do that again, only I want to suck you off properly."

Like I'd ever refuse such a request.

I smirk, palming my dick, feeling it growing hard once more but as I do, I hear my phone buzz. Not just once but over and over.

She glances at it, then at me. "You should get that." She says with a hint to her voice.

No, what I should do is finish this, I should grab her by her hair and give her what she's just asked for.

Only, work calls, duty calls.

Not only will Nico kick my arse if things go wrong but he'll be more than a little curious as to what kept me away, and I can't have that. I need to keep up the illusion, keep up the pretence, I might be blurring the lines right now, but I'm not going to do anything that jeopardises whatever this fragile thing between me and Ruby is.

"I'm giving you homework." I say, as I reluctantly let her go. "I want you to play with yourself while I'm gone, I want you to work out what you like, what gets you off quickest, and when I come back, you're going to show me everything you've learnt."

She blinks, nodding her head just a little.

"Tell me, Ruby, tell me you're going to be a good girl for me and do as I ask."

"I will." She whispers, almost reluctantly, and I can't hold back the cruel laugh. Maybe I will log into the cameras and check, maybe I'll count how many times she comes while I'm gone.

And if I find out she's disobeyed me, well then, I'll make her come so many times she passes out.

I'll make sure she learns exactly what the consequences are for disobeying me.

Ruby

CHAPTER

Twenty-Six

I don't know whether to be relieved or disappointed as he walks out of the door.

I feel like I've run a marathon, I feel like my body is still on the cusp of another orgasm and just having the silk robe against my skin is too much.

How is one man able to manipulate my body like that?

My lips curl as I head back up the stairs and to our room. I need a shower. I need to wash my hair, to sort myself out.

Preston said I was perfect, no, more than perfect. I don't think anyone has ever called me that in my life. Even before everything went to shit, my parents never once praised me to that extent. I want to convince myself that I should feel delighted by it, after all, is it not proof that my plan is working, that Preston *is* falling for me?

But the problem is how *I* reacted. How my stupid heart fluttered, how I clung to those words, clung to him.

I know I'm falling for him, I know that's what's happening and it feels like every alarm bell is ringing in my head because I need to be smarter than that. I have to be. If I give into these feelings then I'll be the one hurt, I'll be the one in danger, again.

I get into the shower, turn the water on and as it cascades over me, I shut my eyes, imagining he's here, indulging in the fantasy that he's still watching me.

I was never interested in sex when I was younger, mostly because my parents made it such a taboo subject. Nice girls didn't talk about such things, nice girls didn't think about such things and nice girls absolutely did not do such scandalous things as touch themselves.

I don't know who my parents intended marrying me off to but one thing was absolutely certain, they expected me to be 'untouched', chaste, the absolute model of propriety on my wedding day.

Would they be happy that I was bound to such a man? I mean, Preston isn't exactly a nobody, is he? He's the Underboss to the Morelli Family, as good as an actual brother to Nico.

And yet, I'm a Holtz, technically with my blood I should be a Mafia Queen, not a Duchess, which is what being married to Preston makes me.

I sigh, rubbing my face, cleaning it with just the water while deciding that my parents approval is rather a moot point considering they're both dead.

And a voice in my head tells me that I need to turn this to my advantage, I need to keep pushing, keep tempting him. If I'm to outsmart Gunnar and Levi, then I have to make my husband fall completely and utterly in love with me.

I have to play the perfect wife, the perfect woman.

With a sigh, I run my hand back between my thighs. He told me to practice, he told me to discover what I like, what turns me on… I can hardly say that it's simply him, his needs, his interest in me, that I'm so touched starved that a little attention is enough to make me putty in his hands.

No, I have to play this cool.

I have to pretend that there's more to me than just a sad little girl, desperate to be loved, desperate to be wanted.

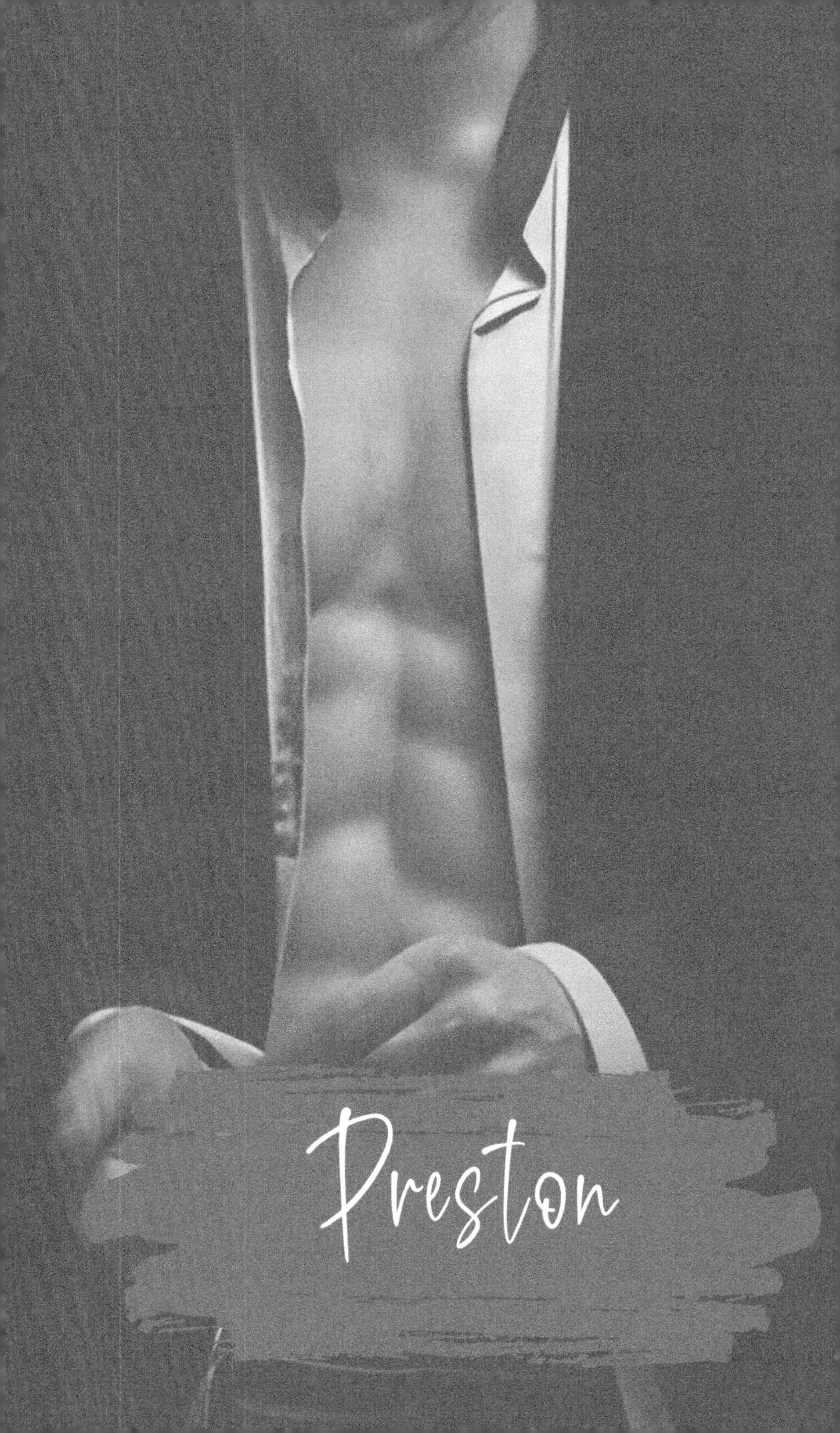

Preston

CHAPTER Twenty-Seven

Gone.

It's all fucking gone.

I stand there, staring into one empty container after another.

First, we were told they were contaminated, then they were quarantined, and now they've done a god damn disappearing act?

I slam my fist into the metal door. Whoever the fuck is behind this has got serious influence, they have to have to be able to pull this off. But who? Who the fuck would even dare?

"Boss?"

Jace stands behind me, obviously nervous.

"You got the footage?" I ask, not turning to look at him.

"Yes, boss."

I highly doubt they'll be anything there but we have to check.

He passes me the tablet and I hit the play button, feeling my anger growing with each second. It's obviously a professional hit, planned right down to the second. I snarl in frustration as I watch the figures moving about, stealing our merchandise without so much as a fight. Where the hell was our security? There should have been twenty armed men here on watch and yet I can't see one.

"Who was on guard?" I ask.

Jace starts listing off the names, a few of which I recognise but most must be new recruits.

"Found their bodies in the canal." Noah says, walking up to us. "All of them took a dozen or so bullets."

I shake my head, kicking at the dirt with my boot. "Nico is going to be pissed." I state.

After the last incident we're running seriously low on supplies. No wonder Levi was so damned desperate to get in bed with us, if they've been hammering his routes as hard as this, I doubt he'll have many diamonds left to trade.

"Check this out," Noah says, pointing to the footage that's still rolling. "See that, he pulled his hood off."

I frown, staring at the figure in question. All of them are stocky, with muscles big enough to show through the dark padded gear they have on. They're wearing balaclavas, but clearly one thinks he's out of view and pulls his up to reveal his face.

We only get a side view, a glimpse at best. Noah hits the pause button and we all squint at the blurry image. For a second my breath catches. I blink, seeing the resemblance, seeing that same nose I know so well.

Surely not? Surely that's a coincidence. Only, I don't believe in them.

I snap a picture with my phone, send it to Nico, and start barking out orders. I need this shit sorted, I need everything cleaned up. We might have been caught with our trousers down but we're not going to shout out about it for the entire city to hear.

It's late by the time I get back. Ruby is in bed, but she's awake with the lamp on like she was waiting for me. As I reach for her, she snuggles in with a contented, almost dreamy sigh, like she can't imagine any place better than my arms.

God, this girl is too fragile, too delicate for someone like me.

"Did you miss me?" I ask, driving that thought away, cursing it, because she is mine. She is.

She nods. "And I did my homework."

The words seem to linger between us. Oh, I know what she's hinting at but right now I'm not concerned about fucking her, I need to hold her, I need to reassure myself that she's here, in my bed, far from all the politics and people that would try to take her from me.

Far from the ghosts of her family too.

"Don't worry about that tonight." I say, taking in a deep breath, feeling that hint of jasmine hit my senses as she relaxes further into me.

And then I reach over, pick up the small box and place it on the covers in front of her.

She frowns staring at it for a second.

"What is it?" She asks.

"Open it and see."

She lets out a tiny huff, that, if I didn't know better, I'd think was annoyance at my reply, but she cautiously takes the velvet box, pops it open and then lets out a gasp so loud it could be a shriek.

"What do you think?"

It's like she can't form words. She just stares at the necklace, her fingers skating the huge diamond that's glinting in the low light.

"You had one before." I state, having done some digging and pulled up some old photos of her family. I was going to have them printed but it feels too much right now, especially with everything going on. "I know this won't replace it but…"

"It's a trilliant cut." She breathes, talking over me in her sudden excitement, and I can hear the awe in her voice which tells me I chose well. Her old necklace was a smaller carat, pear cut, not nearly as fancy as this, though I know it had a deeper, sentimental value.

"You know your diamonds." I murmur, stroking her hair with my hand.

She nods, with a slight smirk I swear that I enjoy more than I should. "Did you expect anything else from a Holtz?"

That makes me laugh. I ease out the chain and motion for her to lean forward so I can clasp it around her neck.

"You didn't need to…" She begins but her fingers are there, touching it, like she can't quite believe this moment is real.

"I did." I reply. "You're my wife, and a Holtz, you should be covered in diamonds."

Her eyes meet mine and I swear for a second I get lost in that look. I pull her in, wrap my arms around her once more and she murmurs her thanks like she still thinks this is all some sort of a dream.

"You're my wife," I repeat. "Whatever you want, whatever you desire, you will have."

Even if I have to kill to keep that promise, even if I have to break the world to ensure her happiness, I'll do it.

I'll do whatever it takes .

Ruby

CHAPTER Twenty-Eight

I don't know what wakes me but something clearly does.

I lay there, in my husband's arms, feeling for the first time like this all might be okay. That despite the odds, if it stayed like this I could be happy, I could be content.

For a moment I watch Preston in the semi-darkness, feeling like he's an enigma. Oh, I know he's deadly, I know the man is ruthless, that he doesn't hesitate to act when he needs to and yet despite that, I feel safe with him, truly safe.

Did my mother ever feel safe with my father? Did their animosity ever switch to caring for one another? I know they were passionate, I know they had their moments but as I've grown up I wonder if it wasn't more necessity driving them than anything akin to love.

As I shift, Preston's eyes open. He's a light sleeper but I guess that comes hand in hand with a profession like his.

I can see the question in his eyes, the way he's searching my face to see if I'm okay. No doubt he's worried I'm off on another sleepwalking episode.

"I'm just going to get some water." I whisper, like that's the reason I'm awake. That I'm just thirsty.

I slip from the bed, pulling a robe around my naked body to shield me from the cool night and I tiptoe down through the ridiculousness that is this house.

In the kitchen, the moonlight is shining through the window enough that I don't need to put any lights on. I grab a glass, going to fill it but just as I turn the tap on something moves.

A hand wraps around my mouth while another pulls me back.

I let out a scream, but it's muffled by whoever has me.

They spin me around and, as my mind fears it's Gunnar, here to enact his revenge, my eyes connect with brown ones so similar to my own.

My heart stops.

My breathing stops.

My entire damn world stops as I stare back at the ghost of a man who should be dead. Who is dead.

He drops his hold, letting me take a step back.

"How, how is this possible?" I whisper.

"I got away." Jett says.

I don't know how to process that. How to even get my head around it. He got away? That's the explanation I get after all this time?

"They shot you, they..."

"I ran, Ruby. I kept running. They didn't find me and I got away."

"Where have you been? Where...?"

"Sssh." He says, hissing because, in my shock, I'm talking far too loudly right now. "It doesn't matter Ruby. None of it matters. It just matters that I'm back, that I'm here."

"Why?"

"Why what?"

"Why are you here?" I ask, looking around us, checking that we're actually alone and Preston's men aren't already making their way to us. God knows how he got in but I don't doubt his presence will be noticed very soon.

He tilts his head like my question makes no sense. "Why do you think? You think I'm going to leave you with that monster? You think I'm going to let Preston Civello keep you as his wife?" He says like it's the most disgusting thing in the world.

"I am his wife." I state, folding my arms in some sort of show of defiance.

He drops his gaze, staring at way the robe is hanging on me, like he knows there's nothing underneath it and I know he doesn't miss the eighteen carat diamond nestled in my cleavage. "Jesus, Ruby." He spits. "You're fucking him, aren't you?"

"So what if I am?" I reply. How dare he turn up, how dare he just reappear after all this time and judge me like I'm some sort of harlot, trading my body for safety, even if that's what I'm sort of doing.

"You know he's a killer, right?"

"So was dad."

His hand slaps the last of the sentence from my mouth.

I clutch my cheek, staring back at him. He's changed so much, hasn't he? He's not the fun big brother I knew. But then again, I'm not the carefree daydreamer I was either. I guess the real world destroyed those parts of us. Crushed them until neither of us were recognisable anymore.

"I'm getting you out." He states. "We're leaving right now."

"No."

He grabs my wrist, trying to haul me across to the French doors and the dark garden beyond. "Once you're away from here, once you have some space, you'll understand."

"No." I snap, yanking myself back, almost crashing into the granite worktop as I stumble. "I'm not leaving. I want to stay. I want to be here. With Preston."

He shakes his head, pulling a face so reminiscent of our father, one I knew to look out for, one I knew meant there was about to be trouble.

"Levi arranged this marriage." He growls. "You really want to help our uncle and this damn alliance he has set up with Nico Morelli?"

"I don't care about him." I cry louder, my pride and my stubbornness making me reckless now. "I care about Preston."

"You're being a fool. A stupid sentimental fool. You think a man like Preston Civello gives two shits about you? You're nothing but a hole to fuck, a thing to own until he wears you out or simply kills you and replaces you with a younger model."

"No."

"Yes."

"I'm not leaving." I state, holding my ground.

This is the closest thing to home I've had and Preston, he's the only person in this entire world that makes me feel safe, that makes me feel like I'm a person of value for myself, not just what my blood is.

I won't betray that. I won't betray him.

Jett snarls again moving to grab me and I dart away, grabbing the glass from the side and throwing it hard onto the marble floor where it shatters into what seems like a million pieces.

"The fuck…?" Jett begins but we both hear it, the movement, the men, people are swarming to where we are. "You stupid idiot." Jett says in a way that doesn't even sound angry, he just sounds disappointed, like I'm some silly little girl caught up in a situation way beyond my understanding.

"Go." I say stepping back, ignoring the spike of the glass that embeds in my foot. "Go before they find you."

He makes a dash for it, sprinting for the door, and I don't look, I don't watch as he disappears.

I don't know what I'd do if they find him, if they bring him back.

Would I plead for Preston to spare him? Would I plead for a brother who I once loved but now feels so much more than a stranger to me?

Would Preston even do it? Somehow I doubt he'd agree if he learnt what Jett's intentions were in being here, if he understood that Jett was trying to split us up.

"Ruby?"

I turn at the sound of Preston's voice. Relief spreads over me as he steps into the room and if that doesn't tell me something then I don't know what does.

He's completely starkers, he didn't even stop to put clothes on when he thought I was in danger and I'll admit my heart reacts more at that fact than it should. I can see the five guards behind him, all ready to attack whatever foe might be lurking in the darkness.

"What happened?" He asks, looking around, searching the space like he already knows something is up.

"I, I dropped the glass." I say, acting like it was a mistake. I know I shouldn't, I know lying to Preston right now is the worst thing to do but some small part of me still yearns for the brother I once knew. Still wants to protect the family I once had.

His shoulders drop, he physically relaxes.

"You've cut your foot." He says, walking up to where the smear of blood from my heel is.

"I…" I fall silent as he sweeps me into his arms, carrying me away and ordering over his shoulder for someone to clean up the mess.

When we get to our room he puts me down on the bed and comes back a moment later with the same first aid kit he produced after I ran away from him. Gently, he cleans my cut while I protest that it's not that bad.

He's on his knees, holding my leg, taking care of me. This man who the entire city fears. This man who simply has to say the word and you're as good as dead.

And yet he's acting like a tiny cut is worth his time. Like I'm worth his time.

He glances up at my face and I wonder what he sees because he frowns just a little.

"I can clean it myself." I say.

He shakes his head. "No, you're my wife, it's my job to take care of you."

"And clean up my messes?" I tease.

"If that's what it takes." He smiles and that harsh, ruthless face turns into something gentle, an expression I doubt many have ever been lucky enough to be granted.

My heart seems to flip, I swallow down the emotion that seems to well up inside. It feels like he's making some sort of declaration, some sort of unspoken vow.

I don't know how to respond, I don't know how to take this, and I sure as hell don't feel worthy of it.

The diamond around my neck suddenly feels so heavy and that lie I told only minutes earlier seems to make my tongue stick to the roof of my mouth.

"You okay?" He asks.

I nod, even though my head is whirling.

My brother is alive.

He's out there.

I want to feel happy, to feel relief that he made it too, but I'm so fearful he will do something stupid, that he will come here again and then Preston will act, he will hurt him.

"Did you really just drop a glass?" He asks quietly.

My eyes widen. I nod quickly. "I was clumsy. I couldn't see because I didn't put the light on."

He scans my face like he can tell I'm not being honest but I can see he's going to drop it anyway. Apparently, he trusts me now and that can only be a good thing. I don't want to spoil it. I don't want to do anything to risk what I have. Though I feel a flash of guilt nonetheless.

"Shall we go back to bed?" I murmur, shuffling back, pulling the covers and holding them for him. He stays still, studying me a moment longer, and just as I think my entire ruse is foiled, he tosses the first aid kit onto the rug and climbs in.

When those strong arms wrap back around me, I know I've made the right decision. I know being here, staying with Preston is the right call. Not just because it's easy, but because I want him, I want my husband, I want this life that he's offering me.

I don't care about Levi anymore.

I don't even care about Gunnar and all the awful things he did.

I'm away from all that.

And more importantly I feel happy, for the first time in so long, I feel like I'm in a good place.

Preston

CHAPTER Twenty-Nine

I leave Ruby to sleep in, getting up with the dawn. I have a mountain of work to catch up on after yesterday's events and besides, I know something happened last night, I know someone was sneaking around. Ruby may have thought she was fooling me but that's far from the truth.

I get into the office, holler out for Noah and Jace, and then sit myself down, staring at the security footage. I can see the shadows, see the person sneaking around and just as I expected, I can see them accosting my wife, before she smashes the glass and we all come running.

But it's the audio that gets me.

Ruby didn't know her brother was still alive, she's clearly been blissfully unaware of that fact but it confirms everything Nico and I suspected since our shipments started coming under attack. Oh, it was easy to figure it out, to put two and two together and that surveillance footage certainly helped. Perhaps this was why Levi was so desperate to make a deal with us, he knew the prodigal son had returned and was afraid that his crumbling empire would disappear entirely.

"I care about Preston."

The words repeat in my head.

Her words.

I'm a fool to get as much pleasure as I do from such a simple statement and yet I feel like a chorus of trumpets are going off in my head. I feel like she's just declared her undying love for me.

And then my eyes focus back on that figure, on her brother. He was trying to take her from me, he was going to steal my Ruby away. I clench my fists, feeling pure rage at the thought.

If I have to, I will hunt him down, I will kill him, hell, I'll kill any man that thinks they can get between me and my wife.

Ruby is mine.

She is always going to be mine.

"Boss?" Noah says, waltzing in like he's just come back from vacation.

About bloody time.

"Where have you been?" I growl.

His eyebrows raise, I'm not usually one to get angry, at least not to show it.

"It's not even gone six." He says, like that's an excuse.

"I'm in." I snap back. "I expect you and Jace and every other fucker to be in when I am."

He gulps, nodding, "Is something up?"

"Something?" I turn my screen, ensuring he gets a perfect view of the man who hours ago was inside my supposedly secure compound. "This man tried to steal my wife last night."

"Who the fuck is that?" Jace asks, apparently appearing out of nowhere too.

"Jett Fucking Holtz." I state.

Noah blinks like he thinks I've misspoken but Jace just shakes his head slightly. "I thought that kid was a goner. I thought they did him in when they killed the parents."

"Apparently not," Noah replies before I can.

"I want him found. I want him brought to me. I'm going to teach him a lesson about what it means to take what's mine."

Noah's out the door before I can finish my sentence but Jace, he's stood, still staring at the screen. "Do you think they know? Gunnar and Levi?"

I shrug. They'd be fools not to suspect it.

"Want me to do some digging?" He asks.

I run my hand over my face. In truth, I don't give a shit what Gunnar and Levi do and do not know. What I care about is the fact that someone got into my house, got to Ruby, and the only reason she's still in my bed right now is because she chose to stay there. She chose me.

"Just find him." I say, before I really do lose my temper.

As I sink back into my chair, I try not to dwell on the fact that my wife lied to me. That she deliberately misled me. I know her intentions were good. She was no doubt shocked by her brother's sudden reincarnation and wanted to protect him. That loyalty shouldn't be underestimated and in a way, it's a good thing, that she is loyal, that she isn't a coward.

I'm going to mould her, hone her, turn that loyalty onto me.

I'm going to make my wife fall so deeply in love with me she won't even notice the blood of her brother dripping from my hands after I've taken away his last breath.

I END UP WORKING LATER THAN I MEAN TO. THOUGH MY MIND KEEPS drifting to my wife, indulging in all the ways we could be spending our evening if we were together, sadly work has demanded my presence.

I send word to Sidney that Ruby shouldn't wait up, but I like the thought of her doing it anyway, of being there, all dressed up, needy and desperate for me to come home and entertain her. Hell, even if she is asleep, I'll wake her up and spend a few hours enjoying her, after all, she deserves a reward for her show of devotion from last night.

My lips curl at the thought, of having her naked and spread wide, of her needy cunt weeping with want.

Perhaps I'll start with my tongue, torture her a little until she's a hot sweaty mess and she's begging me for mercy.

We're sat in the bar, and though it's packed, everyone knows not to stray too close.

These meetings might seem public but they're anything but. This is where we have our little chats, where we speak to the eyes on the ground, where we ensure everything is running smoothly and no shit is brewing in the shadows.

Across from me, Noah is detailing some new conspiracy he thinks he's found. Blaine is twisting a knife into the table like he's trying to carve out its secrets. Nico is beside me and though we're listening, I can tell he has other things on his mind. The alliance with Levi being one. So far they've given us some routes but nothing of consequence. I'm starting to wonder if it's all a bluff, it there's nothing really there and his entire empire is made of smoke and bullshit.

Jace is on the phone, pacing. He keeps glancing at me and then back again. I know he still has some contacts in Holtz's businesses, and I know he's already trying to leverage that as best he can.

When he gets off the phone, he looks physically shocked.

He walks over, crouches down between me and Nico and murmurs about needing a word.

We move to the back room, where it's more secure, and as soon as the door is shut, he starts talking.

"Levi is out."

"What?" Nico says.

"He's…" Jace shakes his head like he can't quite believe it. "He's had a stroke."

"A stroke?" I repeat.

"Yeah, he's in the hospital, they're monitoring him but it doesn't look good. Word is he won't make it till morning."

"Seriously?" Nico growls. "After all that bastard does, he gets to sign out with a nice painless death."

"I don't think a stroke is painless." I say.

"But it's nothing close to the shit that man has inflicted on the world." Nico growls.

"Who is taking over?" I ask, but I already know the answer before the words leave Jace's mouth.

"Gunnar."

"Of course it fucking is." Nico growls.

"We'll need a meeting with him. We'll need to affirm that this alliance still stands." I say.

Nico pulls a smirk. "Worried you'll be losing your wife?" He murmurs.

"Not for a second." I snap.

No one is taking her from me. Even if this does go to pot, I'm not letting Ruby go. She belongs to me now, and woe betide any man that dare tries to suggest otherwise.

"We need to do some digging." I say quickly to cover myself because Nico is giving me a look I do not like. "We need to know exactly what his condition is. We need to know who's staying loyal, if anyone else is vying for leadership…"

"Go to the hospital." Nico says to Jace. "Flirt with the nurses, do whatever you can to get in that room and see for yourself. I want proof. I want photographic evidence that the man is as close to death as they say."

"We should reach out to Gunnar." I state, hating the fact that we need to.

"Yes." Nico agrees but I can hear from the tone that he hates it as much as me. "We need to offer our assistance, play the game."

"And if anyone else is going up against him?" Jace asks.

I look at him. "Find out first. We need to know options."

"This could be an opportunity..." Nico says quietly.

"An opportunity for what?" I ask.

Nico shrugs, telling Jace to piss off and get on with his orders. I watch the man go, knowing that Nico clearly has something he wants to talk about for my ears only.

When the door shuts, Nico sits down pouring out a glass of whiskey for both of us. "Gunnar has no blood connection to the Holtz Family." He states, before taking a sip and watching my face with interest.

"If he's the strongest candidate, you know that won't be an issue." I reply, taking a sip myself.

Nico smirks. "He may look like the strongest candidate but what if there was another, someone with a blood link, someone with power, someone who could offer them a lot more than what they'd get with just his contacts."

"Who?"

"You."

I blink. What the fuck?

"You're married to Frank Holtz's daughter. You have the power and influence of the Morelli Family behind you, not to mention you have the support of numerous other families."

"Are you talking about taking over his business?" Fuck if we did that, the possibilities are endless. At its height the Holtz diamond industry was worth hundreds of millions though we all know Levi has squandered it, mishandled it, halved its value while he was trying to establish his rule.

Nico smiles. "Like I hadn't thought of that from the moment he proposed marriage. Levi has no sons. He has no viable heir. Gunnar may have shoe horned his way in but how much weight will that really hold when Levi isn't there?"

And yet we still don't know why they wanted this alliance so badly. What the hell did they have to gain from this? It can't just be Jett's reappearance, he doesn't have enough power to be a real threat.

"What about Ruby?" I ask.

"What about her?"

"She's my wife, Nico."

He fixes me with a look. "You've been stating that a lot of late, Preston."

"Meaning?"

"Nothing has changed on that front. She's your wife in name only. That was part of the agreement."

"You think I'm going to remain celibate forever?" I growl.

He throws his head back and laughs at my words. "No, Preston, you're fine to get your dick wet, you're fine to fuck whoever you want. But you touch one hair on my goddaughter's head and I'll cut your dick off and shove it so far down your throat, you'll never find it again."

I shake my head. "She's my wife." I snap.

"And she is off limits." He says, slamming his hand onto the table.

I don't know why he's still insisting on this. Why he even cares. It's not like he's squeaky clean when it comes to women. He effectively stole Eleri from this very bar, told her under no uncertain terms that she was his plaything from then on. He's just lucky that she was happy to go along with it and, as it turns out, is even more into public sex than he is.

"If you want the Holtz business, if you want to step up and become the Head, then that's the deal."

"Why?"

He tilts his head as his eyes flash and then I realise what it is, what's going on. He thinks he's protecting her. He thinks that in some way, keeping her off limits is doing his duty to a man who's been dead in his grave for over five years.

"She won't thank you for trying to control her life." I say. Like I haven't been controlling every aspect of hers since I forced that ring on her finger.

He smirks getting up. "Nice try, Preston." He says, walking out and leaving me to follow like a dog that's just had his balls chopped off.

When we sit back down with the others, I whisper to Blaine what's going on. Between the four of us there are no secrets. The only reason Eleri isn't here with her husband is because officially she's in bed, sick with a cold, but the truth is she's pregnant. It's early stages, and neither of them want to reveal their hand before they have to.

Maybe that's why Nico seems more on edge.

But then again, he's always been a rocket waiting to go off, we all are, that's the nature of our lives. If we don't show our strength, if we don't react with speed and force, someone else will steal the rug from under us and we'll be lying in a gutter with a bullet between our eyes.

Some barmaid leans in putting fresh drinks on the table. As she does it she rubs her tits against my arm. The old me would have loved that. The old me would have had her choking on my cock in one of the toilets before she could even pretend to protest.

And yet, now, I don't even contemplate it. She doesn't even register. While I might be desperate to get laid, the only woman who will actually give me the reprieve I need is the one god damn woman I can't have.

I murmur my thanks, barely looking at her face. Nico tells her to go in only the way Nico can and she only just stifles the gasp before disappearing quickly, anxious not to infuriate him more.

He leans in, muttering away into my ear.

I can tell his head is spinning, that in many ways he's as eager as me to be getting on with this new task. It's always the same when the Head of a Family falls. The politics, the scheming, the sneaking around and whispering in the dark. It makes people edgy. It makes people untrustworthy. These are the moments that can make our break you. Say the right thing to the right person, offer the right level of support and someone relatively low on the pecking order can jump right up the ladder and find themselves suddenly top boy.

If Nico has sons that will help secure his future, that is, if they come of age and are strong enough before he passes. And if they're not, well, the future might not look so good. A different Head might see them as a threat, might eliminate them just on the off chance -it's another brutal fact about the life we lead, and another reason why I never wanted to get married and have a family of my own.

This life is messy, complicated, brutal. I don't like the idea of one day being too old and weak to protect the very people who depend upon me.

"Preston," Blaine says, bringing me out of my thoughts. "Isn't that your wife?"

I blink, looking around. What the fuck is he… my eyes widen as I realise it *is* her. She's sat at the bar, at an angle but I can still see her face. Every one of the men sat at our table can see that it's Ruby.

And she's talking to a man, having a full on conversation by the looks of it, and he's even got the balls to put his arm on her stool.

"You're really gonna sit here and let your wife behave like that?" Blaine continues with a grin, stirring the pot the way he loves to.

I get to my feet. Everyone around me is looking from me to the beauty the other side of the room.

The man leans in, he has the audacity to touch her. To touch my fucking wife, right here, in front of me.

And I see red.

I don't stop to think.

I don't stop to breathe.

I storm across the room, fully prepared to wage a fucking war.

Who the fuck does he think he is?

Who the fuck does Ruby think she is, to be here, to be behaving like this when she should be tucked up in my bed, waiting for me to come home like any good wife would.

Ruby

CHAPTER *Thirty*

This is stupid, reckless even, but I'm so sick of being cooped up in that house.

When Sidney told me Preston was working late, I knew exactly what that meant; he was at the bar, the one Eleri spoke about, and some impulsive, perhaps naïve part of me wanted to see it, to see him, to understand more his world and not just be a sidenote in it.

So I did my hair, my makeup, I mean, Annabell helped with that, and I selected what felt like a sexy enough outfit before I got Sidney to have the driver drop me off. Besides, it's not like I'm doing anything wrong, Preston has never told me I can't come here, and with the tracker in my arm, it's not like he can't look and see exactly where I'm at.

My eyes widen as I step inside. It's big, bigger than I imagined in my head. It's darker too, like they're all into ambient lighting but I suspect it's because it helps hide their more nefarious activities.

An ordinary man would worry about the guards missing something, about the poor lighting enabling some assassin to get close, but Nico Morelli is far too high up the food chain for that. Besides, everyone is searched at the door. I doubt you'd be able to even sneak in a tampon without them being aware of it.

Across one entire side is the drinks bar, with more bottles on the wall than I can count. The wood and brass are so well polished you can see your actual reflection in them. People are perched up against the edge, some are sat on the fancy stools, others are lounging against it as they chat away.

Figuring this is the best place to sit and just observe, I walk over and take a spare seat, not too close to anyone, and I look around, trying to spot where Preston might be.

When I do find him, I don't know whether to be shocked or not.

He's sat there, across the room beside Nico and a whole bunch of men I don't recognise. Around them women seem to flit like butterflies. Nico and Preston have their heads bowed together, clearly having a private conversation but that doesn't seem to stop any of the women from trying to get their attention anyway.

I gulp, watching as one leans in brushing her tits against my husband's arm as she places a fresh beer on the table. He glances up, murmurs a thanks before he takes a swig and some sort of monster seems to unfurl inside me. She leans in further. Nico says something and she tenses before walking away but I can't help wondering what Preston would do if Nico hadn't clearly told her to shove off.

Would he have smiled at her, would he have enjoyed her attention, would he have fucked her if she laid it on? And she was laying it on.

I narrow my eyes. I'd never have pegged myself as the jealous type and yet, apparently, I am.

I am incandescently full of rage right now.

My husband of barely more than a month, is here, in this bar, surrounded by women so glamourous I look like a street rat in comparison.

He said he was working late. Is this what he means by working? I bite the tip of my tongue, grind my teeth against it, taking in a low deep breath.

"Trust me babe, you're not his type."

I half jump at the barmaid who's leaning over, her large tits on full display with the black push up bra she has on under the tight white tank top.

"Whose type?" I ask.

She smirks. "Like you haven't been eyeballing Preston Civello from the moment you walked in." She says, looking me up and down like I really am trash.

I glance back across the room to where he's sat. Have I been that obvious about it? Maybe. But apparently my husband has still not noticed my presence.

"He's not into girls like you." She states.

"Girls like me?" I repeat.

"Shrinking violets." She says, flicking her bleached hair back over her shoulder. "Preston likes a girl who can give as good as she gets."

"And how would you know that?" I ask.

She tilts her head as her equally well-endowed friend leans in beside her to be part of this conversation. "Preston likes to share." She says. "And trust me, someone like you, you can't handle a man like that."

"Oh really?" I scoff, feeling a flash of jealousy that I know should be unfounded. What he did before me has no consequence.

He could have fucked half the city and I have no logical cause for complaint.

“You know he’s got a pierced cock?” The first says, “You ever even had sex babe, ever fucked a man with a pierced cock before?”

I gulp because surely the only way they’d know that is if they have been with him. If they’ve fucked him. I look between them both as it sinks in.

They’ve both been with him, they’ve both seen him naked, touched him, been more intimate with my husband than I ever have.

The second girl leans over, patting my hand in a sarcastic manner. “Stick to your basic men.” She says. “Preston Civello is way out of your league.”

I can feel my eyes stinging.

I know it’s pathetic, that these two are goading me, and yet he’s obviously fucked at least one of them.

I glance at the other girls, all five of them laughing and flirting behind the bar. They all seem like carbon copies, massive tits, perfectly arched brows and hair bleached to the point it’s turned white.

Is that what Preston likes? Is that what he’d choose if he wasn’t forced to marry me?

“Even if he was into your type…” The second says, putting a drink in front of me. “He’s off the market. Married some Mafia Princess.”

I bite my lip to hide the laugh. They’ve literally just insulted me then called me royalty within the space of a minute. Years ago I’d have relished that title, hell, I’m pretty certain that’s how my mother referred to me. To us. She certainly acted like we were royalty.

I pick up the glass and sip, pleasantly surprised by the contents. At least they didn’t give me something rancid.

“Is this my consolation prize?” I murmur.

"Might take the sting out of it." The first girl says, smirking like she's done me some sort of favour.

I roll my eyes, turning my back on them, but I don't look at my husband either. Right now, I'm half tempted to get completely wasted and damn the consequences.

Afterall, isn't that what a Mafia Princess would do?

She'd create a scene, she'd make sure everyone knew exactly who she was.

I knock the drink back in one, then order another. The girl smirks again, demanding to see the cash first, like I can't even afford to buy a drink here.

I pull out a crisp fifty and her eyes widen just a little. She clearly didn't expect that, did she?

She takes it from me, then makes a big show of checking to see it's genuine and that makes me laugh out loud.

If only she knew who I was right now, I doubt she'd be so rude.

When the second drink arrives, I sip it more carefully. In my head I like the idea of causing a commotion, of being the kind of woman who would have the confidence to strut up to them all and call my husband out. That's the kind of woman my mother would be - but I'm not that person.

And my husband is not the kind of man you insult in private, let alone in a bar, surrounded by his and Nico Morelli's men.

No, I pull a stunt like that and Preston would make damn sure I regretted it.

"Here all alone, sweetheart?" Someone says, putting a hand around the back of my stool.

I half jump, looking across and see the man leaning in, obviously staring at my tits, like there isn't an entire Victoria Secret's show on display behind the bar.

"I'm just having a drink." I mumble.

"Let me join you. A drink by yourself is boring."

"I'm good, thanks." I say. I don't want to piss the guy off but at the same time, I want to think, to watch my husband and see how long it takes for him to finally notice I'm here - and I can hardly do that while this man is blatantly trying to get in my pants.

"Come on." He says more persistently. "One drink. I'll pay."

I narrow my eyes, was I speaking another language just now? What part of 'no' did he not understand?

"I said no." I say, jutting my chin, but my cheeks still flush because I'm still not confident in asserting myself, I still feel like anytime I answer back, someone is going to knock me down and put me in my place.

His hand lands on my thigh. It feels like it's burning into my skin and not in a good way. "You don't know who you're turning down, lady. I work for Nico Morelli. I can give the kind of things tarts like you dream about. You want jewels, you can have them, you want nice things, you just have to play your part…"

My jaw drops at his words. I dig my fingers into his hand that is even now pushing further up, closer to my crotch.

"I'm not interested in you." I snap.

"Don't be a little bitch." He says. "You came here for a reason. All girls come here for a reason. All doled up like a whore, you think you can flash your tits and you'll bag someone big? I've got news for you girl, you're not worth that, little slut like you, so stop pretending you don't want it…"

His words turn into a yelp as he's hauled backwards off his seat.

"The fuck do you think you're doing?" Preston growls.

The man blinks, looking up at him. "Just putting this little tart in her place." He says, straightening his jacket from where it's all crumpled.

Preston's eyebrows raise. "Little tart?" He repeats, glancing at me, and god do I recoil at the look he gives me.

Does he think I came here for drama? That I led this guy on, intentionally encouraged his behaviour, like I'm playing that sort of a game?

I shake my head, pleading with my eyes for him to see that I haven't done anything, that I tried to tell this man where to go and he wouldn't listen.

"You have no idea who she is, do you?" Preston says.

The man glances at me, sneering, before looking back at Preston. "They're all the same." He laughs.

Preston smirks just a little. It's a cold, calculated look I've seen a few times now and I know it won't end well. He lures you in with that smile, makes you think you're on even footing, when the reality is, you're about to get your arse handed to you. "Is that right?"

"Yeah, you know how it is, they're all happy to spread their legs if they think it's worth their while." He laughs again.

Only Preston doesn't laugh. He pulls out his gun, fixing him with a look that utterly terrifies me.

"That little tart is my wife." Preston growls.

The man visibly pales, stepping back, holding his hands up. "She didn't say, she didn't…"

Preston raises his gun, fixing it on his chest, but his head turns to me and those blue eyes are utterly furious. "Tell me, Ruby, did he offer to buy you a drink?"

I nod.

"And what did you say?"

"I said I didn't want one. I said I wasn't interested." I half stumble over the words as I speak them so quickly.

Preston tilts his head, turning back to the man. "When a woman says she's not interested, that's what she means." He snaps.

"I didn't know. They're all like that, these bitches all play hard to get, they all play these games…"

Preston lets off a warning shot into the ceiling and the entire bar falls deathly silent. "That's twice now you've called my wife names. You've called her a tart and a bitch. You really want to keep going?"

I step backwards, right into the polished brass edge of the bar.

I can feel everyone staring at us now. Even Nico is. They're all watching this play out, watching my husband go total alpha-male.

"You're the wife?"

I look around, seeing the first barmaid from before staring at me with new eyes. Her gaze drops and she stares at the massive diamond on my finger. How she didn't clock it before I don't know. I guess she must have thought the one around my neck was costume jewellery, though how anyone could mistake a real diamond for a cubic zirconia I have no idea.

"I am." I say quietly. I don't hold her any ill will. Maybe that attitude of hers is needed to work in a place like this but I still don't like the fact she's obviously fucked my husband in the past, nor do I like the fact she shouts out so much about it.

"You will apologise to her, apologise to my wife." Preston continues.

"I'm, I'm sorry." The man splutters, barely looking me in the eyes.

Preston jerks his head and two men step up and drag him away.

I watch him go, kicking and pleading before Preston steps in front of me.

"I didn't mean…" I fall silent as he puts the gun away.

"Why are you here, Ruby?" He growls, like he's pissed at me.

"I," I bite my tongue. I don't really know why I came. All the reasons I had seem so stupid now that I'm stood here.

He grabs my arm, yanking me through the place while everyone stares. My heels seem to be the only sound as they clack across the floor. I drop my eyes, I drop my head, more than aware that my husband is super pissed at me and every person here can see it.

So much for not causing a scene.

When we get outside, I take in the barrels, and the crates and all the trash.

"Preston…"

"Why the fuck are you here?" He asks.

"I just came to see…"

"You shouldn't have." He snaps, cutting across my words like I'm not even allowed to explain myself. "And you shouldn't have let that man touch you."

"Excuse me?"

"He had his hands all over you, Ruby." Preston growls, getting right in my face. "How do you think it feels to look around and see my wife with another man's hands on her?"

My anger spikes. I know I should back down, apologise, retreat, but right now I'm too wound up to do any of those things.

I wrench my arm free and slam my fists into his chest. "How do you think it feels to see my husband with another woman's tits in his face?"

He frowns. "Whose tits?"

"That girl. The barmaid."

He shakes his head. "I barely even looked at her." He says dismissively.

"No?" I smirk. "But Nico was the one who told her to shove off. What would you have done if she stayed? Would you have flirted with her? Smiled at her? Fucked her if she spread her legs for you?"

His face turns livid. "You're accusing me of cheating now, are you?"

"If the shoe fits." I yell.

"What the fuck are you talking about?"

"You." I hiss. "You've fucked half the barmaids. How else would they know…?" I wave my hand at his dick, hoping he gets my point.

He pauses, taking in long seething breaths. "They told you that, did they? Was that what this was, some interrogation? My wife decides to come down here and do a little investigation into my life like she's some sort of detective?"

"It's my life too. I'm your wife, remember?" I snap, slamming my fist into the wall the way he always does, only I let out a yelp because it fucking hurts and I was not expecting that.

He shakes his head. "I don't give a fuck about those women. Yes, I fucked them, but it was a long time ago."

I huff, folding my arms. It sounds like an excuse. Like some bullshit reply to explain it all. "Right, so they're good enough to fuck but your own wife isn't?"

"Ruby." He snaps, pinning me against the wall with his hands on my shoulders. "You think I even have time to look at another woman when I'm either working or with you?"

"Men fuck. That's what they do." I state, jutting my chin defiantly. "You don't fuck me so you're obviously fucking someone else." I don't really think that, but my anger and my jealousy is making me say any shit that comes into my head.

He snarls. "You think I don't want to fuck you? You think I don't spend every waking hour dreaming about what your cunt would feel like as I was pounding into you?"

"Yeah, right, the noble Preston Civello, who's so god damn saintly he won't even fuck his wife when she begs him for it."

His hand wraps around my throat, not tight enough to cut off my airway but enough to get my heart racing. "Beg me, Ruby. Beg me now and I'll fuck you like a dirty little whore in this alleyway."

"You wouldn't have the guts." I spit, goading him on, not caring that I'm pushing him further into whatever the hell this possessive rage is.

He wrenches my dress up, yanks it way up over my hips, and then he spins me around, pinning me face first against the dirty brick wall. His hand slaps my arse hard enough to really sting. He kicks my legs apart and I gasp as he tears my thong right off and tosses it.

I hold my breath, shut my eyes, listening out for the sound of him undoing his pants and when I hear it, I know he's not bluffing.

"My wife's so eager to be fucked." He says, lowering his mouth to my ear. "Let's see if she's so eager to come on my cock as she says she is."

I let out a yelp as he pushes himself into me. He's so big, so girthy that he stretches me to the point all the air is choked out of me and those piercings – they're really not helping right now. My nails dig into the concrete, bits of it stick under them as I try to anchor myself.

"Fuck." Preston groans. "You feel so fucking perfect."

"I'm not on the pill." I gasp.

He responds by sliding out and then slamming into me harder.

"Preston…" I cry. "I said…"

"I don't give a fuck what you said." He growls, silencing my protests.

I wiggle, whimpering, trying to get a better angle and he rewards me with another hard slap. "You'll take what I give you, wife. You'll keep your legs spread and you'll let me have my fill until I'm done, do you hear me?"

It's like he's someone else entirely now, gone is the gentleness, gone is the considerate way he checks in on me. I don't know who this Preston is but, as my own arousal grows, I don't care. I want him to fuck me. I want him to use me. I want every piece of him that I can get.

And I need this moment here as much as he does.

He pulls out, one hand wrapping around my right leg to hold it up and the other wrenches my head back by my hair. He slams into me again, showing no mercy.

My face scraps against the bricks, my body takes the full impact and I let out a cry.

"You asked for this, Ruby. You begged for this. How does it feel? To be used like a common little whore?"

I bite my lip, refusing to answer and he lets out a laugh like he already knows what I'm thinking. He grinds against me, hitting something so deep inside I can't hold the moan in.

"You like that?" He asks, his voice still sounding deadly cold. "You like how my cock feels when I'm buried inside you?"

I nod as best I can.

And his grip around my leg tighten. "Say it out loud. Say how much you enjoy your husband's cock. Shout it so the entire bar can hear how much of a desperate little whore you are for me."

"I like it." I say as loud as I dare.

"Louder." He growls, slamming into me and those piercings, fuck, those piercings, they push into me, they push against something I can't explain.

I shudder, feeling so much arousal leaking out that I must be covering us both.

"I like it Preston. I like you using me." I say but I don't shout it. I don't have the oxygen with everything that he's doing to me. "I want you to use me."

He groans as the sound of our flesh slapping fills the air. "You're so fucking wet right now, Ruby. You're dripping."

"Come in me." I gasp as my inner muscles seem to pulsate, seem to grip him like my body knows instinctively how to respond to all of this. "Come in me."

He bites down on my shoulder. I let out a shriek as his teeth bury themselves in my skin. "Keep doing that." He orders, like I have any semblance of control over my body right now.

"Keep fucking me, Preston." I say back. I don't want him to stop. I don't want this to end. And what's more, I'm so afraid that when it does he'll revert back to that protective person he was before, he'll refuse to touch me unless I force it.

I shut my eyes, I let out one desperate moan after another. If anyone is even walking in the street outside they'll hear everything.

"Preston." I gasp.

He smacks my arse again, so much harder and the way I jolt makes those piercings tease my insides to the point I think I actually lose my mind. I start writhing, bucking, moving as much as this overbearing husband of mine will permit me.

"That's right, Ruby." He says picking up the pace, slamming into me so deliciously harder. "Come on my cock, scream like a good little wife and let everyone know who you belong to."

"You." I cry. "I belong to you."

He bites down on my shoulder again. I arch back, rolling my hips, riding him as much as I can as the tears stream down my face.

I'm so close, I'm practically delirious. His left hand drops from his hold around my hair, he wraps it around my throat cutting off my airway for the briefest of seconds and, as if he knows exactly how to manipulate my body, I fall apart. My eyes roll back in my head, I see stars as something cataclysmic shatters inside me.

And I scream.

I scream so loud it feels like I tear my vocal chords.

Preston growls, pushing himself into me, pressing me hard against the wall as he lets himself go and I can feel it, the way his dick pumps, the way those piercings move as he comes inside me.

I can barely get my breath back as I slump into the wall. My head feels dizzy but in the most incredible way. He's still buried inside me, his body is still pressed right into me. I don't want to move. I want to stay here and die in this delirium.

"Ruby." He says quietly, brushing my hair.

I whimper, keeping my eyes closed. It feels too good. It feels too perfect. I don't want to open my eyes and realise this is all some fantasy, that I've simply hit my head and imagined all of this, and I'm really at home, by myself, and none of this has happened.

"Ruby." He says more persistently.

I let out sigh and then he does the unthinkable; he pulls out and I feel suddenly so empty without him.

But I can feel his come leaking out, I can feel it already slick on my thighs.

"Talk to me." He murmurs.

"I think you broke me." I whisper, before letting out a tiny laugh.

His hands wrap around my shoulders, he pulls me back into his chest. "I shouldn't have been so aggressive."

"Don't you dare." I say, turning around, forcing myself to move. "Don't you dare start backtracking."

His lips curl and his eyes seem to sparkle. "You enjoyed me being like that?"

"I said it before, I'm your wife, you're meant to use me as you want."

He shakes his head, cupping my cheek. "I don't want to just use you, Ruby. I want you to want me, I want you to…"

I crash my lips into his. If he didn't get it already then apparently this man isn't as smart as I thought he was. He groans, grabbing my jaw, pushing me back into the wall that seconds ago he had me pinned against and was fucking the life out of me.

"I want you, Preston." I say as we break away. "I want you, however you'll have me."

"In that case…" He says, picking me up throwing me over his shoulder and I shriek at the fact my bare arse is entirely exposed to the entire world. He yanks my dress down giving me some sort of decency. "…We're going home. I want to fuck my wife somewhere better than an alleyway."

"You're the one that dragged us down here." I grumble as he laughs.

Preston

CHAPTER

Thirty-One

Her face is grazed, her knees are scuffed up. She rubs her palms and I can see the damaged skin there too. But when she looks up at me though, she gives me the biggest grin.

"I think you're a masochist, wife." I murmur.

She lets out a little giggle. "Maybe for you."

When we pull up to the house, I practically go all caveman, throwing her back over my shoulder, carrying her up the stairs two at a time, while all the staff who are still awake avert their eyes.

I throw her onto the bed and she bounces onto the mattress, squealing.

"Lose the dress." I order.

She bites her lip, but she's pulling it down, slinking it off her body revealing that she's not wearing a bra.

"My slutty wife shows up at my work with no underwear, does she?" I growl.

She rolls her eyes. "I had underwear. You tore it off me, remember?"

I smirk, getting on my knees on the carpet, forcing her legs so wide she does the splits.

"Preston." She gasps in shock. "I, it's, it's still leaking out of me."

"I know." I say, already watching the way her cunt is still weeping so beautifully.

She's red, bruised, sore from how I fucked her but I wouldn't want her any other way. From now on this is what I want, her body proudly showing off how I use her. Her skin bearing the marks of how her husband worships her.

"Use my come as lube." I order. "Touch yourself, Ruby, make yourself come while I watch."

She sits up, moving her hands, spreading her lips wider with one while the other starts circling her clit exactly as I've touched her before.

"There's a good girl." I say. "There's my perfect wife."

She throws her head back moaning. She's so turned on it takes barely a minute before she starts to flush, before that perfect pussy of hers starts to visibly throb and she comes, pushing out more of my own come as it mixes with her juices.

"So fucking beautiful." I say.

She shudders, reaching out for me. "Fuck me, Preston. I need you."

I grab her hips, pulling her around, I should use a condom, I know she's not on any contraception and ye,t right now, the thought of any barrier between us makes me more mad than I can say.

"I told you to beg, Ruby, do you remember?" I say, lining my cock back up with that needy cunt of hers. "I told you to beg me and you haven't."

"I will." She says reaching up, running her hands over her breasts, teasing her nipples for me to watch. "I'll beg. I need you Preston, please, please fuck me, now that you've started, you can't stop, you can't. Fuck me like you love me. Fuck me the way a husband should fuck his wife."

I lean down over her, grabbing her jaw, staring into those magnificent eyes of hers as I push myself inside her. I missed her reaction last time with how I had her rammed up against that wall and I want to enjoy witnessing every second as I'm sliding inside her.

She gasps, she shudders, she stares back at me as her body adjusts to my cock.

"How's that feel, wife?"

"So good." She breathes, like I've shoved all the oxygen out of her.

I move a little, pulling out an inch then twisting back in, I want her to fully appreciate the piercings, I want her to revel in how they'll pleasure her in all the right places.

"Oh fuck." She groans.

"You like that wife? You like the way my cock teases your insides?"

She bites her lip, nodding.

"I was aggressive with you earlier." I say, dropping my hands to tease those pert little nipples of hers. They're so hard they could cut glass. I tweak them, tightening my grasp as I yank them up until she whimpers and her eyes stream. "If you want me to ease up, if you want me to stop, then you're going to state it by using the word 'red'."

She nods, arching her back, but I can see she's too consumed by lust to truly pay attention.

"Say the word, tell me you understand." I order.

"Red." She gasps.

"There's a good girl." I state, before releasing my hold, watching her tits bounce back. They're so flushed. I slap one and then the other.

She responds to my abuse by dipping her hand down to touch herself and I grin at how liberated she now is, how unashamed she is to take what she wants and not overthink it.

"Anytime, Ruby, anytime you say the word, I'll stop."

"The only thing I want you to stop doing is treating me like I can't handle it when I can." She snaps. "I can handle everything you do to me."

My hand grabs her throat, I pin her back down as her eyes bulge. She's trembling under my touch but she's moaning, rocking her hips, showing me she wants this.

"My little wife is so confident now." I taunt. "So let's see how many times I can make you come. Let's see how long you can last before you're begging for a break."

"No breaks." She gasps. "I've waited too long already. I don't want a break, I want you to fuck me until I pass out, until we both collapse."

Promises, promises wife.

But if that's what she wants, then that's what she'll get, because I've already told her she only has to ask.

I start raising my hips, slamming into her, feeling the way her delicious pussy moulds around me and welcomes me home with every plunge.

She wraps a leg around my back, she digs her nails into my skin and I fuck my wife like a man possessed.

I fuck her like I'll never be able to touch her again.

I fuck her like her pleasure is the only thing I'm living for.

By the time I'm done, she's a sweaty mess. Her eyes are shut. She can barely move from how many times I've forced her body to come. All I want to do is collapse beside her but we can't sleep like this. I can't leave her like this.

I force myself up, force myself to carry her in my arms, and under the warm spray of the shower, I wash her down.

She doesn't open her eyes, she just lays against me, letting me take care of her, letting me show how important she is to me.

Ruby

CHAPTER Thirty-Two

Sunlight streams in behind the curtains. I shift, turning my head and groan at the way my body aches. I feel like I've done ten rounds with a heavyweight champion. Between my thighs, I'm throbbing. But it it's a good throb. A good pain.

"I was too rough." Preston murmurs against my head.

"No." I say quickly. "I just have to get used to it."

He smiles, running his hands down my back, tracing a pattern that he's done before so many times.

"We'll have to practice more." He says. "Train your body to take my cock."

I smirk, spreading my legs wide and feeling the hardness between his thighs. "In that case, I'm ready for another lesson."

Laughter rumbles from his chest, before he's reaching around, grabbing hold of both my arse cheeks. "So eager for me, aren't you, wife?"

In reply, I raise my body up, catching his mouth and kiss him. "I want you. Why would I deny it?"

He tilts his head as I straddle him and then I slide myself down till he's right back where he belongs. My insides scream in protest but I don't care. I know soon enough those piercings will be torturing me in a whole different way.

"Fuck." He groans. "You're a quick learner."

"I had a good teacher." I tease.

He pushes me up, forces me to sit up straight and pulls the covers away so that both of us are fully on view. "You look good like this, Ruby." He says staring at where his cock is buried in my pussy. "So good."

His hands spread my lips wider, he licks his lips as his thumb starts to circle my clit.

"Oh fuck." I gasp, throwing my head back. I'm so sensitive but the minute he touches me I'm desperate for release.

"Ride me, Ruby, show your husband how much better you look with your tits bouncing and your cunt swallowing him whole."

I flush at his words, at the image of what I must look like, but I do it anyway, I raise my hips, I roll my body, I fuck Preston, hoping I look exactly the way he's asking.

"So fucking beautiful." He groans, cupping my breasts, holding them as they bounce.

His thumb continues to tease me, his cock hits that incredible spot inside. I can feel as my orgasm builds, I can feel as every moment of this gets more and more pleasurable. I jerk, letting out a scream as I come with my body slumping into him.

He groans, coming just after me and I fall back, lying on his chest, keeping him buried inside me. His arms scoop around me, his hands cup my arse once more.

As he starts probing my arsehole, I gasp.

"Have you ever been fucked here, Ruby?" He asks.

I shake my head quickly.

His lips curl. "Would you like to be?"

I gulp, unsure how to reply.

"Would you like your husband to fuck every one of your tight little holes? To have you sprawled out on this bed, utterly used with my come dripping out of all three?"

That image both thrills me and scares me shitless. "Do you want that?" I ask.

His response is to push his finger in past my puckered entrance. I jolt in shock but his arm holds me still so I can't move even if I wanted to.

"Relax," He says quietly. "Let me play."

I try to. I really do but how does one relax when someone has their finger in your arse?

He twists it around, stretching me as he explores my body. I bite down the whimper, forcing myself to take it.

"There's my good girl." He says, studying my face. "You'd feel so good with my cock buried there."

"Will it hurt?" I whisper.

He shakes his head. "I'll prep you. I'll make sure you're ready for me."

"How?"

He withdraws his finger and I wince as my arse closes back up.

"We'll start slow. We'll build up to it."

"Can I say no?"

"You can." He says. "You can always say no."

"But you want to do it?"

He circles my arsehole again and I tremble at the strange sensation. "I know you'd enjoy it. I'd make sure of that."

"Fine." I say. "You can fuck me in the arse."

He lets out a laugh, rolling me over onto my side, pulling the covers up. "Like I said, we'll build up to it. Start with plugs."

Butt plugs? He wants to put a damn butt plug in my arse? What the hell have I just agreed to?

"We won't do anything you're not comfortable with." He says gently.

"You've done it before? You've fucked other women like that?"

He nods. "None of them have ever had any complaints."

"Nice recommendation there." I mutter.

He laughs, pulling me in tighter. "Keep up that attitude and I might just stay here all day and work it out of you."

"You can't." I say. "Nico will not be happy if you pull a sicky."

"It's not a sicky. It's doing my marital duties."

"I doubt he'd see it as that."

"No, he wouldn't." Preston says in a tone that's suddenly so serious.

I still, feeling like the air has changed, that the entire tempo of the room has gone up a notch. "Preston?"

"What?"

"What aren't you telling me?" I ask, because clearly there is something.

"Nothing." He says.

I roll over, narrowing my eyes as I face my husband down. "You're lying."

His eyebrows raise. "What did you just say to me?"

"You're lying." I repeat. "I know you are."

He shakes his head, pushing me off, getting out of the bed. "I wasn't supposed to touch you. I wasn't supposed to go anywhere near you."

"What?"

"Nico ordered it. He said you were off limits."

"Excuse me? Why the fuck would he say that?"

A micro expression crosses his face, one I can't read. "He's trying to protect you." He says after a minute.

"Protect me?" I scoff. "He's not my dad, he's not..."

"I know, Ruby." Preston cuts across me. "But if he finds out we're fucking he'll be more than just pissed about it."

"So what, you want to hide this? Hide that you're sleeping with your own wife?" How does that make any sense?

He doesn't reply. He just walks away, goes to the closet and I hear the sound of him pulling out drawers, of him getting dressed. Apparently this conversation is over then.

When he comes back out, he's fully dressed, in his usual black suit, white crisp shirt, and polished oxfords. For a second I gawp at him. He's fucking gorgeous. How is this man my husband? How did I manage to land on my feet considering all the odds were stacked against me?

"You're drooling, wife." Preston teases.

I grin back at him. "And you're late."

He rolls his eyes before tossing something at me that I only just catch.

"The morning after pill?" I say looking at the pack. How did he just have this stashed in his closet?

"I sent one of the maids to get it." He says, no doubt seeing the look on my face.

"Maybe we need something more permanent." I reply.

To my relief, he nods. "I'll sort it." He says before walking out the door, leaving me alone in our bed.

Preston

CHAPTER

Thirty-Three

By the time I get to the bar, I know Nico is going to be pissed. I left without so much as goodbye, I stormed out the place and for anyone who chose to look I'm sure they saw my wife over my shoulder, as I clearly marked my territory like some sort of neanderthal.

Inside, the place is a hive of activity, like something is about to go off. I grab one of our lackey's as he's strolling past.

"What's going on?"

"Our supply got hit." He says. "Last night. Did you not see your phone?"

No, I didn't. I haven't looked at it once. I was too busy revelling in the memories of what it felt like to finally claim my wife.

I jerk my head for him to piss off, chastising myself for acting like a bloody lovesick idiot as I pull my phone out to see the multiple messages and missed calls.

"Where have you been?" Noah asks, coming up to me, looking just as fraught as everyone else around me.

"Busy." I say. Not a lie. I have been busy, busy fucking my wife.

"Nico is looking for you. He's been asking for you for the last hour."

"Where is he?"

Before anyone can answer, a fist comes flying at my face. I stumble back, grasping my jaw.

"You fucked her." Nico snarls. "You fucked my goddaughter."

I draw myself up, preparing for the inevitable backlash because there's no point in denying it. "I didn't do anything she didn't want."

He slams another fist into me. Again, I stumble. All the men around us fall silent, watching this sudden display.

"I told you she was off limits." Nico growls. "I told you she was untouchable."

"She's my wife." I snarl back. "Did you really think I wouldn't do it?"

His eyes widen. He launches himself at me and though I'd dearly love to defend myself and fight back, that's not really an option when it's Nico Morelli beating the shit out of you.

I raise my arms, protecting my face as best I can while taking blow after blow.

"We had an agreement, Civello." He shouts.

I don't reply. I just grunt as each blow lands.

"How long did it take, huh? How long before you got your cock wet?"

"Like you wouldn't have done the same." I snap back.

He pauses, staring at me with a face full of fury. "I would not…"

"You fucking liar." I snarl. "Look at you with Eleri. Look how you were."

"That's different and you know it."

"How is it? How is it different?"

"Because she's not twenty one fucking years of age." Nico says, curling his fist, slamming it into my rib cage.

"Yeah?" I spit back. "And from what you said, if you hadn't met Eleri, Ruby would be your wife now. Tell me, Nico, tell me you wouldn't have fucked her then."

He shakes his head, stepping back. "You…"

Whatever he's about to say, I don't hear it. All I hear is the raging blast of something as it explodes around me. My mind registers what it is, my body moves instinctively to protect Nico, to pull us both to the ground as it feels like an inferno suddenly burns above our heads.

A high pitched shrieking rings in my ears.

I can't do anything but wait until the carnage stops. Only, when it does, the sound is replaced by something infinitely worse. All I can hear are moans, men in pain, men dying.

I get to my feet, throwing off the shit that's landed on top of me.

"Nico." I say, yanking away what looks like half the damned ceiling.

"Help me up." He says, holding his hand out.

I haul him to his feet and for a moment we just stare around us. The bar is gone, half the walls have collapsed, the air is thick with smoke and I can see the flames as they lick up all the spilt alcohol.

"We have to get out of here." I say.

Nico nods but he looks off, like he has a concussion.

At what was once the doorway, he goes to walk out and instinct steps in, I yank him back just as we hear the sound of a machine gun going off.

"The fuck?" Nico growls, ducking down even though he's now far out of the line of sight.

I pull my pistol out, taking aim. If I hit the bastard then another replaces him.

Nico pulls his own gun, resting against some miraculously still standing fragment of the wall and he starts shooting.

"We need back up." I say.

He nods back but he doesn't take his eyes off whoever is out there and he doesn't stop shooting back.

I pull my phone, calling for backup, though I suspect others already have. You can't seriously expect to blow up Nico's bar and not have anyone react to it.

Out front someone moves.

I see the shadows, I hear the shuffling.

I don't have enough damn rounds in my pistol to deal with a full attack.

Someone tries to sneak in around the blown out wall. I slam the back of my pistol into their face, then put a bullet in their head. They collapse as I steal the assault rifle from their now dead grasp.

"They're coming." I shout.

Nico looks across at me before his eyes dart back. I don't know how big this mag is, how many rounds I now have to play with, but I don't have time to check. I take aim, blasting the shoulder of the first arsehole. Whoever is behind him clearly gets the warning and they change tactic, spreading out, coming at us from all sides.

I shoot one after another, ducking down whenever they shoot back. I don't look for Nico. I don't take my eyes away from any of the bastards in front of me.

One comes running at me like he's fucking Rambo and I take great delight in shooting through his stomach. That's what you get for thinking you can simply walk up to me and kill me. Like it would be that easy.

Gunshots ring out around me.

I know more of our men are now alert, are now shooting back. Finally we're actually defending ourselves.

As I glance over at Nico, I can see him caught in a shootout but he's not noticing the man creeping up behind him.

I take aim, pull the trigger and nothing. No bullet. No fucking ammo. I fling the weapon, snatching at a piece of shrapnel and I launch myself at the bastard, yelling as I do.

We land in a heap, narrowly missing the gunfire from whoever is still shooting. Nico turns, staring at us and I bury that piece of metal so far into the man's throat he instantly starts gurgling up blood.

Nico pales as he realises how close the man got.

"He almost had you." I say.

His eyes flash with fury. He stands up, takes aim and finally hits the man he's been trying to kill.

And as the fucker falls backwards, we hear the roar of engines. Finally back up is here.

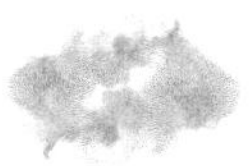

WE'RE SAT ON THE PAVEMENT, STARING AT THE UTTER RUIN IN FRONT of us. There's still smoke billowing out and, as the fire brigade work to make it safe, all we can do is look on.

Around us, the ground is covered in rubble, no doubt from the initial explosion.

The police turned up conveniently right after our men did. They made a big noise, a big fuss and naturally they got fuck all from any of us.

We have them bought anyway but we're still not going to cooperate with them.

Nico told them it was a gas explosion. The look on their faces was priceless.

"They were after you." I say, like he doesn't know it.

He grunts, picking up a small piece of debris that I'd put money on being once part of our bar. He lobs it hard into the smoking mess in front of us.

"You should check on Eleri." I add.

"Already done it. She's safe." He says.

I nod, relieved that she is. The last thing we need is one of us seriously injured. As soon as I sorted backup for here I had Noah go to my house, to make sure it was secure, locked down, and nobody was anywhere near Ruby.

"Who do you think it was?" Blaine asks. He'd luckily been out all day, running errands as he puts it, when we all know he's been ensuring the scum of this city know exactly who's in charge.

"You don't think it was Gunnar?" I say.

Nico frowns. "Seems too soon. How could he have planned this when he only took over yesterday?"

I narrow my eyes, thinking it through. I don't believe in coincidences. I don't believe in simple bad timing. My gut tells me this has something to do with the alliance, maybe it's not Gunnar, maybe it's something else, some other Don whose sensed a change in the wind.

"Who knows about Levi?" I ask.

Nico shrugs.

Blaine pulls a face. "Doubt the other families aren't aware."

Yeah, he's right about that, shit like that spreads. I reckon most of them knew before the sun rose this morning.

"We need to clean this shit up." Nico growls. "I want to know who's behind it, anyone that even knew this was going to happen will pay the price."

I nod. We have to be ruthless now. We have to shut this entire city down. No mercy. No reprieves. They come for us and by god will they suffer the consequences.

"I'm on it, boss." Blaine says walking away, barking out orders.

"You should see a doctor." I state.

"I'm fine." Nico growls.

He certainly doesn't look fine but I doubt I do either. My jaw aches from where he hit me. My ribs are throbbing from where he beat me. Maybe I should be grateful the damn bar was rigged, it saved me from being beaten to a pulp.

"So what are we going to do about Ruby?" Nico growls.

I draw in a low breath. "I love her." I say quietly. "Just as you love Eleri, I love Ruby."

He grunts, tossing another piece of rubble. "Have you told her that?"

"No."

"Why not?"

"It would overwhelm her."

He narrows his eyes. "Did you fuck her on your wedding night, did you lie to me from the beginning?"

"No. I fully intended for this to be what we agreed. I fully intended to just keep it business but she won me over, little by little."

"I knew something was up." He growls. "I could see it. The way you watched her, the way she reacted to you. I thought it was just a crush."

"It's so much more than that."

"Apparently so." Nico snaps, getting to his feet.

I look up at him then get to mine.

"Car's ready." He says, not looking at me, just turning his back and once again expecting me to follow him.

I get, in half expecting us to be going somewhere discreet, out of the city, somewhere he can dispose of my body without too much hassle, so it's more than a little surprising when we pull up to my house instead.

Both of us get out. For a moment I wonder if Nico's going to demand my wife goes with him, that that's the reason he's brought us back here.

The front door opens, Ruby comes running out, throwing herself into my arms and I only just catch her in time.

"It's okay." I say, more than aware that Nico is seeing all of this.

"I was so worried." She whispers, pulling back enough to check me over. Her hand cups my jaw, seeing the bruises Nico gave me hours ago.

"I'm fine." I say.

She lets out a huff before she turns her head, finally seeing Nico stood watching us both intently. He stares at her for a second then meets my gaze, gives a tiny nod, and to my complete shock, he just leaves.

Ruby

CHAPTER

Thirty-Four

"What happened?" I feel like I keep saying it. Keep asking it.

Preston lets out a sigh, sinking into the chair. He looks exhausted. He looks like he's taken a hiding. He holds his hand for me and, as I take it, he pulls me into his lap. "It's been a long day."

I grab his chin, pursing my lips as I see what is unmistakeably bruising across his skin.

"I thought the bar was blown up so how did you get these?" I ask. Wouldn't he be burnt, not bruised if he'd been near the epicentre?

He blinks. "Nico did it."

"Nico hit you?" I gasp.

"He knows, Ruby. He knows about us."

I scowl at that. "You're telling me Nico hit you because you slept with your wife?"

He lets out a chuckle. "Since when did you stop calling it fucking?"

"You know what I mean."

"It's okay. It's sorted."

"Right." I mutter, turning in his lap, getting to my feet.

"Where are you going?" He calls after me.

"Someone has to take care of you." I say walking away, grabbing the first aid kit that he's produced so many times for me.

When I come back, he looks at it in my hands and smirks. "You're playing nurse now, Ruby?"

"Do you want me to?" I tease. "Want me to dress up all sexy?"

His eyes drop to stare at my breasts. "Maybe later." He smirks and I swear my heart flips at the fact we can be like this; relaxed, flirty, a normal couple.

I press an ice pack to his cheek, he's got grazes all over his skin. I open an antiseptic wipe and start cleaning him up, inch by inch and he doesn't even so much as wince but he watches every move I make like this is turning him on.

"My tough old man." I murmur.

He catches my hand, squeezing it in warning. "Less of the 'old', Ruby."

"It's okay," I tease, "Turns out I like my men to be older."

Something flickers across his face, something I can't quite read and it makes me still as flash of fear goes through me. Have I gone too far? Have I offended him with my stupid, unguarded words?

"Tell me, Ruby," He says quietly, "On our wedding night, you said you'd fucked loads of men. That was a lie, wasn't it?"

I gulp, squirming, only his hands move to grab me, to hold my hips and force me to stay exactly where I am.

"What does it matter?" I whisper, dropping my gaze as my cheeks heat.

"And when you arrived in this city, you tried to run away with a boy..."

I can't keep the gasp in. The shock that makes my stomach drop. How the fuck does he know that? How long *has* he known that? Poor Finn, with everything else going on I'd barely thought about him. I'm truly a selfish piece of shit, aren't I?

"It's okay," He reassures but I can hear the tone, I can hear the hint to his voice, he may be speaking the right words but there's an edge to them.

"Who, who told you?" I stammer. Was it Gunnar? Is he in contact with him? Is he stirring the pot, making things worse for me? But why would he, if he thinks I'm spying for him... only, I'm not, am I? I haven't replied to his messages, he's lost all radio contact.

Perhaps this is his new game, turning my husband against me and forcing me to comply because I have no other option?

"It doesn't matter." Preston says. "I just wanted to hear it from you, to understand..."

"Finn was just a friend." I gasp out quickly. "He wasn't. We didn't..."

He lets out a sound that could be relief or it could be annoyance, I can't tell.

"They killed him." I suddenly sob, as that memory flashes of him in a headlock, of that gun pressed into his face, and that guilt hits me. Maybe that's why I hadn't thought about him. Because I'd gotten him killed, I'd done nothing to stop it. "They killed him because he was trying to help me."

He pulls me in, wraps his arms around me like I'm the battered person here, and I cling to his hard body, shutting my eyes so tightly.

"It was him, wasn't it?" Preston says, "He was the one you slept with."

I know I should tell him the truth, I know right now is the perfect opportunity and yet I can't do it. I can't speak the words, I can't admit it, and most of all I can't bear to see the look in his eyes, the disappointment, the shame, the disgust when he learns what was really going on.

So I do it, I take the cowards option and I nod back. It's a tiny movement, a tiny gesture, but I can feel the way it damns me all the same.

I expect him to react to my admission, to show his anger at my blatant disrespect but, instead, he just holds me, like I'm precious, like I matter, like he actually cares about me as a person and not just what I represent as a Holtz.

I love you.

I don't even know where the words come from, where the thought comes from but as I force myself to look my husband in the eyes, I know it's true. All these stupid feelings, all this stupid emotion I've been fighting, it's no good, it's utterly useless.

This man has broken down my walls, somehow, without even trying, he's done it, he's made me *feel* again.

I blink away the tears, trembling more in fear at how vulnerable I am, how precarious everything suddenly feels.

And then I'm kissing him, crashing my lips into his, needing to shut my head up, and stop always seeing the worst possible outcome. So I love my husband? So what? Surely that's a good thing, surely that's the best case scenario? But loving makes me vulnerable, loving makes me weak.

His hands tangle in my hair as he deepens it, and his tongue battles mine for dominance. I can't help the moan as I give in and let him win.

But as we break apart, I can still see that serious look on his face. "I need to tell you something."

I can see from his face that whatever it is, it can't be good. I bite my lip, waiting for whatever awful news he's going to speak about now.

"Your uncle is dying."

"What?"

"Levi had a stroke." Preston states.

My eyes widen. I don't know whether to laugh out loud or rally against the fact that that bastard has once again gotten off too easily.

"Ruby?"

"I, give me a moment." I say, scrambling from his lap, turning my back on him. My mind feels like it's whirling. My body feels like it's trembling. I don't understand why I'm not jumping for joy.

The bastard is dying, the bastard is dying.

"Who is taking over…?" I ask.

"Gunnar."

Of course. Of course he is. So he gets my family's wealth, he gets my family's power, everything that was stolen from me. I clench my fists, letting out a snarl of frustration and then jolt as I feel Preston's hands on my shoulders.

"I'm sorry." He says, like he understands why I'm so wound up. Like he has a clue.

I stare back at him, trying to tell myself that the idea forming in my head is madness, that I'm rocking the boat when right now, I'm safe in the harbour, far from the storm, that none of it should matter now.

"You could do it." I half-whisper.

"What?" He frowns and a micro-expression I can't read flickers across his face before that mask comes down.

"You could take over." I state.

His eyes react, his jaw tightens. "Ruby…"

"Hear me out, you have Nico on your side, you have me, a Holtz, as your wife…"

"Ruby." He growls, clearly telling me that I've crossed the line.

"What?" I say. "Why not? Why not take it back?"

He shakes his head, pulling me in, burying my face into his chest. "This isn't a discussion for now."

"This is exactly when we should be talking about this. Gunnar is weak right now, they only follow him because of Levi…"

"Ruby." He snaps. "Enough. Enough."

"But…"

His hand wraps around my mouth. He stands over me and, though I know he's pissed, all I can feel is that heat rapidly spreading through my core.

"I've spent the entire morning having the shit kicked out of me in one way or another." He states. "I want to spend the rest of my day buried in my wife, losing myself in her body, not arguing about something that doesn't matter. Do you hear me?"

I nod quickly, even though I want to argue more.

It might not matter to him, it might not seem of importance, but this was my family's legacy, my inheritance by all accounts, and it's being stolen. Again.

He picks me up and I squeal as he carries me back up the stairs.

In the bathroom, he turns the shower on, before he practically tears my clothes from my body and shoves me inside.

The water is freezing, it makes me physically shiver as it hits me but within seconds it warms up enough that I don't mind. Besides, my nipples are now seriously hard and I like the way Preston is staring at them.

"I'm dirty." He comments. "Clean me, wife, and if you do a good job I'll reward that pretty mouth of yours."

Preston

CHAPTER Thirty-Five

I could tell her. I know I could.

But in my head it seems more logical to keep things as they are. Besides, I won't get her hopes up and then see them dashed.

She's too fragile for that, she's too broken.

I want to do this the right way, I want to tell her when it's complete, when we've won. I want to take her hand and see the joy in her eyes when she realises all of her inheritance is being returned, that every wrong that was done has been punished.

So I keep my mouth shut, keep my thoughts to myself and enjoy as my wife starts scrubbing my skin, worshipping me with such devotion and for the first time, I have no conflicting thoughts, no fear that anyone will take her from me.

She is finally mine, and soon, I'm going to make her a queen.

She sinks to her knees, her wide, begging eyes staring up at me, and though I've imagined this moment over and over, nothing prepares me for the beauty of it as she parts her lips, and slowly, delicately, she slides me over her tongue.

My hands find her hair. I don't mean to grip so hard but I know it's hurting as I start driving myself further and further down her perfect little throat, desperately seeking my climax. I can hear her gagging. I can see her tears streaming down her cheeks, mingling with the spray of the shower but I don't give a fuck.

She isn't actually fighting me, she isn't giving any signals that she wants me to stop.

And besides, from what I can tell, Ruby has never had a cock in her mouth before so I'm going to teach her exactly how to take me, exactly how I like it.

I pin her in, one hand pressed against the tiles, forcing her to arch her back as I pick up my pace.

She looks so damn good on her knees. Too good. Now that I've had her like this, I'll want her like this all the time.

She gasps, grabbing hold of my arse to try and anchor herself.

"You can take it." I growl, still giving no mercy. She will take it, she will take every thrust, every gag, she will swallow me down and choke like the good little wife I'm making of her.

When I finally come, I roar out, pouring my come down her throat and like the good girl that she is she swallows it. Not that I give her much of a choice.

She slumps back, her tits heaving as she stares up at me but I don't let her get her breath before I yank her up, wrap her legs over my shoulders and bury my face between her thighs.

"Oh fuck, Preston," She shrieks.

I can't reply. I can't say anything, and nor do I want to. I'm too busy eating the life out of her cunt, devouring her. It takes barely a minute before she starts writhing, gasping, falling apart for me.

With one hand, I reach up, grabbing her by the throat, and I hold her in place as I force her to come.

She screams out. Her legs tighten around my own neck, and she rides my face as she seeks more pleasure.

When I put her down, she's so unsteady I have to hold her to me so that her legs don't collapse.

"Preston," She breathes. Her nails dig into my skin, her head is resting against my chest.

I hold her still, but my hand wraps around her stomach, and though I should let her have a moment, I can't wait, I just can't.

I pick her up, slide her back onto my cock and she hisses as I settle inside her.

"It's too good." I groan. She is too good.

She doesn't respond behind a whimper and as if that spurs me on, I start fucking her just as mercilessly as before.

The sound of our wet flesh slapping against each other mingles with the groans and grunts as I take my wife one more time.

"I can't, I can't." She sobs but I don't care what she says, because she will. She will come for me. She will give me this.

I slam into her pussy, and despite her protestations, I can feel how close she is.

"You like me using you." I state. "You enjoy it, Ruby. Admit it."

"Yes," She sobs, like it's some sordid little secret.

"You're my wife." I growl. "My wife to use as I see fit. And using you like this…" I start punctuating each word, ensuring that, though I can't say the 'L' word, it's there, that feeling, that need, that obsession. "Using you like this makes me happy, and you want your husband to be happy, don't you?"

"Yes." She cries as her body becomes more erratic, as wave after wave starts to take over.

"Come, wife, prove how much you enjoy being my slut."

She shakes her head, those pretty tears stream down her face once more but, just as always, she's obedient in this, and she starts screaming, writhing, proving that every word I spoke is true.

I groan in response, only just managing to hold myself back from spilling my load.

"I'm going to fill you up, wife." I say, putting my hand on her belly. "And one day soon I'll put a baby in there."

Her eyes widen. She lets out a gasp.

"Would you like that? To grow fat with my child?"

She nods just a little like she's trying to convince herself more than she is me. "But not yet." She breathes.

"Not yet." I agree.

I'm not ready for children yet despite my age, besides I want to enjoy my wife, enjoy just her company and her body for a while.

We'll make our kingdom secure, ensure we are untouchable and then, and only then, will I start breeding her, will have her pretty little body swollen and full with our heirs.

I LEAVE HER TO SLEEP, THOUGH IT'S A HARD THING TO DO. SHE LOOKS so peaceful, so content, tucked up in my bed, right where she belongs.

When I get to the office, Noah is already waiting, and we spend hours going through every one of Gunnar's cronies, going through all the little details we know, working out where the cracks are, and what weaknesses we can exploit.

Unsurprisingly, most of Gunnar's men are loyal to him. When we make our move, most of them will be eliminated. But there are a few, a handful who are already giving off signals that they're not happy to see the Holtz empire in his dirty little hands.

It's nearly five when Jace comes racing in through the door.

He glances at the papers, sees the lists of names and a flicker of curiosity covers his face, before he quickly fixes his gaze on me.

"It's all over." He says.

"What is?" I reply.

"Levi. He passed an hour ago."

My eyebrows raise. I guess I'm not surprised. All the commentary from the hospital was he was unlikely to make it. But I *am* annoyed that the bastard couldn't even wait on more day.

"Well?" Jace says, grinning.

"Well, what?" I ask.

"I take it you're making a play for the family heirlooms?" He states.

"Of course he is." Noah bristles. "His wife is a Holtz."

"Gunnar won't just roll over." Jace warns like we're all fucking idiots. "He'll be expecting something like this."

"What do you suggest?" I ask, curiously.

He shrugs, acting more nonchalant than is believable. "Just saying. That's all."

Noah rolls his eyes but it makes me wonder all the same – am I being naïve? Am I missing something? Between Nico and myself we have an army poised to step in, to takeover. He's already done the brunt work, speaking to the other families, smoothing things over and ensuring there will be no reprisals and yet, something niggles all the same.

I feel like we're missing something obvious.

"Any word on the brother?" I ask. Surely if anyone's going to throw a spanner in the works, it'll be him?

"Nothing." Jace says, shrugging. "We tracked the vans but they all came up empty. The man must be having help from somewhere."

Of course he's got help. No way the bastard is able to simply attack our enterprises all by himself.

For a moment I wonder what will happen when we do catch him, does Ruby love me enough now to forgive me murdering her brother? Will it even come to that?

I snarl, already knowing the answer. Of course it will. Jett is a threat, not only to me, but to Ruby. He won't simply sit by and let her takeover their family's empire.

No, he'll rise up and challenge her… and then we'll have a damned civil war.

Sibling against sibling. Holtz against Holtz. I don't want to see the sadness and betrayal in Ruby's face when that day comes.

No, better I finish this before it even starts.

Better I eliminate him from the board before he can make any further moves.

"Keep looking." I say to Jace. "And the rest of you, get back to work." I add before grabbing my things. Suddenly I need to be there, back with my wife, ensuring that no one has tried to steal her while I've been away.

But when I pull up to the house, I see the waiting car. My eyes narrow and though I know this could be about anything, why else would he be here?

I get out, shut the door, and stride towards the arsehole smirking at me.

"What are you doing here?" I ask.

"Is that any way to speak to your ally?" Gunnar says, tilting his head.

"I have nothing to say to you." I state, walking past, the sooner he's put in his place the better. Besides, he must know we're pulling the rug out from under him, surely he's not that stupid? I'm half tempted to pull out my gun and put a bullet in his head right this very second.

He follows behind me, shadowing my steps inside the house and though I'm itching to push him out, I need to be smart here, as far as he's concerned we're all still in bed together, that nothing has changed with Levi's passing.

I don't want to reveal our hand too early and fuck everything up.

I just need a few more days, a bit more patience.

"I came to see Ruby." He says loudly.

That makes me pause. "What the fuck do you want with my wife?"

Is that his game, is he trying to undo our deal, is he trying to renegade on everything? Well, he can fuck right off. No one is taking Ruby from me. No one is taking my wife.

"She didn't tell you?" He says.

"Tell me what?"

"Your wife invited me for dinner." He states as if it's the most natural thing to come out of his mouth.

I blink, wondering if I've misheard him but I know what he said. "What?" I snarl, just as I sense her, as I see her from my peripheries.

Ruby

CHAPTER
Thirty-Six

I wander down the hall, frowning at the sound of voices. Preston has been gone all day and I didn't expect him back so early, or that he'd be with visitors.

Only when I spot them, I freeze. My heart physically stops and it's all I can do not to run. Not to scream.

"Hello, Ruby." Gunnar says, tilting his head the way a predator does.

Preston narrows his eyes like he's as pissed about this as I am.

"I would have thought you'd be more forthcoming with your husband…" Gunnar continues and I swear my stomach lurches at those words, at what awful things he's about to divulge.

"About, about what?" I stammer.

"About me being here, about you inviting me to dinner tonight."

My eyes dart to Preston. Is that the lie he spun? Is that what Gunnar said when he showed up here?

"Ruby?" Preston asks, but Gunnar cuts across him like this is his house, his domain.

"It must have slipped her mind, what with Levi's passing."

I draw in breath and I get a mouthful of his stench but that fear, that old lingering panic is steadily taking over.

I don't know what to say.

I don't know what to do.

Mentally, I can feel my body shutting down, my mind withdrawing, going back to that same place of safety in my own head.

Preston walks up to me, murmuring in my ear. "Is this what I think it is?" He asks coldly.

I blink up at him, even more confused.

"Are you setting this up for me to take over?" He half-growls.

I can hear from his tone that he's not amused. That right now he must see this all as some sort of conspiracy, like I'm some conniving bitch pulling strings behind the scenes to get what I want.

I shake my head quickly. "No." I whisper.

He narrows his eyes before turning away and gesturing for Gunnar to follow him. When we walk into the dining room, I sit beside Preston and I don't say a word. I don't look at either of them.

I want so desperately to be anywhere other than where I am. And more than that, I hate the fact that he is here, in this place I considered a sanctuary.

Gunnar seems to talk away, discussing the alliance, how he wants to continue it as if Preston works for him now, as if the three of us are part of the same family.

I spoon a mouthful of food up, shovelling it in, and somehow manage to swallow.

When Preston slides his hand over my thigh, I physically jolt like I've been shot. Like someone has electrocuted me.

"Ruby?" He murmurs quietly, studying my face.

"She was always like that." Gunnar says leaning on his elbows. "She's skittish, aren't you, Ruby?" He teases.

I don't respond, I stare at a smear of gravy on the edge of my plate. This meal feels like it's taking forever and I know whatever point Gunnar is trying to make, he's not done it yet. Right now, it's just score pointing, him showing how much power he still has over me and how stupid I've been to pretend otherwise.

"Tell me, Preston, how are you finding her?"

"In what capacity?" Preston asks.

"As a wife, is she doing her duties. Is she satisfying you as you expect?"

I flush more. I clench my fists as Preston looks between us.

"What exactly are you asking?" He growls.

Gunnar shrugs before taking a long slurp of his wine. "Her mother was a whore, it's only expected that she acts like one too. If I were you I'd keep a close eye on her though because as soon as your back is turned, I guarantee she'll be fucking half your men."

I gasp. A tiny barely audible sound but it's all I can make. It feels like my throat is closing up with fear. It feels like every wall in this house is crashing down on me.

And a big part of me would welcome it.

To be buried.

To die here, under this rubble and never have to come back up again.

Preston draws himself up, and I can see he's furious now. "Do not ever speak of my wife like that." He snaps.

Gunnar smirks, looking at me then back at my husband. "I see she's charmed you then. Good work, Ruby, you were quick this time." He winks.

The chair screeches as Preston pushes it back. He gets to his feet, but as he does, his phone rings. You can feel the tension as he stares Gunnar down, as it's clear he wants to beat the shit out of him but something else is dragging him away.

"What?" He barks down the receiver.

Someone mumbles back from the other end.

Preston shuts his eyes, runs his hand over them then lets out a frustrated sound. "Fine." He hangs up before turning to me. "I have to go."

I nod, smiling as best I can, acting like it's no big deal when all I want to do is beg him to stay, or better, take me with him, take me out of this awful situation.

"Go." Gunnar says, leaning back in his chair. "There are some things I have to discuss with your wife. Matters about Levi that I'm sure would bore you."

"Do you want him to stay?" Preston asks me.

I want to scream, I want to tell him exactly what this is but my voice won't work, my fear is too great, it feels like I'm spiralling, reliving all that horror and I'm buried so deep in the darkness I don't know how to climb out.

"Go, Preston." Gunnar says. "Your wife will still be here to fuck when you get back."

He searches my face one last time, glances at Gunnar then lifts my jaw up to plant a chaste kiss on my lips. "I'll be as quick as I can." He states before walking out.

The minute the door shuts, the minute I'm alone, it feels like everything shatters.

"Isn't that sweet?" Gunnar says quietly. "He treats you like you're actually worthy of respect."

"Get out." I say, getting to my feet, grabbing the knife for good measure.

Gunnar laughs, moving quickly, and within seconds I'm fighting to get out of his grasp. He slams me down onto the same table we've all just been eating at and the plates rattle from the impact.

"Stupid little bitch." He spit, clawing the knife from my grasp. "Did you really think you could just ignore me forever?"

"You have no power over me." I hiss back.

He wrenches my hair back and it feels like my very scalp is on fire.

"Is that so, Ruby? You think you just slink off here, fuck Preston Civello and make a nice little life for yourself?" He snarls.

I whimper, digging my nails into his hands but he won't let go. He won't let up.

He pushes me back onto the wood, wrenching my dress up as I kick out, as I fight. "Stupid little whore." He says. "Did you forget who you belong to? Who really owns you…"

"I'm married to Preston." I gasp. "I belong to him now."

He laughs, undoing his zipper, getting his cock out as I try so hard to escape his grasp. "You belong to me, bitch, you always have."

He rams himself into me. He's not nearly the size that Preston is but the force of it and the brutality makes this so horrifically painful.

"I'm not yours." I cry. "I'm not."

He grabs my face, slamming it back into the wood. "I will break you if I have to. I will break every bone in your body, just like last time."

The air can't get in, my heart is racing too fast, my body is screaming in protest at what Gunnar is doing to me. My tears are streaming down my face but there's nothing I can do, just like always I'm helpless.

Pathetic.

"You belong to me, Ruby. You can't escape me."

I shut my eyes, hating that it's true, that even now, even here, in Preston's home, he's walked right in and can do whatever he wants.

I was a fool to believe I was safe, a fool to think this wouldn't happen.

His body presses into mine, his stench covers me. He groans as he comes and he wipes himself on my arse then steps back, assessing his handiwork.

"In two days' time you're going to meet with Eleri Morelli." He instructs. "You're going to take her out. There's a fancy new restaurant on Broad Street. You'll have lunch at noon and we'll be waiting."

My stomach knots. I can hear what he's not saying, that they're going for her, whether they're going to simply kill her or kidnap her, either way they're making moves and I'm the one who's going to set it all up.

He grabs my face, slamming it back into the table. "Did you hear me, Ruby?" He growls. "Did you hear what I said?"

I nod. "I heard you." I whisper.

"And if you don't do it, if you think you can ignore me again, I'll savage your body so badly you'll never recover. I'll toss you to my men and they can do what they want with you."

I gulp, hearing that same threat he's used before, the one he knows will work because I can barely take what he forces on me, how would I ever survive all his men as well?

I crumple to the floor, my body physically unable to take anymore.

He kicks me with his boot, sneering at how pathetic I am.

"Useless slut." He spits. "I've a good mind to put a bullet into your head and you can join the rest of your useless, rotting family."

I don't respond. I don't have anything left to fight this. He does his trousers back up, strides out and he leaves me there, on the floor.

Only, I can't stay here, I can't let Preston know what's happened. As quick as I can I cover myself up, wipe my face, putting down that mask I've created so carefully and I slip out of the room, up the stairs and force myself to wash, to clean, to make myself presentable for when my husband returns.

He can't know about this.

He can't realise what I really am.

I have to pretend better than I ever have before. I have to smile and lie better than ever.

Because my husband will kill me if he realises what this is, what I'm up to.

I know it in my heart.

He'll kill me and throw my body to the dogs.

Preston

CHAPTER Thirty-Seven

I didn't want to leave but I could hardly not when someone was going for our warehouses. I raced down, all guns blazing, only it turned out to be a false alarm.

The minute Jace gets there I can't hold back, I can't keep in my frustration. I slam my fist into his jaw and the impact sends him flying backwards.

"Next time you call me up, acting like something big is going on, you check first." I snap. I'm not some god damn lackey. I'm not some low level criminal used to racing around this city, trying not to be caught with my dick in my hands.

"Preston." He stammers but I cut across him.

"Sort this shit out." I growl, waving my hand to all the men who are stood waiting for orders after we burst in like there was a full on war inside.

He glances around then nods. "I'm on it boss." He murmurs.

"You better fucking be." I growl before turning around and heading back home.

It took me the best part of an hour to get out here. It'll take another god damn hour to get back. I hate the fact that Ruby is there, with Gunnar and though she didn't say anything, didn't seem to protest, the more I think about it, the more it sets my teeth on edge.

I grab my phone, calling up Noah, and he picks up after two rings. "Boss?"

"Go to my house." I order. "Gunnar is there with my wife. I want to make sure nothing happens."

It already feels too late.

In my gut it already feels like I've left her to the jackals and when Noah calls back barely ten minutes later, I know shit has gone down.

What have I done leaving her like that?

"What's he done?"

"He's left Boss." Noah says. "The house is empty."

"What?" I snarl, taking out my anger on the one man who isn't responsible.

"The lights are off. Sidney says she went to bed not long after you left."

It doesn't make sense. Something in my gut tells me that but if something had happened there would be evidence, and besides, Ruby wouldn't have just slinked off to bed. I know her too well now.

I get into my car, speed back across, jumping every red light, practically crashing my car in my haste. I all but smash my way through the gates and then I'm out, wrenching the door open, bellowing Ruby's name.

Only, I'm met with silence. Eery fucking silence.

I stalk up the stairs and Sidney meets me on the landing.

"Where is she?" I bark, "Where is my wife?"

"In bed," He says quickly, like he doesn't understand what all the commotion is about.

I push past, sprinting down the hall. I don't know what I'm expecting to find, I don't know what the hell has happened but every instinct in me is screaming out as I storm into our bedroom before coming to an abrupt stop.

She's curled up in bed, the covers all around her but I can tell she's not asleep.

"Ruby?"

She shifts, giving me a glimpse of her tearstained face and within seconds I'm there, wrapping my arms around her.

"What happened? Did he hurt you?" I ask. If he laid a finger on her, he's a dead man.

She sniffs, burying her face in my chest.

"Tell me, Ruby, tell me what's going on."

"I," She shakes her head and I can feel how much she's trembling. "I don't want to do it," She whispers so quietly.

"Do what?"

She starts sobbing more, becoming inconsolable and I tighten my grip. "It's okay, I've got you, I've got you." I repeat. I don't know what the fuck Gunnar did, what the fuck he said, but by the time this is all over, I'm going to make him pay for every insult he's inflicted on my wife.

"Preston," She gasps, clinging to me.

"You're okay." I state, "I've got you, I've always got you."

Ruby

CHAPTER
Thirty-Eight

I hide out, pretending to be sick but I don't think I'm fooling anyone.

Preston is being so careful around me and if anything, it makes it all worse. So much worse. I can't look him in the eyes. I can't even smile at him because I feel like a traitorous bitch.

But I also know I can't do it, I can't betray him.

Gunnar is going to hurt me, he's going to let his men hurt me too and though it puts the fear of god into me, I don't see any other way out of this.

On what is essentially judgement day, I say goodbye to Preston as normal and then as the hours slip by, I descend into what feels like complete and utter madness.

My chest tightens, my fear goes into a frenzy, I swear I'm having an actual heart attack and I find myself knocking back one drink after another. Paralysed by the thought of whichever way this plays out.

If I could, I would run, but Preston has already put paid to that idea – there's no escaping this house, no escaping whatever this day brings.

I know I'm meant to meet with Eleri but I have Sidney message, telling her that I'm sick.

She replies straight away that she can come over instead and I say no, fearing that if she does, if she comes here, then Gunnar may alter his plan to this location. That she'd still be in danger. And I can't have that.

Oh, I know Gunnar is going to make me pay, I know however this plays out, I'm dead, but I can't do it, I can't drag Eleri into it, I can't betray Preston after everything he's done for me.

No, sacrificing myself is the only option now.

I have no other cards left.

Preston

CHAPTER Thirty-Nine

No one knows we're coming. At least no one should.

And yet, as we take over the Holtz compound, there isn't a single person to stop us. A single man putting up a fight. It's like they just left the gates of Rome open and allowed the barbarians to waltz right in.

I frown, staring around, as an eery feeling settles in my bones. They should be fighting. They should be protecting this.

Where the fuck is Gunnar?

Where the fuck are all Levi's men?

There's no way they've simply fled and left all of this for us.

We stalk through into the main house, our footsteps echoing against the concrete walls.

The place is a shit-show, rubbish, furniture, you name it is strewn around like a tornado swept through.

"Over here."

I pick up pace, rushing to where Nico's voice came from and as I come to a stop on the threshold, I can't help but grin.

The room beyond is set up like a hospital suite. Machines that should be beeping away are all switched off. Syringes and medicine bottles are scattered across the floor. And in the middle, still hooked up to a dormant machine, in a massive bed, is the bastard himself.

His eyes are shut. His skin is a strange off white and the darkness beneath his eyes tells me what I already knew; he's dead. Levi is gone.

Blaine walks up to him, flickers one lid open and then slaps him around the face.

"Yeah, he's a goner." He states, like we all can't see it.

"I guess that answers it." Nico murmurs.

"Answers what?" I ask.

He looks over at me with a smirk. "Why the compound is deserted, no doubt Gunnar is regrouping, ensuring he has everything in place to take over."

I'll admit, I'm itching for this fight, itching to finally settle this. Ruby has been off for days now. I know she's not mourning Levi, I know that's not what's going on, but what better way to cheer her up than to tell her I've got it back, I've got back everything they stole from her, and that I'll be head of the Holtz Family, with her beside me.

My chest swells, my stupid heart reacts and I can see it, how she'll gasp, how she'll smile, how her entire face will light up.

Her comments the other day already told me enough – she wants this.

She wants me to do it.

In my pocket my phone buzzes, I pull it out, half expecting to see some message about Gunnar but as the words form in front of me, I frown. What the fuck?

My fingers fumble as I tap the screen, calling Jace back. "What the fuck are you talking about?" I growl down the phone the second he picks up.

"I'm sorry, boss." He says. "I didn't want to believe it either but it makes sense."

"I want proof." I need proof. I won't believe a word of it unless he can show me he's right.

"She's been passing on information for weeks." Jace says. "And today, she was meant to be meeting with Eleri. They were meant to have lunch, only the restaurant they're supposed to be eating at just blew up."

"Blew up?" I repeat. What the fuck does that mean? Is my wife dead? Is Ruby lying in the gutter right now?

"They didn't show. Perhaps she got cold feet."

"How do you know all of this?" I growl. Bit bloody convenient that he's got all the answers.

"Gunnar. He told me. You wanted me to chummy up to him and that's what I've been doing."

"I don't believe it." I state.

"Then talk to your wife." He replies. "Talk to Ruby. You'll know by how she reacts that it's true."

Oh, I'll talk to her alright. I'll prove that he's wrong. That my wife is innocent. That this is all bullshit.

Preston

CHAPTER *Forty*

I storm into the house. Though there were men on the gate, inside it's deserted.

Sidney meets me almost immediately, but I brush him out the way.

"Ruby." I holler. Where the fuck is she?

I search the library, the kitchen, everywhere that would make sense and just as my panic begins to rise, I find her, in the snug, sat in complete darkness.

For a moment I stand there, watching her, hearing that accusation in my head.

But she wouldn't do it, she wouldn't. I trust her. I trust what we have.

Ruby wouldn't betray me. Not like that.

I flick on a lamp and she flinches at the sudden brightness, shielding her face with her arm.

"Ruby?"

She looks up, her eyes unfocused but full of tears. She's sat on the floor between the couch and the coffee table. There's a bottle in her hand but I can see it's all gone. She's drunk the lot.

"I…" She slurs like she can't even string a sentence together because she's so damned inebriated.

"What's wrong?" I ask, fearing whatever words are going to come out of her mouth.

"I lied." She stammers. "I lied and I don't want to do it anymore."

"Lied about what?"

She drops her gaze, staring at her feet. "It wasn't supposed to be…" She hiccups. "He's going to be so mad at me."

"Who?" I growl.

"Gunnar." She barely whispers his name but it's like a damned stake in my heart.

This can't be happening. This can't be…

"What the fuck are you talking about?" I snap.

She shuts her eyes, trembling. "I didn't want to do it but he was trying to make me. He was trying to force me…"

"Force you to do what?" I snarl and then I hear the word I've been dreading, the word I never believed she'd speak. "Betray…" She gasps almost incoherently.

It's like everything shatters. Like my entire world crumbles around me and I don't think, I just react, hauling her to her feet.

Jace was right. Ruby is a mole.

The bottle slips from her grasp, smashing to the floor. She whimpers more, trying to bury her face into my chest, only, I won't let her.

My heart turns to stone as I realise how stupid I've been. I don't know how she got hold of anything of worth, perhaps I confided something – though I don't remember doing so…

Christ, did she ever even care for me or was that all an act? Was I so damned stupid to fall for a pretty face?

She can't walk. She can't even stand.

She must have drunk herself into a stupor to block out all the guilt about what she knew was going down today.

I pick her up, throw her over my shoulder, carrying her through the house and down into the basement.

I have a room down there. A cell for necessary moments like this.

I yank her arms above her, tying her wrists with rope, making sure my treacherous wife is properly secure to the chain that hangs down from a reinforced beam in the ceiling.

She isn't even fighting me as I do it. I lift her head and can see she's passed out.

As I let her go she drops forward, her arms taking the full weight of her body.

I roll my sleeves up, every ounce of love I felt for this woman turning, twisting into hate.

How the fuck could she do this?

How the fuck could she work for them? After what they did to her family?

I snarl, slapping her hard across the face. My hand leaves an imprint that's vivid across her cheek. I'm not above hurting women when it's needed, when it's called for. They may be called the fairer sex but they're just as capable of violence when the situation calls for it.

And my wife here is proof that they can be just as untrustworthy.

But somewhere deep inside, my heart twists, because I fell for it. I fell for this creature of deception.

She lets out a whimper as she comes back around. As her eyes focus on me she starts to tremble enough that the chain above her rattles.

She looks horribly drunk now, she looks like she's at the stage where she's not fully in control of herself and yet reality is biting so hard.

Her eyes dart about the stark room then they settle back on me. Fear flashes in them. Maybe it's finally hitting her how truly fucked she is.

She licks her lips, her hands twisting against the ties I know are cutting into her skin.

"What the fuck have you done, Ruby?" I growl.

She shakes her head.

"Tell me." I shout.

Her chest is rising and falling heavily. The little slip of a dress she has on should make me feel something akin to sympathy after everything we've been through, but right now, it just makes her look more like a she-devil.

"What were you lying about?" I ask. "What information did you pass onto Gunnar?"

She shakes her head more violently. "I didn't. I promise you, Preston…"

My hand slaps her again. I don't want to hear her pleas, I don't want to hear the way she says my name. She betrayed us, she openly admitted it and now, suddenly, she's trying to pretend otherwise?

"Please…"

"None of that." I growl. I don't want to hear how sorry she is. I don't want to hear her beg. There'll be time for that later. Right now, she needs to tell me how involved she is and what else Gunnar is up to.

"Did you help him plan the attack today?"

Her eyes widen. She gulps. "He didn't…" She swallows. "I tried to stop him."

"Like hell you did." I snarl.

She squirms in the restraints. Her body jerks. The chain twists and her feet lose traction on the floor. She kicks out falling backwards, crying out in pain as her arms take the full impact of it.

I grab hold of the front of her dress, yanking her back.

"If I have to beat the answers out of you, then I will." I say.

"I don't know anything." She cries. "I don't know what he did…"

I grab her jaw, forcing her to look at me. "You already told me you do." I state. "You already admitted you've been lying to me."

Her eyes flash with fear. She sobs harder but no matter how many times I slap her, she refuses to admit anything.

I step back, already knowing what I have to do, what will make the girl give me the answers I want.

Ordinarily, we have Blaine for this kind of work.

He likes to get his hands dirty.

But I'm just as effective as he is, though his methods might be more crazy than mine, when I need to, I know exactly how to extract information, how to make someone talk.

My phone rings in my pocket and I pick it up as I walk over to where the knives are hanging.

"Nico." I say.

"Where the fuck are you?" He asks. I pretty much stormed out of the compound without a word, too desperate to get to my wife, too eager to prove that Jace was wrong, that Ruby wouldn't fuck me over like that.

God, what a fool I've been. What a complete fucking idiot.

"You need to get here." I reply.

"Where?"

"My house." I turn around, making eye contact with my wife. Her gaze drops to the blade in my hand and I see her head shake again. "Ruby is involved."

"What?"

"Just get here." I hang up before I have to say anything further. If I hold off on this, if I don't take this step now, I know my foolish love for this woman will override all sense and I won't be able to do what is necessary; I'll be as much of a traitor to Nico as my wife is.

"Preston." She whimpers.

"This is your last chance, Ruby." I say holding the blade in a way that I know will scare her the most. "Tell me everything you know or so help me god I will cut every last secret out of you."

She screws her face up. "I didn't… please you have to believe me."

Only, I'm done hearing her excuses, hearing her pathetic attempt to try to trick me.

Does she think I'm so stupid I'd believe her?

Does she think that she's dug her claws into me that deep that it will override my loyalty to Nico?

She's not who I thought she was.

She's not the woman I fell in love with.

This woman here is all Gunnar's creature and none of mine.

She bites her lip at first slice of the blade, like she's refusing to make a sound, but within seconds she gives in, screaming, jerking, trying to get away.

"It's very simple, Ruby." I say, keeping that ice cold grip on my heart, refusing to let my love for this woman override my senses. Override my loyalty. "Tell me what you know and all of this will end."

"I don't know anything." She screams.

I take another cut. Another awful slash down her back. Crimson blood flows over her perfect skin, mingling with the sweat and the dirt at her feet.

And yet still, the woman refuses to talk.

By the time Nico bursts through the door, she's covered in blood. It's dripping from her body as she hangs limply from the chain.

"Fuck." Nico growls.

"She knows." I say, turning to face him. "She knows everything."

"What has she said?"

I shake my head because somehow my wife seems to be the strongest fucking person I've ever met, she hasn't said a thing, nothing beyond pleas and whimpers. I even tried whipping her to see if that would make her talk but she gave me nothing.

Not a word beyond her screams.

He narrows his eyes, stepping up to her. I'm not even sure she knows he's in the room. He grabs her face staring at her dazed, unfocused eyes.

"Ruby." He says. "Talk to me and all of this will end."

She sobs, shuddering. "That's all I wanted. I just wanted it to end."

"What?" I ask.

She looks at me but it's like she isn't really registering me, like she doesn't have the energy to focus beyond the tip of her nose.

"How much blood has she lost?" Nico asks.

I shrug. It wasn't like I was keeping count. I needed answers. I *still* need answers. And as yet, my darling wife has given me nothing.

Nico drops his hold, pulling his phone out, dialling a number I know is for the doctor. When he hangs up he turns back to face me. "You're certain she's involved?"

"Yes." I snap. "She told me Gunnar…" I trail off as my mind suddenly registers that he was here. He came to this damned house.

Is that when he told her what to do, is that how he communicated it all? He came up with a plan and then got his little bitch to play her part?

I all but shove Nico out of the way, grabbing her by the throat as I put my face right into hers. "He was here." I state. "He came to this house, didn't he?"

Her eyes widen, more fear than I thought possible shows in those beautiful irises.

"What did you tell him, Ruby? What exactly did you divulge?"

"He didn't…"

I let out a laugh, stepping back. She can deny it all now. "I have footage of it." I state. "I have this entire house under surveillance."

She starts trembling like I'm about to catch her in some new lie -and we both know that I am.

"Preston…" She gasps.

I tilt my head. Here we fucking go.

"Please, please don't watch that."

"Why the fuck would I not?" I reply.

She shuts her eyes, her breath coming so fast like she's having a full blown panic attack. "I don't want you to see." She whispers, hanging her head.

"Bit fucking late for that." I state. I'll see it alright, I'll witness every moment of her treachery and she'll no longer be able to deny it.

"Please…" She begs as Nico jerks his head at me and I storm out.

Whatever the fuck she's hiding, we're about to find it all out now.

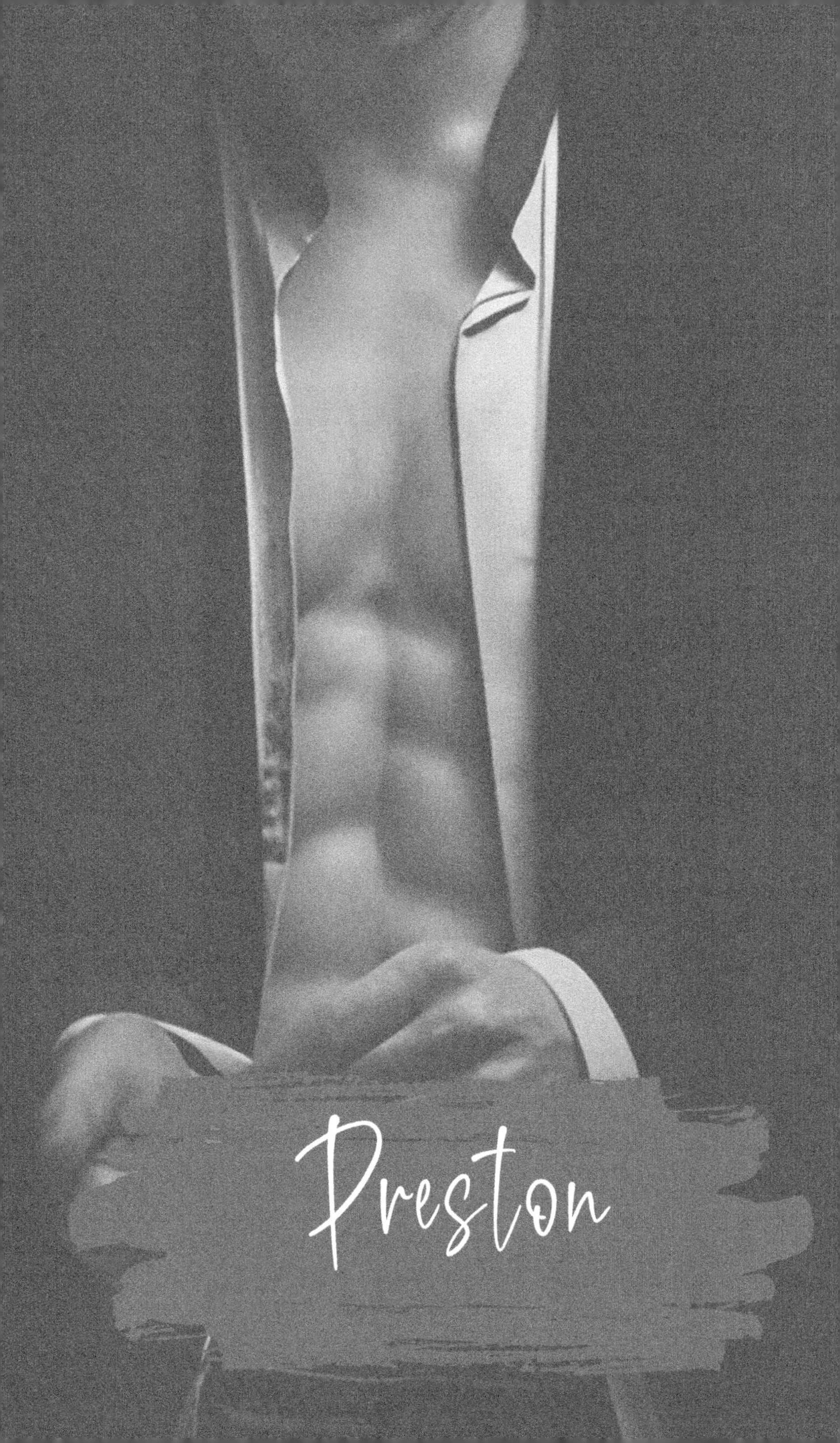

Preston

CHAPTER
Forty-One

The surveillance room is the other side of the basement. I cut across it, not caring that my own hands are dripping blood.

Ruby's blood.

When I tap in the code, the door clicks open. My phone has access to an app for the livestream but all the old footage can only be viewed here, from the main database.

I tap in the date, scanning through the files. It takes me barely a minute to find the time I'm looking for.

My hand smears blood across the keyboard. My fingers drip blood into the indents of the mouse. At least once I know the truth, I can confront Ruby and all of this will be over. She'll admit what she's done.

She'll crumble and then, and only then, will I let the doctor see to her.

My phone rings, buzzing in my pocket.

I snatch it up, grunting down the microphone to whoever it is while hitting play then fast forward. There must be twenty minutes of my interaction with Gunnar before I leave and the juicy bit plays out.

"Boss?" Noah says.

"What?" I growl back.

"He's gone."

"Who's gone?" I ask, losing my damned patience. Like I have time for cryptic games.

"Jace."

"What…?"

"He fled. Took an entire crate of diamonds with him."

"What the fuck are you talking about?" I ask, dropping my gaze from the screen. Why the fuck would Jace do that? Why…

"We think he's been tipping them off, whoever is behind the attacks on Levi's shipments."

What? Why? What does Jace have to do with any of this?

My eyes dart back to the screen. At what I so stupidly misunderstood. At what I so stupidly believed was some plot between Ruby and Gunnar.

I had high definition cameras installed, so not only is the picture crystal clear but the sound is absolutely perfect too.

And if anything it makes what I'm watching that much more horrific.

He's attacking her. He's assaulting her right here, in my home.

Why the fuck did she never tell me? Why the fuck did she hide this from me?

My heart hammers in my chest. My stomach drops. I step back, seeing the blood all over me with new eyes.

Ruby's blood.

Ruby.

I did that. I fucking tortured her.

She wasn't disloyal. She didn't betray me. If anything I'm the one who betrayed her.

"Boss?"

I don't reply. I just hang up, running back down the corridor, back to where my wife is bound, and injured and scared out of her life.

"Ruby." I yell, as I burst into the room. Nico looks at me. Ruby can't even lift her head.

Fuck, I'm a monster.

I'm everything my wife has spent her entire life trying to escape.

It feels like entire world collapses around me and I know all of this, all this horror is of my own making.

Ruby

CHAPTER

Forty-Two

I hear him calling my name but I can't move.

I don't have the strength to even raise my head.

Everything hurts so much.

I can feel my blood still trickling down my back. I can feel my body shaking so hard that the metal holding me up is rattling like some macabre symphony above my head.

"What is it?" Nico asks my husband, only he doesn't reply, he just crouches down in front of me like he's finally seeing me as a person, like he's finally seeing every horrific part of me. Every bit I've tried to keep hidden.

"How long?" He asks.

I gulp, not wanting to admit it.

"How long?" He snarls.

"From the beginning." I whisper.

He lets out what sounds like a groan of pain, curling his hand into a fist and he slams it into the solid concrete floor.

"What is it?" Nico repeats again but Preston doesn't answer.

His hands reach up, he unhooks me from the chain, unties me carefully, holding me far more considerately than he was tying me up. I collapse into him with my body far too heavy for me to keep upright.

My head hurts so much from all the alcohol and the amount of blows to my face.

One of my eyes is swollen so big I can't even open it properly. My lip is split and I can taste the blood on my tongue.

But it's nothing compared to the state of my back.

To how my husband has tortured and mutilated my flesh.

"What is going on?" Nico growls.

Preston stares at me like some part of him doesn't want to speak it, to betray this new horror that I've buried so deep.

"He was raping her." He says.

Nico turns his head, staring from me to Preston. "Who was?"

"Gunnar."

Preston doesn't quite meet my eyes as he carries me up out of the basement and back up the stairs and despite myself, I cling to him, I wrap my hands around the softness of his shirt like my life depends upon it.

When we reach the master suite, my eyes widen. I can't understand why he's carried me back here and not simply dumped me in one of the spare rooms. Am I not disgusting to him? Am I not repulsive?

Seconds later, Nico walks in, followed by a man I know is the doctor. His eyes widen just a little at the state of me but he clearly keeps whatever is in his head to himself.

He's quick to pull out his bag, to start stemming the bleeding, to preparing a needle which he tells me will numb the pain, like that's ever helped me before.

I lay on my front, half dazed as he stitches my skin back together, piece by bloody piece.

Preston is there, standing, arms crossed, watching like his entire world is over.

"I have to get back." Nico says.

Preston looks across at him and nods.

"I want to know how she is." He states, fixing Preston with a look I can't read.

Again, my husband nods and then Nico Morelli looks at me, his eyes narrowed, not in hate, not in anger, but concern, like I deserve it, like I'm someone such a man as him might care about.

He turns and walks out and as if that's the permission I need, I let the pain and the tiredness take me.

I let the heaviness sweep over everything.

I let myself succumb to sleep, hoping that maybe I won't wake.

That maybe god is finally done with me.

That whatever awful things I did in another lifetime, my debt is now paid and I'll be reborn into a new life, one not full of hardship, of pain, of the worst unimaginable fear that never seems to cease.

Preston

CHAPTER Forty-Three

I can't take my eyes from her. I can't bear to let her out of my hold.

She whimpers in pain and I know it's my fault.

That I did this.

I'm the worst kind of monster imaginable.

How could I ever believe it, how could I ever even think she'd do such a thing?

I get up, grabbing the meds the doctor left and draw up a syringe. Apparently pills won't cut it when you've done the kind of damage I have.

Her face is screwed up. Half of it is black with swelling from where my hands have laid into her.

I wish I could take it back, I wish I could take it all back and start again but it's too late. It's far too fucking late.

I pull the cover off, trying to be as delicate as I can but she still wakes as the needle slips into her skin. I hear the hiss, I hear the whimper, and I press the plunger down quickly before pulling it out.

"I'm so sorry." I say for what feels like the thousandth time.

But I could say it a thousand times more, a million times more, and it still would not be enough.

I brush her hair back from her face, her brow is sweaty like she has a fever. She flinches at my touch, trying to move away and for that, I can't blame her.

I grab a damp cloth and carefully dab her skin. "I won't hurt you." I murmur soothingly. "I'll never hurt you."

"But you did."

Her words cut through me worse than any knife.

I steal my breath, trying to explain what the fuck I was thinking, "I thought you were a mole. I thought…"

"I told you." She cries. "I told you over and over."

"I'm so sorry." I say again. I don't know how to make her believe me, I don't know how to fix this. If I even can fix this.

She whimpers again and I know the pain meds aren't kicking in, that even with that, I'm not helping her.

"Tell me what to do." I say. "Tell me. I'll do anything to make this right."

Her tears start to fall at those words. "There's nothing you can do." She whispers.

I choke, grabbing hold of her, hugging her so tightly in my desperation. "I won't let you go. You're my wife. I won't let you leave me."

Only, those words make her cry harder. Instead of comfort, it feels like a curse.

I'm damning us both in this moment.

Condemning us both.

I don't let her go, I don't release her from my grasp until I can hear from her breathing that she's fallen asleep once more. It's going to take weeks, maybe even months for all the damage to heal.

I'll pay whatever I have to, I'll find the best doctors to treat her, I'll jump through whatever hoops she says to fix this.

I just need my wife back.

I need her back.

When she wakes again, I can see she's not all with it. That the drugs are having full effect.

Her eyes struggle to focus, she keeps licking her lips, wetting them with her tongue.

I hold a glass for her to sip and she does it more out of instinct than anything else. Taking huge gulps, her throat bobbing as she swallows again and again.

"He wanted me to seduce you." She says quietly. "He wanted me to make you fall in love with me but that's not what happened." She gasps. "I fell in love with you. Almost from the start, I loved you. I loved you."

I cup her cheek, hating the way she flinches from my touch.

She used the past tense and not present.

My head already tells me what that means, that I've destroyed that too, that my actions have decimated any feelings she had for me.

I don't deserve her love, I don't deserve anything from her.

"Why didn't you tell me?" I ask. "Why didn't you say what Gunnar was doing, how he was hurting you?"

She screws her face up as more tears fall. "I couldn't. You were a stranger, and by the time you weren't, I knew you'd despise me. What sort of a man wants a wife like that?" She spits like she's disgusting, like she's so full of self-loathing she can't even think straight. "I couldn't tell you. I couldn't trust you."

I hang my head, hating myself because I should have seen this, how the fuck did I not see all this? It was right under my god damn nose this entire time.

"I was loyal to you. I was. When he came round…" She trails off her face contorting into something horrific. "He put a phone in amongst the boxes they dropped off but I hid it. I didn't communicate with him once, that's why he showed up here."

"Where did you hide it?"

She licks her lips, "In the library. I turned it off, put it behind the copy of 'Huckleberry Finn'."

Her eyes glaze over, she shuts them for a second like they're too heavy to keep open.

All this talking isn't helping her.

She's not resting right now, she's using far too much energy trying to explain herself.

"Sleep, Ruby." I say, wanting to touch her, wanting to hold her hand, to comfort her but I don't dare.

"You were so kind." She whispers. "I expected you to be like them. I expected you to treat me like he did."

"I will never hurt you." I say but I hear the awful lie in that, because I did, I hurt her worse than any of her family did. "I will protect you, Ruby, from now on you'll never have to be afraid again."

She doesn't look at me, she has her eyes shut fully.

I can't tell if she's asleep but the tears are still falling.

She's still crying even now.

Preston

CHAPTER
Forty-Four

"How is she?"

I don't reply.

My wife is broken.

She has been for a long time.

And instead of taking those broken pieces and helping to put them back together, I took a sledge hammer to them and shattered her into smithereens.

I'm not sure she will ever recover and I certainly don't deserve to keep her if she does.

I slam my fist into the wall.

How the fuck did I not see this?

I knew she was traumatised, I knew she was scared of me to start with but I thought it was because of what she'd witnessed all those years ago. I thought it was just that.

I never considered they would have hurt her in such a way.

"I'm going to kill him. I'm going to gut him." I state.

"Then sit down." Blaine says, grinning. "Because we have a plan."

I narrow my eyes, staring from him, to Nico, to Eleri.

"Go on." I growl but I don't sit. I'm too angry to sit. Too angry to stay still.

Eleri's looking at me like I'm an absolute piece of shit and I know I deserve every second of her derision.

"We found where Gunnar is hiding." Nico says, leaning over the table.

I narrow my eyes, still not convinced by the fact he's simply up and leaving. It's too simple, too easy. He's invested too much into Levi's empire to wash his hands and let us take it.

"There's a shipment going out tomorrow. Enough diamonds for him to set himself up. It's not taking the usual routes but…"

I barely hear the words because I don't give a shit about diamonds, I don't give a shit about anything beyond the woman lying, half dead in my bed because of me.

"We're going to be there, waiting for him."

I stare back at Nico, visualising what he's saying, "He'll have men." I state.

"We'll have more." Blaine grins.

"And after tomorrow, you'll be head of the Holtz Family." Nico declares.

I want to wince at that, to react with guilt, I have no right to such a position and yet, I'm still Ruby's husband, if I can win this for her, if I can get back her birthright maybe that will help atone for my sins.

"What about Jace?" I ask.

I want him hunted down too, I want him strung up, I want him to suffer just as much as Gunnar for what he's done.

"We're still looking." Blaine states. "Fucker got away but we'll have him soon enough."

Soon enough isn't good enough.

Every second that man breathes, every moment he is free is an insult to my wife, a further knife in her back.

I open my mouth to state it and Nico gives me a look to shut the fuck up. Apparently, right now they're more concerned with the diamonds than giving my wife the justice she deserves.

Eleri starts laying out the map, detailing exactly how it's going to go down. Who's going to be where.

I stand mute, watching it play out, while making no input.

And when we're done, I head straight out the door, not bothering to even say goodbye.

I know Ruby will be awake, I know she'll be wondering where I am, and though I had my reasons to leave the house, it doesn't feel enough.

Ruby

CHAPTER Forty-Five

I know he's here. I can feel his presence filling up all the dark spaces in the room.

As I shift to get more comfortable, he's right beside me, fluffing the pillows, trying to help.

And then our eyes connect.

The bruising around my face has gone down enough so that I can at least see properly but I'm quick to drop my gaze.

"Ruby," He murmurs, taking my hand, asking what I need, if I'm hungry, if I'm thirsty and I can't bear it. The tone, the desperation, any of it.

"You tortured me."

I don't mean to say it, to voice it, but the words slip out anyway.

"I'm so sorry." He says, "I'm so fucking sorry."

I don't reply. There's nothing I can say.

On some level I get it, if he truly believed I was the traitor, then I deserved everything I got, I deserved a bullet to the head.

But the joke is, it wasn't me, despite how much Gunnar was trying to make me do it, despite everything, I trusted Preston, I gave him my loyalty and he didn't hesitate to turn on me.

"Did Levi know what Gunnar was doing?" He asks. "Did he let him…"

"No." I say, cutting across him. "I don't think anyone knew. Though I'm not sure if he'd have done anything if he did."

"He's going to pay for it, he's going to pay for everything he's done." Preston spits.

I can hear the fury in his voice, the venom too.

I shut my eyes, feeling like this cycle of pain and death never seems to end. It never seems to stop. I really was fooling myself these few months, believing that I could ever have something as unachievable as happiness.

Looking back, I should have played it differently, should have known that such a life was not for me. Instead of running I should have just ended it. Taken a side exit. Killed myself and spared everyone else all this trouble. Preston would have been fine without me, Levi would have died anyway, and Jett, wherever he is, well, he wouldn't have cared, probably he would have been relieved not to pretend anymore, not to have to waste anymore time on me.

I let out a long exhale, one that sends a flash of white-hot pain through my spine, and once more those useless tears slide down my cheeks.

"Just do it." I whisper.

"Do what?" He asks.

"Kill me. Get it over with."

He reacts like he's the one in pain, like he's been shot. "Why the fuck would I do that?" He snarls.

I start crying harder, my tears becoming an uncontrollable sob. "Please, just end it. I want it to end. I want it to stop. I can't do it anymore…"

He growls, wrapping his arms around me like it might bring me comfort.

"I'll make it stop." He states. "I'll protect you. I'll never let anyone hurt you again."

Those words should be a comfort.

They should help soothe everything, only if anything, they make it worse.

I start choking up, crying for the girl I was, the stupid naïve idiot who saw this man as my saviour, who saw this marriage as my chance of survival.

"I'll let you get some rest." He says once I've cried myself into exhaustion.

I turn, knowing that rest will not come.

Peace will not come.

I need pain meds. I need water.

When I voice that, he's quick to leave, quick to get the pills and a glass.

He pops them out of the blister pack, sliding each one into my mouth and raising the glass, helping me to drink.

When he puts the glass back on the stand, I can tell he feels as helpless as me right now.

THE COVERS ARE WRAPPED AROUND ME WHEN I WAKE. BUT THAT'S not the only thing. Preston's arms are holding me, keeping my body pressed into his so tightly.

The pain is there, my back is in agony and my face is throbbing.

I try to stifle the whimper but I can't hold it back and it comes out as a pained sob. My husband tries to soothe me, only, I can't help but flinch from his touch.

Afterall, he did this, he tortured me.

With regret in his eyes, he gets up and crouches beside the bed, staring at my face.

"I'm so sorry." He says for what must be the millionth time.

Only, apologies won't fix this.

Apologies won't undo the damage, won't heal my flesh.

And I think it's worse hearing him say it, hearing the strong, possessive man that I've grown used to, sounding so broken.

Preston

CHAPTER
Forty-Six

I hate leaving her. I hate walking out that door, knowing that I'm not there to protect her.

But in this, I have no choice.

I'm going to make Gunnar pay for what he's done, make him truly suffer. And maybe then that will be enough.

The stupid fuck saunters into the yard like he owns the place. Like this city is his and not ours. He only has a few dozen men beside him and it takes barely a minute before we have them subdued and disarmed.

Of course Gunnar smirks up at me like he thinks I can't do shit and when I land that first punch, it feels more than satisfying to hear the crunch of his nose shattering.

We toss him into the back of a van.

His men we dispose of because why the fuck would we trust them?

I'm half tempted to drag him back to my house, to let Ruby witness this moment, to let her see justice being melted out, only, I think the sight of him will do more harm than good, and besides, she can't leave her bed and I sure as hell am not letting him anywhere near our room.

So instead, we take him to Blaine's residence.

He naturally has an entire outbuilding dedicated to enacting every kind of imaginable and unimaginable pain and he delights in showing me all the fancy machinery he's created. Apparently the man likes to experiment.

While I'm tempted to put some of it to use, I brush it aside.

I want this to be personal.

I want to deliver every cut, every bruise with my own hands. I want to feel every moment of this, remembering how I hurt my wife, and how this fucker hurt her more.

The room he's in is bare, cold, with a perfect stream of light coming down from the skylight.

I prowl around the edges, keeping to the shadows. I can see in his eyes that he still thinks he can beat me.

I want to kill that hope, I want to beat it out of him, break him the way he broke my wife.

I pick up a wrench, feeling the weight of it, as I take aim, he seems to brace himself and as the metal crunches against his bone, he lets out a more than satisfying groan of pain.

But it isn't enough.

It will never be enough.

I could hold this man here, could torture him from now until the very end of time and it would still not grant Ruby the justice she deserves.

'He wanted me to seduce you.'

Ruby's words repeat in my head. That he planned this, he forced her to be his spy knowing exactly what I would do when I found out.

He sent her off like a sacrificial lamb, not giving a fuck what happened to her.

I guess the only fuck up was Levi dying along the way.

But then, was that really a fuck up? If Ruby was taken off the board, then Gunnar was perfectly positioned to take over.

I grip his jaw, pushing hard against the pressure points. "Where you behind it?" I ask. "Did you make it look like Levi had a stroke?"

He laughs back, and all the saliva and blood collecting in his mouth makes a gurgling sound.

"Finally figured it out?" He spits. "Wondered what took you so long. I even left you the evidence to find..."

The phone. The fucking phone - he did that on purpose. He left it like breadcrumbs for me to follow.

Fury explodes in my head.

He wanted me to do it. He wanted me to attack Ruby.

He wanted me to think that she was the traitor because then she'd no longer be a threat, and I, in turn, wouldn't have any cause to fight him for Head of the Family.

Is that why Jace did what he did, why he made sure I'd act?

My fist slams into his face, I feel the crunch of my own knuckles as I make impact and while some part of my brain says I'm being stupid to be using my bare hands, I need this pain, I deserve this pain.

I've been a fucking idiot.

I've been a complete fool.

And it's Ruby who's suffered because of me.

His head swings back, I swear his neck almost snaps but he grins back at me. "You really thought she was something, didn't you?" He taunts. "The way you looked at her, you fell for the stupid whore…"

He can't finish his sentence before I'm swinging for him once more.

"How does it feel, Preston, knowing I broke her in, I had your wife first?"

"You're going to pay." I spit, reaching for the wrench. "For every bruise, every cut, every moment you took from her."

He groans, jerking in the chair but there's nothing he can do to escape me.

I know somewhere in the shadows Nico is watching. I know part of him wants his own revenge right now, after all, Ruby is his god daughter and this piece of shit defiled her for years.

"How many times?" I bellow. "How many times did you touch her? Did you rape her?"

He smirks, his shattered teeth dripping blood down his chin. "She liked being my whore." He states as if I'd believe it.

I grab the pliers from the side, force his mouth open and start ripping out his teeth, one by one. I don't need answers from him. I don't need words.

All I want is pain.

His pain.

My pain.

It doesn't matter.

Nothing matters.

We throw his body into the incinerator, and I stand back watching the flames, imagining it's the very pits of hell swallowing him up.

"We'll make an announcement in the morning." Nico murmurs.

"About what?"

"You being head of the Holtz Family."

I don't respond. I just turn and stalk away. Like I give a shit about diamonds, about power, about anything.

None of that matters to me anymore.

The only thing I care about is my wife, about earning her forgiveness, about proving that she can trust me, and earning back her love.

Ruby

CHAPTER
Forty-Seven

I can hear someone moving about, walking about.

I open my eyes as much as I can and my heart thumps as I see it's not my husband. He's not the one in my bedroom right now.

He crouches down, narrowing his eyes, brushing back my hair from my face as I hiss in pain.

"What the fuck happened?" Jett asks.

I gulp, shutting my eyes. How is he here? How did he get in? Preston has this house guarded better than Fort Knox.

"He did this, didn't he?" He spits. "Your husband did this."

I wish I could say otherwise. I wish I could shout out that that's a lie, that Preston would never hurt me, but I can't.

He shakes his head, snarling, before he scoops me up and with the drugs still in my system I can't fight him.

More pain racks through my body at the way he's holding me and I cry out.

"I don't want to..." I begin and he curses, cutting across me.

"Enough, Ruby. He's done enough."

He carries me out of our bedroom, down the stairs and my eyes widen as I see the bodies, as I see the people who used to smile at me, who used to fetch me tea, who helped take care of me.

When my eyes find Annabell lying lifeless, face down in a pool of blood, I can't properly register it. I can't believe it.

"What have you done?" I cry.

"What was necessary." He snaps back.

I try to get free, I jerk in his arms and the cuts on my back seem to rip open with every move I make.

"Let me go, Jett. Please." I beg.

"I'm taking you away," He says, acting like he's helping me. "I'm taking you somewhere you'll be safe."

I scream out, pummelling my fists into his chest as my back rips more.

When we step outside there are more bodies, all the guards are dead. He's killed them all.

A man walks up to us, needle in hand and Jett nods quickly.

"No." I scream.

"Get on with it." Jett snaps and I shut my eyes as I feel the thing spike me, as I feel them drugging me so that I'll be easier to steal.

I WAKE IN A PANIC.

Everything comes flooding back as I look around the strange space I'm in. Someone rebandaged my wounds. Someone has wrapped my entire torso up and I realise with a sickening feeling that they stripped me while I was unconscious.

"Hey baby."

My eyes snap to my right.

For a second my head won't register that it's her. That she's there. Another ghost from my past has suddenly resurrected herself.

"Momma?" My voice cracks as I say the word I haven't spoken in over five years.

She looks good. She looks really good. The rich patterned material of her dress makes her dark skin glow. Her hair is braided so intricately and she has huge diamond and gold dangly earrings that catch the light.

"It's me, baby, it's me." My mother says, getting up from the seat she's no doubt kept a vigil at, and she hugs me tight enough that my back protests.

"How, how is this possible?" I sob.

First Jett and now her? How is my family alive? How have they never even reached out or tried to help me until now?

"I ran baby, after Levi attacked us, I ran." She states.

"You left me behind." I say, before I can stop myself.

She nods, wiping a tear. "I had no choice. He took everything, he murdered your father."

"Like I don't know." I snap. "I saw his body. I saw him, lying there, with half his face blown off."

"I'm so sorry, baby." She says, taking my hand, soothing me.

"You left me." I say again.

"I couldn't get you out."

"Did you even try?" I ask.

She meets my gaze then drops it and that tells me all I need to know.

That she didn't.

She didn't even attempt it.

She put her own life above mine, decided I wasn't worth risking her own skin for.

My anger flares, the grief that I've carried all this time twists inside me. "Was Jett with you this entire time?" I ask.

She nods. "We got out of the country, we had allies in Europe who we knew could help us."

"What about me?" I scream, as my anger suddenly takes over. "What about me?"

She wrings her hands, her face contorting with guilt. "Levi had you. We couldn't get you out, to even try would be…"

"What?" I cut across her. "What would it be?"

She gets up turning her back to me, staring out the window as if it's suddenly all too much for her. As if she expected this reunion to go better, that I'd be so overjoyed she's alive, I'd overlook the fact she left me for the jackals.

"Do you know what they did?" I ask. "Do you know how they treated me?"

"I couldn't do anything, Ruby." She says so calmly, like my pain means nothing to her. "I would have, believe me."

"I don't." I say crossing my arms, feeling the way my skin protests at how my muscles move underneath it. "You left me to Levi, you let them hurt me, beat me, rape me."

"No." She hisses, covering her ears like that will make it all go away.

"You did that," I shout. "You let them do that."

The door slams open. Jett comes in as if he's suddenly her loyal defender, her knight in shining armour.

"You're awake." He says, stopping at the end of the bed. "How are you feeling?"

"How, how am I feeling?" I repeat, looking from him to her.

Is this a joke? Is this all some god awful joke?

"I feel like shit." I scream. "I just found out that she's alive, that you both have been, and apparently you were safe and well this entire fucking time."

"Ruby." My mother says, telling me off like I'm still a child. Like she has the right to parent me.

"You need to calm down." Jett states.

"No." I say, pushing my body up, forcing myself to move. "I need to go back. You're taking me back."

I can't trust these people. I can't trust anyone.

My legs sway under me as I force myself to stand.

I'm wearing a pair of shorts so at least my bottom half is decent. My head spins for a second and I grab hold of the bedside table to steady myself.

"Not a chance." My mother says dismissively.

"You really want to go back to him?" Jett sneers. "After what he did to you?"

"You're one to talk." I growl. "You abandoned me, you left me for dead. I doubt you cared what happened to me."

"We couldn't get you out." My mother says.

"Did you even try?" I say, as my tears spill down my cheeks.

She sinks onto the edge of the bed and, as she places her hand on my arm, I jerk away.

"Don't you dare fucking touch me." I hiss.

"I see you've picked up his foul language then." She mutters.

"Along with a few other things." Jett adds.

"Like what?" I spit.

"Like your husband's blind loyalty for Nico Morelli." Jett replies.

"What does that have to do with anything?" I ask. "At least he knows what the word means."

My mother shakes her head, scoffing. "You stupid girl." She says. "You have no idea, do you?"

"No idea about what?" There are more secrets? More revelations they want to just drop on me?

"Nico Morelli is the reason all this happened." Jett states. "He's the reason our father got killed. He's the reason Levi has gotten away with it so long."

I blink, staring at her for a second before I start laughing. They're mad. They have to be.

My mother leans over and slaps me hard across the face. I gasp out feeling like my brain slams into my skull. My cheek is still heavily bruised from what Preston did. How I don't collide with the wall I don't know.

"You didn't have to do that." Jett says quietly.

"Yes, I did." She snaps back. "If Ruby won't act like an adult..."

"An adult?" I repeat, scowling.

"Nico had the power to stop everything." My mother says. "He knew what Levi was going to do. I told him. And instead of helping us, he sat by and watched it happen."

I narrow my eyes, not believing a word of it. Besides, even if he did know, it wasn't Nico's place to step in. He had no links to our family, he bore us no allegiance.

Rival families rarely got involved when an internal war broke out. It was always safer to stay out of it and wait for the victor to emerge.

"And when it was all over he washed his hands." She adds. "He didn't try to help. He did nothing to save you."

"Why would he?" I ask. She's making him the villain when the reality is, she's the one who let me down. She's the one who left me. Her own flesh and blood.

"He's your godfather, Ruby." She says, jabbing her finger right in my face. "He swore to your father that he'd look after you. Look after us."

"What?"

"They had a pact, the pair of them. He'd be your godfather but when you came of age he was meant to marry you."

My eyes widen. Nico Morelli? I was meant to marry him? My stomach churns, not because the man is disgusting but the thought of it, of being with someone other than Preston makes me feel physically sick.

"And then Levi came along and offered him a juicy carrot. A nice way to soothe his conscience after the deed was done."

"They had an alliance." I say.

My mother laughs, she throws her head back and laughs like this is all just a big joke. "Levi needed Morelli more. We've been taking back everything he stole. The mines, the businesses, he's haemorrhaging funds just to keep himself afloat. That's why he had you sold off, he knew we were getting close so he made sure you were placed well out of our reach."

"He's dead. Levi is dead." I say. "He had a stroke."

They look at each other in shock. Apparently, that's news to them.

"So it's over." My mother grins. "The bastard bowed out before I could gut him."

"Gunnar has taken over." I spit.

"Gunnar isn't a threat." Jett says waving his hand. "He never was. The man's a thug, a coward. No one would follow him."

"Yeah?" I say, taking a step towards them as my fury turns to icy rage. "You know what else he is brother? You know what else that man did?"

He frowns, shaking his head slightly.

"It doesn't matter." My mother says, talking over me like what I have to say it's even worth their time. "It's over. All of it is over. We have won."

"It's over?" I repeat. "That man raped me for years. He brutalised my body in the worst ways…"

"Enough." My mother says, drawing herself up, clapping her hands together. "Enough. I don't want to hear it. It doesn't matter."

I don't think. I don't even care about the consequences, I launch myself at her, clawing at her face. "You did that. You allowed that to happen." I scream as she tries to fight me off.

Jett wraps his arms around my body, pulling me back and I kick hard, trying to throw him off.

"She's feral." My mother says, standing back, staring down at me like I disgust her. She has a long scrap down her cheek from where my nails made contact and I can see the blood beading up on the surface.

"What do you expect?" Jett says, tossing me back onto the bed. "She's been living with Preston Civello."

I land in a heap, my heart is racing, I'm panting as the adrenaline floods through my body. I know I've moved too much, that I've torn through whatever tiny bit of healing my back has done.

"Get the doctor." My mother barks.

I don't try to get back up, I just lay there as what feels like a lifetime worth of grief and despair hits me.

"What has she done?" A man says walking over, grabbing hold of me.

"Don't touch me." I hiss. I'm sick of them all manhandling me, touching me as if I'm just an object they can pass around and treat as they see fit.

Jett tuts, grabbing my arms, stopping me from getting away as the stranger starts undoing the bandages.

"I told you her skin needs time to heal. She needs constant bedrest until it does or she risks infection."

"Tell that to my sister." Jett says, meeting my gaze as I glare at him.

My mother leans down, squatting in front of my face as second by second the man strips me back to topless.

"You used to be such a good girl, Ruby. You used to be so well behaved." She says.

I bite my tongue, thinking about all the other things I used to be too. All the things that were stolen away, all the things I endured while she picked up her skirts and ran like a coward.

"You're not to speak of the past." She continues. "I don't want to hear what you went through. I don't want to know about any of it."

"Too hard on your conscience, mother?" I spit.

She grabs my mouth, squeezing my lips together and I cry out as my battered flesh once again protests. "Shut up, Ruby. You will shut up and you will behave."

I jerk my head back and the doctor makes a loud comment about my needing to stay still.

"I'm not a child anymore." I say, ignoring him entirely. "You don't have any power over me."

She snorts. "You'll find you're wrong there, baby. I'm still your mother and I'm the head of this family."

"Our father was the head and this family ceased to exist the day he died." I shout back.

She folds her arms, looking at my brother who scowls.

"What are we going to do with her?" He asks, sighing.

She shrugs almost nonchalantly. "It doesn't matter. The deal is sorted. Once Civello and Morelli are taken care of, she can argue all she wants. I'm sure her new husband will have ways to bring her in line."

"New husband?" I gasp. What the fuck does that mean?

My mother nods. "You think I didn't have this all planned, baby? You think I would leave you in the disgusting arms of Preston Civello forever?"

"He's not disgusting." I snarl back.

"He mutilated your body." Jett growls. "He tortured you and yet you still defend him?"

"At least he realised his mistake, at least he apologised." I state. "You both left me to die."

My mother turns her back, hissing. "I'm not going over this again. You're like a broken record."

"Are we done?" Jett says to the doctor.

I don't know what he slapped over my skin but every cut, every wound is burning worse than ever.

"I need to bandage her back up." He says.

Jett grunts, hauling me back up and baring my breasts to the entire room. "I'll hold. You wrap." He says, like any of this is okay.

I shut my eyes letting them do it, self-preservation taking over my pride but let's face it, it's better I'm wrapped up and covered than exposed in front of all these arseholes.

Only, when they've finished, Jett produces a load of rope. "You hold her down." He says to the doctor.

"What are you doing?" I ask.

He glances at me, then wrenches my arm up against the headboard. "You need to stop moving, Ruby. This ensures you do that."

"You're tying me to the bed?" I snarl.

"It's for the best." My mother says.

The doctor nods. "Give it some time, let your body heal."

I jerk and the doctor leans all his weight onto me. "Don't hurt yourself."

"Fuck you." I spit.

"Ruby." My mother says. "Stop being so ungrateful."

Ungrateful? Is she mad? I let out a shudder deciding a different tactic.

"What if I need to pee?" I say. "What about food?"

"We'll take care of you, baby." My mother cups my cheek. "We'll untie you when you need the bathroom and we'll handfeed you ourselves."

"I'm not an invalid." I growl.

"No." She smiles. "You're my daughter, and now I have you back I'm going to make up for all those years I couldn't look after you."

"Nothing will make up for what you did." I cry as Jett finishes with my hands and starts tying my feet so I'm spread eagled on my front across the mattress.

"There." He says proudly and all three of them stand back looking down at me, smiling.

They are mad.

Every single one of them.

They're bat shit crazy but there's nothing I can do. No way I can get out of these bindings and even if I could I don't have the strength to stand, let alone make any sort of escape attempt.

Ruby

CHAPTER Forty-Eight

"How are you doing, baby?" She says, standing at the end of my bed.

I glare back at her. Is she for real? It's been two days, Two days of being spoon-fed like a baby and watched as I hobble to the toilet, like they think I might throw myself out the window.

Not that that's an option because the damn thing is nailed shut.

My neck is killing me from the angle I'm holding my head at. My hands and feet have gone numb and no amount of wriggling them seems to fix it. Every time they cut me loose, the blood rushes back and I get the most excruciating hit of pins and needles.

"I want to go home." I say.

"You are home, Ruby." She replies.

"My home is with Preston."

She tuts, tapping her foot irritably. "Enough. We've been through this."

"You could work with them." I say. "Nico would listen, if you went to him I'm sure he'd agree…"

"To what, Ruby?" She cuts across me. "You think he'd just let me have takeover, that he'd allow that?"

"He won't stop you." I say. "He'd make a deal."

She laughs before her face goes hard. "I've already made a deal. I'm already getting what I want and I don't have concede anything to that bastard."

I draw in a low breath. "How could you do this?" I say quietly. "How can you do this to me?"

She sinks onto the bed beside me, brushing my hair back off my face. "I'm doing this *for* you. I'm ensuring our future."

"I have a future. With my husband."

She shakes her head, slamming her hand down onto the bed right by my face. "When will you give that up?"

"I won't."

"He doesn't love you. No man truly loves you, Ruby. That's the nature of what they are. All women are a means to an ends. If you're smart, you'll realise where your place is and you'll learn how to rise in spite of them."

"Preston loves me." I say back.

I know it.

I know he does because if he didn't, he would have just walked away after what he did to me.

He wouldn't have gotten on his knees, he wouldn't have taken care of me.

She sneers. "Even if he did, he won't for much longer. He's already shown you how he deals with betrayal. Imagine how he'll react when he realises you've lured him to his death."

My eyes widen. All I can think about is the tracker in my arm. Is that what she means? Is that what I am right now, a trap waiting to spring. I slump into the mattress, feeling that awful hopelessness hit me again.

"There's a good girl." My mother says, no doubt seeing the defeat in my eyes.

"I have to pee." I say quietly.

She gets up, slowly undoing the ties. "Come on then."

As soon as they're off, I jump up, pushing her out the way. She lets out shriek, grabbing my arm and I smash my fist into her face.

But the door crashes open.

Two men I don't know grab hold of me and I'm slammed back into the mattress face first.

"What the fuck?" Jett says, as he marches in.

"Little bitch." My mother says, grabbing my hair wrenching my head back. "You keep this up and you're going to regret it."

"Like you will when you double cross Nico." I shout back.

She pushes my face into the duvet, pushes so hard she's suffocating me. I jerk but the men hold me still.

I kick out but it does nothing.

Black spots punctuate my eyes. My heart is pounding in my chest. My head is screaming.

And then it stops.

Everything stops.

Blackness takes over everything and I drift off. I give in. I welcome it.

Ruby

CHAPTER

Forty- Nine

It takes all my strength to stand still, to not glare, to not lash out at the man gawping at me.

The drugs are still in my system, still making my head feel hazy, still making my eyes struggle to focus. I swear I'm swaying slightly but either no one notices or no one here cares.

Jett stands off to the side, arms folded, frowning as he watches me and I can't tell if it's because he's ready for me to act out or he's hating this as much as I am.

But my mother flits about making sure this significant new being gets her full attention.

He steps up, grabbing my face, staring at me like I'm some precious jewel he's trying to find a flaw with. All the tattoos covering his skin seem to morph into one, as if they've come to life.

"...and her back?" He asks.

"The wounds are healing well." The doctor replies. "And though there will be scarring, it is only her back..."

He drops his gaze, blatantly staring at my breasts. "I'm sure she'll make it up in other ways." He murmurs. "Besides, the diamonds will help."

I grit my teeth, pulling back from his grasp, unable to hide the snarl and his eyebrows raise.

"Ruby." My mother says in warning.

"No," The man smirks. "It's okay, I like them high spirited. It makes them more fun when you break them." He says, grabbing hold of me again, pushing his body into mine. "You're like a pure bred horse. Flighty, spoilt. I'll beat that out of you if I have to."

And then it hits me who he is.

Why he's so familiar.

"Jace?" I don't know how I know his name, maybe some subconscious part of me remembers my husband calling him. Because that's where I know him from. Preston. He works for Preston.

Maybe this is some trick, he's playing my mother, pretending to be on their side and soon, he'll sneak me out and rescue me?

He doesn't react. Doesn't show any hint that he even heard me.

"Phone." He says holding his hand out.

Someone puts the mobile in his palm and he wraps his arm tighter around my body. "You remember your orders?" He says.

I nod. I remember every word. Everything my mother told me barely an hour ago, even though none of this makes any sense.

"And any hint, any attempt to tell them what's really going on and I'll put a bullet in your pretty skull, this whole deal be damned."

I nod again. I'm not so stupid as to be blatant about it. Jace must be helping me. It's the only thing that makes sense. I'm not going to ruin my only chance of escape.

He dials the number, holding the phone to my ear and I shut my eyes, hating the way everyone is watching me right now.

When I hear my husband's voice, my heart actually leaps. I let out a whimper before I can stop myself and someone in the room snarls. The hands around me dig in tighter and it takes everything I have not to react.

Afterall, Jace is helping me.

He might be pretending right now, but he's Preston's man. He's on my side.

"Ruby?" Preston says in shock.

"It's, it's me." I say back, focusing on him.

"Where are you? Are you hurt, are you…" He falls silent, no doubt remembering exactly how hurt I was the last time he saw me.

"I'm okay." I state, forcing myself to get some sort of control. I have to do this right or Preston will be dead and it will be entirely my fault. "I just, I needed to get out."

"Of course."

"I, I'm sorry." I say. "I just saw red. I saw red, Preston. That's why I left. I needed a little thinking time."

Please let him hear it, please let him hear what I'm not saying, the hidden message in my words.

Jace's hands squeeze around me in warning. I'm going off script. I know and so does he. The feel of a gun pressed against my neck sets my heart racing even faster.

"Where are you, Ruby?" He asks after a moments' pause.

"I, I can't tell you that." I reply, reverting to back to the plan, their plan. "But I want to see you, to talk."

"When?"

God, he sounds so desperate, he sounds like he believes everything I don't want him to and he doesn't hear anything else.

"There's a park near to where I am. I'll message the address. Be there tomorrow at ten am. We can talk."

"I'll be there, Ruby." He says. "I'll be there."

"I love you." I say before I can stop myself. I need him to hear it. I need him to know, even if this goes wrong, even if everything crashes around us, I need him to realise that I forgive him.

That we are so far from all the shit that he put me through, all that torture.

"I love you too, Ruby, I love you so much…"

Before he can finish, Jace hangs up the phone.

"How sentimental." He says, before running that gun down my cheek. "I wonder how long it will take for you to make such declarations about me?"

"Go to hell." I snarl before I can stop myself.

He tuts, grabbing my face, planting a disgusting kiss on my lips as I try to get away.

It's an act. It has to be.

But we both know Preston would gut him for touching me like that.

"After tomorrow, that's exactly where Preston will be. Where he and Nico will be." My mother says clapping her hands together. "I hope you're proud of yourself, Ruby, you've played a pivotal role in bringing them all down."

I can't stop the tears as they fall. I can't hold them back as it hits me that Preston didn't realise what was going on. That this is a trick. He's going to come tomorrow and these bastards are going to murder him.

"Take her back to her room." My mother says, waving her hand in frustration.

"Allow me." Jace says.

We shuffle out of the room, me being compliant, wondering if this is the moment, that we take a right instead of a left, that we head down instead of up.

Only, that's not what happens.

"Jace…" I gasp. We could do it now. I know we could. We could be out of here and away before my family even realise.

"You that eager for me already?" He murmurs.

"What?" I gasp, shoving him as hard as I can.

He spins me around, pinning me against the wall and drops his eyes to stare at my chest once more. "Do you know how hard it was, to watch, to wait, to know he was going home every night to fuck you?"

"What…?"

His mouth turns into a grin that makes my stomach lurch.

"You're Preston's man." I say, like my stupid brain can't think of anything else.

"Wrong." He says, slowly dragging a finger down from my neck to my cleavage.

"But…" He has to be. He works for Preston, why would he be screwing him over?

"You're mine, Ruby." He says, lowering his mouth to my ear. "That was the deal I made. I passed on information, I spied on Civello and Morelli for years, I helped steal millions of diamonds from your uncle, all so I could have you."

"What the fuck are you talking about?" I snarl.

He grabs my wrists, yanking them up, wrenching them above my head and I scream out as my skin protests.

"That's the deal your mother made." He says getting right in my face. "She gets the mines and I get you, along with a few diamonds of course."

No. No. It can't be.

Why the fuck would my mother agree to that?

But then my mother is a greedy, heartless bitch. Of course she did.

My mind starts racing, trying to figure this all out. Is he the reason Jett has been able to access the house so easily? The way he managed to bypass all of Preston's security?

"Get the fuck off me." I snarl.

He lets out a laugh. "No point fighting it, Ruby. This time tomorrow you'll be on your knees, choking on my cock if you know what's good for you."

I screw my face up, raise my knee, and slam it into his groin. Like hell I'll ever willingly do that.

He groans, doubling over but he's forced to let me go and I seize the opportunity to run.

But I barely get a few metres away before I see Jett stood, blocking my path, glaring at Jace like he wants to gut him.

"Please..." I begin, only he's quick to grab me, quick to haul me back to my room while behind us Jace starts shouting out exactly how he's going to treat me this time tomorrow.

"Jett," I plead as he starts forcing me backwards, trying to get me to lie down nicely on the bed so he can tie me back up like a good little prisoner.

"Jett..."

"What do you want?" He snarls.

"This isn't you." I state.

He shakes his head, glaring at me. "How would you know? You think I'm still the same brother I was all those years ago?"

"No," I whisper, "But I know some part of you hasn't changed."

"I'm doing what's right."

"You're not." I cry. "You're helping them, you're selling your own sister..."

"For revenge." He snaps. "To ensure Nico Morelli pays for what he's done to our family."

"And what about you and mother?" I spit. "Do I not get justice for what you've done to me?"

He shakes his head, "You'll understand, in time, you'll see this is the only way."

"I'm your sister." I scream. "I'm your flesh and blood, and you're helping them."

He narrows his eyes as something akin to guilt flashes across his features but he still picks up the handful of fabric and forces it into my mouth all the same.

"I'm sorry, Ruby," He mutters as he ties me down. "It's for the best. It's the only way."

Preston

CHAPTER *Fifty*

"She used our safe word." I say.

I see how they react to that. Like they think we were into hardcore BDSM when in fact it was nothing like that, I just wanted her to feel safe, to feel in control, like any of my actions at end came even close to that.

"She said red. Twice. And her tracker is gone."

"You put a tracker in her?" Nico growls.

"What did you expect me to do after she ran?" I retort, almost surprised he hasn't done the same with Eleri.

Blaine smirks leaning right over the desk. "Fuck me, Preston, I never took you for that kind of a man."

"What kind?"

"As possessive an arsehole as I am."

Eleri stiffens. "You bunch of misogynistic…"

"Not now, love." Nico says, cutting across her, which I can see only infuriates her more.

"He put a tracker in her, like she's his possession." Eleri snarls.

"She is." I state. "I had to know where she was, I had to keep her safe."

She scoffs. "Keep her safe? You controlling, manipulative bastard."

"Eleri." Nico growls. "Hold your god damn tongue, woman. You want to crush his balls then fine, wait till this shit show is sorted and you can go right ahead."

"She can crush my balls anytime." Blaine says.

Nico goes very still, drawing himself up. "What the fuck did you just say about my wife?"

Blaine gulps, realising that second how far he's stepped out of line. "I..."

"Enough of this shit." I growl. "What are we, kids in a fucking playground? My wife is out there, we still don't know who has her but it's clear what they're after."

"The Holtz diamonds." Eleri says, nodding.

"The Holtz diamonds." I agree.

"And no doubt their entire fucking enterprise." Nico adds.

"So how about we park the ball crushing, huh?" I say.

Nico smirks, Eleri folds her arms under her huge tits, and Blaine, he looks like he might just thank me for saving his arse.

My phone buzzes in my hand. I open the message and see the address that my wife has supposedly just sent to me.

When I look it up, it's pretty much as she said, a park, nothing significant or noteworthy and that in itself says it all. There are no buildings nearby. No random bystanders. Just trees, wildlife and a river to contend with.

"Well?" Nico says.

I smirk, looking at all three of them. I know what this is. What exactly I'm walking into and I'll do it, I'll go with my hands held up and my chest bared, willing to die if that's what it takes to see Ruby one last time, to get her safe, to get her free.

"It's an ambush." I say, spinning the phone, letting them all see for themselves. Like we thought it would be anything other than a trap.

"We could still…" Eleri begins but I cut across her.

"This goes exactly as we planned." I state, looking at Nico who nods.

Ruby

CHAPTER
Fifty-One

The breeze catches in my hair. I shiver in just the little flimsy dress they made me wear.

Apparently, I'm doing the full damsel in distress look today. Underneath the scooping neckline, the bandages are gone. My skin hasn't healed but it needs fresh air according to the doctor and it's itching so badly I have to sit on my hands to stop myself from tearing it all back open.

When I managed to snatch a look at my back in the bathroom this morning, the bright red stripes made my heart stop. My entire back is scarred. I doubt they'll ever fade but even if they do, the skin is raised enough that even the naked eye will see the damage.

I gulp, feeling my throat bob against the tight collar they fitted around my neck.

My mother took great delight in showing its effects, and, as I fell to the floor gasping from the electricity that had pulsated through my body, she knew she'd played her hand well.

Except, I've got a few cards of my own.

I clench my fists, hoping that I have the guts for this. That I don't revert back to the cowardly creature I used to be.

Though I can't see them, I know they're there, hidden amongst the trees. My mother, my brother, and that arsehole Jace. They're all watching, alongside the snipers, with their fingers on the trigger, ready for if I fuck this up.

As the sound of twigs snap, my heart picks up.

I take an involuntary step before I force myself to still.

I have to be calm.

Patient.

I have to pretend that I'm as docile and submissive as my family think.

Preston's outline comes into view. I bite my lip to stop myself from crying out and as our eyes connect, I try to convey so much. I try to warn him, to tell him to turn back, to go away, to leave me here.

His eyes drop, they take in the skimpy dress and my body beneath it, before he notices the leather around my neck.

"Preston." I murmur his name but I don't say it loud enough for anyone to hear above the sound of crashing water from the waterfall a few metres away.

He stops. Pauses. Looks around for a fraction of a second. He's not nearly close enough to touch but right now, that's a good thing.

That keeps him safe.

Keeps him alive.

"I missed you." He says.

"I missed you too." I reply.

He lets out a sigh. "It doesn't have to be like this."

I nod. In so many ways I would choose a different fate, a different ending, but my life was never one of fairy tales and miracles.

And what better way than to die with purpose?

To die for something significant rather than because someone has simply decided it.

No, to die for Preston, to die to save him, that makes this bearable, that makes this fear inside me containable.

"Have they hurt you?" He asks.

I frown, my head shaking slightly. My family can read into it what they will. After all, soon I'll no doubt have a bullet in my brain, and nothing will matter.

"If they've laid a finger on you..."

"That's enough." My mother says, stepping out from where she's been hiding.

He takes a sharp inhale of air then looks back at me in surprise.

"She's..." I begin but my mother sends a quick shock through the collar and I yelp before falling silent.

"That's enough." My mother repeats. "We're not here to talk about Ruby."

"Funny," Preston smirks. "I thought that's exactly what I was here for. To talk to my wife."

"She won't be your wife for much longer."

Preston's jaw ticks. He glances back at me and again, I shake my head. I don't want him to think I'm happy with that, that I'd agree to that, that despite everything he's done, I'd willingly walk away from him.

"What do you want, Diana?" He growls.

"I want my revenge." She snarls. "You and Nico really think you could just take what you wanted, steal from me and I'd just crawl away..."

He smirks. "No," He murmurs. "But we wish you had. We gave you an opportunity. We gave you a chance five years ago."

"And then you helped Levi." My mother spits.

Preston takes a step forward and she holds the little device in her hand up, flashes it like it's a gun. "One more step Preston and I'll make Ruby pay."

"Leave her out of this." He replies.

"Why? She's a part of this, she always has been. You and Nico made sure of that."

"What the fuck are you talking about?"

She glances back at me, a smile gracing her lips. "You all thought you could trade my daughter like she was one of those diamonds from our mines. My husband tried it first, then Levi. Now you think she belongs to you, that because you forced a ring on her finger, she's your family now and not mine."

"You started this, Diana. The minute you tried to steal your husband's business."

I let out a gasp of shock at that revelation and another flash of pain hits me from the damned collar.

"Shut up." My mother hisses at me.

"Do that again and I'll kill you." Preston growls.

"Why? Because you're the only one allowed to hurt her now?" My mother snaps.

I wince, hating the way his eyes react, the guilt that he clearly has and then that mask comes down. My husband becomes the cold, ruthless man I know him to be. The man I need him to be.

The man I both love and fear.

"I said it before, Diana," He says. "Leave Ruby out of this."

My mother smiles, taking a step back, pulling me in front of her like a human shield. "You want my daughter so badly? You care for her that much, Preston?"

"I would die for her." Preston growls.

My mother grins. "You have no idea how true that statement is."

Preston pulls out his gun, pointing it right at us. For a second I wish he'd do it, that he'd pull the trigger, but I know that will only result in carnage.

"Let my wife go."

"Not so fast, Civello." Jace says, stepping out from where he's been hiding. "She might be your wife now but by sundown she'll belong to me. I'll be the one who gets to enjoy that nice little body of hers, despite how you've mangled it."

Preston's eyes widen, he stares at him in shock. "You?"

"Who do you think has been helping Diana? Ensuring all Levi's power trickles away, ensuring all those mines he thinks he stole appear worthless."

"Preston." I whimper.

His eyes connect with mine. I can see how much fury is residing there. "You made me think she betrayed me." He snarls. "You made me believe my own wife was passing on secrets…"

Jace lets out a laugh that sends a shiver through my spine. It was him? He's the reason Preston tortured me?

"Didn't work though, did it." Jace says before spitting on the ground at his feet. "Stupid bitch was meant to hate you after that, but all she does is go on about how she wants to be with you."

Was that really the point? To split us up? To make me turn on him?

I guess on some level it did work, because even now, a part of me still fears me husband.

But I love him too.

I love him more.

I love him enough to sacrifice my life to save his, despite what he's done to me.

"Give me my wife or I will blow your fucking head off." Preston growls, moving to take another step, to fall right into the trap they've laid for him.

I scream out in warning, forcing my body to move.

As the electricity hits me, I can't even think straight, but I don't stop, I let the searing pain tear through my body as I throw myself at Preston.

We land in a heap, in a mass of dirt and leaves. I can feel the way my back has torn open, I can feel the way my blood is trickling down my skin.

Half the ground gives way beside us leaving a gaping hole that I know is littered with spikes, and we're now trapped between it and the raging river behind.

"Ruby." Preston murmurs.

A second later gunshots go off. I duck, hiding myself against his body but he's not just lying there, he's pointing, shooting, fighting just as much as everyone else is.

"Run, Ruby." He says.

I shake my head. "Not without you."

"No one is going to hurt you." He states. And we both know the reason why that is, that I'm the prize, the reason all this shit is going down.

I can see Preston's men now. I can see Nico, coming out of the trees. And that man, Blaine, he's practically dancing in the hail of bullets like he's the very god of death himself.

My mother's men fire back. Even she has her own gun and is busy taking pot shots.

I can't tell who is winning or losing but we're pinned here, trapped, while the shooting goes off around us.

"Run, Ruby." Preston growls again.

"I won't leave you. I won't." I state.

"You've already done enough." He murmurs, cupping my cheek. "You already told me over the phone what this is."

So he did hear it. He did understand.

Relief spreads across my face at the fact he knew I wasn't setting him up. That I was doing whatever I could to warn him.

And then that smile is wiped right off my face as a white hot searing pain hits me from the collar. I scream out, wrapping my hands around it, as the tears stream down my cheeks.

"Ruby." Preston shouts.

A shadow covers us and, as the pain recedes I lie, panting, staring up at my mother.

"You never were obedient." She chides me. "Perhaps your new husband will do a better job of teaching you than your old one has."

"I'm her husband." Preston growls, throwing his arms around me protectively. "No one is taking her from me."

"No?" My mother muses. "What if we were to take *you* from her? Eliminate you from the equation."

"Stop," I gasp. "Please, please just stop. You can have the diamonds, you can have it all. I just want Preston. I just want…"

"I don't give a fuck what you want, Ruby." My mother hisses. "This isn't about your wants, this is about mine. What I need. What I deserve."

"And that's a cold hole in the ground." Preston spits.

My mother laughs. "No, I will have so much more than that. Now that Levi is dead, I will finally have what I set out to gain five years ago."

"Take it." I hiss. "Take it all, just leave us alone."

She scoffs. "Like your husband and Nico Morelli would ever allow that." She spits. "You think I don't realise they're already trying to secure my mines, trying to take it all."

I frown, glancing at Preston and I can see from his face that it's not a lie.

He *is* trying to take it, he's trying to claim all my family's inheritance.

My mind flits back to that conversation, when we found out Levi was dead, when I told him he could take everything from Gunnar and he refused to even discuss it.

Has he been lying this entire time?

Making his own moves behind my back?

Why? Why would he keep it from me?

"See what he is?" My mother sneers. "You claim to love him but he doesn't love you. He loves what you represent. What you can offer him. All those pretty little diamonds and the power that comes with being married to a Holtz."

"He loves me." I state. I know it.

He wouldn't have come here if he didn't. He wouldn't have risked his life like this.

Preston takes my hand, his gun pointed at my mother but I know unless he gets a clean shot, she'll pull the trigger, even if he gets her first.

"How could you?" I snarl at her. "How could you betray our family like that?

She smirks, shrugging. "Your father was going to divorce me. He was going to just push me aside, like we hadn't built this empire together."

"So you killed him?"

"No, Levi got to him before I could. He knew what I was up to. He knew Frank wouldn't have the balls to fight me so he murdered his brother and stole you."

"And you just left, you just ran."

She shrugs. "What else did you expect? You think I was really going to stick around and wait for Levi to kill me too?"

"You left me." I gasp, feeling that awful betrayal again.

"You were a child. And besides, Frank had already sealed your fate by signing you over to Nico. It was your bad luck that Levi got to you first."

"My bad luck?" I repeat, feeling my anger rising. She dares to insinuate that's what it was, like she wasn't even partly responsible for everything that went down. Everything I endured.

"Drop it." Jett says, from right behind us.

My heart sinks as I take him in. He's really doing this, he's really on her side?

He takes a step forward, boxing us in, not that it makes much of a difference because none of Preston's men can get near us right now.

And besides, they're too busy trying to save their own asses to be thinking about ours.

"I said drop it, mother."

My eyes widen. So do my mother's. She turns snarling. "What the fuck?"

"You really think you can win this?" He says.

"You're betraying me? After everything I've done for you…"

"You killed our father." He snarls, glancing at me then back at her. "I only went with you because I thought Levi did that, that this was our best option…"

"It *is* our best option."

He smirks. "No, I don't think so. You thought you could steal from your own flesh and blood, that you could manipulate us all but I see what this is now. I see what's really been going on."

She draws herself up like some bird of prey unfurling her wings, ready for attack. "You're just as bad as she is." She spits.

"It's over mother. You lost."

She lunges just as Jett throws himself at her. The gun goes off before he even lands on top of her and Jett groans, falling into a heap.

"Jett." I scream, trying to scramble to where he is but Preston grabs me, pulling me back.

"I will kill you both if I have to." My mother states, pointing her gun back at us.

"What about your deal?" I sneer. "I doubt Jace will want a dead bride."

"After today I will have control of everything. With enough diamonds, I doubt he will care who he's fucking."

She turns the gun on Preston and I throw myself on top of him to shield him, just as he pulls the trigger to take her out with his own.

Both guns echo around us. I scream out as the bullet hits me and I crumple. I don't know if Preston manages to shoot her, I don't know who's even alive, if Jett is okay, if any of us are.

I fall, I tumble, I slip into the raging water as more pain than I thought possible takes over my body. I gasp for air but I can't keep my head above the water. My limbs don't work. I fight to get out, I fight to stay afloat but I can feel myself sinking.

And for a moment, I think that this is it, this is my fate, to drown, to be swallowed up by the rapids.

Only, something wraps around me, something pulls me back out.

"Ruby?"

I hear his voice but it's so far off. I blink, staring at his unfocused face.

And then that darkness does come. Once more it shrouds me and once more I welcome it.

Preston

CHAPTER
Fifty-Two

The machine beeps enough to irritate. I sit, staring at the tiny waves undulating up and down like I understand what I'm looking at, when in reality, all it's telling me is her heart is still beating.

That she's alive.

Nico walks in, standing right by the door, keeping on the peripheries because he knows he's intruding.

"How's the brother?" I ask, cutting through the silence.

"Alive." He says. "He's out of surgery now. Lost his spleen but apart from that…" He trails off as my wife shifts, as her leg kicks out violently like in her head, she's still fighting a battle all on her own.

"And Jace?" I ask.

He smirks. "I gave him to Blaine. Thought he could do with some reward after all of this."

I grunt. At least that will keep the man entertained for a few days.

"Preston…"

"Whatever it is, I don't want to hear it." I say, knowing that I run the risk of pissing him off.

"You have to deal with the mother. It's your call. Whatever you choose to do."

I narrow my eyes, pressing my hands together. Would Ruby forgive me if I killed her? Does she still hold some love for her despite everything the woman has done? I grit my jaw, trying to figure it out, but as always my wife's thoughts seem to allude me.

"Leave it with me." I murmur.

"And the business?"

I don't reply. I don't show any reaction to that question.

Everything Frank Holtz created, everything Levi and Diana stole is now mine because of the woman lying right here in front of me.

The woman who sacrificed herself for me.

Who threw herself in front of the bullets meant for me.

And yet when the situation had been reversed, when her life was in my hands, I'd not hesitated to pick up that knife and carve into her skin, like she'd meant nothing.

Nico murmurs something. I don't listen. I don't register it. I just stare at the woman I should have protected, hearing her screams, hearing her pleas, hearing every horrific moment that I inflicted on her.

When he leaves, I don't know.

I'm only vaguely aware that it's me and her. Alone again.

And slowly she starts to stir, she starts to wake.

I brace myself for whatever words come out of her mouth, whatever future she decides we have.

Because as much as I can't bear the lose her, it's her choice where we go from here.

She deserves at least that much from me.

Ruby

CHAPTER
Fifty-Three

I know he's there. I know he's probably been sat, stewing, waiting for me to wake for hours.

As I shift enough to look at him, he meets my gaze and my stupid heart flips.

Even in his despair, he still takes my breath away.

"Preston," I say, unsure if it's a curse or a declaration of love.

"How are you feeling?" He asks, moving closer, though still obviously hesitant.

I blink, staring down at where a drip is embedded into my arm.

A machine beeps in the background.

A constant, annoying counter that marks every second that we fall to silence.

"How long was I out?" I ask, ignoring his question entirely.

"A while. They had to operate to remove the bullet." He states. "But you'll make a full recovery."

I guess I should be grateful for that.

"And my mother?" I continue. I remember the sound of gunshots, the echo of it in my head. Preston pulled the trigger at the same time as she had.

Is she dead?

Did my husband murder my mother on top of everything else?

He narrows his eyes for a moment. "She's alive." He growls. "You can decide what we do with her. If you want her to be punished, or if you want us to let her go."

My eyebrows raise. He's giving me that? He's letting me make such a decision?

"I want her dead." I say before I can hesitate, before I can second guess it, before my stupid head tries to pretend that she deserves any different outcome.

He pauses, scanning my face like he thinks I might change my mind, only I won't, I know I won't.

"She's the cause of this." I state, "She betrayed my father, then she left me with Levi, she left her own child…" My voice catches but I fight back the emotion that threatens to takeover. "I want her dead." I state again.

It's the least he can give me, the least I deserve.

He nods, pulling out his phone, and he sends a message to god knows who. I know he won't have her killed yet, he'll give me the option of deciding how, but for now it doesn't matter, the decision is made and that's all I care about.

"Ruby…" He begins but I cut across him. Whatever he has to say, I'm just not mentally ready for it.

"How is Jett?"

He sighs. "He's alive too. He's recovering but he shouldn't have any lasting injuries."

"I can't believe she shot him." I whisper but that's not true.

I do believe it.

I do believe that the woman I've come to know over these last few days is capable of murder.

"You knew he was alive." Preston says.

I nod.

"For how long?"

"A while. He broke in that night I pretended to drop a glass in the kitchen." I admit.

"Did you know your mother was alive as well?"

I shake my head. "No. I only found that out once Jett kidnapped me."

He gets up, moving to stare out the window for a moment before he turns around as if whatever words he needs to say, he has to physically prepare himself for.

"Ruby," He murmurs, taking my hand, dropping to his knees beside the bed.

Despite my best efforts I flinch, it's not even his touch that makes me flinch, it's just human touch in general. I'm so used to it resulting in pain now that my mind can't register that something else might be the result.

"...The Holtz business is yours. All the diamonds, all the mines, all of it belongs to you."

I blink back, wondering if I've misheard him. "What?"

"I'll sign it over. I'll have the paperwork drawn up."

I open my mouth to argue but then it hits me; this moment here is a crossroads, a chance for me to stop playing the victim.

I've been passed around like a trophy, from one damned man to another. I'm so sick of feeling helpless, of being powerless, of always being at the whims of men, when it's my inheritance they're after.

Mine.

If I'm the Head then I'll no longer be the one taking orders, I'll be giving them.

I gulp, wondering if I'm being reckless. Naïve even. I'm twenty one years of age. Would they even let me? Would they let a woman takeover?

But I know if I had a dick they would, they wouldn't even question it.

And besides, Nico rules with Eleri as his queen. Would it not work similarly with me and Preston, me as Head, and him as my help?

I meet Preston's searching eyes and give a curt nod back.

I want to do it.

I want to be in charge for once.

I want to take all the broken pieces of my family's empire and rebuild it, create something beautiful from all the carnage and destruction.

"I'll have our divorce papers drawn up as well." He says quietly.

"No." I gasp. I don't want that. Anger flashes through me as once more he's making the decisions, deciding my future with no negotiation.

He looks at me as if I might be mad.

"I…" He begins but I cut across him.

"Does it not matter what your wife wants?" I snap back.

A micro expression crosses his face. One of pain. One of anguish. "I have no right to call you that, not after what I did."

"Preston," I sigh. "It's not for you to make that decision. It's mine. I'm the one you hurt. I'm the one you tortured. I get to decide what your punishment is, and, when you deserve forgiveness."

"I don't." He says, dropping his gaze like he really is defeated.

"Yes, you do." I reply. "You saved me, even when you didn't realise you were doing it, and you walked into that trap, you came back for me when you could have left me to Jace and my mother."

"I would never have done that." He states.

I squeeze his hand. "And I will never leave you." I say. "Not until I die. Isn't that how our kind of marriages work?"

His lips twist, for the first time in what feels like forever, he smiles. "I love you, Ruby. I love you so much."

"I know." I croak, as I fight back that wave of emotion. "And I want to fix this, but I have some conditions."

I can't go back to being that scared, pathetic creature I was before.

I have to make him see that I'm no longer that person.

"And what are they?" He asks.

"Jett." I say. "If my brother wants to stay, then you find a place for him. You help him to fit in."

He scowls. "That man stole you from me."

"He thought he was helping me."

"How can I trust him?"

"He's my flesh and blood." I state. "I want to at least give him a chance of redemption." After all, he clearly had no idea what my mother was really up to. He clearly had no inkling that she was planning to usurp my father all those years ago. Perhaps if he did, things would have turned out differently.

He grunts. "Fine." He says. "What else?"

"We're a team now. You and me. From now on, we discuss things, we decide things, together. No more hiding information, no more keeping me locked up in that house."

My lips smirk as I realise he couldn't keep me locked up if he tried.

I'm the one with the power now.

I'm not some silly little girl, chained to a man twice her age, forced into circumstances she can't understand.

I'm in control now and it's time I proved that.

"Like what?" He asks, like he doesn't know.

"Like the fact that Nico is my godfather, for one." I state.

Yeah, he reacts to that, he shows with his face that he knew all about it, that officially the plan was I marry Nico when I was old enough.

"Alright." He replies, holding his hand out like this is a serious deal we're making.

When we shake, he smiles, before leaning to capture my lips in a chaste kiss. I cup his chiselled jaw with my hand and I can feel his stubble prickling my skin. He's normally clean shaven. Immaculate. It's odd to see him so unkempt.

But as I drop my hand, I wince, feeling that familiar pang from my back. How those wounds protest.

"I will get you a doctor." He begins. "I will pay for the best plastic surgeon…"

"No," I say firmly. I don't want that. I was never that vain, I was never so caught up in how I looked that I would risk going under the knife and for what? To try to remove some part of our story.

No, these scars are like a battle we've both endured and I want to wear them with pride.

They're proof of my own fight, proof that I'm more than what I appear to be.

That I'm a fighter and, though I may have forgotten that for a while, I don't any longer.

Ruby

CHAPTER

Fifty- Four

It's hard to settle the nerves. Hard to keep the serene look on my face too and not let out a squeal.

I know just beyond this room are the other Families. The other Heads. Among them is Nico and that alone gives me some comfort that there's a friendly face in all of this – at least somewhat friendly that is.

I wring my hands for what must be the tenth time while my brother watches but keeps his mouth shut.

Whatever thoughts he has, he mercifully decides not to speak them out loud.

As the door opens, I turn my head, and my heart flips as my eyes land on Preston. He's in a dark grey suit, looking more deadly and somehow more majestic than ever.

"Jett," He says, jerking his chin for my brother to leave us and he quickly disappears out of the room.

They're still not at ease with one another, still finding their way. I guess it doesn't help that Noah is technically his guard, watching him to make sure he plays by our rules because as yet, even I don't trust him fully.

"You look beautiful." Preston murmurs, closing the distance.

I give a weak smile that betrays my nerves and I glance down at the silver satin dress that hugs my figure like a second skin.

"I think the red would have been…" His fingers silence the last of my words.

"Perfect." He says, before sinking to his knees.

It's been two months. Two months since we executed my mother, since we took back everything Gunnar and Levi stole.

Since I became head of the Holtz Family.

And now here I am, acting like I have a clue what I'm doing, pretending that all of this is normal, that a female Head, a Queen even, has the right to rule on her own accord.

But then, why shouldn't I?

My father might have been old fashioned but I don't doubt he would have been more than proud to see what I've become, what I've achieved.

Preston's hands skate up my leg, slowly, almost cautiously, he does the straps of the heels up and I hold my breath, trying not to react to the feel of his fingertips brushing against my skin.

We haven't touched, haven't kissed, haven't done anything since I got out of the hospital a few weeks ago, and though he's barely left my side, he's acting like a bodyguard, not a husband.

My back is fully healed, my injuries from where my own mother tried to kill me are also all healed.

I lean down, catch his face with my hand, and the hint of his stubble pricks my fingers.

But I see that look, that flash of something, before he forces himself to meet my gaze.

"When will you forgive yourself?" I half-whisper.

He shakes his head slightly. "It's not…"

"I already have." I cut across him. "I forgave you weeks ago."

"Ruby…"

I draw in a deep breath, straightening myself up as if I'm preparing for battle. "Am I not Head of this Family now?" I ask.

His lips curl at my tone before he catches himself and that hard mask replaces the softness. "Yes."

"And are you not meant to obey me?"

"Yes." He says again.

"Then follow your orders and do as I ask."

He lets out a huff in response as though what I'm asking for is utterly impossible.

"Fuck me, Preston. Fuck your wife."

"I have no right to call you that." He snaps. "No right to touch you either. I don't deserve you, I don't deserve to touch you, I don't deserve your love…"

"Deserve?" I repeat, feeling my own anger flare. He's so lost in his own head he can't even see what this is.

I'm literally offering him redemption and he's too damned stubborn to take it.

I step back, sit on the desk and glower at him. "You want to play hard to get, is that it? You want to draw out your pain, prolong your suffering, and for what?"

I can see in his eyes that that's it.

So I pull the skirt of my dress up. Slowly. Inch by inch, letting it gather around my waist. The fabric is so thin I didn't dare wear any underwear and his eyes widen when he realises that I'm completelty bare.

"Don't pretend that you don't want to fuck me." I say, lowering my hand, drawing it between my thighs and to where I'm already growing wetter by the second.

I can hear his breath catch.

I can see the way he's holding himself back, like he's so desperate to just reach out and grab me but he doesn't dare.

"You used to watch me, remember?" I taunt, as I slowly start to play. "You wouldn't let yourself touch me then, either. You tried to act all noble but it wasn't long before you gave in."

He groans as his shoulders slump. "I don't deserve…"

I drown out those words with a long moan that I know will send the man rabid.

He edges closer, his knees shuffling like he's just trying to get a better look and I spread my thighs as wide as they'll go.

As I start fucking myself with my fingers, we can both hear the sound of it, the sound of my pussy begging for more. "Fuck me, Preston. Take what you want and just do it."

He snarls, clenching his fists, and I reach out, run my wet fingers over his lips and he sucks them in like he's a dying man.

"Don't I taste good?" I whisper. "Don't I deserve to feel pleasure after all the pain I've been through?"

"Ruby,"

"Fuck me, Preston. Stay on your knees if that nurses your conscience enough, but for god sake, give me this."

His hands grab at my thighs. I yelp as his fingers dig into my flesh and he buries his face in my pussy, sucking my clit, devouring me like it's his very first taste and he needs every drop.

"Yes," I cry, not caring that we're almost certainly being heard in the other room. Not caring that I'm keeping everyone else waiting.

I grab at his hair, directing his mouth and I roll my hips to spur him on. His tongue pushes inside me and it's the most incredible feeling. I arch my back, I lay myself flat against the desk and lose myself as he eats me out.

"Make your Queen come." I gasp. "Show her how sorry you really are."

He groans, his hands tightening around my thighs, and I delight in the knowledge that the bruising he's inflicting on my flesh will stay there for days after.

My orgasm hits me like a tsunami.

Wave after wave of ecstasy punctuates through my body and I scream out, riding Preston's mouth, needing more, needing him.

It feels like the first time, it feels like that desperate first climax when I was half petrified of him and yet already falling stupidly in love with those piercing blue eyes, with that chiselled jaw, with him, my husband.

"Preston," It sounds like a battle cry. It sounds like a prayer.

I don't care if they all hear me, if everyone in this building hears me fall apart.

He lifts himself up, pulls my body and manoeuvres himself so that he's above me, and, as he drags his cock out, he fixes those devastating eyes on me.

"You let me back in, Ruby, you let me fuck you again and that's it. No going back, no divorce, no freedom…"

I snarl, grabbing his throat. My hands might be small but the feeling of dominance doesn't escape me as I squeeze just a little.

"You think I'm playing games?" I say back. "I already told you what I wanted. You're mine, Preston. Just as I am yours. I'm not looking for freedom, I'm not looking for a quick fuck."

He draws himself up, his mouth twisting into that familiar smirk.

"Is that so, wife?" He says, before crashing his lips into mine in a devastating kiss.

I moan, twisting my tongue, letting him ravish my mouth, and as he does he pushes himself inside me.

"Oh god," I gasp. It's been too long. It's been what feels like forever.

Within seconds we both go into a frenzy.

I tear at his shirt, almost rip the buttons off with the need to see him, to feel him.

One of his hands twists in my hair, wrenching my head back as he peppers my neck with kisses.

His thumb finds my clit and he begins circling, almost torturing me with his touch, while he's slamming into my pussy.

"Ruby," He groans, "It's so good, you're so fucking good."

"Come in me," I gasp. "Come in your wife, and prove your love."

I don't know if it's my words or the fact that he's close but he bites down onto my shoulder, bites hard enough that I yelp, and then he's coming, pouring himself into me.

For a moment we both lay there, him still on top, still buried to the hilt.

"Don't…" I say, as he starts to slide off me but he fixes me with a look.

"They're waiting." He states.

For some reason I find that thought amusing. That they're all stood around, these powerful men, waiting on me.

"Fine," I mutter, more to myself.

Preston rearranges his clothes then offers his hand for me to take. Thankfully my dress isn't crumpled but I run my hands down it all the same, smoothing the cool fabric.

"Shall we?" I say, like I had this all planned out.

He crosses the room, opens the door and holds it for me.

Beyond, I can see the grand space, the ornate furniture, and the low murmur of voices suddenly turn to silence.

Evidently, they've realised I'm about to grace them with my presence.

I draw in a deep breath, straighten my spine and as I do, I feel it; his come, slowly leaking out of me.

As if that spurs me on, I strut out of the room, leaving Preston to follow in my steps.

I'm ready now. I'm ready to face them all.

From now on, the world is going to meet with an entirely different Ruby Holtz. Not a Mafia Princess, not a pretty little jewel to be passed around and bartered with.

No, I'm a queen now. And I will ensure nobody ever forgets that.

THE END

BLURB FOR

I was a journalist, I had a life, friends, and then all of that was taken from me.

No, not taken, stolen.

The Brethren found out about my exposé. They realised I was getting too close to their nasty little secrets - and so they made sure I disappeared.

Except, they didn't just grant me the mercy of a shallow grave. Oh no, instead they handed me over to Magnus Blake, practically gift-wrapped me for him.

And he's got plans for me. Big plans.

He says I'm his new pet project. He says he's going to break me, torture me, use me in every disgusting way he can think of.

There's no escaping him. I know he's too powerful to beat.

But as the days draw out, as the nights get colder, I can feel something worse taking hold of me. I can feel how my body responds, how my emotions are twisting.

I don't want to want him.

I don't want to crave him.

But the darkness is eating away at my sanity.

And in the end, it doesn't matter what I feel anyway; my life belongs to him. Every breath belongs to him.

WHAT TO EXPECT:

DUAL POV

Pitch black triggers

Captor / prey

Stockholm syndrome

HFN

Read on for a sneak preview…

GET YOUR COPY

SNEAK PEAK AT

Deviant

My knees slam into the hard floor. I don't want to cry out but I can't keep it in and it comes out like a strangled noise from behind the gag.

My wrists are tied behind my back so tightly that I swear my fingers are going to drop off from lack of blood. I try desperately to move them, to ease the pressure but it makes no difference whatsoever.

Something beats into me. It might be a stick, it could be something metal, but I double up. Then a boot slams into my side.

My top is pulled back from behind and something sharp drags down my skin as I realise they're cutting my clothes off.

I jerk out, I try to fight but what can I actually do when I'm practically hog tied? Within seconds I'm stripped naked and I shiver, trying to curl up and hide myself in any way I can.

A hand gropes my breast. I scream out, ramming my head back into whoever is stood behind me but they obviously see it coming.

"Stupid fucking bitch." I hear the curse above the rough fabric sack they've wrapped around my head.

I don't know where I am but I can make a damned good guess.

As if answering that thought, the sack is ripped off. My eyes dart about, I desperately try to adapt to the sudden brightness.

I'm in the hall. Their hall.

I knew it and yet my heart sinks all the same. It's so much worse seeing it in real life and not just from the few stolen images.

I am so fucked.

Maybe if I'd left sooner, maybe if I'd just run… no, they would have found me anyway. There's no escaping this. No escaping them.

They're the Brethren after all, they run the entire world, control all of us.

This hall is normally filled to the rafters. It looks like a church, with a high vaulted ceiling and ornate, gothic carvings. It must be sixteenth century but I know it was never used for worship, at least, not worship of anything beyond their own greed and power.

My mind flickers to the photos, the ones Clay managed to take during one of their ceremonies, and a chill runs up my spine. I don't know what they have instore for me but I know it's going to be horrific.

There's ten of them, ten men, all masked, all robed, surrounding me.

"Someone's been sniffing around where they don't belong." One of them says, nudging by me.

I glare back but it still feels reckless, but then, what does it matter? They're going to kill me. I know that much. I know I'm not making it out of here alive.

From above, something drops. It's been dropping, no, dripping for a while but I've ignored it.

I glance up and pure, unadulterated fear grips me.

I fall back, shake my head, lose all sense of reason but I can't tear my eyes from the horror.

It's Clay. So they got him first.

He's strung up, suspended between ropes that span the width of the roof. His skin has been flailed. He's been tortured for what must have been hours.

And it's his blood that keeps dripping down onto the flagstone beneath us.

"Please..." the words escape my lips but it comes out as a desperate, pathetic wail.

One of the men starts laughing.

Another tilts his head, takes a step forward and grabs my face.

"What other end did you expect? You think you can poke the dragon and not get burnt?"

I gulp. I knew what I was doing was risky, I knew that, but it wasn't about me, was it?

One of them yanks the gag from my mouth.

"Fuck you." I spit as soon as I can get my tongue to work.

All my fear is still there, but I refuse to let them see it, refuse to give in. They want to kill me, fine, but my pride won't let me die a coward.

Cold metal presses against the back of my neck. I still, recognising that it's the barrel of a gun. Could I be this lucky to simply face a bullet? Have a quick, painless death?

"Blow her fucking head off." The same man orders but another steps forward, into the light.

"Wait," he says.

I know that voice, I know it was well as my own. I can't keep the tremble as it sinks in exactly who he is; Magnus Blake.

So he's here too?

The others turn to look at him. With their masks on, I can't see their expressions but I know he holds enough sway to get whatever he wants.

"The crime was against me, was it not?" Magnus states.

"It was against all of the Brethren." The main man replies.

Magnus shakes his head, producing papers, my papers, and he flicks through them. "Most of this is about me, about my activities."

"What does it matter?"

"It matters," Magnus says, staring right back at me now. "Because I want my own justice."

"Justice?" I splutter. What justice does he think he deserves? He's got more blood on his hands than half the population of Rykers.

He closes the distance, grabbing my face in a vice like grip. "This woman insulted me, I demand recompense."

"Fuck you," I snarl but no one else is paying attention to me.

The others are all mumbling, discussing between themselves.

"Her sentence still stands." The main man says.

"Of course." Magnus replies. "I'm just going to take my time before I carry it out."

No.

No.

This can't be happening.

I flail, I jerk my head back and smash it into his stupid mask but someone grabs me and holds me tight.

"The more you fight, the worse it will be." He taunts, whispering into my ear.

Worse? It can't get any worse?

I'm dragged out, hauled out and tossed into the back of a van. My face slams once more into a hard surface and for a second I lay there, dazed, immobile, while pain explodes behind my eyes.

My arms are pinned under me, my legs feel like they're refusing to cooperate.

In my head all I can hear is the same word screaming over and over, 'run'.

And then I realise that he's here, watching me from the still open door.

"I wonder how long you'll last." He murmurs.

I don't reply. I just glare back. If he thinks I'll break down and start crying, if he thinks I'll beg for my life, he's got another thing coming. He may be able to bully this entire world, but he won't bully me, he won't.

He grabs my hair, wrenches my neck so that I'm forced to face him full on, while he drops his gaze to take in my naked body. From the angle he's at I don't doubt he's got a perfect view of everything I have.

I shift quickly, shutting my legs and he tuts with annoyance.

With one hand he pinches my nipple and I whimper with the sharp hit of pain.

"Not bad." He says, like he's sizing up a cut of meat.

"Get your fucking hands off me." I hiss.

Only, that just makes him smirk. This is a joke to him, isn't it? He's so fucking used to doing whatever he wants that even now, even my kidnapping and potential murder is just another day at the office.

"Do you know how long I've waited for this?" He asks, finally take his disgusting hands off me.

I frown in confusion. What the fuck is he talking about? I know the Brethren has only just found out about me, there's no way they would have let me continue, no way they would have risked it.

"I'm going to break you…" He says so calmly, it makes the words coming out of his mouth even worse. "…I'm going to carve away every little piece of what makes you, you, I'll destroy every tiny bit of hope you have, and only when I decide, only when you suffer enough, will I grant you your death..."

Get your hands on this book here

OTHER BOOKS

Twisted Love Duet
Downfall: Book One
Uprising: Book Two
Reckoning

Mafia Romance
Vendetta: A Mafia Romance
Coercion: An Age Gap Mafia Romance

The Fae Girl Series
A Place of Smoke & Shadows
A Place of Truth & Lies
A Place of Sorcery & Betrayal
A Place of Rage & Ruin
A Place of Crowns & Chains

ABOUT THE AUTHOR

Ellie Sanders lives in rural Hampshire, in the U.K. with her partner and two troublesome dogs.

She has a BA Hons degree in English and American Literature with Creative Writing and enjoys spending her time, when not endlessly writing, exploring the countryside around her home.

She is best known for her romance / fantasy novels 'The Fae Girl' Series but has also published a series of spy erotica novels called 'The BlackWater Series'.

For updates including new books please follow her Instagram and

For updates including new books, please follow her Instagram, TikTok, and Twitter @hotsteamywriter.

Authors Note

Thank you so much for reading 'Coercion'. I hope you enjoyed it as much as I enjoyed conjuring up all the twists and surprises.

With this book I really wanted to take the standard 'virginal damsel' and turn her into something more real, something more tangible. To make her a modern day heroine and not just a pretty trophy princess.

If you enjoyed this book, why not subscribe to my newsletter where you'll be the first to hear about new releases and any giveaways I'm running. There will also be lots of ARC opportunities coming up so watch out for these!

I would be eternally grateful if after reading this you left a review.

Reviews really are an author's lifeblood, not just because it helps beat back the crazy amount of imposter syndrome we all have but because it helps us get noticed / builds our community on places like amazon and ensures we can continue creating more stories for you to read and indulge in.

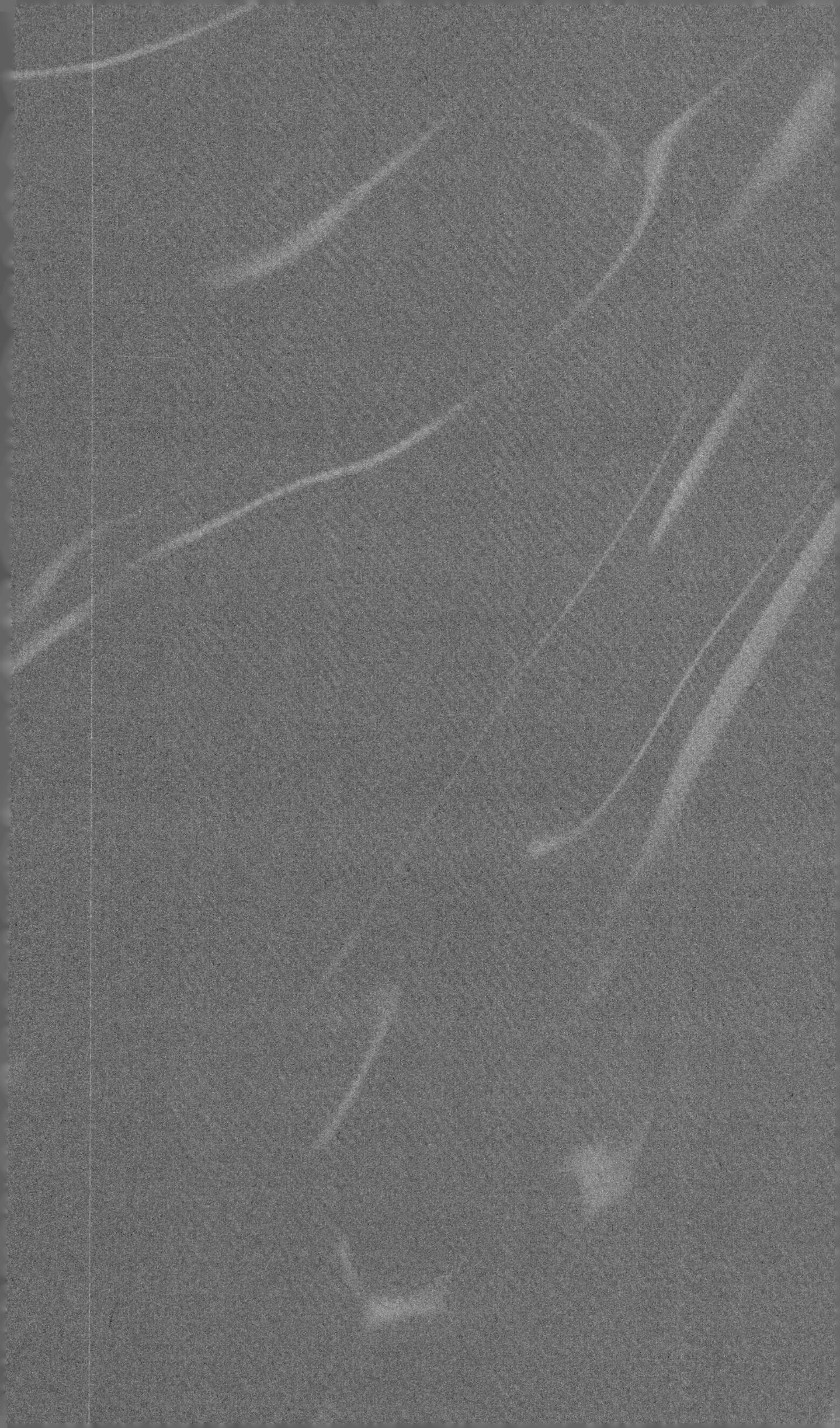

Made in the USA
Coppell, TX
17 May 2024

32495522R10236